KT-117-434

RIVER OF DARKNESS

RENNIE AIRTH was born in South Africa and worked for a number of years as a foreign correspondent for Reuters. He now lives in Italy. *River of Darkness* is the first novel in the highly acclaimed Inspector Madden trilogy.

Also by Rennie Airth

THE BLOOD-DIMMED TIDE

THE DEAD OF WINTER

RENNIE AIRTH

RIVER OF DARKNESS

PAN BOOKS

First published 1999 by Macmillan

First published in paperback 2000 by Pan Books

This edition published 2009 by Pan Books
an imprint of Pan Macmillan, a division of Macmillan Publishers Limited
Pan Macmillan, 20 New Wharf Road, London N1 9RR
Basingstoke and Oxford
Associated companies throughout the world
www.panmacmillan.com

ISBN 978-0-330-46562-5

Copyright © Rennie Airth 1999

The right of Rennie Airth to be identified as the
author of this work has been asserted by him in accordance
with the Copyright, Designs and Patents Act 1988.

The acknowledgements on page 529 constitute an extension of
this copyright page.

All rights reserved. No part of this publication may be
reproduced, stored in or introduced into a retrieval system, or
transmitted, in any form, or by any means (electronic, mechanical,
photocopying, recording or otherwise) without the prior written
permission of the publisher. Any person who does any unauthorized
act in relation to this publication may be liable to criminal
prosecution and civil claims for damages.

3 5 7 9 8 6 4

A CIP catalogue record for this book is available from
the British Library.

Typeset by SetSystems Ltd, Saffron Walden, Essex
Printed and bound in the UK by CPI Mackays, Chatham ME5 8TD

This book is sold subject to the condition that it shall not,
by way of trade or otherwise, be lent, re-sold, hired out,
or otherwise circulated without the publisher's prior consent
in any form of binding or cover other than that in which
it is published and without a similar condition including this
condition being imposed on the subsequent purchaser.

Visit www.panmacmillan.com to read more about all our books
and to buy them. You will also find features, author interviews and
news of any author events, and you can sign up for e-newsletters
so that you're always first to hear about our new releases.

To the memory of my mother and father

LONDON BOROUGH OF SOUTHWARK	
SK 1973313 5	
ASKEWS & HOLT	08-Jul-2011
AF MYS	£7.99
3241641	B

Acknowledgements

I would like to express my thanks to
Sue Lines, Assistant Curator, Royal Military Police
Museum, Roussillon Barracks, Chichester,
and to
Major P. E. Atteridge, AGC (RMP),
for their valuable assistance.

I'm back again from hell
With loathsome thoughts to sell;
Secrets of death to tell;
And horrors from the abyss.

Siegfried Sassoon, 'To the War-Mongers'

Part One

Part One

What passing-bells for these who die as cattle?

Wilfred Owen, 'Anthem for Doomed Youth'

Blue Anchor Library
Market Place, Southwark Park Road,
London, SE16 3UQ

Account: ****0371

River of darkness

Due date: 06/10/23

Total items borrowed: 1

15/09/23 11:20 AM

1

THE VILLAGE WAS EMPTY. Billy Styles couldn't understand it. They hadn't seen a living soul on the road from the station, and even the green was deserted, though the weather was the kind that normally brought people out of doors.

The finest summer since the war!

The newspapers had been repeating the phrase for weeks now as one radiant day followed another, with no end to the heatwave in sight.

But here in Highfield, sunshine lay like a curse on empty cottage gardens. Only the headstones in the churchyard, crowding the moss-covered stone wall flanking the road, gave mute evidence of a human presence.

'They're all at the house,' Boyce said, as though in explanation. He was an inspector with the Surrey police, a thin grey man with an anxious look. 'Word got around this morning.'

Boyce had come to the station to meet Inspector Madden and Billy. In a chauffeured Rolls-Royce, no less! Billy wanted to ask who'd sent it, but didn't dare. With less than three months' experience in the CID he knew he was lucky to be there at all, assigned to a case of such magnitude. Only the August bank holiday, combined with the heavy summer-leave schedule, had brought it about. Scotland Yard had been thinly manned that Monday morning when the telephone call came from Guildford. Minutes later Billy had found himself in a taxi with Madden bound for Waterloo station.

He glanced at the inspector, who was sitting beside him staring out of the car window. Among the lower ranks at the Yard, Madden was reckoned to be a queer one. They hadn't met before today, but Billy had seen him striding down the corridors. A tall grim man with a scarred forehead, he seemed more like a monk than a policeman, the young detective constable thought. An impression that gained strength now each time the inspector's glance fell on him. Madden's deep-set eyes seemed to look at you from another world.

He had a strange history – Billy had heard it from one of the sergeants. Madden had left the force some years before after losing his wife and baby daughter, both in the same week, to influenza. The son of a farmer, he had wanted to return to the land. Instead, the war had come, and afterwards he'd returned to his old job with the Metropolitan Police. Changed, though, it was said. A different man from before. Two years in the trenches had seen to that.

They had cleared the village, leaving the last cottage behind. Rounding a bend in the road, the chauffeur braked. Ahead of them, blocking the narrow country lane and facing a set of iron gates, a crowd had gathered. Whole families were there, it seemed, the men in shirtsleeves and braces, the women wearing kitchen aprons and with their hair tied up in scarves and handkerchiefs. Children stood hand in hand, or else played together on the dusty verges. A short way down the road two little girls in coloured smocks were bowling a hoop.

'Look at them,' Boyce said wearily. 'We've asked them to keep away, but what can you expect?'

The chauffeur blew his horn as they drew near and the crowd parted to let the car through. Billy felt the weight of their accusing stares.

'They don't know what to think,' Boyce muttered. 'And we don't know what to tell them.'

The drive beyond the gates was lined with elms, linked at their crowns like Gothic arches. At the end of it Billy could see a house built of solid stone, clothed in ivy. Melling Lodge was its name. Madden had told him. A family called Fletcher lived there. *Had* lived there. Billy's mouth went dry as they approached the gravelled forecourt where a fountain topped by a Cupid figure, standing with his bow drawn, sprayed silvery water into the bright sunlit afternoon. Blue uniforms stirred in the shadows.

'We brought a dozen men down from Guildford.' Boyce nodded towards a police van parked at the side of the forecourt. 'We may want more.'

Madden spoke for the first time. 'We'll need to search the land around the house.'

'Wait till you see the other side.' Boyce groaned. 'Woods. Nothing but woods. Miles and miles of them.'

Madden's glance had shifted to a group of three men standing together in a shaded corner of the forecourt. Two of them wore light country tweeds. The third sweated in a double-breasted serge suit. 'Who are they?' he asked.

'The old boy's Lord Stratton. Local nob. He owns most of the land hereabouts. That's the Lord Lieutenant with him. Major-General Sir William Raikes.'

'What's he doing here?' Madden scowled.

'He was a weekend guest at Stratton Hall, worse luck.' Boyce pulled a face. 'He's been raising merry hell, I can tell you. The other one's Chief Inspector Norris, from Guildford.'

As Madden opened the car door, Raikes, red-faced and balding, came striding across the gravel.

'About time,' he said angrily. 'Sinclair, is it?'

'No, Sir William. Madden's the name. Detective Inspector. This is Detective Constable Styles. Chief Inspector Sinclair is on his way. He'll be here shortly.' Madden's glance roamed the forecourt.

'Well, for God's sake!' Raikes fumed. 'What's keeping the man?'

'He's getting a team together. Pathologist, fingerprint squad, photographer . . .' The inspector made no attempt to disguise his impatience. 'It takes time, particularly on a bank holiday.'

'Indeed!' Raikes glared at him, but Madden was already turning away to greet the older man, who had joined them.

'Lord Stratton? Thank you for sending the car, sir.'

'It was nothing. How else can I help you, Inspector?' He held out his hand to Madden, who shook it. His face showed signs of recent shock, the eyes wide and blinking. 'Do you need any transport? I've a runabout at the Hall. You're welcome to use it.'

'Would you mention that to Mr Sinclair? I'm sure he'll be happy to accept.'

'Now see here, Madden!' Raikes tried to force himself back into the conversation, but the inspector ignored him and went on speaking to Lord Stratton.

'There's something I need to know. The woods behind the house, do they belong to you?'

'Upton Hanger? Yes, the ridge extends for several miles.' He seemed eager to help. 'I keep a pheasant shoot over by the Hall' — he pointed in the direction of the village — 'but this side the woods run wild.'

'What's your policy on trespassing?'

'Well, technically it's private property. But the villagers have always had the run of the woods. Over on this side, at least.'

'Would you change that, sir? Make it clear no trespassing will be allowed and ask the police to enforce it.'

'I understand.' Stratton frowned. 'Better to keep people away.'

'I was thinking of the London press. They'll be here soon enough.'

'Boyce!' Chief Inspector Norris spoke.

'I'll see to it, sir.'

'One other thing.' Madden drew Lord Stratton aside. 'There's a crowd of villagers outside the gates. Could you speak to them? Tell them what's happened here. There's no point in keeping it a secret. Then ask them to go home. We'll be questioning them later. But they're no help to us standing out there blocking the road.'

'Of course. I'll see to that now.' He set off up the drive.

Watching, Billy could only marvel. How did Madden do it? He wasn't a nob himself, that much was certain. There was a rough, unpolished air about the inspector that set him apart from the likes of his lordship. But when he talked, they listened! Even Sir William Whatsit, who could only stand there glowering.

'Chief Inspector,' still ignoring Raikes, Madden turned to Norris, 'could we have a word?'

He moved away, and after a moment's hesitation Norris joined him. The Guildford chief was red in the face and sweating heavily in his thick serge suit.

'I'll need some details, sir.'

'Speak to Boyce.' Norris blinked rapidly. 'Good God, man! You can't treat a lord lieutenant that way.'

Madden regarded him without expression. Norris opened his mouth to speak again, then changed his mind. He spun on his heel and rejoined Raikes, who stood with his back ostentatiously turned to them, glaring up the drive at the retreating figure of Lord Stratton.

Madden nodded to Boyce and led the way out of the forecourt around to the side of the house. When they came into a pool of shade he paused and took out a packet of cigarettes. Billy, encouraged by the sight, lit up himself.

'I was told four in the house.' The inspector was speaking to Boyce.

'That's right.' The Surrey inspector took out a handkerchief. 'Colonel and Mrs Fletcher. One of the maids, Sally Pepper, and the children's nanny, Alice Crookes.'

'Who found the bodies?'

'The other maid, Ellen Brown. We haven't talked to her yet. She's in hospital in Guildford. Under sedation.' He wiped his face. 'Brown returned this morning. Mrs Fletcher had given her the weekend off – Saturday and Sunday – but she was due back last night, and the other maid, Pepper, was to have had today off. Brown missed her train – she's got a young man in Birmingham – and only arrived this morning. She was seen passing through the village, running from the station, looking to be in trouble with her mistress, I dare say. Half an hour later she was back again, not making much sense by all accounts.'

'Half an hour?' Madden drew on his cigarette.

Boyce shrugged. 'I don't know what she did when she found them. Fainted, I would guess. But she had enough sense to get herself to the local bobby. He lives at this end of the village. Constable Stackpole. He didn't know what to think – whether to believe her, even. He said she was raving. So he got on his bicycle and pedalled like blazes. He rang Guildford from the Lodge. I was the duty officer and I informed

9

Chief Inspector Norris and he rang the chief constable who decided to call in the Yard right away.'

'When did you get here?'

'Just before midday. Mr Norris and I.'

'You went through the house?'

Boyce nodded. 'We didn't touch anything. Then Sir William arrived with Lord Stratton.'

'Did they go inside?'

'I'm afraid so.'

'*Both* of them?'

Boyce looked shamefaced. 'Mr Norris tried to stop them, but . . . Anyway, they didn't stay long. It was getting to be ripe inside. The heat, you know . . .'

'Anyone *else*?'

'Only the doctor.'

'The police surgeon?'

'No, Stackpole couldn't raise him – he lives in Godalming – so he rang the village doctor.'

'What time did he get here?'

'She.' Boyce glanced up from his notebook. 'Her name's Dr Blackwell. Dr Helen Blackwell.'

Madden was frowning.

'Yes, I know.' Boyce shrugged. 'But it couldn't be helped. There was no one else.'

'Was she able to cope?'

'As far as I can tell. Stackpole said she did what was necessary, confirmed they were all dead. It was she who found the little girl.' He consulted his notebook. 'Sophy Fletcher, aged five. Apparently she's a patient of the doctor's.'

'The child was in the house?'

'Hiding under her bed, Stackpole said. She must have been there all night . . .' Boyce looked away, biting his lip.

Madden waited for a moment. 'You said "children".'

'There's a son. James, aged ten. He's been spending a few weeks with his uncle in Scotland. Lucky, I suppose, if you can call it that.'

'Do we know if the girl witnessed the murders?'

Boyce shook his head. 'She hasn't said a word since Dr Blackwell found her. The shock, I imagine.'

'Where is she now?'

'At the doctor's house. It's not far. I sent an officer over there.'

'We must get her into hospital in Guildford.'

Madden killed his cigarette on the sole of his shoe and put the stub in his pocket. Billy, watching, followed suit.

'Any idea of time of death?'

'Dr Blackwell says between eight and ten last night – based on rigor. Couldn't have been before seven. That's when the cook left. Ann Dunn. She lives in the village. I've had a word with her, but she couldn't tell us much. She fixed them a cold meal, then took herself off. Didn't notice anything unusual. Didn't see anyone hanging about.' Boyce glanced back towards the drive. 'The gates were open. They could have driven in.'

'They?'

'Has to be more than one man.' Boyce looked at him. 'Wait till you see inside. Most likely a gang. There's stuff been taken. Silver. Jewellery. But why they had to—' He broke off, shaking his head.

'How did they get into the house?'

'They broke in from the garden side. Come on, I'll show you.'

Boyce led the way to the front of the house, out of the shade on to the sun-washed terrace. It was late afternoon, past four o'clock, but the cloudless summer sky held hours of daylight yet. Shallow steps led from the terrace to a lawn bordered by flower-beds with a fishpond in the middle. Further on another set of steps led to a lower level bordered by a shrubbery. Where the garden ended the woods of Upton Hanger began, rising like a green wave, filling the horizon.

'See! They smashed in the French windows.' Boyce pointed. 'They're not cracksmen. Not professionals.'

One of a pair of tall glassed doors at the front of the house had been knocked off its hinges. The empty frame lay across the doorway. Broken glass glittered in the sunlight. Madden crouched down to examine it. In the silence Billy heard the sound of flies buzzing. It came from inside the house. He wrinkled his nose at the rotten-sweet smell.

'We can't leave 'em there much longer,' Boyce observed. He watched Madden with narrowed eyes. 'Not in this heat. There's a mortuary wagon standing by in the village. Should I bring it up to the house?'

'Better wait till Mr Sinclair gets here.' Madden stood up. 'You can begin fingerprinting, though. Start with the people who've been in the house.'

A grin replaced the anxious frown on Boyce's face. 'Does that include the Lord Lieutenant and Lord Stratton?'

'Certainly.'

'Sir William told Mr Norris they hadn't touched anything.'

'I'm sure he did. Print them both.'

Madden glanced at Billy. 'Constable?'

'Sir?' Billy straightened automatically.

'We'll go inside now.'

2

As Billy stepped over the broken door frame into the house, the smell of decaying flesh triggered a rush of nausea and he had to dig his fingernails into the palms of his hands to stop himself retching.

Eyes watering, he tried to block out the stench and concentrate on what was before him. They had entered the drawing-room, that much he could see. Madden was bending over the body of a young woman sprawled on the floor in the middle of the room. She lay on her side with her legs splayed like a runner in mid-stride, hands clutching at emptiness. Billy noted the black dress and frilled cuffs. This must be the maid, Sally Pepper, he told himself.

His glance took in the tray and coffee things – silver pot and two small cups and saucers – strewn across a cream-coloured carpet edged with vine leaves. The spilled coffee had spread into the shape of a flower. Black petals for a funeral wreath.

He knew the woman had been stabbed, Madden had told him earlier, but he couldn't see where. Then he noticed the inspector examining a small tear in the maid's uniform over her chest. It looked as if the black cloth had masked the flow of blood.

Billy was struck by how little had been disturbed.

Take away the smashed door and the pitiable figure on the carpet and the room was relatively untouched. Chairs and tables stood in their places. Nothing was disarranged. A cabinet where china was displayed remained shut, with the glass unbroken. Above the carved stone fireplace a pair of shepherdesses graced the mantelpiece beneath a painted portrait of a woman sitting on a sofa with two young children, a boy and a girl, on either side of her. All three were fair-haired.

Billy was starting to sweat. If anything, the smell was getting worse. He saw Madden's eyes were on him.

'If you're going to throw up, Constable, do it outside.'

'I won't, sir. Truly.'

Madden's glance implied disbelief. Billy gritted his teeth. He watched as the inspector started to move away from the body, then changed his mind and returned to it, this time to look at the back. He bent and peered at the area between the shoulder-blades. Billy wondered why. There was nothing to see there. He took a deep breath, then checked himself hurriedly as the surge of nausea returned.

He couldn't understand it. In three years on the force he'd seen his share of corpses, not all of them pretty. Week-old cadavers found in abandoned tenements. Floaters hauled from the Thames. Earlier that year he had worked on his first murder case since moving from the uniform branch to the CID. An old pawnbroker battered to death in his shop in the Mile End Road. His skull had been reduced to a red pulp, yet Detective Constable Styles hadn't turned a hair. Why now?

Searching for an explanation, Billy was left with the feeling that it had something to do with the enormity of what had happened in this house. He had seen it in the faces of the villagers and of the men who waited outside. Even Madden's grim features had registered a sense of disbelief as he recounted the bald details on their taxi ride to Waterloo. It was something that *shouldn't* have happened – that was the closest Billy could come to explaining it – not in the peaceful Surrey countryside, barely an hour's train ride from London. Not in England!

Madden rose. Skirting the body, he went to an inner door that stood open and paused on the threshold. Billy joined him. In front of them was a hallway with a passage branching off it, running the length of the house. To their left, a trousered leg protruded from a doorway. Madden went towards it, walking in the middle of the carpeted passage, his eyes on the floor in front of him. Billy stayed on his heels.

They came to the body of a middle-aged man lying on his stomach with his arms outstretched in the shape of a cross. His head was twisted to one side, the lips drawn back in a rictus of agony. A stab wound in the middle of his back had left a dark stain in the checked hacking jacket he wore. Some deep internal injury was signalled by the gush of blood from his mouth on to the surrounding floorboards. At the very edge of the pool of dried blood, a curved indentation was visible.

'Do you see that?' Madden pointed. 'Someone's walked there.'

'One of the killers, sir?' Billy peered over his shoulder.

'I doubt it. The blood was already dry. Make a note for Mr Sinclair.'

Madden stepped carefully over the body. Billy followed, fumbling for his notepad. They were in an oak-panelled study, furnished with a desk and two stuffed-leather armchairs. The walls were hung with photographs, mostly of men in military uniform. Some showed them sitting on chairs, stiffly posed. Others were less formal. There were pictures of polo matches and clay-pigeon shooting. Madden seemed more interested in a pair of shotguns mounted on a wall rack.

'Was he trying to reach one of those, I wonder?' He spoke the thought aloud.

'Or the telephone, sir?' Billy seized on the chance to participate. He indicated the instrument standing on the desk.

Madden grunted. He was still looking at the gun rack, frowning.

'Something's missing from the mantelpiece, sir.' Billy tried again. He was feeling better. The smell was less strong in here. 'That mark on the wallpaper . . .'

'A clock, most likely.' Madden spoke without turning. 'There might have been other stuff up there. Silver cups. The maid will know.'

He led the way out and walked back along the passage, checking each room as he came to it. He paused at only one, the dining-room, where plates and cutlery from the previous night's meal lay on the uncleared table.

At the far end of the corridor was a swing door. The inspector pushed it open and went through. Billy, following on his heels, retched involuntarily and almost threw up as a pungent reek assailed his nostrils. They were in the kitchen. The afternoon sun poured through unshaded windows on to a table where the remains of a roast chicken rested on a platter beside a glistening ham. As Madden approached, a cloud of flies rose into the air and then settled on the food again. Beyond the table a chair had been knocked over on its back and directly behind it a woman's body lay on the flagstoned floor, half propped against the wall. Grey-haired, plump-featured, she was dressed in a bloodstained white blouse and an ankle-length skirt of dark blue material. Her face wore a surprised expression.

'The nanny,' Madden murmured. He glanced at Billy, who had chosen that moment to shut his eyes while he tried to control his heaving stomach. 'Give me your handkerchief, Constable.'

'Sir?' Billy's eyes shot open.

'You've got one, haven't you?'

'Sir!' He gave it to Madden, who wet the cloth at the sink and handed it back to Billy.

'Put that over your nose, son.'

'Please, sir, I don't need—'

'Do as I say.'

Without waiting to see if his order was carried out, the inspector crossed the room to where the body lay.

Brushing aside the flies he bent down and unfastened the blouse, drawing it apart. From where he was standing Billy could see the wound, neat as a buttonhole, between the tops of the veined breasts. Madden stayed staring at it for a long time. When he rose his eyes had that unseeing 'other world' look, and Billy was relieved. The damp mask across his nose made the stench in the kitchen bearable, but the handkerchief felt like a badge of shame. As soon as they were back in the passage he tugged it off.

They returned to the hallway and he followed Madden up the stairs to the floor above. When they came to a landing the inspector paused.

'Do you see?' he asked, pointing.

Billy peered into the shadows. Embedded in the pile of the wine-coloured stair carpet were tiny pin-pricks of reflected light. 'What are they, sir?' he asked.

'Seed pearls. From a bracelet, I should think. They've been trodden in. Watch your step.'

At the top of the stairs there was another passage, like the one below, running the length of the house.

'Wait here,' Madden told Billy.

He walked down the corridor to his right, checking the rooms, and then returned to the stairway. At the first doorway on the other side he paused.

'Over here, Constable.'

The inspector's voice carried a note that gave Billy time to prepare himself. He walked the few steps to the door and followed Madden into the room. At first he could make nothing of the twilight gloom. The curtains, which must have been drawn the previous evening, still blocked out most of the daylight. Then, as his eyes grew accustomed to the half-darkness, he saw the body. *Mrs Fletcher*, Billy thought. The colonel's lady. (The painting in the drawing-room was fresh in his mind.) She was lying on her back on the bed, flung across it, it seemed, with her legs parted and her arms spread out, the fingers clenched. A silk dressing-gown of Oriental design, embroidered with red flowers and tied at the waist with a sash, was spread out on the bed on either side of her like a half-opened fan. Her legs and the bottom of her stomach were bare. The sight of her pubic hair made Billy blush and turn away. He couldn't see her face – her head was hanging over the other side – but when he followed Madden around the foot of the bed he saw the fair hair cascading down.

'Keep clear,' Madden warned him sharply. 'There'll be blood on the floor.'

Billy was just wondering how the inspector knew that – could he see in the dark? – when the answer became clear. Staring down at the livid gash in the white column of flesh, he felt a sense of violation stronger than anything he had experienced that day.

'Why'd they do that?' Billy couldn't stop himself. 'Why'd they have to cut her throat?'

*

Boyce was waiting for them when they came out on to the terrace again. The sun was lower in the sky, the shadows lengthening.

'Mr Sinclair rang from Guildford,' he told Madden. 'He'll be here soon.'

'You can start the men searching the gardens.' The inspector lit a cigarette. 'But stay out of the woods for now.'

Boyce wondered what Madden had made of the shambles inside the house. He searched in vain for any hint in the dark, withdrawn eyes.

'You don't think they came that way, do you?'

The inspector shrugged. 'If they drove in the front gates, why come round to this side to break in? They could have knocked on the door.' To Billy, he said, 'Find that village bobby – what's his name? Stackpole?'

Billy returned in a few minutes with a tall, moustached constable. Madden greeted him.

'Do you know these woods?' he asked.

'Well enough, sir.' Stackpole eyed him warily. Word had spread about the Scotland Yard inspector who'd told the Lord Lieutenant where to get off.

'Come along, then. You too, Styles.'

A gravel path through the shrubbery at the bottom of the garden led to a wooden gate. On the other side of the wall they found a uniformed constable patrolling a small expanse of meadow grass bordering a shallow stream. He was a young man, not much older than Billy himself, and with similiar colouring – fair skin and reddish hair. His face was flushed by hours spent in the broiling sun.

'Excuse me, sir.' He hurried over to them.

'What is it, Constable?'

Madden had paused to take off his hat and jacket and hang them on the gate. When he rolled up his sleeves Billy saw a random pattern of scars spread over his forearm the size and shape of sixpences.

'A footprint, sir. Down by the stream. I noticed it earlier.'

'Show me.'

The constable led the way down the gently sloping bank. He pointed. 'There, sir, next to the stepping-stones. Coming this way.' The stream, diminished by weeks of drought, had shrunk to half its normal size. The earlier course of the water was marked by a surface of smooth dried mud. It was on this that the faint imprint of a footmark showed beside one of a line of flat stones crossing the stream. Madden nodded his approval.

'Well spotted, Constable.'

'Thank you, sir.'

'Go up to the house. My compliments to Mr Boyce and ask him to send a couple of men down here with some plaster-of-paris. Tell him the footprint's shallow but well defined and if they're careful they should get a good cast of it.'

'Right away, sir.' The constable set off briskly.

Madden went down on his haunches. Stackpole joined him, squinting at the stream bed.

'He might have missed his footing, sir. Coming across last evening, just as it was getting dark.'

'Big man.' The inspector frowned. 'Size eleven, I should say. That looks like a boot mark.'

Stackpole pursed his lips. ''Course, it could be anyone's.'

Billy felt the prick of envy. First the young constable. Now the village bobby!

Madden led them across the stepping-stones to the opposite bank. Almost at once they were in the wood, moving uphill through a stand of saplings that ended when they came to the tall beeches. A sea of fern and brush covered the ground on either side of the path, which was well used and easy to follow. The air was hot and still.

'Do the villagers come up here often?' Madden spoke over his shoulder.

'A fair bit, sir.' Stackpole kept pace with the inspector's long stride. 'Time was when the whole hanger was a shoot, but that was before the war. Now his lordship only has two keepers and they don't come over this way, except once in a while.'

Panting at the rear, trying to keep up with them, Billy had to watch for branches whipping back in his face. When he caught the cuff of his jacket in a bramble thicket, the constable paused to help disentangle him. He was grinning under his helmet. 'City boy,' he whispered.

Billy flushed a deeper red. He saw that Madden was watching them from above, hands on hips.

The hill steepened as they neared the top of the ridge. Madden stopped. He sniffed the air. 'Constable?'

'Yes, sir. I smell it . . .'

Stackpole cast about him with narrowed eyes. Billy caught a whiff of something. They were in the middle of a steeply sloping forest of pines. The carpet of ferns stretched unbroken on either side of them.

'Can't tell which way the wind's blowing,' the constable complained.

'Quiet!' Madden spoke sharply.

They stood in silence. Billy heard a low rustle in the undergrowth away to their left. Madden picked up a stick and threw it. A raucous cry broke the stillness, followed by the flapping of black wings as a pair of crows rose from the ground and flew off, threading a path through the lofty pines.

Madden and Stackpole looked at each other.

'Let's take a look,' the inspector said.

Madden left the path and began wading through the waist-high ferns. Keeping his eye fixed on the spot where the crows had appeared, he worked his way up and across the slope. Stackpole stayed close behind. Billy, struggling in the rear as before, lost his footing on the steep slope and had to grab at a root to keep himself from sliding down. His hat fell off. He caught it with his other hand. For a moment he lay spread-eagled like a starfish on the hillside. The others paused and looked back.

'It's all right, sir,' Billy gasped. 'I'm coming.' He could see Stackpole chuckling.

By the time he caught up with them they had stopped and were standing with their backs to him looking down. Madden held out a hand to check Billy's puffing uphill progress. The young constable saw they were at the edge of an area where the undergrowth had been flattened. The body of a small white dog lay on the ground in front of them. Beyond it was the corpse of a man, clad in a soiled cloth coat. He lay on his back with his head pointing down the slope. His hands, clutching at his chest, had torn apart his blood-soaked shirt. Where his eyes had been there were only pits. Billy blenched at the sight of the sockets, filled with congealed blood.

'Do you know him, Constable?' Madden's tone was detached.

'Yes, sir.' Stackpole, too, had paled. 'Name of Wiggins. James Wiggins. He's from the village.'

'What would he be doing up here?'

'Poaching, most likely.' The constable mopped his brow. 'That coat of his has got the deepest pockets in the county. Like as not we'll find a bird in one of them. Must have come across here from his lordship's shoot to dodge the keepers.' He pointed a finger at the dog. 'That's Betsy, Jimmy's bitch. Wonderful nose for a pheasant, or so Jimmy always said.'

'You've had dealings with him?'

'You could say that.' Stackpole grunted. 'He's been up before the bench. But not nearly as often as he should have. Hard man to lay a hand on.' The constable bit his lip. 'Poor Jimmy. I always said he'd come to a bad end.'

Madden was peering at the ground in front of them. Something had caught his eye. He bent down and slipped his hand into the trampled ferns, then withdrew it holding a cigarette stub delicately between his fingertips. He held it up to the light.

'Three Castles. One of his?'

'Not likely. Pipe and a tin of Navy Cut – that was Jimmy's style.' Stackpole's brow was knotted in a frown. 'Sir, I don't see how this could have happened.'

Madden, occupied with folding the stub into a handkerchief, glanced at him questioningly.

'I just can't see anyone creeping up on Jimmy. You wouldn't have got within twenty feet of him. If *he* didn't spot you, the bitch would have.'

Madden put the handkerchief carefully into his trouser pocket. He said, 'I think it was the other way round.'

'Sir?'

The inspector turned so that he was facing down the slope. The others followed the direction of his glance. Melling Lodge lay directly below them, clearly visible through a gap in the pine forest. Billy could make out a group of men in plain clothes standing on the terrace. A line of blue uniforms moved slowly across the sunlit lawn.

'I think whoever killed them was sitting here, waiting for dark.'

Stackpole nodded slowly, comprehending. 'Betsy would have picked up their scent,' he said. 'Come looking to see who it was.' He touched the small body with the toe of his boot. A thin trickle of blood had dried on the white jaw. 'When she was stabbed she must have squealed, kicked up a racket, and Jimmy came running.'

Madden was frowning. 'I didn't see a dog at the lodge,' he said. 'Did the Fletchers have one?'

'Yes, sir, Rufus. An old Labrador. But he died not long ago.'

Leaving Billy posted by the body, Madden and the constable returned to the path. The inspector wanted to climb to the top of the ridge. It took only a few minutes, the pines thinning out as they scaled the stony crest. On the other side was a vista of farms and woodland stretching for miles. In the distance, hazy in the afternoon light, they could just make out the blurred contours of the South Downs.

Not far from the base of the ridge a cluster of cottages stood with a square church tower in the middle.

'That's Oakley, sir,' Stackpole said, without prompting. 'I was born there.'

Madden pointed to a narrow track that led from the hamlet through fields of ripening corn to the edge of the woods beneath them.

'Could you get a car along there?'

The constable shook his head. 'Tractor, maybe. Car springs wouldn't take the ruts.'

They went back down the path and crossed the slope to where Billy was standing by Wiggins's body. Madden paused for only a moment. 'Stay off the flattened area,' he told the young constable. 'It needs to be searched. I'll be sending some men up.'

Billy felt his cup of bitterness brim over. The inspector had finally found something he was fit for. To stand watch over a body until others came to do the police work.

'Isn't there something I can do, sir?'

'Yes, keep the crows off him,' Madden called back as he hastened away. 'They go for the eyes.'

Stackpole clapped him on the shoulder sympathetically as he went by. 'Not yours, lad,' he said, with a wink.

3

CHIEF INSPECTOR SINCLAIR drew Madden aside, leading him down the shallow steps from the terrace on to the now deserted lawn. They made an oddly contrasting pair: Madden, tall and rumpled, with his jacket slung over his shoulder; Sinclair, slight and no more than medium height, almost the dandy in his tailored pinstripe suit and soft felt hat. They stood close together, casting a single shadow in the dying sunlight.

'A question. Have we any idea what we're dealing with here?' The chief inspector's restless glance took in the squad of uniformed police who had moved off the grass and were searching the shrubbery at the bottom of the garden. At Madden's behest he had just dispatched two CID sergeants to deal with the body in the woods. 'An armed gang, I'm told, a robbery gone wrong.' He nodded towards the terrace where Boyce and Chief Inspector Norris stood watching them. 'In that case, perhaps someone would explain to me why there's stuff in the house in plain view worth more than what was taken. Did you see the china in the drawing-room? And that brace of Purdeys on the gun rack? Good of them not to loot the place, wouldn't you say? Especially since they had all night

29

to do it.' Angus Sinclair's consonants had the precision of cut glass. A native of Aberdeen, he'd been a policeman for more than thirty years. 'Your thoughts, John?'

Madden lit a cigarette before replying. Sinclair studied his face. He noted familiar signs of strain and deep-seated fatigue in the dark, shadowed eyes. They were aspects of Madden he had come to recognize, souvenirs of the war, as permanent and unalterable as the scar on his forehead.

'Starting with the door, sir,' Madden's deep voice rose little above a murmur, 'why break it down? It wasn't locked. Then the victims' hands and arms. Apart from Mrs Fletcher, they were all killed the same way, but there isn't a cut or scratch on any of them.'

'Your point?' Sinclair cocked his head attentively.

'Whoever did this was in a hurry. The victims had no time to react or defend themselves. I think those downstairs were all dead within seconds of the door being smashed in.'

'Which means the killings were deliberate. That was the intention from the outset.' The chief inspector paused, reflecting on what he had said. 'So much for a robbery gone wrong! Anything else?'

'The weapon, sir. It was unusual. No injuries to the hands and arms, as I said. And then there's Colonel Fletcher, killed from behind in that way.'

'Would you care to be more specific?' Sinclair frowned. 'Have you any idea what it was?'

Madden shrugged. 'I'd rather hear what the pathologist says. I don't want to put ideas in his head.'

'Or mine?' The chief inspector raised an eyebrow. 'But as regards Colonel Fletcher, I take your meaning. You'd think he would have faced his attacker. Why did he turn and run?'

'He might have been trying for one of the guns in the study.'

'Even so, an old soldier . . . You'd expect him to take on a man with a knife. If it was a knife . . .' Sinclair grimaced. 'An armed gang? Could they be right?' He gestured towards the terrace.

Madden shook his head. 'I think it was one man,' he said.

The chief inspector looked hard at him. 'I was hoping you wouldn't say that,' he admitted.

Madden shrugged.

'I have the same feeling.' Sinclair's gaze shifted to the house. 'It's got the smell of madness about it. That's one man's work. But we have to be sure. What about the woman upstairs, Mrs Fletcher? There could have been two of them.'

Again Madden shook his head. 'He broke the door down and killed the maid in the drawing-room, then went for Colonel Fletcher. The colonel tried to reach the study – where the guns were – but he only got as far as the doorway before he was caught from behind. As for the woman in the kitchen, the nanny, I doubt she even knew what was happening. You can see the surprise in her face.'

While Madden was speaking Sinclair had taken a briar pipe from his pocket. He stood now, tapping the empty bowl in the palm of his hand.

'Aye, but that still doesn't explain Mrs Fletcher. She wasn't killed like the others.'

'I think she heard the disturbance and came down the stairs. That's where they met. Did you notice the pearls in the carpet?'

The chief inspector nodded. 'From a bracelet, I'd say. It must have broken. I think he seized her there and dragged her upstairs to the bedroom. Tell the pathologist to look for bruises on the wrists and arms.'

Sinclair examined the bowl of his pipe. 'If you're right, then since he didn't kill her on the stairs, he must have had something else in mind. Rape, by the look of it. Poor woman. Well, we'll know soon enough.' He slipped the pipe back into his pocket. 'That would explain why she wasn't stabbed. He wanted her alive. But what did he use to kill her with?'

'A razor, I'd say.'

'Yes, but whose? The colonel's? Or did he bring his own?'

The chief inspector expelled his breath in another long sigh. He watched as a plain-clothes detective stepped over the broken door frame to deposit a white envelope in a numbered cardboard box, one of four standing in a row on the terrace. Close by was a leather holdall, Sinclair's 'black bag', containing equipment he deemed necessary for a murder investigation: gloves, tweezers, bottles, envelopes. The new scientific approach to crime detection was slowly gaining ground, though not without meeting resistance. Juries remained suspicious of forensic evidence. Even judges were inclined to give it little weight in their summings-up.

'I've sent for the mortuary wagon.' Sinclair was speaking again. 'We'll do the post-mortems in Guildford tonight, as many as we can. I want to run the investigation from down here, at least in the early stages. Bring a bag when you come tomorrow. You'll be sleeping in the pub.

'Meantime, there's that little girl to think about. Get over to Dr Blackwell's house, would you, John? Find out if the child saw anything. And arrange to have her moved to hospital right away. We can take the doctor's statement tomorrow. I must get back.' He glanced up at the house again. 'I want to keep an eye on that pathologist. He's new to me. I asked for the sainted Spilsbury, but he wasn't available. On holiday in the Scilly Isles, if you please! I had to take one of his assistants at St Mary's.' As he spoke, photographer's flash powder, like sheet lightning, lit up a window. 'All this and the Lord Lieutenant, too!'

'You met him, did you?' Madden donned his jacket.

'He was leaving when I arrived. With inky fingers and a foul disposition. He said you were impertinent. No, *damned* impertinent.'

'He went inside the house – did he tell you *that*?'

Sinclair was amused. 'You are aware, are you not, that he's head of the magistracy and chief executive for the county of Surrey? Take care, John. That type likes to make trouble.'

Madden scowled. 'I've had a bellyful of that type.'

'Then again, someone stepped in that pool of blood

in the study. I might send an officer after him to look at the sole of his shoe. That should spoil his supper.'

Madden's glance, straying to the bottom of the garden, was arrested by the sight of Styles sitting on a bench at the edge of the lawn. The constable's red hair was plastered to his sunburned forehead. He was picking burrs from his socks.

'Aye, I'm sorry about that.' Sinclair had followed the direction of his gaze. 'I shouldn't have landed you with a green one. There was no one else on hand this morning. I'll have him replaced tomorrow.'

Madden shook his head. A smile touched his lips. 'No, leave him,' he said. 'He'll do.'

4

THE FORECOURT was becoming crowded. A second police van was drawn up behind the first, and on the other side of the fountain a big Vauxhall tourer was parked against the creeper-clad wall. The numbers of uniformed police had thinned, but several plain-clothes men were gathered in a group near the front steps. Searching for Stackpole, Madden found him beside a trestle table on which plates of sandwiches and a large tea urn rested.

'Courtesy of the village ladies, sir. Would you care for a mug?'

'Thank you, not now. I have to see Dr Blackwell. Could you tell me the way to her house?'

'I'll do better than that, sir.' Stackpole emptied his tin mug and wiped his moustache. 'I'm going there myself. Mr Boyce sent a man over this morning, but he needs to be relieved.'

'You could do with a break yourself, Constable.'

'Oh, I'm all right, sir,' said Stackpole, who was thinking the same applied to Madden. The inspector's dark eyes seemed to have sunk even deeper into his gaunt face. 'And at least I'll get my supper later, which is more than can be said for this lot.'

He led the way out of the forecourt and through a

kitchen garden. A gate in the high brick wall opened on to a path that joined the road some distance past the entrance to Melling Lodge. Looking back, Madden saw that the crowd of villagers had dispersed. But now there were several cars parked outside the gates.

'That'll be the London press,' he said.

The winding lane ran between hedgerows. The two men tramped along it side by side. After a while, Madden spoke: 'Just between us, Constable, we're not inclined to treat this as a robbery. It looks as though the killings were deliberate, even planned.'

Stackpole sucked in his breath. 'That's hard to believe, sir. If you'd known the family . . .'

'Well liked, were they?'

'More than that. Miss Lucy – Mrs Fletcher – she was born here, at Melling Lodge. The house would have gone to her brother, but he was killed in the war. When she and the colonel settled at the Lodge, it must have seemed like coming home to her. And as for the village – well, you won't find a soul who wasn't that pleased to see her back.'

They had come to a belt of forest, a spur of woodland spilling down from the slopes of Upton Hanger. The road bore to the right, but Stackpole pointed out a narrow track in the woods ahead. 'That's a short cut to the doctor's house, sir. It'll save us ten minutes.'

The path, dark as a tunnel, ran beneath a dense canopy of beech and chestnut. The sun had almost set. When they came to a garden gate, Madden paused. He took out his cigarettes. 'Constable?'

'Thank you, sir.'

'I was told you were with Dr Blackwell when she found the child.' He struck a match for them.

'So I was.' Stackpole drew in a lungful of tobacco smoke. 'I'd already been looking for her when Dr Helen – Dr Blackwell – arrived, and we started searching again. It was the doctor who found her, under her bed in the nursery. Poor little girl. She'd squashed herself up against the wall and was lying there with her eyes shut. She must have heard us calling, but she didn't make a sound. When Dr Helen pulled her out she was stiff all over and there were dust balls in her hair. She wouldn't say a word. The doctor wrapped her in a bedspread and put her in her car and drove her straight here.'

'Have you known Dr Blackwell long?'

'Since we were children, sir.' The constable grinned. 'Miss Helen's from the village. Fine doctor, they say.'

'But not yours?'

'Well, no, sir.' Stackpole looked embarrassed. 'I mean, the wife and children go to her, but somehow it doesn't seem right, her being a woman . . . Besides there's her father, old Dr Collingwood. He still sees a few patients.'

They put out their cigarettes. Madden unlatched the garden gate. Close by, a huge weeping beech spread its branches over a corner of the lawn. He saw the house outlined against the darkening sky. Like Melling Lodge, it faced the woods of Upton Hanger, deep and mysterious at this hour. The same stream they had crossed earlier that day divided the ridge from an orchard at the bottom of the garden, which was bounded by a low stone wall.

They walked up the sloping lawn to the house where the curtains remained undrawn on a wide bow window. Light from inside washed across a broad terrace lined with flower-pots. Roses clung to a trellis. The air was heavy with the scent of jasmine.

As they drew near the house a dog began barking and a door opened. Stackpole touched his helmet.

'Evening, Miss Helen.'

'Hullo, Will.' The doctor was a tall silhouette against the light. 'Down, Molly!' she commanded as a black pointer slipped out of the door behind her and came prancing up to the men.

'This is Inspector Madden, from London. Sir . . . Dr Blackwell.'

They shook hands. Helen Blackwell had a firm grip.

'Come in, please.' She ushered them into the drawing-room. 'I've been expecting you. I only wish the circumstances were less appalling.'

Madden took off his hat. 'I'm sorry you had to be called in this morning, ma'am,' he said. 'I expect they were your friends.'

'They were. It was dreadful.' Helen Blackwell had thick fair hair, drawn back and tied with a ribbon behind her head. Her eyes were an unusual shade of blue, Madden noted, dark, almost violet-coloured. He registered her good looks, but was struck more by the signs of character in her face. Her glance was direct. 'I've known Lucy Fletcher all my life. We grew up together, people used to take us for sisters.'

She fell silent, but he saw she had something more to say and he waited.

'I didn't examine the bodies thoroughly this morning. It wouldn't have been right. Can you tell me, was Lucy . . . Mrs Fletcher . . . ?'

'Assaulted?' Instinctively he avoided the more explicit term. 'We don't know. The pathologist will conduct the post-mortems in Guildford, probably tonight.'

Stackpole coughed. Dr Blackwell turned to him.

'I believe there's an officer here, Miss Helen.'

'In the kitchen, Will. You'll find Edith there. Ask her to make up a plate of sandwiches, would you? And have some yourself.'

As the constable left them, Madden began to speak, but she checked him with a gesture. 'Sit down, Inspector. Please. You must be exhausted.'

Gratefully, he obeyed. Dr Blackwell went to a drinks tray. She poured whisky from a decanter into a glass and brought it to him. 'Consider that a medical prescription.'

Her smile, open and friendly, took him by surprise. She seated herself beside a table where a group of silver-framed photographs stood showing young men in officer's uniform. Madden's eye shifted away from them quickly, but she had caught the direction of his glance.

'Those two on the left are my brothers. David was killed on the Somme. He's the younger. Peter was a pilot. He only lasted three weeks. My mother died of a heart complaint the year before the war and now I can only think of it as a blessing.' She was silent. Then she gestured towards another of the photographs. 'And that's my husband, Guy. He was killed, too. A stray shell, they said.' Her glance met Madden's. 'Scenes from an English drawing-room, circa nineteen twenty-one.'

He could find no words.

'I was thinking of them today when I went to the Lodge. How the thing I hated most about the war was the way it plucked up people at random and destroyed them. How I'd thought that that, at least, was over.'

There was a knock on the door and a maid came in carrying a tray with sandwiches on it. She put the plate on a side table near Madden. Dr Blackwell gathered herself. 'What can I do for you, Inspector? Would you like me to make a statement?'

'We're concerned about the Fletcher child. We'd like her moved to hospital in Guildford as soon as possible.'

'I'm afraid that's out of the question.'

Her response was so swift that Madden had to check to assure himself he'd heard her correctly. He put down his glass. 'Dr Blackwell, this is a *police* matter.'

'I understand that. It changes nothing.' She spoke in a calm voice, but her expression was unyielding. 'Sophy was in a state of profound shock when I found her this morning. She was quite unable to move or speak. The stiffness – it's a form of hysterical paralysis – has eased somewhat, but she hasn't said a word, and I don't know when she will. The very worst thing now would be to put her among strangers. She knows me and everyone in this house and she trusts us. There's nothing that can be done for her in hospital that can't be done here.'

'She's a possible witness—'

'I'm aware of that. You're welcome to keep a policeman here. More than one, if you wish. But I won't have her moved.'

The steadiness of the doctor's gaze seemed to set a seal on her words. In spite of his surprise, Madden had listened carefully to what she said, while noticing that her pale silk blouse was embroidered with a pattern of green leaves. He came to a decision quickly. 'I believe you're right,' he declared. 'I'll say as much to my chief inspector.'

The severity of her expression dissolved at once into the same open smile as before. 'Thank you, Inspector.'

'But I must see the child.'

'Of course. She's in bed. Come with me.'

She led him out into a hallway and up the stairs. Following, Madden caught a whiff of jasmine, like an echo from the terrace outside. They stopped at a closed door in the passage above.

'One moment, please.' She opened the door and glanced inside. 'Come in. Try not to wake her.'

'Isn't she sedated?'

'I gave her something earlier, but it'll have worn off by now. She's sleeping normally. I'd like that to continue.'

Madden followed her into a bedroom where a night

light burned. A dark-haired young woman in a maid's uniform got up from a chair as they entered. Dr Blackwell motioned to her to sit again.

'This is Mary,' she whispered. 'Sophy knows her well. They go for walks in the woods together when she comes to visit.'

He went closer to the bed. At the sight of the blonde head buried in the pillow an old grief awoke in him and he stood for a long time, bent over her, listening to the faint rhythm of the child's breathing, so precious it seemed.

Watching him, Dr Blackwell was startled by the look of pain that crossed his face. Earlier her curiosity had been aroused. She had wondered about this rough-looking man who bore the stamp of the trenches in his dark, shadowed eyes. A year spent working in a military hospital had taught her to recognize the signs, but she'd been surprised to see them on the inspector's face. The police had been one of the reserved professions.

Now, all at once, another image came to her, raw and shocking, causing her to flush and bite her lip. And she thought then how cruel life could be. How heartless and uncaring.

5

MADDEN LIVED WITH GHOSTS. They came to him in dreams: men he had known in the war, some of them friends, others no more than dimly remembered faces.

Most were the youths with whom he had enlisted, shop assistants and drapers, clerks from the City and apprentices. Together they had marched through the streets of London in their civilian clothes to the bray of brass bands, heroes for a day to the flag-waving crowds, full of pride and valour, none dreaming of the fate that awaited them in the shape of the German machine-guns. Valour had died on the Somme in the course of a single summer's day.

One of the few survivors in his battalion, Madden had mourned the death of his comrades. For a time their loss had seemed like an open wound. But as the war went on he ceased to think of them. Other men were dying around him and their deaths, too, came to mean little. With no expectation of staying alive himself his emotions grew numb and by the end he felt nothing.

He never spoke of his time in the trenches. Like many others who came back, miraculous survivors of the carnage, he had tried to put the war from his mind, doing his utmost to block out all memory of it. Offered his old job back, he had hesitated before accepting. His decision to leave the Metropolitan Police before the war had been taken in the hope of finding a new life in the familiar surroundings of the countryside. And although he came to accept the choice he had made, finding in the day-to-day demands of investigative work at least a partial shield against the charnel house of memories that threatened to engulf him, he could not shake free from the cold hand of the past. Always he sensed the abyss at his feet.

Sleep brought no respite, for what he kept from his mind by day he was forced to relive in his dreams where he was haunted by the faces of old comrades and by other, more terrible images from the battle-field, and from which he would wake, night after night, choking on the imagined smell of sweat and cordite and the stench of half-buried corpses.

For a while he had hoped all this would pass. That his memories would grow dim and peace of mind return to him. But he lived in the long shadow of the war, and as time passed and the shadow deepened he came to see himself as permanently injured, a casualty of the conflict, which had failed to kill him but left him none the less damaged beyond repair.

Increasingly solitary, he saw his life as all that was left to him: a tattered sail that might bear the wind but would bring him to no haven.

6

AT NINE O'CLOCK the following morning, Chief Inspector Sinclair addressed the team of detectives assembled in the Highfield church hall.

'Some of you with experience in murder inquiries may already have recognized the particular problems we face in this case. Most murders, as we know, are either domestic in origin or are committed in the course of some other crime. We can probably rule out the first in this instance. And while robbery was certainly a factor at Melling Lodge, there are reasons to believe that this was not the principal motive. Indeed, it seems likely that whoever broke in did so with the intention of killing all those present in the house.'

His words drew a murmur from his audience. The group of a dozen detectives included plain-clothes men from Guildford CID and a contingent from Scotland Yard, comprising Madden and Styles and a detective sergeant named Hollingsworth. They were accommodated in straight-backed chairs facing a dais where Sinclair sat at the centre of a table, flanked by Chief Inspector Norris on one side and a senior uniformed officer on the other. Also on the stage, but sitting apart, were Lord Stratton and a middle-aged man whom Boyce identified as Sir Clifford Warner, the Surrey chief constable. A thin file lay on the table in front of Sinclair. Beside it was a canvas bag tied with a drawstring.

'In a case of this nature there's bound to be speculation. You will have seen some of it in the morning papers. Apparently we're looking for an armed gang.' The chief inspector paused. 'That may or may not be true. Let's hope it is. One of them is sure to open his mouth before long. I see, too, that the Sinn Fein is being held responsible in some quarters. It might be useful if I gave you some background on Colonel Fletcher. He was born in India and was commissioned in the Indian Army before returning to England, where he transferred to the regular army. He served in the war in the Signals Corps and then settled with his family here in Surrey. Neither he nor his wife has ever set foot in Ireland so far as we can determine.'

Sinclair smoothed his neatly trimmed cap of grey hair. His eye fell briefly on Madden, who was sitting in the front row of chairs beside Boyce. The inspector looked pale and drawn.

'This investigation will be run initially from Highfield. The vicar has put this hall at our disposal, and I intend to use it as the main interview room and also as a central collecting point for all information. Mr Boyce will be in charge here, along with Inspector Madden, whom most of you have met. They'll be assisted by Detective Sergeant Hollingsworth from Scotland Yard. The uniform branch will be working with us in the early stages under the direction of Chief

Inspector Carlyle, of Guildford.' Sinclair indicated the uniformed officer beside him. 'For the past hour his men have been searching the woods behind Melling Lodge. That will go on all day – and for as long as necessary thereafter.

'A word about the interviews. The villagers have been informed, and they'll be turning up in relays starting in about fifteen minutes. I want to know how they spent the weekend, and in particular where each and every one of them was between eight and ten on Sunday night.' He paused to give emphasis to his next words. 'Every person in the village must be spoken to. We need to know if they saw or heard anything out of the ordinary, no matter how trivial.

'A more general line of questioning will deal with the matter of strangers. In a small rural community like this, outsiders are quickly noticed. Were any seen on Sunday, or the preceding days? With the help of the Surrey police we're going to be asking the same questions in the surrounding villages. Unfortunately, either by chance or design, this could not have occurred at a worse time for us.' The chief inspector frowned. 'I refer, of course, to the bank-holiday weekend. Half the country seems to have been on the move, and I'm afraid we'll find even Highfield has had its share of visitors and passers-by.'

He opened the file and took out a sheet of paper. 'Here is a partial list of items taken from Melling Lodge. It was supplied by the cook, Mrs Dunn. She can't be sure about the upstairs – we'll have to check that with the maid Brown when she's brought back here from Guildford. Mainly silverware and some of Mrs Fletcher's jewellery.' He glanced up. 'Not the best bits, incidentally. It's being circulated to jewellers and pawnbrokers in the normal way. Consult it if you need to.'

He removed a second sheet of paper from the file.

'Fingerprints lifted from the house are being checked against the occupants and others who were known to be regular visitors. That will take a while. We also have a footprint.' He held up the sheet of paper. 'This is a sketch of the cast taken of a print in the stream bed at the bottom of the garden. Size eleven, military-type boot. Notice the heel.'

Sinclair displayed the drawing which showed an arrow-shaped wedge missing from the rim of the heel.

'This will have to be checked against the boots of all the men in the village, as well as Colonel Fletcher's footwear. Mr Boyce will organize that.' He paused again. 'A number of cigarette stubs were found near the body of James Wiggins in the woods above the house. They have been sent to the government chemist for analysis. They were all the same brand – Three Castles – which Wiggins didn't smoke. Find out who smokes cigarettes in the village and what brand they favour.'

The chief inspector extracted a further piece of paper from the file. He studied it for several seconds.

'I have here a preliminary report from Dr Ransom, the pathologist,' he went on. 'A description of the wounds inflicted on the three victims downstairs at

Melling Lodge and on Wiggins. I expect to receive a further report on Mrs Fletcher's injuries by courier from Guildford later today. The four victims I refer to were all killed with the same weapon, or an identical one. Dr Ransom characterizes this as a relatively narrow blade – no more than an inch wide – with one angle acute and the other blunt. The depth of the wounds varies between four inches, in the case of Alice Crookes, the nanny, whose body was found in the kitchen, and six inches, in the case of Colonel Fletcher. No exit wounds were found. Dr Ransom is unable to say whether the wounds were inflicted by a right- or a left-handed man. This is because they were struck with "a remarkable degree of uniformity" – I'm quoting now – "being both straight in relation to the skin surface and horizontal". He adds one further observation: "in each case some lateral damage to tissue was caused when the weapon was withdrawn."'

Sinclair replaced the sheet of paper carefully in the file. His glance met Madden's briefly.

'Dr Ransom agrees with Inspector Madden and myself that these wounds are typical of those caused by the standard British Army sword bayonet. I have one here.' Sinclair loosened the drawstring on the canvas bag and took out a sheathed bayonet. He withdrew the glittering steel from the scabbard and held it up. 'Notice the similarities to the murder weapon as described by Dr Ransom. One angle blunt,' he ran his finger along the top of the bayonet, 'the other acute. It may strike you as strange that a weapon of this length – it's twenty-one inches, in fact – should be used to inflict such relatively shallow wounds. Inspector Madden will explain.'

Madden rose to his feet and faced the detectives. He spoke in a monotone. 'What I have to say will be familiar to anyone who has served in the ranks. For the rest of you, I'll describe briefly the training given to infantrymen in the last war. The average soldier, armed with rifle and bayonet, will automatically thrust the weapon in as far as it will go. Run his enemy through, in fact.

'He has to be taught not to do this. Skin and muscle cling to the blade making it difficult to extract. The correct method, as taught by the Army, is a short, stabbing thrust followed by a half-twist to break the friction as the weapon is withdrawn. All the wounds we have been discussing show these characteristics.'

One of the Guildford detectives held up his hand. 'Sir, are you saying a bayonet fixed to a rifle was used in these killings?'

'I am.'

'Were they all killed by the same man?'

'I believe so.' Madden paused. 'You heard what the pathologist said. "A remarkable degree of uniformity." I'll go further and say that whoever killed them was an expert in the use of this weapon. In each case only one thrust was required. Either the man was highly trained, or, more likely, was once an instructor himself. Possibly an Army sergeant.'

Again there was a murmur from the assembled detectives. Madden glanced at Sinclair and sat down.

'Right!' The chief inspector looked at his watch. 'If there are no more questions, I suggest we get started.'

*

'Thank you, Chief Inspector. A fine summary, if I may say so.' Sir Clifford Warner paused at the top of the church hall steps to shake Sinclair's hand. Lord Stratton hovered at his shoulder. 'You'll keep me informed?'

'Of course, sir.'

The Surrey chief constable glanced curiously at Madden as he moved away.

'They were talking about you earlier, John.' Sinclair was filling his pipe from a leather pouch. 'Warner wanted to hear about your run-in with the Lord Lieutenant.'

'Has Raikes lodged a complaint?'

Madden's pallor seemed more striking in the morning sunlight. Sinclair wondered if he had been disturbed by the thought of the bayoneted bodies. They were colleagues of long standing, their acquaintance going back to before the war when Sinclair's eye had first been caught by the tall young detective, fresh out of the uniformed branch. Much had happened to Madden since then.

'Not that I know of, and not that I care. Let Raikes get back to doing what he does best, slaughtering innocent birds and beasts and stay out of police business.' The chief inspector struck a match. 'Oakley, you say?'

'Yes, sir.' Madden drew on the cigarette he had lit

some moments before. 'It's on the other side of the ridge. I'd like to get over there. I think our man might have come that way.'

'You'll need a car, then.'

'Lord Stratton's offered to lend us one.'

'So he has. What's more I've accepted. God knows, we'll get no help from the Yard.' Scotland Yard's attitude towards motorized transport – they saw no reason why any policeman should be supplied with a vehicle when he had two perfectly good feet – was a pet grievance of the chief inspector's. Second only to his dogged and so far unsuccessful campaign to have a central police laboratory established. 'He took your side, by the way, Stratton did. He said Raikes was wrong to go inside the house and wrong to invite him along. Called him a blockhead. Quite brightened my morning, his lordship did.'

Madden trod on his cigarette. 'What about the press, sir? Have you spoken to them yet?'

'I'm meeting them at noon. Just for now, and between us, I'll not discourage the notion of a gang, if anyone brings it up. One man on his own – now that's a disturbing thought.'

They moved aside as the first group of villagers come to be interviewed gathered at the foot of the steps. Dressed as though for church, Sinclair noted. Suits and ties for the men, hats for the women. He made his own silent prayer: *Let just one of them remember something, anything, a face, a description . . .*

A young woman knelt to tie on a toddler's bonnet. The sight caused Sinclair's face to harden.

'I'll be seeing Dr Blackwell later,' he said. 'I'm not happy about that little girl staying in her house. She ought to be in hospital. It's something the doctor should understand. Can't she be persuaded to see reason?'

'Not an easily persuadable woman, sir.' Madden's face was a mask.

'Is she not?' The chief inspector's eyes lit up. 'We'll see about that. I intend to have words with this dragon.'

7

THE CAR WAS PARKED in the cobbled courtyard of
the village pub, where Madden had left his bag with
the landlord earlier that morning. It was a well-worn
Humber with a dent in the rear mudguard. Lord
Stratton himself, bareheaded, stood talking to two of
the villagers. When he saw Madden he came over.

'Inspector, I must apologize for what happened
yesterday.' His thin, seamed face showed the ravages
of a sleepless night. 'Raikes had no business taking
me into that house, and I had no business accepting.
Well, I've paid for it.'

'Sir?'

'I can't get it out of my mind. The sight of the
bodies . . . Poor Lucy Fletcher, laid out like a sacrifice.
What kind of man would do a thing like that? Then
I find myself thinking perhaps there were more than
one . . .'

'We don't know yet that she was raped, sir.'

'No . . . no . . . of course.' He thrust his hands into
the pockets of his tweed jacket and stared at the
ground. 'The villagers keep asking me . . . There are
some things one doesn't want to know.'

'How are they taking it?'

'Badly.'

Madden sought and obtained directions to Oakley. He drove along the same road he had travelled the day before, past Melling Lodge, where two uniformed policemen stood on duty at the closed gates and a man lugging a heavy press camera leaned against a car parked on the grass verge. A mile or so further on he came on another set of gates and another uniformed constable. He stopped the car and got out.

'Is this where Dr Blackwell lives?' Madden could see the house at the end of an avenue of limes. He only knew it from the other side.

'Yes, sir. We've got a man inside, but Mr Boyce sent me over to watch the gates. The doctor was bothered by the press this morning, they wanted to know about the little girl.'

A mile further on he came to a signpost for Oakley, turned left and followed a road that led through a saddle in the wooded ridge down to the broad open plain he had seen the day before from the top of Upton Hanger. Another signpost directed him on to a dirt road and he drove through fields where the corn had already turned golden from the long, rainless summer.

The hamlet of Oakley comprised no more than a dozen houses grouped around the church tower. Madden brought the car to a stop beside a white-washed building with the picture of a stage-coach and the name 'Coachman's Arms' painted in faded lettering on the wall. As he was setting the handbrake a police sergeant stepped out of the doorway of a cottage across the road. He looked at Madden inquiringly. The inspector got out of the car and produced his warrant card.

'Gates, sir. From Godalming.' The sergeant touched his helmet. 'It's this Highfield business. I've been sent over here to talk to the locals. They don't rate a village bobby.'

'You'll ask them if they've seen any strangers?' Madden drew him into the shade of a chestnut tree growing in front of the church.

'Yes, sir. And anything out of the ordinary they might have noticed these past few days.'

'We're specially interested in any cars that might have passed through the village.'

'Shouldn't be too many of those, sir. Mind you, it was a bank holiday.'

'Also cars parked at the roadside. Perhaps even off the road where they mightn't be noticed.' Madden became aware that Gates was looking over his shoulder. His glance had turned to a flat, hard stare. The inspector turned his head and saw a man standing in the doorway of the Coachman's Arms with his hands in his pockets watching them.

He faced the sergeant again. 'I'm going to take a walk through the fields, but I'd like a word with you before you leave. How long will you be here?'

'An hour should do it, sir. Then I've got to go to Craydon – that's a few miles away – and ask the same questions there.'

'Have you any transport?'

'Just a bicycle.'

'Wait for me here. I'll give you a lift over.'

Madden walked back the way he had come, on the dirt road, and continued along it until he found an even rougher track, which branched off through the fields towards the wooded ridge. The deep treads of tractor tyres were graven in mud that had dried and set like marble. Ditches a foot wide criss-crossed the rutted surface. At one point the track petered out entirely and the tractor marks continued across ploughed furrows until they picked up the path again. Stackpole had been right. No car could have passed this way.

Feeling the sun like a weight on his back, Madden took off his jacket and walked steadily towards the ridge. Passing a small spinney he heard a jay call, and another answer. He was tempted to stop for a cigarette – the wood looked cool and inviting – but instead he pressed on and arrived at the foot of the ridge.

He saw that it was steeper on this flank than on the Highfield side and also less densely wooded. Standing in the shade of an oak tree he marked the upward zigzag line of a footpath as it traversed the slope above. He looked left and right along the hillside, but could see no sign of any other pathway in the vicinity.

The inspector began a careful examination of the area where he stood, scanning the ground in a gradually widening circle, and then extending his search along the base of the ridge at the woodline, looking for the tell-tale sign of a cigarette stub. He found several, but none were of the Three Castles brand.

The footpath up the slope proved equally bare of clues. The dusty surface bore the marks of blurred footprints – it looked like a well-used way – but none showed the distinctive damaged heel outline discovered in the stream bed. It took him twenty minutes to scale the ridge, and half that time to make the return journey.

He sat down then in the shade of the oak tree and took out his cigarettes. The green leaves overhead seemed to remind him of something: the image of Helen Blackwell in her patterned blouse came into his mind with a pleasant jolt. He lit a cigarette.

Far away, beyond the golden fields, a faint blur on the horizon showed where the downs began. He watched a hawk circling in the air above. Etched clear against the brilliant blue sky, it wheeled and wheeled in ever-tightening turns. Wheeled . . . and dropped! Wheatstalks shivered and were still. The hunter had its prey.

Madden extinguished his cigarette. He'd yet to catch the scent of his.

*

In Oakley, the door of the Coachman's Arms stood open. Sergeant Gates was seated at one of the tables in the taproom. Smoke-blackened beams supported the grubby ceiling. The smell of stale beer and tobacco soured the air. The man Madden had seen standing in the doorway earlier lounged over the bar, his elbows resting on the stained surface. He was in his early thirties with black slicked-back hair and a knowing smile.

'This is Inspector Madden,' Gates said tonelessly.

'Sir, this is Mr Wellings, the landlord. I was about to question him.'

'Go ahead, Sergeant. Don't mind me.' Madden sat down.

Wellings directed his smile at the inspector. 'Still half an hour to opening time, I'm afraid. But if Sergeant Gates is prepared to turn a blind eye, I dare say I could draw you a pint.'

'No, thank you, Mr Wellings.' Madden didn't return the smile.

'We're interested in any customers you might have had over the weekend,' Gates began. 'Visitors, not locals.'

'Starting when?'

'Saturday.'

'I had the Farnham Wheelers Club through here at midday. About a dozen of them. They parked their bikes outside and came in for a drink. And there was a party of four in a motor-car. Two men and their wives, I reckon. They had the ploughman's lunch.'

'Was that all?' Gates looked up.

'No, there was another couple in the evening. Bloke on a motorbike with his girlfriend on the pillion. Took me aside, he did, and asked me if I had a room for them. I told him I didn't run that kind of establishment. I did say he could try his luck in Tup's Spinney.' Wellings smirked.

Madden waited to be enlightened, but Gates went on: 'Sunday, then?'

'There were more. Quite a few. Four parties in cars between midday and two o'clock. Six men and four ladies, as I recall. Two of the parties were travelling together, heading for the coast. And then in the evening there was one other car with a man and his wife and their son. But all they wanted was directions. They'd lost their way.'

'Did you see any other cars during the day? Travelling through the village, but not stopping?'

'Or motorcycles?' Madden said.

Wellings paused, frowning with exaggerated concentration. He shook his head. 'No, I can't say that I did. But, then, I'm stuck in here during opening hours. Don't see too much of what's going on outside.' The smile was back.

Sergeant Gates looked at Madden, who nodded.

'Thank you, Mr Wellings.' He closed his notebook.

'What did you think, sir?' he asked Madden outside.

'I thought he was lying.'

'I agree, but about what?' The sergeant wrinkled his nose. 'He's a right sow, if you'll pardon the expression. The last two landlords quit because they couldn't make the place pay. But somehow he manages to, and you have to ask yourself how.'

'After-hours drinks?'

'That, and he'll sell you a carton of fags at below market price, or so I've been told. We think he handles stolen goods, but we haven't been able to lay a finger on him thus far.'

'There's a list out of items taken from Melling Lodge. If any of them turn up locally, pull him in. Never mind if there's a connection or not. Put him through it.'

'It'll be a pleasure, sir.'

Madden donned his jacket. 'What was that he said about the man with the motorbike and his girl?'

'He should try his luck in Tup's Spinney.' Gates gestured. 'That's over in the fields. Well known to the local lads and lasses, if you take my meaning.' He grunted. 'Wellings has an eye for the ladies himself, they say. Especially if it's someone else's wife. Nasty piece of work.'

They loaded the sergeant's bicycle into the back of the Humber, and Madden drove him the few miles to Craydon. Returning by the same road, and passing through Oakley, he saw Wellings on the pavement outside the village shop talking to a young woman with bobbed hair. He paused in his conversation and watched Madden's car as it went by.

8

MADDEN PARKED the Humber where he had found it, in the courtyard of the Rose and Crown in High-field. As he climbed out of the car, the door of the pub opened and a lanky man in a city suit came out. He had his tie loosened and his hat tipped back on his head.

'Mr Madden, is it? Reg Ferris. *Daily Express*.'

He held out his hand. Madden shook it briefly. They hadn't met before, but he knew Ferris's name and recalled that he was no friend of the chief inspector's.

'Bad business.' The reporter's darting eyes went from Madden to the car and back as though he hoped to glean some information from putting the two together. 'I'm told it was like an abattoir in there.'

Madden reached into the car for his jacket.

'We're waiting for Mr Sinclair. He's said he'll meet us.'

'Then I dare say he will.'

Ferris leaned against the car. He put his hands in his pockets. 'This is different, isn't it?' He watched to see how Madden would react.

'Different?'

'You've not had a case like this before – admit it.

Slaughtering a whole household, and for what? A few bits of silverware? It doesn't make sense.'

The inspector put on his jacket. 'Goodbye, Mr Ferris.' He walked away.

The reporter called after him: 'From what I hear you don't know where to start.'

*

Madden found the chief inspector on the church hall steps talking to Helen Blackwell. The doctor was wearing a man's white linen jacket with the cuffs rolled up over a light summer dress. She greeted Madden with a smile.

'Dr Blackwell has been giving us a statement.' Sinclair's grey eyes held a hint of wry amusement. 'She has also explained to me her reasons for wanting to keep Sophy Fletcher at her house, rather than send her to hospital. I found her arguments . . . persuasive. The child will stay here.'

'Thank you again, Chief Inspector.' The doctor shook his hand warmly. Her eyes brushed Madden's. 'Good morning to you both.'

Sinclair's nod was approving as he watched her walk away. 'A fine-looking lassie.' He gave Madden a side-ways glance. 'Dragon indeed! You might have warned me, John.'

'Nothing from Oakley, I'm afraid, sir.' Madden was smiling. 'The press are waiting for you at the pub. I bumped into Ferris.'

'Is that rodent here?' The chief inspector's face darkened. 'It must be the smell of blood.'

'He's already guessed we've got problems.'

'He doesn't know the half of it. Come with me. There's something I want to show you.'

Inside the hall a low hum of voices sounded from a line of tables where detectives were taking statements. Madden saw Styles, bent over a pad, sitting opposite an elderly woman in a black coat and hat. Inspector Boyce was at another table before a growing pile of statement forms. With a nod to him, Sinclair picked up his file and led Madden to one side, out of earshot. He removed two typewritten sheets of paper clipped together from the folder and handed them to the inspector. 'Have a look at that.'

It was the post-mortem report on Lucy Fletcher. Madden spent several minutes studying it. Sinclair waited until he had finished.

'So he never touched her.' Eyes narrowed, the chief inspector stood with folded arms. 'Ransom looked everywhere. Vaginal swabs. Anal swabs. He even tested the poor woman's mouth. Not a trace of semen.'

'He grabbed her, though, just as we thought,' Madden said. '"Bruises on the upper arms . . ."' he quoted.

'He grabbed her and dragged her up the stairs to the bedroom and cut her throat. Why *didn't* he rape her? There was nothing to stop him. She was naked under that robe. What was he doing there? Why was he in that house?'

Madden was silent.

'He killed her with a razor, Ransom thinks. But it

wasn't the colonel's – that was with his shaving things in the bathroom. We found no trace of blood on it. He brought his own.'

Madden put the report back in the file. 'Did you show this to Dr Blackwell?' he asked.

'Yes. Why?'

'They were childhood friends. She needed to know.'

Sinclair sighed. He pointed to the pile of forms in front of Boyce. 'Go through those, John. See if you can find anything. I must talk to the press. When I come back we'll sit down together. The assistant commissioner's called a meeting for tomorrow morning. The Yard is making its concern clear,' he added drily. 'I expect to be told they want an early result.'

'I doubt they'll get one this time.' Madden weighed the file in his hand.

'Spare a thought for me tomorrow when I'm telling them that.'

*

The tea urn had appeared again; it was sitting on a table by the door. Madden poured himself a mug and took a sandwich from the heaped plate beside it. He collected the pile of forms from Boyce and settled down in a quiet corner.

The statements, short for the most part, were mainly testaments to the unchanging nature of village life. Most of those questioned had seen the Fletchers at church on Sunday morning – for the last time, tragically. Several of them had spoken to Lucy Fletcher afterwards. 'Such a lovely lady,' Mrs Arthur Skipps, the butcher's wife had said, unprompted, and the detective interviewing her had let the remark stand.

Such a lovely lady.

Tom Cooper, the Fletchers' gardener, had been one of the last to see them alive. Although he was free on Sunday, he had gone over to Melling Lodge in the late afternoon to water the roses growing beside the kitchen-garden wall. The long drought had made it a difficult summer for him and he was determined not to see his labours go for nothing. Colonel Fletcher had found him busy with a watering-can and chided him in a friendly way for working on his day off. The colonel had been in his 'usual good spirits'. Later, Mrs Fletcher and her daughter Sophy had walked by and Cooper had waved to them. They were talking about the puppy the Fletchers were planning to buy for Sophy and her brother when they returned from Scotland at the end of the summer.

Lord Stratton, in his statement, said he had taken the Lord Lieutenant and his wife to dine with the Fletchers on Saturday evening. It had been 'a pleasant occasion'. The Fletchers had talked about their plans to drive through France later that summer to visit friends in Biarritz.

Helen Blackwell, who had also been at the dinner, was more forthcoming. Sophy Fletcher was to have spent the whole summer with her uncle and aunt – Colonel Fletcher's brother and his wife – at their home outside Edinburgh. An attack of measles had kept her in Highfield, however, and her brother James had been sent on ahead. She was due to have travelled to Scotland by train the following week in the company of her nanny, Alice Crookes. Shortly thereafter the Fletchers had planned to leave for France.

The last part of Dr Blackwell's statement, an account of her urgent summons to the house on Monday morning, was given in cold medical language. She had examined each of the victims in turn and pronounced them dead. Rigor was starting to recede and she had estimated the time of death at a little over twelve hours earlier. She said 'something' had made her look under the bed in the nursery. She employed the same phrase as she had used with Madden to describe Sophy's condition when she found her. 'Profound shock.'

The question of strangers in the village over the weekend was dealt with in several of the statements. Frederick Poole, the landlord of the Rose and Crown, reported a busload of passengers in a Samuelson motor coach stopping at the pub for lunch on Saturday. The company had alerted him ahead of time. As far as he knew, all those who alighted from the bus had boarded the vehicle again later. Apart from that, there had been upward of a score of motorists and cyclists who had called in at the pub on Saturday and Sunday. None had stuck in his mind. All had continued their journeys.

Freda Birney, the wife of the owner of the village shop, Alf Birney, reported seeing two hikers picnicking by the stream between the outskirts of the village and Melling Lodge on Sunday just before twelve o'clock. She had been taking the dog for a walk before preparing lunch for her family. Madden made a note to have the hikers traced and questioned.

Running his eye over the next statement in the pile, he paused, went back and reread it carefully, checked the name of the interviewing officer, and then put it to one side.

*

Billy Styles pushed the form across the table, watched the man sign it, said, 'Thank you, sir, that'll be all for now,' then leaned back in his chair and stretched. His tenth interview of the day. Harold Toombs, the village sexton. Billy had had to fight to keep a straight face as he wrote it down. Toombs had spent the weekend working in his garden. He had neither seen nor heard anything out of the ordinary.

It was a matter of amazement to Billy that he was still part of the investigation. After his experiences of the day before he had expected to find himself back in the CID pool at Scotland Yard.

Detective Sergeant Hollingsworth, who'd brought him the news, seemed equally surprised. A stocky, nut-faced man with twenty years on the force, he affected to find Billy's presence among them a source of wonder. 'Can't think what the guv'nor has in mind. No bloodhounds in your family tree, are there, Detective Constable Styles? No hidden talents we're not apprised of?'

On receiving word, Billy had experienced a moment of elation, quickly followed by one of foreboding as he contemplated the prospect of spending another day under the dark glance of Inspector Madden.

But thus far, beyond a polite, 'Good morning, sir,' from Billy, and a distracted nod in response from the inspector, they hadn't exchanged a word, and Billy had found himself mildly bored as he recorded the villagers' bald accounts of the long, sun-drenched weekend.

Now he saw Madden, sitting in the corner of the hall, beckon to him. He rose from the table and went over. 'Sir?'

Madden held out a statement form. 'Yours, I think?'

Billy glanced at it. 'Yes, sir. May Birney. Her father owns the village store.'

The inspector eyed him. 'Well, did she, or didn't she, Constable?' he asked.

'Sir, she wasn't sure.' Billy shuffled nervously. 'First she said she did, then she changed her mind. Said she must have been mistaken.'

'Why did she do that? Change her mind?'

'Sir . . . sir, I don't know.'

Madden stood up so abruptly Billy had to spring backwards. 'Let's see if we can find out, shall we?' With a nod to Boyce he strode from the hall. Billy hurried after him.

The village store, a few minutes' walk away down Highfield's only paved road, was situated between the pub and the post office. Alf Birney, plump, with a fringe of grey hair like a monk's tonsure, came from behind the counter to show them into a curtained-off room at the back of the shop.

'It's not right this should have happened,' he muttered. 'Not to a lady like Mrs Fletcher. Not to any of them.' He shifted a carton of custard powder off a chair to make room for Madden. 'I can remember when she was a child. She used to come to the shop every Saturday to buy her sweets. Little Lucy . . .'

He left them there, and a minute later his daughter came in. May Birney was no more than sixteen. She was dressed in a dun-coloured work smock, her bobbed hair cut in a fringe across her pale forehead.

'Get it straight in your mind now, girl.' Her father's voice came from beyond the curtain. 'Tell the inspector exactly what you heard.'

Miss Birney stood before them, nervously twisting her fingers. Madden looked at Billy and nodded. Taken by surprise – he'd assumed the inspector would handle the questioning – Billy cleared his throat. 'It's about this business of the whistle you say you heard. Or didn't hear.' He spoke loudly, and watched her flush and steal a glance at Madden, who was seated at a table in the middle of the room.

'You were out walking the dog, you said,' Billy prompted her.

May Birney stared at her feet.

'Tell us again what happened.'

The girl said something inaudible.

'*What?*' Billy heard himself almost shouting. 'I didn't hear. What did you say?'

'I said I told you before but you said I was imagining it.' She spoke very quickly looking down.

'I never said that—' Billy checked himself. 'I asked

you if you were sure you'd heard a *police* whistle and you said, no, you weren't—'

'I said *like* a police whistle.'

'All right, *like* a police whistle, but then you said perhaps you'd been mistaken and you hadn't heard it at all. Do you remember saying that?'

The girl fell silent again.

Billy stepped nearer. He felt Madden's eyes on him. 'Now listen to me, May Birney. This is a serious matter. I don't need to remind you what happened at Melling Lodge on Sunday night. Stop saying you're not sure or you don't remember. Either you heard something or you didn't. And if you're making all this up . . .!'

The girl turned bright red.

Madden spoke. 'Would you like to sit down, May?' He drew up another chair for her. After a moment's hesitation, the girl complied. 'Now let's see, I'm a little puzzled, what time did this happen?'

'Around nine o'clock, sir. Might have been a little later.'

'Was it still light?'

'Just getting dark.'

'You were walking the dog?'

'Yes, sir, Bessie. She's getting old, you see, and needs to be taken, but if you put her outside, she just flops down, so Mum and me, we take her down to the stream and make her walk a bit.' She kept her eyes on Madden's face.

'Then you heard what sounded like a police whistle?'

'Yes, sir, like that. The same sort of sound.'

'Just once?'

May Birney hesitated, her brow creased in concentration. 'Well, sir, it was like I said' – she shot a glance at Billy – 'first it was there, then it sort of faded away, and then it came back just for a moment.'

Madden's brow creased. 'Was there a breeze blowing?' he asked.

The girl's face lit up. 'Yes, sir, that was it. That's what happened. It came and went on the wind. I heard it twice. But it was so faint . . .'

'You wondered if you'd heard it at all?'

She nodded vigorously. Shooting another defiant glance at Billy, she said, 'I just wasn't sure.'

'But you are now?' Madden leaned forward. 'Take your time, May. Think about it.'

But she paused for only a moment. 'Yes, sir,' she said. 'Now I'm sure. *Positive.*'

On their way back to the church hall, Madden paused outside the Rose and Crown. A low brick wall enclosed the cobbled yard in front of the pub and he sat down on it and took out his packet of cigarettes. 'I believe you smoke, Constable?'

'Thank you, sir.' Surprised and pleased, Billy fumbled with his matches. Madden accepted a light. He sat for a while in silence. Then he spoke.

'This job we have,' he drew on his cigarette, 'it gives us a lot of power in small ways.'

'Sir?' Billy didn't understand.

'It's tempting to use it, particularly with people who . . . who don't know how to defend themselves.'

Billy was silent.

'Do you understand what I'm saying, Constable?'

He shook his head.

'Don't take the easy way, son.' Madden looked at him now. 'Don't become a bully.'

The cigarette in Billy's mouth had turned to gall.

'Now go and see if Mr Boyce has something for you to do.'

9

THE FOLLOWING MORNING the inspector went from cottage to cottage on the Melling Lodge side of Highfield, inquiring whether any of the occupants had heard a whistle on Sunday evening.

The third door he knocked on was opened by Stackpole. The village bobby, still in his shirtsleeves, carried a small curly-haired girl in the crook of his arm whom he introduced as 'our Amy'.

'Can't help you, sir,' he told Madden. 'It wasn't me that whistled, that's for certain. Sunday evening the wife and I were over having supper with her parents. They live on the other side of the green.'

A tow-haired boy peered out of a doorway behind him. Madden heard a baby's wail.

'Pardon me for saying so, sir, but young May Birney isn't what I'd call a reliable witness. Got her head in the clouds half the time, that young lady. She's sweet on a lad who works for one of Lord Stratton's tenants, but her parents are dead set against him. I've seen her down by the stream, mooning about.'

Madden smiled. Like all good village bobbies, Stackpole made everyone else's business his own. 'In the end, she seemed quite sure she'd heard it,' he said.

'Could have been something else,' the constable

suggested. 'Jimmy Wiggins whistling up his bitch. Or one of his lordship's keepers.'

'Perhaps.'

The inspector gave an account of his visit to Oakley the day before. 'I didn't take to Wellings. He didn't strike me as being truthful.'

'I'm not surprised,' Stackpole observed. 'Lies as he breathes, that one.'

'Gates said he handles stolen goods.'

'You weren't thinking . . .?' The constable raised an eyebrow.

'The stuff taken from Melling Lodge?' Madden shrugged. 'It did cross my mind. What's your view?'

Stackpole shifted the little girl to his other arm. 'I'd say if someone offered Sid Wellings a set of silver candlesticks, or a piece of jewellery, he'd snap it up. But by the time you talked to him he must have known what happened at the Lodge and if he had any connection with it, even by chance, he'd have been wetting himself.'

Madden nodded. 'All the same, next time you're over there, speak to him. Ask him the same questions. What was he doing over the weekend? Who did he see passing through the village? Let him know we're not satisfied with his answers.'

Stackpole looked at the inspector curiously. 'Do you still think he came through Oakley, sir?' And then, after a pause: 'It is "he" we're looking for, isn't it? Not some gang?'

'We believe it's one man,' Madden confirmed. 'But keep that to yourself for now. About Oakley, I'm not sure. He had to have some kind of transport. We think he was carrying a rifle, and when he left he must have had what he took from the Lodge. I don't think he could have come into the area on foot, even through the fields, without someone spotting him.'

'A *rifle*, sir?'

'He killed them with a rifle and bayonet – we're fairly sure of that. All except Mrs Fletcher.'

'Is he a soldier then?' Stackpole scowled.

'I doubt it. There's no military camp anywhere near. An ex-soldier, more like it.'

'Plenty of them about.' The constable pressed Madden to come in for a cup of tea, but he declined the offer. Stackpole himself was due at Melling Lodge to join the party searching the woods. 'Between you and me, sir, it's a waste of time. Even with Lord Stratton's keepers helping. Most of these lads are town-bred. They'll more likely step on something than see it.'

An hour later Madden was back at the church hall. He had found no one to confirm May Birney's story of the whistle. Sergeant Hollingsworth was seated at the table where Boyce had been the day before. The Guildford inspector was supervising a check of all boots in the village.

'He's got a fingerprint team with him, too, sir. They'll take the prints of anyone who called regularly at the Lodge.'

'Anything else?' Madden began leafing through the pile of statements on the table.

'Only the lady doctor, sir. She came by, asking for you. It's to do with the little girl.'

'What about her?' Madden looked up quickly. 'Is something the matter?'

Not that I know of, sir.' Hollingsworth scratched his head. 'Dr Blackwell just wants a word with you. But she said it was important.'

*

Madden broke the police seal on the front door of Melling Lodge and went inside. The house lay in semi-darkness, with the curtains pulled. The metallic smell of blood was still strong in the hot, musty air.

Standing in the flagged hall, he pictured the scene as it must have happened. The man with the rifle bursting into the drawing-room from the terrace, glass and wood splintering, the maid with the coffee tray turning, mouth open, ready to scream—

In! Out! On guard!

The commands he'd once been taught came back to him, accompanied by a sickening image.

The killer had caught Colonel Fletcher before he could reach the guns in the study, then the nanny in the kitchen, running from room to room down the long passage.

In! Out! On guard!

Why such haste? Madden wondered. *What was driving him?*

Racing up the stairs he had encountered Lucy Fletcher, dropped his weapon and seized her by the upper arms. He was big and strong, judging by the size of the footprint in the stream bed, if it was his. Madden saw him picking up the woman by the arms and holding her clear of the floor – they had found no heel marks dragged across the carpet – carrying her into the bedroom and flinging her across the bed like . . . Lord Stratton's words returned to him: like a sacrifice.

He saw the white throat hideously slashed, the cascade of golden hair . . .

The nursery, papered with daffodils and bluebells, was at the end of the passage upstairs. It contained two beds, one unmade. Dolls and stuffed toys sat in a row on a wooden shelf. A model aeroplane hung from the ceiling. Madden took a laundry bag off its hook behind the door, emptied it and put in fresh clothes from the cupboard and two pairs of girl's shoes retrieved from a foot locker. Other items went into a brown paper bag he found on top of the cupboard.

A uniformed officer had been posted in the forecourt outside. At Madden's direction he made a list of everything taken from the nursery, which the inspector signed.

'I'm removing these articles from the house,' he told the constable. 'My compliments to Mr Boyce and see that he's informed.'

*

The avenue of limes led to a pleasant half-timbered house with a garage on one side where a red Wolseley two-seater was parked. The maid, whom Madden had seen upstairs on his previous visit, answered the door-bell. She led him straight through the drawing-room out into the garden. Dr Blackwell was seated in an arbour at one end of the terrace with a little girl beside her. Sophy Fletcher had waist-length fair hair. She was dressed in a blue muslin frock belted with a yellow sash.

At the sight of the inspector she sprang from her chair and threw herself on to the doctor's lap, burying her face in her shoulder.

Shocked, Madden halted. 'I'm sorry, I didn't mean to alarm her.'

He turned to go back inside the house, but Helen Blackwell called out to him, 'Don't go, please.'

To the child, she said, 'Sophy, this is Inspector Madden. He's a policeman.'

The little girl, her face still hidden, gave no response. Madden could see her body trembling.

'Come and sit down,' the doctor urged him. 'I want Sophy to get used to being with strangers again.' Privately she wondered if it wasn't the inspector's grim aspect that had upset the child. She saw that Madden was carrying a bag in each hand.

'You'll have some lemonade with us, won't you?' She sought to lighten the deep frown with a smile. 'Mary, pour the inspector a glass, would you?' A jug and glasses stood on the table in front of them.

Madden tugged open the laundry bag. 'I brought some of Sophy's clothes from the Lodge,' he explained.

'How very kind of you.' She was touched by his gesture. 'I was going to ask about that. This is something Mary ran up.' She patted the blue muslin back. 'Luckily Sophy left a pair of shoes here on her last visit.'

'You wanted to talk to me?'

'Yes, please. Later . . . ?' She glanced down at the fair head. 'Could you stay a little while?' He nodded. 'I have a patient to see in the village, but I shan't be long.'

She watched as he sat down and began emptying the brown-paper packet he had brought. He took out several dolls and a teddy bear and began arranging them in a circle on the grassed flagstones in front of him. Mary hovered. The inspector looked up. 'Do you have any old tea-cups?' he asked. 'The more chipped the better. And perhaps a jug of water?'

Dr Blackwell nodded to the maid, who went into the house.

'Sophy . . .' She nudged the small figure on her lap. 'Look what the inspector's brought.'

The child didn't move. Her face stayed sealed to the doctor's shoulder.

The maid returned with a tray bearing an array of china. She put it on the ground beside Madden. He began to lay out the crockery, rattling the cups and saucers as he did so. Helen Blackwell felt a small movement. The child had turned her head. She was watching out of the corner of her eye.

Madden put a cup and saucer in front of each toy, then placed the jug of water in the centre of the circle.

'Someone will have to pour,' he announced.

Mary started forward, but Dr Blackwell checked her with a gesture. The little girl was stirring. She climbed slowly off the doctor's lap. Keeping a wary eye on Madden she approached the circle of figures and dropped to her knees in front of them. She studied the group for several seconds. Then she picked up the teddy bear and placed him at the head of the circle near Madden's feet. Her eyes met his. Whatever she saw in the inspector's sombre glance seemed to reassure her and she lifted the jug of water and began to pour.

Dr Blackwell rose. 'I must go and see my patient,' she said, without urgency. 'Can I leave you here for a little while, Inspector?'

He nodded in answer.

'Sophy, I'll be back soon.'

The child, absorbed in the business of filling the cups, made no reply.

When the doctor returned half an hour later she found the arbour deserted. Mary was standing at the edge of the terrace with folded arms looking out over the garden. Helen Blackwell joined her and saw Madden and Sophy, hand in hand, at the bottom of the lawn, near the orchard.

'Did he take her down there?' she asked the maid.

'No, she took him, ma'am.' Mary smiled. 'She's showing him the garden.'

'Is she talking to him?' Dr Blackwell hardly dared to hope.

'No, just pointing.'

As she spoke, the little girl lifted her hand and indicated the weeping beech at the edge of the lawn. They went there together and vanished from sight beneath the drooping branches. After a minute they reappeared. The child stood close to Madden with her head bowed while the inspector bent over her and carefully picked the twigs from her hair.

'*He*'s talking to *her*,' Mary observed.

Dr Blackwell said nothing. She found herself feeling breathless in the hot midday sun.

'Let's go inside.' She drew the maid away. 'I don't want her to see us watching.'

From the drawing-room window they observed the little girl lead Madden back to the terrace. At the bottom of the steps she halted and reached up her arms to him. He lifted her easily, and in a moment she had attached herself to him, winding her arms about his neck and pressing her cheek to his shoulder. He stood still, as though stunned, then turned and slowly mounted the steps to the terrace. Helen Black-well saw the tears on his cheeks.

'Oh, ma'am . . .' Mary said beside her.

The doctor moved away from the window.

'Mary, would you go and ask Cook to get Sophy's lunch ready?' she said. 'I'll bring her through in a moment.'

As soon as the maid had gone Helen Blackwell sat down in a chair and lit a cigarette. She felt drained of energy. She wanted to sit quietly and think.

But there was something she had to do at once, an urgent problem that needed solving, and after less than a minute she extinguished the cigarette, ran her fingers through her hair and went out on to the terrace to speak to Inspector Madden.

10

'SHE WANTS TO SEND the child to *Scotland*? Och, John, I can't let her do that.'

'It might be the best thing, sir.'

They were sitting in what Mr Poole, the landlord of the Rose and Crown, called the snug bar, a panelled recess at the back of the taproom. He had set it aside for the use of the police. The main bar was shut – it was the middle of the afternoon – but they could hear the barmaid at work cleaning up. She was singing a song Madden remembered from the war.

> K-K-K-Katy, my beautiful Katy,
> You're the only g-g-g-girl that I adore . . .

'What will I tell the Yard?'

'What Dr Blackwell told me. It's her professional opinion. The child would be better off with her family – she still has a brother alive, remember – and also more likely to recover if she's away from here.'

Sinclair frowned discouragingly. 'You say her aunt and uncle are coming down from Scotland for the funerals?'

'Yes, on Friday. Dr Blackwell would like Sophy to go back with them.'

'The child hasn't said a word yet?'

'No, but Dr Blackwell thinks she will soon. Start speaking . . .'

'Well, then?' Sinclair raised his eyebrows.

'The doctor believes it's unlikely she'll talk about what happened that night. In fact, she may have blocked it out of her mind. Repressed memory, I believe it's called.' Madden paused. 'Dr Blackwell's already spoken to someone in Edinburgh – a psychologist – who could start treating the child right away.'

'Takes a lot on herself, your Dr Blackwell does.'

'Not mine, sir. Very much her own woman, I'd say.'

'Would you, now!' Sinclair snorted. 'Damn it, everything she says makes sense.' He took out his pipe and began to fill it. 'This doctor in Edinburgh . . .?'

'Another woman, sir.' Madden smiled. 'A Dr Edith Mackay. She had a full medical training and then studied to become a psychologist. Apparently she specializes in children. Sophy's aunt and uncle are only half an hour out of Edinburgh. She could see the child regularly.'

'Very well.' The chief inspector held up his hands in surrender. 'But if the girl says one word about what happened that night . . .'

'Her uncle will get in touch with the Edinburgh police immediately. Dr Blackwell promised that.'

Sinclair lit his pipe. 'Anything else?'

'Only this.' Madden took two folded pieces of paper from his jacket pocket. 'Dr Blackwell gave Sophy a pad and some crayons and she started drawing straight away. Always the same thing, the doctor said.' He handed the papers to Sinclair who examined the child-ish scribbles. The same balloon and string design covered both sheets of paper with little variation.

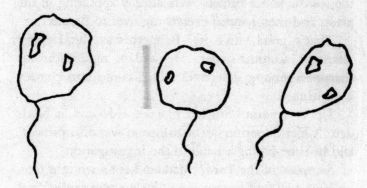

'What does it mean?'

'Dr Blackwell has no idea. But she thought we ought to see it.'

The chief inspector handed the papers back. He said, 'I'm about to break the law. I'm going to ask Mr Poole to serve us a drink. Then I'll tell you what happened at the Yard this morning.'

*

'Like the curate's egg, it could have been better and it could have been worse.'

Sinclair set two glasses of whisky on the table in front of Madden. He shut the hatchway to the tap-room, picked up his pipe from the ashtray and sat down.

'Parkhurst started off chairing the meeting' – Sir George Parkhurst was the Assistant Commissioner,

Crime; effectively head of the CID — 'but he only spoke for ten minutes. Held forth on the undesirability of massacres in the Home Counties, pointed out that the words "police baffled" were already appearing in the press, and then handed everything over to Bennett.'

'That's good, isn't it?' Bennett was the Deputy Assistant Commissioner. He had a reputation for sharpness among detectives who'd come into contact with him.

'Up to a point.' Sinclair glanced sideways at Madden. 'Chief Superintendent Sampson was also present, and he'll be taking a hand in the investigation.'

'Sampson of the Yard?' Madden kept a straight face.

'You may find it amusing,' Sinclair said acidly, 'but take it from me, the man's a menace. I dare say he's already pictured the headlines. "Another Triumph For Sampson Of The Yard!"'

'They're not putting him in charge, are they?'

'Not yet — but he hasn't suggested it. He wants to sniff around a little first, get the feel of it. After all, other headlines are possible. "Sampson Of The Yard Falls Flat On His Face. Sampson Of The Yard Doesn't Know His Arse From A Pineapple."' The chief inspector looked wistful. 'He's playing it canny for the moment. He and Bennett will oversee the investigation, but it's still ours.'

He tapped out his pipe in the ashtray.

'I gave them a summary of our inquiries to date. That we've no reason to suspect any local involvement in the murders. We think they were killed by an outsider. Norris, from Guildford, was there. He still believes more than one man was involved. Said the victims downstairs and Mrs Fletcher were almost certainly killed by different people. Sampson agreed with him.'

'Why did he do that?' Madden scowled.

'To create difficulties for us?' Sinclair shrugged. 'Who knows? I should warn you, he doesn't care for me. Wouldn't mind seeing *me* fall flat on my face. The point is, we're still officially searching for more than one man. So be it.'

He emptied his glass.

'But the important thing was, Bennett supported us on the bayonet theory. Over Sampson's objections, by the way – he said the medical evidence was inconclusive. Did you know there were more than sixty thousand soldiers in mental hospitals at the end of the war? Most of them shell-shocked, poor devils, but there must have been some of the other kind. Bennett's going to talk to the War Office. We'll get a list of patients who've been released and start running them down. He'll also ask them to look into Colonel Fletcher's military service record. Did he have a run-in with one of his men? Some deep-held grudge?' The chief inspector shook his head. 'Motive's still our main problem. I told them that. Revenge is a possibility, but this notion of an armed gang losing their heads and going berserk is pure balderdash, and Bennett knows it. Those killings were deliberate.'

11

AT THE CORONER'S INQUEST, held in Guildford the following day, verdicts of murder by person or persons unknown were returned in the case of all five victims. The coroner, an elderly man with red-veined cheeks and a drooping eyelid, spoke of the horror felt 'not only in Highfield, but here in Guildford' at the 'heartless, brutal murders of Colonel and Mrs Fletcher'.

'He seems to have forgotten about the maid and the nanny,' Sinclair remarked to Madden afterwards. 'Not to mention Mr Wiggins, the poacher.'

They were standing in the street outside the court-room. Madden nodded to the Birneys as they went by with a group of villagers, heading for the station. The public benches had been crowded.

Helen Blackwell had been one of those testifying. She had arrived with Lord Stratton and a tall, silver-haired man whom she seemed to resemble. Now she brought him over.

'Chief Inspector, I'd like you to meet my father, Dr Collingwood.' Sinclair shook hands. 'And this is Inspector Madden.'

Dr Collingwood told them he had been driving

through France with friends when word of the murders had reached him. 'I thought I'd got over the shock, until I drove past Melling Lodge yesterday evening.' He had the same dark blue eyes as his daughter, and he looked at her with concern. 'My dear, this has been harder on you than you realize. You seem quite worn out.'

It was true, Madden thought. She was paler than he remembered, tense and stiff-backed, and for the first time her manner with him was cool and distant.

'Don't treat me like a patient,' she scolded her father. 'Anyhow, my main worry's over now, thanks to Mr Sinclair.' She turned to the chief inspector. 'I can't thank you enough for agreeing to let Sophy go to Scotland.'

Sinclair tipped his hat to her and bowed. 'You should thank Inspector Madden, ma'am. He was a most persuasive advocate.'

Dr Blackwell looked at her watch. 'We ought to go. Sophy gets anxious if I'm away too long.'

Dr Collingwood moved off towards Lord Stratton's Rolls-Royce, which was parked nearby. Sinclair accompanied him. Dr Blackwell lingered.

'I almost forgot,' she said. 'Sophy keeps doing those squiggles. But today she produced something different. Or, rather, it's the same, only bigger.'

She opened her handbag and took out a sheet of drawing paper. It bore a single, enlarged version of the smaller figures the child had drawn earlier.

'I can't think what she means by it.'

She gave the drawing to Madden, who studied it.

'It looks like a balloon,' the doctor said. 'But why does she keep repeating it?'

Madden stared at the drawing, frowning. 'Has she ever done anything like this before?'

'I don't think so. Mary says not. To tell the truth, I haven't the faintest idea what's going on in her mind.' *Or yours, Inspector*, Dr Blackwell thought, as she turned away and went off to join her father and Lord Stratton.

12

WALKING BRISKLY, briefcase in hand, Chief Inspector Sinclair threaded a path between the headstones and joined Madden where he was standing in a corner of the Highfield churchyard.

'Has something happened, sir?' Madden had been expecting him earlier – in time for the funeral service – but there had been a message from Scotland Yard to say the chief inspector would be delayed.

'Later, John.'

Sinclair nodded to Lord Stratton, who was with a small group of mourners making their way from the graveside. The sexton was already at work filling in the twin graves of Charles and Lucy Fletcher. A silent line of black-clad villagers filed through the churchyard gate.

'I've something to show you.' He hefted his briefcase.

Lord Stratton led one of the group aside, a lean, suntanned man with greying temples.

'That's Robert Fletcher, the colonel's brother,' Madden told the chief inspector. 'He and his wife came down from Edinburgh yesterday. They're going to leave things at Melling Lodge as they are for the time being. They want to get Sophy back with her brother as soon as possible.'

They watched as the two men crossed the church-yard to where a black-suited figure stood in the shade of a cedar tree. Madden recognized the florid features of Sir William Raikes, the Lord Lieutenant.

'I'd better go, too, and pay my respects to his nibs.' Sinclair glanced at his companion. 'No need for you to trouble yourself, Inspector.'

Madden was glad to be left on his own. The funeral scene took him back to his youth. He'd been too young to remember his mother's death, but his father had perished in a barn fire when he was sixteen. The boy, home on holiday from the Taunton grammar school where he was a scholarship pupil, had helped to drag the body from the blazing timbers. The sight of the charred corpse, shocking to him then, now seemed like a foretaste of what had awaited him on the fields of northern France. His father had been buried in late summer. It had been a day like today.

Helen Blackwell's face, white beneath a veil, appeared before him. 'Inspector, I've come to say goodbye.' Her voice was strained. 'My father and I are going up to Yorkshire to stay with friends for a few weeks. I imagine you'll be gone by the time we return.'

Madden stared at her. Finally he spoke. 'Yes, we're moving out this weekend. The Surrey police will stay on for a time.'

'I hardly dare ask – have you made any progress?'

'Some . . .' He checked himself. He felt the need to be open with her. 'Hardly any, I'm afraid. It's a case where the answers aren't obvious.' He wanted to say more, to detain her further, but the words dried in him.

She smiled briefly and held out her hand. He felt her firm grip for the last time.

'Goodbye, then, Inspector.'

She rejoined her father. Madden followed her figure with his gaze as they left the churchyard together.

*

'It makes fascinating reading, doesn't it?'

Sinclair stood with his hands on his hips while Madden sat studying the typewritten pages. Both men had removed their jackets in the stifling heat of the snug bar.

'Good of Dr Tanner to let us know finally. A pity he couldn't have told us earlier. But, then, the government chemist is a busy man. It moves me to think that one day the police will have their own laboratory. It moves me even more to know I haven't a hope in Hades of being alive to see it!'

'Tanner's sure about it being tobacco ash?' Madden asked.

'I put the same question to him. He said there's no doubt in his mind. He'll swear to it.'

'What made you look there?' Madden was curious, but not surprised. The chief inspector's meticulousness was legendary.

'The lavatory bowl was clean, but there seemed to be dust on the rim. Now that was strange, I thought. The rest of the bathroom was spotless. So I took some scrapings and sent them off with the other stuff.'

'Colonel Fletcher didn't smoke, did he?'

'No, he gave up three years ago, on doctor's advice. Nor did Mrs Fletcher.' Sinclair cocked his head. 'And somehow I couldn't see the upstairs maid sneaking a quick fag in the master's bathroom. No, it was our man, all right. He likes a cigarette now and again – you'll see.'

'"Traces of blood in the handbasin and on the hand towel . . ."' Madden was reading from the chemist's report. '"Blood group B . . ."'

'We were lucky there. Mrs Fletcher was the only one in the household with that group. It's quite rare. He cut her throat and then washed and dried his hands.' Sinclair began to pace up and down the small room. 'He was in hell's own hurry coming in, but afterwards he had the leisure for a wash and brush-up. Time for a smoke, even.'

Madden looked up. 'The robbery was a blind, wasn't it?'

'It's starting to look that way,' Sinclair agreed. 'Mrs Fletcher's jewellery case was lying open on the dressing-table. He grabbed a few pieces. The same downstairs. A brace of candlesticks, that clock off the mantelpiece in the study, Colonel Fletcher's shooting cups. Anything that shone or looked fancy. He should have thought a little while he was doing that. Put himself in our shoes.'

'What's he done with the stuff, I wonder?'

'Thrown it away?' Sinclair shrugged. 'I'll wager it won't turn up at the pawnbroker's. Not unless he's careless or greedy, and I've a nasty feeling he's neither.'

The chief inspector took out his pipe and pouch. He pointed with the pipestem at the file. 'And now comes the really interesting part. Read on, Macduff.'

Madden bent over the report again. Sinclair filled his pipe. From the taproom next door the sound of voices signalled the arrival of opening time.

'My God!' Madden looked up. 'Can we be certain of these times?'

'Reasonably so – Tanner's own words. I spoke to him on the telephone.' The chief inspector lit his pipe. 'It's a question of the moisture content of the tobacco. Three of the cigarette stubs found by Wiggins's body were recent, no more than forty-eight hours old. Four had been lying there longer – up to three weeks. Tanner's sure about those. It's the other six he won't commit himself on, except to say the condition of the tobacco suggests a longer period still. I tried to press him, but he wouldn't be pinned down. They could be many weeks old, he said, even months.'

'*Months?*' Madden grasped the implication at once. 'He must have sat there and watched them,' he said. 'Long before he *did* anything. There's a good view of the house and garden from where Wiggins was killed. He must have come back to the same spot over and over . . .'

'And watched them . . . as you say.' Sinclair took his pipe from his mouth. 'I've no idea what we're dealing with here,' he admitted. 'But I know this much – we'll have to think again.'

13

PROMPTLY AT TEN O'CLOCK the following Monday morning, Sinclair and Madden were shown into the office of Deputy Assistant Commissioner Wilfred Bennett at Scotland Yard. Office space at the Yard was assigned on the basis of seniority, in ascending order. The lowest ranks worked at the top of the building where they had the most stairs to climb. Bennett occupied a comfortable corner suite on the first floor with a view of the Thames and the tree-lined Embankment.

He was speaking on the telephone when they went in, and he motioned them to an oak table lined with chairs that stood by the open window. London was still in the grip of a heatwave and no breeze stirred the white net curtains. Coming to work that morning, Madden had sat on the upper deck of an omnibus, but even there he had found the air humid and stifling. He thought with regret of the quiet upstairs room in the Rose and Crown, which he had occupied for the past week. Waking from tortured dreams he had sensed the countryside breathing silently around him, the woods and fields stretched out like a sleeping giant under the starry sky.

As Bennett hung up, the door opened and Sampson

entered. The chief superintendent was in his mid-fifties, a heavy-set man with brilliantined hair and a muddy complexion. He greeted Sinclair and Madden warmly. 'Another scorcher! And they say it's going to get worse.'

Madden had had few dealings with him, but he knew that the air of bonhomie was a front. Sampson's reputation at the Yard was that of a man whom it was wise not to cross.

Bennett seated himself at the table with his back to the window. His glance rested on Madden for a moment, taking in his hollow-eyed appearance. Sampson sat down beside him.

'Until this case is resolved, I intend that we should meet every Monday morning at this time to review the progress of inquiries and discuss whatever action needs to be taken.' Slight, no more than forty, with dark, thinning hair and a quick, decisive manner, Bennett was known to be one of the coming men at the Yard. 'Chief Inspector?'

'Since we last talked, sir, there have been some new developments. I'll run through them for you.' Sinclair opened his file. Elegant in a dove-grey suit, he had the knack of looking cool on the hottest day. 'First, the footprint by the stream. Thanks to Inspector Boyce and the Surrey police, we've established that the boot that made it doesn't belong to anyone residing in Highfield. While we can't assume it was worn by the man we're seeking, there's a strong likelihood it was, and if it should prove to be his, it's almost as good as a fingerprint. You'll recall the sketch of the cast I showed you, with the wedge missing from the heel?'

Bennett nodded.

Sampson spoke. 'The "man"?' His small eyes, black as currants, were crinkled with puzzlement. 'I thought it was agreed at our last meeting that it's likely more than one person was involved.'

'Yes, sir, but as I said, there have been new developments.' Sinclair regarded him blandly.

'Go on,' Bennett said.

'We've identified all the fingerprints lifted from Melling Lodge apart from three sets. One of them is a child's — we're assuming it belongs to the Fletchers' son, James, who was not in the house at the time of the attack. The other two have been sent to the Criminal Records Office. They're being checked now.

'On Friday I received from the government chemist, somewhat belatedly, the results of tests made on various items sent to him for analysis. In consequence, Inspector Madden and I have made certain deductions. Qualified, of course. But disturbing none the less.'

He gave a brief summary of the chemist's report relating to the ash and blood traces found in the bathroom and the cigarette stubs retrieved from the woods.

'Sir, this man, and I say *man*,' he glanced at Sampson, 'because I cannot conceive that this crime was carried out by a gang or group of men, was in the neighbourhood of Melling Lodge many weeks beforehand. He seems to have made repeated visits in order to observe the Fletcher residence. I'm increasingly inclined to view the robbery as a blind, an attempt to mislead us. I believe his sole intention was to murder the members of the household.'

Sampson spoke again. 'Pure supposition,' he said genially.

Bennett looked uneasy. 'There's a lot of theorizing in what you say, Chief Inspector—'

'And precious little evidence to back it up,' Sampson cut in. His tone was friendly, almost jocular. 'Come on, Angus, we don't know who smoked those cigarettes. We don't know whether one or more men broke into the house, and we don't know that they didn't panic in the middle of what started out as an ordinary robbery.'

'Strictly speaking, that's true, sir,' Sinclair agreed. He seemed unruffled. 'And you're right. We lack hard facts. An eyewitness, for example. So far we've found no one who noticed anything amiss, or even out of the ordinary that day. I find it hard to believe that a gang of men could have moved in and out of the area without someone spotting them. But *one* man – now that's possible.'

Sampson pursed his lips, plainly unconvinced.

'Then, if it was a gang, shouldn't we have heard something by now?' Sinclair continued.

'Not necessarily. Not if they're professionals.'

'If they were professionals, sir, they would have done a better job of robbing the place.'

The chief superintendent's muddy complexion darkened. 'Are you finished?' he inquired.

'Not quite.' Sinclair turned to Madden. 'Inspector?'

Madden consulted his notebook. 'The Fletchers owned a dog,' he said. 'A Labrador. It died about three weeks ago, apparently of old age. In view of what Dr Tanner had to say about the cigarettes, I tried to get in touch with the local vet, but he's on holiday, in the Hebrides.

'However, I spoke to the Fletchers' gardener, Cooper, and he was able to tell me where he and the colonel had buried the animal. We dug up the remains on Saturday morning and I had them brought up to London for Dr Ransom to examine.'

'That must have made his weekend,' Bennett observed.

Madden's smile flickered briefly. 'He rang me this morning, sir. He found a heavy dose of strychnine in the dog's stomach. There's no doubt it was poisoned.'

'There's no doubt it *ate* poison,' Sampson interrupted in a tired voice. 'You're making assumptions again, Inspector.'

'Possibly, sir.' Taking his cue from Sinclair, Madden adopted a conciliatory tone. 'But I did speak to Lord Stratton and he assured me that his keepers are categorically forbidden to lay poison of any sort on his land.'

Bennett cleared his throat. 'All right, I've heard enough. From now on, unless we discover anything to the contrary, we'll proceed on the assumption that this is the work of one man.'

'As you wish, sir.' Sampson ran a hand across the slick surface of his hair. His face was expressionless.

'Now, I've been in touch with the War Office,'

Bennett resumed. 'They sent one of their people round, a Colonel Jenkins. He'd already looked into Colonel Fletcher's military record and found he was one of the most popular officers in his regiment. With *all* ranks – he made that point. As for our other request, he'll have a list of names of discharged mental patients ready for us by the end of the week.'

He rested his elbows on the table.

'No doubt you've all read the Sunday papers. The general opinion seems to be that we're in the dark, and for the time being I'm afraid we'll have to swallow that. We can hardly tell the public that a madman armed with a rifle and bayonet is roaming the country-side. I'll put out a statement later about various lines of inquiry being pursued. Do you agree, Chief Inspector?'

'Yes, I do, sir.' Sinclair sat forward. 'But I'd like to add to what you've said. We must be careful at all times what information we put out. We've no reason to assume the man we're looking for doesn't read the newspapers. He'll want to know what *we* know about him. Let's keep him in the dark as much as possible. Either you or I can speak to the press, when necessary. Other officers should be directed not to discuss the case.'

'Very well. I'll so order it.' Bennett suppressed a smile. He stood up. 'That will do for now. We'll meet again next week. Chief Inspector, a word before you go . . .'

Bennett moved to his desk. The other men rose. Sampson and Madden left the room. The deputy waited until the door had shut behind them. 'I take it that last remark was aimed at Mr Sampson.'

'Sir?' Sinclair looked mystified.

'I'm told the chief superintendent has many friends among the press.' Bennett sat down at his desk. 'Sampson of the Yard – isn't that what they call him?'

Sinclair thought it best not to respond.

'I'll issue an order as you suggest. But don't count on him obeying it. He's the senior superintendent in the force and he may not consider it even applies to him. He has, moreover . . . special connections in this building. You'd do well to remember that. We both would.' Bennett looked wry. 'In any case, it's not that that I want to talk to you about.' He sat back. 'Are you sure you've picked the right man to assist you in this case?' he asked bluntly.

This time the chief inspector's surprise was unfeigned. 'Madden's a fine officer, sir.'

'I don't deny it. Or he was . . .' Bennett held up his hand quickly. 'I know his history, Chief Inspector. What happened to him before the war. His wife and child . . . I can't *pretend* to know what he suffered in the trenches, what any of them suffered, though it's plain to see on his face. But there's no point in beating about the bush. A lot of people think he was lucky to be taken back into the force at his old rank.' He glanced at Sinclair. 'I'm not one of them, incidentally. But when I look at him now, he seems exhausted. Burned out. So I ask you again – is he the right man?'

Sinclair took his time replying. 'I've known John Madden since he was a young constable,' he said finally. 'I picked him out because I thought he had the talent to make a good detective, and I was right. It's an odd trade, ours. Hard work will get you only so far. There comes a moment when you have to be able to see through the facts, the mass of them that collect, to find what's important, what's significant. Madden has that gift. I was bitterly disappointed when he decided to leave the force.' The chief inspector paused. 'With the bank holiday there weren't many names to choose from among those on duty, and Madden was the obvious pick. I've thought about it since. Whether I'd have chosen someone else if I'd had the opportunity. The answer's no, sir.' He looked straight at Bennett. 'I have the man I want.'

The deputy nodded his head briskly. 'That's plainly spoken,' he acknowledged. 'Let's hope you're right.'

14

A LIST OF PATIENTS discharged from mental wards in Army hospitals, running into several thousand, arrived from the War Office three days later. It was delivered by Colonel Jenkins in person. He deposited the thick manila envelope on Sinclair's desk, but declined the chief inspector's invitation to sit down.

'I've been detailed to help you in any way I can. I thought we'd better meet.'

Even in civilian clothes, the colonel cut an unmistakably military figure in his sharply pressed trousers and Brigade of Guards tie. His manner was curt, with an edge of impatience, as though he thought his time could be better spent. Madden eyed him coldly.

'He's an old staff officer,' he told Sinclair, after the colonel had gone. 'It's written all over him. We didn't see much of them in the war. They never came near the front.'

Working out of Sinclair's second-floor office, Madden and Sergeant Hollingsworth began the lengthy task of breaking down the list of discharged patients into subsections to be sent to the various police authorities around the country.

'We'll ask them to find out if any of these men have a history of violence,' the chief inspector said.

'Though, given recent events on the continent of Europe, and the fact that they were all soldiers, the question seems redundant.'

Madden asked for Detective Constable Styles to be assigned to assist them. Sinclair was amused. 'I see you haven't given up on that young man yet.'

'He'll make a decent copper one day,' Madden insisted. 'He just needs standing over.' He glanced at the chief inspector. 'I seem to remember someone doing the same for me once upon a time.'

In another life, he might have added. The years before the war seemed far off now. He'd been a husband and father then, but that, too, was in a different world when he had been a different person. The abyss of the trenches lay between.

On Friday morning, soon after they had gathered for work, the telephone rang. Hollingsworth answered it.

'For you, sir.' He handed the instrument to Madden. 'It's that constable in Highfield.'

*

Stackpole was waiting to greet him as he stepped off the train.

'It's a pleasure to see you again, sir.' He shook Madden's hand warmly. 'We've got him this time.' The constable's broad, tanned face was split by a smile. 'Knowingly making a false statement, obstruction of justice. With any luck we can put the little weasel away for a spell.'

'Yes, but I want to know exactly what he saw that

night.' They walked quickly down the platform towards the exit. 'Have you talked to Lord Stratton? Can we use his car?'

'No need, sir.' Stackpole's smile flashed beneath his thick moustache. 'Dr Blackwell's offered to give us a lift.'

Madden stopped. 'I thought she'd gone to Yorkshire.'

'I should have gone to Yorkshire.' Helen Blackwell stepped out of the deep shadow of the platform shelter in front of them. She held out her hand to Madden. 'I would have gone to Yorkshire. But my locum managed to fall off a horse and break his leg and it's taken till now to find a replacement. He's due to arrive this afternoon.'

Remembering her pale face in the churchyard, he was pleased to see the colour back in her cheeks. She looked flushed in the bright morning sun. They went out of the station into the road. The Wolseley two-seater was parked in the shade of a plane tree.

'Meanwhile, as Will says, I'm going to Oakley. I have two patients to see there. I've a feeling they're the same people you want to speak to, but although I've used all my wiles on him, he refuses to tell me.'

'Now, Miss Helen!' Stackpole blushed bright red. He left them to pull out the car's dicky and dust off the seat.

Dr Blackwell watched him, smiling. 'Poor Will. He kissed me once, when I was six and he was eight, and he doesn't know to this day whether I remember it or not.'

Madden burst out laughing, overcome by the pure pleasure of being in her company again.

She looked at him critically. 'You should do that more often, Inspector,' she said.

*

During the short drive to Oakley, Madden told her the reason he had come from London.

'So you got the story first from Fred Maberley?' She spoke over her shoulder to Stackpole, who sat crouched in the dicky, clutching at his helmet. 'He rang me, too. And then I had a call from Wellings. He seems to think his wrist's broken.'

'He'll have worse than a broken wrist by the time I've done with him,' the constable growled in her ear.

She glanced at Madden and smiled. 'I hope Fred wasn't too rough with Gladys.' Her gloved hands spun the steering-wheel and they left the paved surface for the dirt road that led to Oakley. 'He sounded shamefaced when he rang me.'

'Got what she deserved, that young lady,' Stackpole offered. 'What did she expect – going off to Tup's Spinney with a piece of trash like Wellings?'

'Shame on you, Will Stackpole. Just because Fred's her husband doesn't give him the right to hit her.'

'No, but . . .' Stackpole subsided in the dicky.

The single road through Oakley showed more signs of animation than on Madden's previous visit. Several women, weighed down with shopping bags, clustered in front of the village store. Further up the road, outside the Coachman's Arms, three men stood talking, their heads close together, like conspirators. Dr Blackwell parked in the shade of a chestnut tree growing on the lawn in front of the small church.

'Would it be all right if we saw Gladys Maberley first?' Madden asked her.

'Perfectly. From what I can gather, Mr Wellings is the more gravely injured of the two.' He hadn't seen her this way before. She was in a light, almost joyful mood. With a smile at them both she picked up her doctor's bag and walked off towards the pub.

Stackpole led the way to a whitewashed cottage at the end of a row of houses. The front door was opened by a broad-shouldered young man with blunt features. He was dressed in rough farm clothes.

'Fred, this is Inspector Madden, from London. We'd like a word with Gladys.'

He muttered something inaudible. Head bowed, he led them into a small kitchen where the young woman with bobbed hair Madden remembered seeing with Wellings was sitting at a table. She had a cut lip and a blackened, swollen eye. The other eye was red and swimming with tears.

'Well, Gladys Maberley!' The constable removed his helmet. 'You look like you could do with a cup of tea.'

As the woman started to rise, the young man spoke for the first time. 'Let me, Glad,' he muttered. He busied himself with a kettle at the sink.

'This is Mr Madden,' Stackpole said. 'He's come all the way from London to talk to you, Gladys.' He put his helmet on the table and pulled out a chair for the inspector and another for himself. 'So tell us what you've been up to – and mind!' The constable wagged a warning finger. 'Don't leave anything out.'

Twenty minutes later they were standing outside the door of the Coachman's Arms. Stackpole was grinning with delight. 'I can't wait to see the look on his face, sir.'

Inside, the smell of stale beer lingered in the taproom. Wellings was seated with his right arm resting on a bar table. Dr Blackwell was at work, strapping his wrist in a tight bandage.

'Not broken, just sprained,' she said to them, as they came in. 'Mr Wellings will live to fight another day.'

'I want to lay a charge.' Wellings shook his other fist at Stackpole. 'Have you got that? He came at me with a shovel. That's a weapon in my book. Do you hear what I'm saying, Constable?'

'I hear you, Mr Wellings.' For the second time that day Stackpole removed his helmet. He had stopped grinning.

Helen Blackwell snapped her bag shut. 'I'll leave you now,' she said. She went out.

Wellings ran his fingers through his slicked-back hair. Stackpole spoke to him. 'You'll remember Inspector Madden?'

'Who?' Wellings looked over his shoulder and noticed the inspector for the first time. 'What's he doing here?'

'We'll ask the questions.' The constable sat down at the table.

'I'm not answering any questions until I hear what you mean to do about Fred Maberley.' Wellings looked defiant.

Madden seated himself. 'Two weeks ago you made a statement to Sergeant Gates. In view of what Gladys Maberley has just told us, I now realize that you failed to tell the truth on that occasion.'

'Says who?'

'Shut your gob, you piece of filth.' Stackpole spoke in an even tone. 'Just listen to what the inspector's saying.'

Wellings flushed. He glared at the constable.

'You knowingly made a false statement to the police. That constitutes an obstruction of justice, a serious matter at any time, but given the circumstances of the case we're investigating, exceptionally grave. You will very likely go to prison, Mr Wellings.'

'What?' He turned white. 'I don't believe you.'

'I will ask you now – what were you doing on the night of Sunday, July the thirty-first? I am speaking of the late evening, after the pub was closed.'

Wellings licked his lips. His glance strayed to the bar. 'You wouldn't have a fag, would you?' he asked.

Madden took out his cigarettes and placed them on the table with a box of matches. He waited while Wellings lit up.

'Gladys and I' – he took a long pull on the cigarette – 'we went to Tup's Spinney.' He blew out the match.

'What time?'

'About half past eleven, maybe a little earlier.'

'Where was Fred Maberley?'

'Asleep.' Wellings's smile flickered and went out.

'While you were there did you see or hear anything?' Madden asked.

Wellings nodded. 'A motorbike. Just after we got there. It went past us through the fields.'

'In which direction? *Away* from Upton Hanger?'

Wellings nodded again.

'What make of motorcycle? Did you notice?'

He shook his head.

'What *did* you see?' Madden persisted.

Wellings puffed on his cigarette. 'When I heard it, I got up and went to the edge of the trees. I thought it might be someone else coming to the spinney. You know . . .' He grinned knowingly at Madden, but received no sympathy from the inspector's glance. 'There was a moon up, I saw it clearly. A motorbike and sidecar.'

'A *sidecar* – you're sure of that?'

'Yes, I'm sure. At first I thought there was someone in it, you know, a passenger, but then I saw there wasn't.'

Madden and Stackpole looked at each other.

'Let me get this clear,' the inspector said. 'There was *something* in the sidecar?'

'That's right – a shape. That's all I could see. Like I said, at first I thought it was a passenger. But it just didn't look right, not for a person. It was too low. There wasn't much showing over the rim of the sidecar.'

'How fast was it travelling?'

'Not fast. He was watching for the ruts.'

'*He?* You saw the rider?'

Wellings shook his head. 'Just his shape. Big bloke. He was wearing a cloth cap. That's all, Mr Madden, I swear. It was only for a few seconds, then he was gone, heading back towards the road.'

Madden stared at him. 'You could have told us this two weeks ago,' he said.

Wellings said nothing.

The inspector stood up. 'Stay here.' He signed to Stackpole and the two of them went outside into the road. The constable filled his lungs with fresh air.

'I suppose he'll get off now, the little bastard.'

'Not at all.' Madden shook his head firmly. 'No bargain was struck. We're going to charge him. But don't tell him that yet. Get his statement first. *Then* tell him, but leave it for a few days. He may remember something more.'

Stackpole's grin returned. He took out his notebook.

'Before you go back in, I need a telephone.'

'There's only one in Oakley, sir, at the post-office counter. That's in the store. You'll have to go through the Guildford exchange.'

Five minutes later Madden was connected with the Scotland Yard switchboard. He caught Sinclair on his way out to an early luncheon appointment.

'We need to get the Surrey police on to this, sir. They'll have to go over their tracks, question the same people in the same villages. On this side of the ridge, at least.'

'But now we've something specific. A motorcycle

and sidecar. A big man in a cloth cap. Well done, John!'

'We've Stackpole to thank, sir. He doesn't miss much.'

'I'll be sure to mention that to Norris when I speak to him. What was he carrying in the sidecar, I wonder?'

Madden thought. 'Assuming he had a rifle with him, he wouldn't want to cart it around in the open. Perhaps a bag of some kind?'

'Hmmm . . .' The chief inspector mused. 'It was after eleven when Wellings saw him. Say he quit Melling Lodge around ten o'clock, what was he doing for the next hour? It wouldn't have taken him that long to get back to his motorcycle.'

They fell silent. Then Madden spoke: 'I'll be back in a couple of hours, sir—'

'No, you won't, John. There's nothing we can do from here at present. You need a break. Take the weekend off. I'll see you at the office on Monday morning.'

'But I think I should—'

'Inspector!'

'Yes, sir?'

'That's an order.' Sinclair hung up.

Coming out of the shop, Madden saw Helen Blackwell sitting in her car in the shade of the chestnut tree. Two women stood with folded arms chatting to her, but they moved off as he approached. She accepted, with a smile, his offer of a cigarette. When he bent over to light it, he caught a whiff of jasmine, reminding him of the evening he had gone to her house.

'I don't know whether it's unusual,' he began, 'but you are the first woman doctor I've met.'

'Not unusual at all. Twenty years ago there were barely a dozen of us in the whole country. Of course, the war helped.' She drew thoughtfully on her cigarette. 'It's terrible to say that, but it's true.' She glanced up at him with a smile. 'My grandfather was a gentleman, you know. That's to say he did nothing. When Father came down from Cambridge and said he wanted to be a doctor the old boy nearly had a fit. He thought it was almost as bad as going into trade. And the funny thing was, Father was just the same. "You can't," he said. "You're a woman." But we got over that.'

Sunlight filtering through the chestnut leaves touched her hair with gold. He already regretted the moment of their parting. He wondered if he would ever see her again.

'I took over the practice after the war. Most of the villagers seem happy enough with the change. That is, apart from one or two.'

She was smiling broadly and he saw she was looking at Stackpole as he approached from the direction of the pub.

'How's my patient, Will?' she called out.

'Sicker than when you saw him, Miss Helen.' The constable tapped his jacket pocket. 'I've got his statement, sir, signed and sealed.'

'We think the man we're after came through here

on a motorcycle,' Madden explained to her. 'It's a start.'

'Don't wait for me, Miss Helen,' Stackpole said.

'Are you sure, Will?'

'I've still got Gladys Maberley's statement to write out, and then I want to have a word with Fred. Get him calmed down. The post van will be through in an hour. I'll get a lift back to Highfield.'

Madden shook his hand. 'Good work, Constable. You'll get those statements off to Guildford?'

'First thing in the morning, sir.' He touched his helmet and was gone.

Madden walked around to the passenger side. She reached over and opened the door.

'You don't have to go back to London right away, do you?'

It sounded more like a statement than a question, and Madden shook his head.

'Come back to the house and have lunch with me.'

She smiled at him as he climbed in and then, unaccountably, laughed.

'What is it?' he asked. And when she didn't reply, 'Why are you laughing?'

'I'm ashamed to tell you.' She started the car. 'I was thinking about my locum falling off his horse.'

15

SHE SEATED HIM in the arbour on the terrace with a glass of beer.

'I'll be back in a minute.'

Madden looked out over the sunlit garden at the woods beyond, rising like a green wave. The heat of the day was still building. He sipped his beer. It was a moment of peace, rare in his life, and he wanted to arrest it and clasp it to him: to stop time in its tracks. He heard a noise and looked round, expecting to see her. But it was Mary, the maid. She was carrying a wicker hamper and a plaid blanket.

'Good afternoon, sir.'

'Hullo, Mary.'

She smiled at him and put down the basket with the blanket on top of it, then went back inside the house, but returned in a moment with a pair of cushions.

'I thought we'd have a picnic.'

Helen Blackwell stepped from the doorway on to the terrace. She had shed her skirt and blouse of the morning and was wearing a cool chemise-type dress of white cotton. Her hair, freed from the ribbon she used to tie it back, lay on her shoulders. Madden saw that her legs were bare.

'Thank you, Mary,' she said to the maid. 'That will be all.'

She picked up the cushions and the blanket. Madden assumed the burden of the hamper. Together they went down the steps from the terrace. As they started across the lawn the black pointer he remembered from his first visit rose from a pool of shadow beneath a walnut tree and joined in the procession behind them.

They reached the orchard at the bottom of the lawn and passed beneath plum trees heavy with sun-ripened fruit. The buzz of wasps sounded loud in the dappled shade. A stone wall marked the boundary of the garden. She opened the gate and let him through, then closed it quickly before the dog could follow them.

'Not you, Molly.'

The animal whined in disappointment.

'Stay!' she commanded, without explanation. She smiled at him. 'You can't come on a picnic dressed like that. At least take your jacket off.'

He did as she said, then stripped off his tie as well and draped both garments over the green wooden gate.

They were close to the edge of the shallow stream. On the other side, the woods came down almost to the water, but where they were a carpet of meadow grass extended for a short distance downstream. He followed her until their way was blocked by a thicket of holly bushes.

'This is the tricky bit,' she said. She slipped off her shoes and stepped down from the bank into the stream. 'Be careful, the stones are slippery.' She moved slowly through the ankle-deep water, holding the cushions and blanket in a bundle above her head. When she was past the bushes she climbed up on the bank again.

Madden took off his shoes and socks and put them on top of the hamper. He rolled up his trousers and stepped down into the cool water. She was waiting on the bank, hand outstretched, to take the basket from him.

'I used to come here with my brother, Peter, when we were children. It was our secret place.'

They were on a small patch of grass enclosed by bushes. Close to the bank, water-lilies tugged weakly at their stems in the faint current of the stream.

'He was the pilot, wasn't he?'

'You remembered . . .' Her deep blue gaze brushed his. 'That was such a terrible night. All I could think of was how we'd been young together – Lucy and Peter and David and I – and now they were all dead. And then I looked into your eyes and saw that you must have been in the war, too, and I couldn't stop thinking about all those dead . . . the ghosts we live with.'

He wanted to speak, but could find no words, and he looked away.

She studied his face for a moment, then began to spread the blanket and cushions on the grass. Madden retrieved his shoes and socks. About to put them on, he was arrested by the sight of her sitting beside him. She was leaning on one hand, her legs tucked to the side, looking down, her face hidden by the fall of thick, honey-coloured hair. In the stillness that enveloped them the whirr of a pigeon's wings sounded loud overhead. Not knowing what to do or say, he unfastened the sleeve of his shirt and began to roll it up.

'Shrapnel.' She spoke, and he felt the touch of her fingers on his forearm where the scars were spread like strewn coins.

'I worked in an Army hospital for a year. I know all the wounds.' Her fingers stayed on his skin. Her touch went through him like fire. 'And that scar on your forehead . . .' She took her hand off his arm and raised it to his head, sliding her fingers under the lock of hair that fell across his brow and running them gently across the skin. 'That's most likely a shell fragment, too.'

Madden began to tremble. Her face was close, but their eyes didn't meet. Her glance was fixed on his forehead. He saw a faint line of sweat on her upper lip and the golden hairs on her forearm. He put his arm around her waist, clumsy, unsure of what he was doing, but when he bent to kiss her, her hand went from his forehead to the back of his neck and she pressed her lips to his, meeting his tongue with hers, kissing him deeply.

She drew him down and in a moment they were lying stretched on the blanket, side by side. He could feel his heart racing, the blood drumming in his ears. Then she moved again, pulling him over her until she was on her back and he was above her. They continued to kiss. When he put his hand on her hip she caught it with hers and held it and then brought it to her stomach and pressed it there. He began to fumble with her dress, but she reached down herself and drew it up and then took his hand again and brought it to her bare stomach at the top of her pants and guided it down inside them. He felt the stiff curly hair and then the wetness.

She reached for him, and he broke their kiss to tear open his trousers. When she took him in her hand he groaned. She let go of him to push at her pants and he joined his hand with hers and together they stripped them off her. She spread her legs to receive him and cried out when he entered her.

He never knew how long they were together. To him, it seemed only moments, and then his body was shaken by spasms and he felt her bucking and reaching for him. She cried out again.

They lay together, unmoving. In the silence he heard a blackbird call in the woods across the stream. Her breathing, hot in his ear, slowly abated. His weight lay on her, crushing her, he thought, but when he sought to shift it she held him imprisoned in her arms.

'Stay with me,' she pleaded, and they lay together. Her thighs held him fast, both slippery with sweat.

Finally she relaxed, sinking under him, and he moved and lay alongside her. She turned her head so that her face was close to his and when he kissed her she responded, bringing her hand up to his cheek, stroking him. He looked down at her body. Her long

legs, one bent over the other, were flushed in the
sunlight. Moisture shone in her dark golden bush. He
could smell his semen mixed with their sweat. He was
close to tears.

'John . . .?' Her eyes were open, she was smiling at
him. 'Your name is John, isn't it?' Her soft laughter
in his ear gave him the release he needed and his
laughter joined with hers. 'Oh, God! I wasn't sure I
had the nerve . . . and you wouldn't *speak*.'

'Speak?' At first he didn't understand. And then,
when he did, he couldn't tell her that he had never
imagined such a scene. Had never pictured himself
lying in her arms, lying between her legs. That he no
longer thought of his life as holding such possibilities.

'I knew it that first night. It was awful, I suddenly
found myself wondering what it would be like to . . .
make love with you. And then I remembered poor
Lucy lying there with her throat cut and Charles and
the others and I couldn't believe I was thinking that.'
She was silent, looking away. Then she turned her
head and smiled into his eyes. 'They talk about the
demon rum, but I think it should be the demon sex.'
He put his arms around her. She rested her head on
his chest. A light breeze stirred the bushes around
them, bringing relief from the heat. 'After the war,
after Guy was killed, I had an affair with a man. I
needed someone. But I found it didn't work, I didn't
really care for him, and I had to stop it . . .'

Madden thought of his own barren life. But he
couldn't bring himself to speak of it. Instead, he asked,
'There's been no one since?'

She laughed softly against his chest. 'How did St Paul put it? Marry or burn?' Then her brow creased and she looked up at him. 'Oh dear, I never even asked, I just took it for granted – *you*'re not married, are you?'

He shook his head. 'I was. But it was years ago.' He needed to tell her. 'We had a child, a little girl. They both died of influenza. It was before the war.'

She held him in her steady gaze. 'I saw that when you looked at Sophy. I didn't know what it meant. *She* knew . . . she felt something. The way she went with you . . .'

She kissed him and then released herself from his arms, sitting up and covering her legs as she did so. She ran her fingers through her hair.

'I must pull myself together. My new locum will be here in an hour and I have to get him settled in. Then Lord Stratton's giving me a lift to London. I'm spending the night with my aunt and catching the train to Yorkshire tomorrow morning.'

She smiled down at him.

'You were laughing earlier because the other one fell off his horse,' Madden said. 'Why?'

'If he hadn't, you and I wouldn't be here now.'

'But that was before . . .' He was amazed.

'Yes, but I knew this was going to happen.' Her eyes held his. 'Are you shocked?'

He drew her down to him.

She said, 'I never even gave you any lunch. There's still time.' He felt her breath on his lips. 'Or we could make love again. Though I don't know . . . can we?'

Smiling, she slipped her hand between his legs and took him gently, like a bird, in her folded palm.

'Oh, yes . . .'

*

They left the hamper with the blanket and cushions by the garden gate.

'I'll get Mary to collect them later. I haven't the strength now.'

She watched, smiling, as he put on his tie and jacket, and then they walked arm in arm through the dappled shade of the orchard until they came in sight of the house, when he started to pull away from her. She kept his arm in hers and drew him into the shade of the weeping beech, near the side gate.

'I'll be away for a fortnight.' She kissed his cheek. 'When I get back I'll find some excuse and come up to London.'

He watched her turn and leave, the pain of loss already sharp in him. He was afraid she would soon start to regret what she had done. That the next time he saw her it would be only to hear excuses and embarrassed explanations.

As though she had read his mind, she turned and came back to him. 'Hold me for a moment.'

He wrapped his arms about her and they stood like that. Then she drew back and kissed him full on the mouth.

'In two weeks,' she said.

16

MADDEN AWOKE IN TERROR, thinking he was under shellfire, and then lay sweating in the darkness as the rumble of approaching thunder grew louder.

His sleep had been tormented by a familiar nightmare, a racking image that dated from the first time he had been wounded when he had lain in a casualty clearing station and watched an Army surgeon, his white smock drenched with blood, saw off the leg of an anaesthetized soldier. Awake, Madden could recall the surgeon completing the operation and tossing the shattered limb into a corner of the tent with other amputated fragments. In his dream the bloodstained figure kept sawing and sawing while the soldier's mouth stretched wide in a soundless scream.

Peace returned to his mind with the memory of Helen Blackwell's kisses and the feel of her body pressed to his. Along with the throb of renewed desire came a yearning for the anchor of her calm, steady glance.

*

The room where he awoke was the same one he had used before in the Rose and Crown. He had returned to the village intending to catch a train to London.

Instead, either on a whim or because he could not tear himself away, he had spoken to the landlord, Mr Poole, and fixed to spend the night there.

During his hours of sleeplessness an idea had come to him – he'd been thinking of his childhood, and days spent in the woods with his friends – and after breakfast he walked up the road from the pub to the village shop, where Alf Birney, tonsured and aproned, greeted him from behind the counter.

'We thought you'd all gone back to London, sir.' His voice held a hint of reproach.

'We'll be back and forth, I expect.'

'You haven't caught any of them yet, have you, sir?'

'Not yet, Mr Birney.'

Madden bought half a loaf of bread, a tin of sardines and a packet of biscuits. Coming out of the store he was hailed by Stackpole, who was walking by. 'I didn't know you'd stayed on, sir.'

'It was a spur-of-the-moment decision. Mr Sinclair gave me the weekend off. There's something I want to do.' He looked at the constable, bronzed and smiling under his helmet. He felt a warmth for this man who had kissed Helen Blackwell. 'Are you busy today?'

Stackpole shook his head. 'Saturdays are usually quiet. We've got the wife's sister and her brood coming over at lunchtime. Now, if I could find a good excuse to get away . . .' He grinned.

'Let's walk along,' Madden suggested. 'I'll tell you what I have in mind.'

Stackpole listened carefully while he explained.

'I see what you mean, sir – he didn't care about

tossing his cigarette stubs around so if he'd eaten anything there we ought to have found some traces. Maybe a tin or a crust or an empty packet.'

'More than that,' Madden admitted. 'We haven't put this about, but we're fairly sure he kept coming back to the woods over a long period so that he could watch the Fletchers.'

'And I never knew it!' The constable looked grim.

'No fault of yours,' Madden hastened to assure him. 'He must have taken good care not to be seen. I think Wiggins only came on him by chance.'

'Still, I see what you mean, sir. He might have had some other spot up there. A hide, or a lair.'

'How well did the police search the woods?'

'Search?' Stackpole's snort was contemptuous. 'They just tramped around, flattening things. They gave up after four days, and none too soon, if you ask my opinion.' He raised his hand in greeting to a pair of men sitting on a bench in the forecourt of the pub. 'Tell you what, sir. If you wouldn't mind, I'd like to get out of my jacket – you could do the same – then we could go up there and take a look around.'

They walked on until they reached the Stackpoles' cottage near the end of the village. While the constable got ready, his wife sat with Madden in the small parlour. A plump, curly-haired young woman with a deep dimple, she seemed unawed at finding herself in the presence of a Scotland Yard inspector.

'Just you see you get home in good time, Will Stackpole,' she called through the doorway. 'There's the lawn needs mowing, and the baby's chair's broken again.' To Madden, she said, 'You've got to keep after them.'

The constable came in in his shirtsleeves carrying a brown-paper packet. 'I see you bought some things at the shop, sir. I've got a few bits myself. We'll have enough for a bite of lunch.'

'What's this, then?' his wife inquired of the ceiling. 'A picnic in the woods?'

She missed the inspector's deep blush.

*

A uniformed constable sent from Guildford was on duty outside Melling Lodge, but Stackpole said there wouldn't be one there after the weekend.

'We'll just lock up the gates, and I'll keep an eye on the place. Mr Fletcher will come down from Scotland to see what needs doing. The Lodge will go to young James, I'm told, but that won't be for years. Can't see anyone wanting to live there. Not for a while, anyway.'

Water still sprayed from the fountain in the fore-court. The Cupid figure, bow drawn, cast a shadow on the white gravel at their feet. Madden noticed that the ivy clothing the walls of the house was freshly trimmed.

'Tom Cooper's been told to keep up the garden,' Stackpole informed him. 'Poor old Tom, he hates having to come here now. This was a happy house. Anyone in the village will tell you that.'

They walked down the terraced lawn to the gate at the bottom of the garden and crossed the stream on the stepping-stones. A rumble of thunder broke the stillness of the morning. Clouds like hewn marble darkened the sun.

Madden paused at the foot of the path. 'Now, my idea is, if he laid up anywhere it wouldn't be on this side, towards Lord Stratton's land and his keepers, it would be in the other direction.' He pointed west along the ridge, away from the village. 'Let's climb up a bit, then look for a way across.'

All along the length of the path the ferns and undergrowth on either side had been trodden down.

'That lot from Guildford, they just spread out in a line and walked up the hill,' Stackpole said, in disgust. 'Then, when they got to the top, they spread out some more and came down again.'

'How much of the woods did they search?' Madden was sweating freely in the stifling heat.

'No more than a mile across. The keepers scouted around a bit, but they didn't find anything.'

Two-thirds of the way up the slope they came to a track branching to the right, and Madden took it. The trampled undergrowth continued for some distance, then the ferns sprang up again and the forest seemed to draw in on them. The inspector kept his gaze on the ground ahead, though the footpath showed no sign of recent use. The narrow track was littered with dead twigs and leaves.

Thunder boomed, louder than before. The air was close and still. Stackpole swatted a midge. 'You can't see more than a few yards,' he complained, his glance probing the bushes on either side of them.

'Look for a broken branch,' Madden advised. 'Anything that seems disturbed.'

The path began to descend and they came to a natural bowl in the side of the hill, circled by a ring of lofty beech trees. The track went around it, resuming its straight course on the far side. Taking a short cut, the two men walked across the shallow depression. Successive generations of dead leaves had given the surface a soft, yielding quality, and midway across Madden was assailed by a sudden sharp memory of a trench, springy with bodies like a mattress, and the eyes of dead men staring up at him. These fragments of a past he had tried to forget came without warning, often accompanied by dizziness and a feeling of vertigo, and he hurried to regain the footpath.

'How far have we come?' He saw that Stackpole was looking at him with concern, and realized he must have paled in the few seconds it had taken them to cross the bowl.

'More than a mile, I'd say, sir. Dr Blackwell's house is below us.' He pointed down. 'You can see it from further on.'

Lightning crackled in the darkening sky, followed almost at once by a loud peal of thunder. A sudden gust of wind brought a shower of leaves and twigs from overhead.

'Let's find some shelter,' Madden suggested.

A short distance along the path they came to another clearing where a huge sweet chestnut stood. The spreading branches, decked with graceful leaves shaped like spearheads, provided ample protection from the fat raindrops that were starting to fall.

'Good place to stop for a bite, sir.' The constable was still anxious about his companion.

'Why not?'

They settled down under the tree. Madden peeled back the top of the tin of sardines. Stackpole sliced bread with his pocket knife. The constable had brought two bottles of beer with him. They ate and drank, sitting comfortably with their backs against the deeply scored trunk, while the sky at first grew darker, and then brightened. By the time they had finished eating the sun had come out again, but at that moment it began to rain in earnest and they sat in the shelter of the great tree and watched the drops falling like a shower of golden coins through the sunlight.

'It won't last,' Stackpole predicted with the assurance of a countryman, and after a minute he was proved right. The rain ceased. Perversely, however, the sky began at once to darken again and the thunder continued to roll.

Madden had been thinking. 'I don't believe he'd have picked a spot too far from Melling Lodge. Can we find a path to the top of the ridge? I'd like to have a look around up there.'

'We passed one a quarter of a mile back.'

Gathering the remains of their lunch, they set off again, retracing their steps. Lightning flashed, followed by a detonation of thunder. Madden increased his pace, striding out along the path. They had come to the circle of beeches where the footpath bent like a

bow, and this time the inspector followed it, avoiding the bowl of leaves. The dusty track had darkened in colour with the earlier shower. Madden's eyes were fixed on the ground ahead of him. Suddenly he halted.

'What is it, sir?' Stackpole hurried forward.

'*Stay where you are!*'

The constable stopped in his tracks. He stood rooted.

Madden crouched down. On the damp earth in front of him, fresh as a newly minted coin, a footprint had appeared. The heel had a piece missing. His eye skipped swiftly past it and he saw others. They were coming in his direction. He looked over his shoulder at the path behind him: his own footsteps showed in the damp dust, but no others.

'Sir, what is it?'

'*Quiet!*'

Madden looked to his left: there was only the circle of beeches with the empty bowl at their centre. To his right the slope rose steeply to a line of ilexes, their leaves blowing silver and green in the gusting wind. A dense growth of holly filled the spaces between their trunks, forming an impenetrable screen. As he stared at the thicket a familiar sound came to his ears, borne on the breeze: the oiled *click* of a rifle-bolt being drawn back.

'*Down!*' he roared. '*Get down!*'

Madden dived to his left, where the nearest beech tree stood, and as he did so the silence exploded.

CRACK! CRACK! CRACK!

The shots came in rapid succession and the ground

beside Madden's head erupted as he rolled frantically towards the tree. Another shot rang out and a chunk of bark as big as a fist struck him in the face. Next moment he was safe behind the massive trunk.

He looked back and saw the constable lying flat on the path, his face white and shocked.

'*Move!*' he yelled. '*The trees!*'

Galvanized by the command, Stackpole rolled over. The earth where he had lain leaped into the air as the sound of two further shots coincided with a loud crack of thunder. The constable scrambled to his hands and feet and plunged behind a tree trunk.

Madden counted in his head: *six*.

He looked around him. He was near the edge of the bowl, but where he was it was shallow, only inches deep. Stackpole was luckier. A few paces from where he crouched behind the tree, the floor of the depression was at least a couple of feet below the rim. Madden's experienced eye skipped from the row of ilexes to the lip of the bowl, working out angles of fire. His terror of a few moments ago had been replaced by a familiar numbness.

'Will!' He used the constable's name, speaking in a low voice. 'Can you hear me?'

'Yes, sir.' The hoarse whisper barely reached him.

'Stay behind that tree, but move back into the dip behind you. When you're there, get down on your stomach and crawl around the edge. Be sure to keep yourself pressed up tight against the side. Don't worry, he won't be able to see you from where he is. When you get to where the path straightens, stand up and run like hell!'

Stackpole was silent.

'Will?'

'I'm not leaving you, sir.'

'Don't be a damn fool.' His officer's voice came back to him easily. 'Do as I say. *Now!*'

The constable began to back away from the tree trunk. When he reached the edge of the bowl he slid down into the depression and began to crawl on his stomach, away from Madden, back the way they had come. Another shot rang out and bark flew off the side of the tree where he had been crouching.

Seven. A Lee-Enfield rifle held ten rounds in its magazine.

His mind cold, Madden waited for the inevitable to happen. Soon now the man would descend from the screen of holly to hunt them down. When that happened, he planned to spring to his feet and run along the path in the opposite direction to Stackpole, splitting up the available targets. He knew their attacker was expert with a bayonet. Whether he was also a marksman was something he would discover in the next few minutes. Still in the grip of the numbness that had taken hold of him after the first shots, Madden viewed the prospect with a fatalism bordering on indifference.

Thunder echoed, further off now. Then he heard another sound: the smashing of undergrowth. It came not from the line of ilexes but from higher up the slope. Taking a gamble, Madden sprinted across a dozen feet of open ground to the next beech tree in the circle. Pressing his body to the trunk, he waited for the answering shot. None came.

Again he heard noise, more distant now. He peered around the tree and caught a glimpse of a figure high up, near the crest of the ridge.

'He's moving!' he shouted. 'I'm going after him.'

Madden flung himself at the slope, tearing through the waist-high ferns, forcing a path through the dense undergrowth. Skirting the barrier of holly bushes, he came on the path left by his quarry, a line of snapped branches and flattened ferns leading up the hill, and he followed it. Stackpole's shout sounded behind him.

As Madden neared the crest the underbrush thinned and the ground became slick with pine needles. Emerging from the straggling firs he saw the figure of a man running along the top of the bare ridge half a mile away. He was carrying a bulky object slung across his shoulder.

'I'm coming, sir . . .' Stackpole's voice was close, and a moment later he joined the inspector red-faced and gasping.

Wordlessly, Madden pointed. They set off in pursuit.

The line of the crest was uneven, broken by bumps and hollows, and twice they lost sight of their quarry as the ground dipped, only to see him again toiling up the next rise. Then he changed direction suddenly, veering off to the right, and when they reached the spot they found they were at the top of the path that ascended the ridge from the fields around Oakley. The hamlet lay beneath them surrounded by the broad sweep of farmlands.

The cough and stutter of a motorcycle being kicked into life sounded faintly.

'Blast!' Madden sank to his haunches.

'There he goes!' Stackpole started down the path, but the inspector called him back.

'It's no use. You won't catch him.'

They watched as a motorcycle and sidecar emerged from the treeline below and moved slowly along the rutted track through the cornfields. The rider, hunched over the handlebars, did not look back. Madden cupped his hands like binoculars over his eyes. 'See what you can make out. Anything at all.'

The constable copied him. They crouched in silence.

'Cloth cap,' Stackpole panted. 'Just like Wellings said.'

'Black bodywork on the sidecar. What make of bike is that?'

'Harley-Davidson . . . I think. Hard to be sure from here. There's something in the sidecar, sir. Could be a bag.'

Madden stood up. 'I've got to get down to Melling Lodge and ring Guildford. I want you to stay here. We have to know what road he takes when he reaches Oakley. As soon as you're sure, come down to the house.'

'Yes, sir.' Stackpole's gaze was riveted to the valley floor.

Madden turned and went plunging down the steep hillside.

*

Blue uniforms milled in the forecourt of Melling Lodge. To the chief inspector, as he stepped from his car, it seemed as though the scene of two weeks before was being re-enacted. The familiar form of Inspector Boyce materialized from the pale shadows cast by the limpid evening light.

'Sir.' He shook hands with Sinclair. 'We've been in touch with the Kent and Sussex constabularies. There'll be officers on the look-out for him all over the south-east.'

Sinclair spied Madden's tall figure approaching.

'John?' His voice held a note of concern.

'I'm fine, sir.' They shook hands. 'Not a scratch. He missed us both.'

Sinclair looked at the two men. 'Any chance of him heading north or west?'

'It doesn't seem likely,' Madden replied. 'Stackpole saw him take the Craydon road. That rules out Godalming and Farnham to the west. If he passed through Craydon he'd come to the main road between Guildford and Horsham. He could have turned north there, but they're watching for him in Guildford. So either he turned south, towards Horsham, or he kept going east to Dorking and beyond.'

'That's assuming he sticks to the main roads,' Sinclair felt bound to point out.

'Quite, sir. If he knows the back roads . . .' Madden shrugged.

'And he could cut up to London, if he wanted.'

'I don't think so.' The inspector shook his head. 'He's a country man.' Then he shrugged a second time. 'I'm guessing,' he admitted.

Boyce coughed. 'We've something already, sir. Three witnesses saw him ride through Oakley this afternoon, two women and a man.' He took out a notepad. 'Same basic description. Big fellow in a brown jacket and a cloth cap. One of the women thought he had a moustache. Brown hair, she said. About the bike, the women just saw a motorcycle and sidecar, but the man – he's a young chap called Maberley – he said it was a Harley, no question. There was a brown leather bag in the sidecar, the top of it was sticking out. Maberley saw that – he was interested in the bike, so he looked hard. Said the bag was like a cricket bag.' He checked his notepad. 'Oh, and the sidecar's painted black or dark blue.'

'And what do we have up there?' Sinclair asked Madden. He nodded towards the woods of Upton Hanger.

'A big hole that's been filled in, Stackpole says. He went up again and found it in a thicket above the path, well hidden.'

Madden explained how he'd stopped to examine the footprints. 'He must have seen us from above and realized we'd picked up his tracks. It's possible he recognized Stackpole as being a policeman.'

'How so?' the chief inspector asked.

'We know he's spent time in the woods, but he might have been in Highfield, too. If so, he'd know the village bobby by sight.'

The constable, like Madden, still in his shirtsleeves, appeared before them. 'I've got hold of a couple of spades from the toolshed, sir,' he said to Sinclair. 'We're ready when you are.'

Boyce looked at his watch. 'Nearly seven.' He called to one of the uniformed officers. 'Bring some flares from the van. We're going to need them.'

*

It took them forty minutes to reach the circle of beeches. From there Stackpole led the party up the hillside, past the line of ilexes, to an area dense with holly and tangled brush. Earlier, the constable had discovered a way into the thicket, a narrow entrance made to resemble an animal's track and masked by dead branches. The men had to crawl in one at a time.

Sinclair and Madden were the last to enter. The chief inspector had lingered at the bottom of the slope to examine the beech tree where Madden had sought cover.

'A narrow shave,' he observed, running his fingers over the bullet-gouged trunk. 'You must have had some anxious moments, John.'

Madden recalled the eerie calm that had possessed him. It was a throwback to his time in the trenches, and the realization sent a chill through him.

The mound of earth discovered inside the thicket

was about ten feet long at its base and in the rough shape of a triangle. Some soil had already been shifted and lay in a heap beside it.

'Looks like he was digging it up when you disturbed him,' Boyce remarked, dusting off the knees of his trousers. 'What's he got down there, I wonder? Not another body, I hope!'

The answer wasn't long in coming. The first constable detailed to dig struck a metallic object with the first thrust of his spade. He bent down and hauled out a silver branched candlestick from the loosened soil. A few seconds later a second was uncovered. Then three silver cups were unearthed, all bearing inscriptions noting that 'Captain C.S.G. Fletcher' had won them in target-shooting contests. They were found beside a rolled-up cloth, which contained a collection of jewellery comprising a garnet necklace, two gold rings, seven earrings – only four matched – and a locket on a golden chain.

Lastly, a mantelpiece clock, mounted in Sèvres china, was pulled from the clinging soil. The porcelain was cracked and a piece was missing.

'That's all that was on the list,' Boyce commented.

Under the canopy of trees it was rapidly growing dark and Sinclair gave the order for the naphtha flares to be lit. Thrust into the ground at intervals around the site, the naked flames brought an air of ceremony to the grim proceedings, as though some blood sacrifice was being offered to the deities of the forest.

The digging continued, with the officers working in pairs now, jackets shed and sleeves rolled up. Six feet down the spades struck another obstruction. This time the object proved harder to dislodge, but eventually a broad strip of corrugated iron was uncovered and passed up. Brushed clean and laid out on the ground, it became the receptacle for a variety of other items retrieved from the loose earth near the bottom of the hole: a piece of tar soap, a length of two-by-four, several wooden slats, cut to measure, numerous cigarette stubs, a piece of bacon rind, a bottle of Veno's cough medicine, a half-eaten jar of cherry jam, empty tins of Maconochie's stew.

One of the diggers handed up an earthenware jar.

'What's that for?' Boyce wondered aloud.

'Rum.' Madden spoke from the shadows. 'A half-gill unit. Standard issue.'

Sinclair glanced at him. The inspector stood on his own in the shadows, away from the flickering light. His face was expressionless.

The two men working in the pit handed their spades up and began climbing out.

'I reckon that's all, sir,' one of them said to Boyce.

'Wait!' Madden came forward and peered down into the hole. 'I want all that loose soil cleared out, Constable. Back you go.'

Boyce started to say something, but the chief inspector held up his hand to silence him.

The two constables resumed their labour. Madden stood over them while they shovelled earth out. After a few minutes, he said, 'Right, that'll do.' He helped the pair out and then jumped down into the pit himself. 'Let's have one of those flares over here,' he said.

It was Sinclair himself who brought it over. The others gathered around. The excavated hole was in the shape of a blunt T, the two arms branching out only a little beyond the thick central trunk, where Madden was now standing. He pointed behind him to the head of the T where a broad step had been cut into the back wall.

'That's where he slept,' he said. 'Those wooden slats are for duckboards, to keep the floor dry, and the piece of tin is for the roof.' He came forward. 'And this is a firestep.' He mounted a low projection at the foot of the T, bringing his head and shoulders up over the lip of the trench. 'What we have here is a dugout.'

'Like in the war, sir?' The question was Stackpole's.

'Like in the war.' Madden's voice was scored with bitterness. 'That muck you see – the soap and the stew and the rum – it's what they had in the trenches. Even down to the cough medicine – we used to live on the stuff.'

He looked up at Sinclair. 'I'll tell you what he did, sir. He took a swig of rum, the way we used to before an attack, and then he went down there and blew his bloody whistle and charged into that house and killed the lot of them. And that's not all—' Madden pulled out his wallet from his back pocket and extracted a folded sheet of paper which he handed up to the chief inspector. 'Do you remember those drawings Sophy Fletcher made? This is another one.'

Sinclair held up the paper to the light. The men gathered around, peering over his shoulder.

'That's a gas mask,' Madden said. 'When he broke in he was wearing one, and that's what the child saw – some goggled-eyed monster dragging her mother down the passage. It explains why she hasn't said a word since.'

Part Two

But now hell's gates are an old tale;
Remote the anguish seems;
The guns are muffled and far away,
Dreams within dreams.

And far and far are Flanders mud,
And the pain of Picardy;
And the blood that runs there runs beyond
The wide waste sea.

Rose Macaulay, 'Picnic July 1917'

Part Two

1

Dressed in her maid's uniform and white lace cap, Ethel Bridgewater sat at the kitchen table reading yesterday's *News of the World*. Her attention had been caught by a half-page advertisement for something called the 'Harlene Hair-Drill', which promised users of the company's products 'a luxurious wealth of gloriously beautiful and healthy hair'.

For some time now Ethel had been considering having her own hair bobbed – more and more of her friends were doing it – but she was reluctant to take the step. Though a plain young woman, she possessed a head of rich chestnut hair and felt instinctively it would be a mistake to get rid of this crowning asset.

She was reading the advertisement for a second time when the door to the stableyard opened and Carver came in. He didn't speak, and neither did she. They seldom exchanged a word, going about their duties in silence when they happened to meet.

Glancing up, Ethel received a shock. Carver's looks had been transformed since their last encounter before the weekend. His moustache had disappeared and, shorn of this covering, his mouth was revealed as thin with a marked downward turn at one corner where a small scar was visible. It was entirely in keeping with their relationship that it did not even occur to the maid to pass comment on his changed appearance.

Ethel rose from the table and began to busy herself preparing tea for her mistress, Mrs Aylward. Carver opened the stove door and took out a plate of food which had been left there for him. He ate at irregular hours, and the cook, Mrs Rowley, who lived in the neighbourhood and would not be back to prepare dinner until later that afternoon, had been taught to leave his meals warming in the oven. He brought the plate over to the table, collecting a knife and fork from the kitchen cutlery, and began to eat.

Ethel hurried over the tea things. Once she had taken the tray into the drawing-room there was dusting work she could do upstairs. In truth, she didn't like to find herself alone with Carver for any length of time. If asked why, she would have found it difficult to give a reason. Certainly he had never offended her in any way. But his presence had a strange – almost physical – effect on her. After a while the air seemed to get closer, as though some unseen agent were consuming the oxygen, and Ethel would find herself becoming breathless. As soon as the kettle boiled, she made the tea and took the tray out.

Carver, whose real name was Amos Pike, carried his dirty plate to the sink and cleaned it. He washed and dried his utensils, returning everything to its place. Using the hot water remaining in the kettle he made himself a cup of tea and brought it to the table. He picked up the newspaper and read it carefully, paying particular attention to the news columns. Satisfied, he washed and dried his cup and went outside into the yard.

Mrs Aylward's house, though modest in size, boasted a set of stables at the rear. Built by the previous owner, an enthusiastic horseman, they were no longer used for that purpose and had been converted into a storeroom and garage. Pike lived in a room on the floor above.

Employed primarily as a chauffeur, he was also charged with keeping the garden tidy. But his duties there were minimal, Mrs Aylward's interest in horticulture being confined to a conservatory that she had added to the house, attaching it to the side of her studio.

His job that day was to clean the greenhouse windows and he had already done the inside. Now he set up his ladder on the gravelled path that ran alongside the structure and mounted the steps with a bucket and mop. He worked automatically, his brow grooved with some inner preoccupation, his glance unfocused.

Pike had unusual eyes. Flat and brown, they seldom gave any clue to what he was thinking. Many people found them disturbing.

2

Deputy Assistant Commissioner Bennett rose as Sinclair and Madden entered his office. 'Inspector! I'm relieved to see you in one piece.' He came round from behind his desk and shook Madden's hand.

'A pity you didn't nab him when you had the chance,' Sampson offered. The chief superintendent, in a mustard-coloured suit and matching tie, was already in his chair. He grinned to show he was making a joke. 'There were two of you, weren't there?'

Bennett looked at him sharply, but made no comment. He took his own chair at the table by the window. The others joined him.

'Well, Chief Inspector?'

Sinclair opened his file. 'On the positive side, sir, we now *know* it's only one man we're looking for, and the military connection is solidly established. Mr Madden assures me that what he built in the woods was an Army dugout, down to the last detail. One of the villagers reported hearing a police whistle at the time of the attack. Police whistle, Army whistle — they're one and the same. He seems to have acted as though he were going "over the top".' The chief inspector's tone indicated his distaste for the cliché. 'Apparently he wore a gas mask at the time.'

He took two pieces of paper from his file and passed them across the table. 'Those are drawings which the Fletcher child made later – as you know, she hasn't spoken yet. We didn't know what they meant until Inspector Madden realized they were an attempt by her to draw a gas mask.'

Sampson scowled. 'We haven't seen these before,' he said.

'I didn't include them in the file,' Sinclair admitted. 'They seemed to have no bearing on the case.'

'We'll have everything in future if you don't mind, Chief Inspector.' Sampson's small eyes had turned hard.

'As you wish, sir.'

Bennett stirred restlessly. 'But what are we dealing with here?' he demanded. 'What's this man about? Is he a lunatic? Have we any idea?'

Sinclair shook his head. 'He may prove to be, sir. But I'm inclined to regard him as sane. Frighteningly so. Whatever mayhem he committed in Melling Lodge, all his preparations leading up to it, as well as his getaway, show the most detailed planning.

'And considering the events of Saturday, I'd say he kept his head to a remarkable degree. Instead of persisting with his attack on Mr Madden and the constable, he cut his losses and ran for it while he still had a chance to escape. We have eyewitness reports of him riding through both Oakley and Craydon and the most extraordinary thing, as far as I'm concerned, is that apparently he was going at no more than twenty miles an hour. Granted he didn't want to attract attention, but he must have felt an enormous urge to put his foot down. The man's an iceberg.'

Sampson clicked his tongue with impatience.

'Now, as to sightings, I'm afraid the news isn't good. After Craydon he effectively disappeared. That's to say, we've had any number of reports of motor-cyclists travelling about the countryside, but given it was a Saturday afternoon, that's hardly surprising. Some of them were stopped by the police, but without result. He seems to have vanished.'

Bennett hesitated. 'At our last meeting you indicated that the robbery was designed to mislead us. Are you still of that view?'

Sinclair looked unhappy. 'That seems less likely now,' he conceded. 'But I'm still puzzled as to why he would risk returning to Highfield.'

'No, really, we can't have that.' Sampson came to life, striking the table with his fist. 'There's a perfectly obvious explanation and it's staring you in the face. The man's a *thief* – I've said so from the start. He buried what he stole because he didn't want to be caught with it on him. Two weeks later he went back to collect it. He assumed the police would have left the area by then, and he was right. Madden's presence in the woods was pure chance. My God, he even brought a bag with him so he could load the stuff and take it away. Just look at the *facts*, man.'

He thrust his head forward, brilliantined hair glinting in the sunlight that came through the window.

'Let me offer you another suggestion, Chief Inspector. Have you considered that this man may be simply a loner who holed up in those woods? Who saw Melling Lodge as a tempting target and set out to rob it, but lost control of himself? I'll grant you he may be deranged. But calling this hole a dugout! Why not say he simply built himself a shelter? Of course he has an Army background – the same is true of most able-bodied men in this country. He built what he'd been taught to build – a place to sleep and protect himself from the weather. And as for this *gas mask*!' He picked up the single large drawing and squinted at it. 'I'm glad you know what it is, Madden, because I'm damned if I do.'

He put down the piece of paper and turned to Bennett. 'What *is* certain, sir, is that the child was a key witness and she was allowed to go to Scotland out of our control and protection. I have strong reservations about that. I think it was an error of judgement. But it's done.' He made a dismissive gesture. 'Let's concentrate now on what we *know* and what we can *find out* and stop cooking up wild theories unsupported by evidence.'

There was silence. Bennett coughed. He looked at Sinclair.

The chief inspector was gazing at the ceiling. 'A loner holed up in the woods who has a motorcycle. No, I don't think so.' He shifted his glance to Bennett. 'Sir, this man has a job, I believe. He seems to move only at the weekends. Now, it's true he may have returned to collect what he stole. But we must look at the crime as a whole. The bayoneted victims were all killed within seconds of each other – the evidence is clear on that point. He didn't "lose control". He broke into that house with the *intention* of killing the occupants, and we still don't know why.' He paused deliberately. 'As for Sophy Fletcher, I made my decision on the basis of medical advice – that returning her to her family was the best measure we could take, both for the child herself and as regards the possibility of our obtaining any testimony from her in the future. I've heard nothing to make me change my mind.'

He fixed his cool grey eyes on Sampson. The chief superintendent's muddy complexion turned brick red. Bennett looked from one to the other. He seemed to be enjoying the confrontation.

'Very well.' He shifted in his chair. 'What now?'

Sinclair consulted his file. 'We're still going through the list of discharged mental patients supplied by the War Office. Other police authorities are helping. That's a long job. We've put out a general description of the man we're looking for, and the motorcycle and sidecar. Harley-Davidson, through their agents, will supply us with a list of purchasers in the last three years – since the end of the war. We'll start with that, concentrating on the Home Counties. We may have to extend it later.'

'He could have bought it second-hand,' Bennett observed.

'We'll check those registrations, too. But we have to face the fact he may have stolen the machine, and it may be on false plates.' Sinclair straightened the papers in his file. 'Inspector Madden has come up with an idea that we think might be worth pursuing,' he went on. 'Of course, we've already consulted the Crime Index and there's no criminal on record with a modus operandi remotely resembling this man's. But in spite of that, we'd like to put out a general inquiry to other forces to see if they have anything similar to this case in their records.'

'Surely—' Bennett began, but Sampson cut him off.

'That sounds like a waste of time to me. Several people slaughtered in a house? I think we'd have heard about it, don't you?'

'Yes, indeed, sir.' Sinclair turned his tranquil gaze on the chief superintendent. 'But what if he tried and failed? I'm thinking of an abortive attempt, or perhaps an assault with a weapon similar to the one used at Melling Lodge. Some case still unsolved and unexplained.'

Bennett was pondering. 'How would you do it?' he asked. 'Through the *Gazette*?'

'Yes, sir.' The *Police Gazette*, containing particulars of crimes and criminals sought, was circulated daily to all forces of Britain and Ireland. 'We'll list some general information about the case, type of wound and so on, and see if it draws a response.'

Sinclair closed his file. He paused, as though gathering himself. 'Sir, there's one further point I'd like to make. While every effort should be made to track this man down by orthodox police methods, we should recognize the special problems we're faced with and be prepared to look at other ways of approaching the inquiry. Taking up the point you made earlier, as to whether he's sane or not, I think it's time we considered calling in an expert in the field of psychology.'

There was silence in the room. Bennett shifted uneasily in his chair. Sampson, beside him, raised his head slowly and fixed his gaze on the chief inspector.

'We have a unique situation here,' Sinclair went on, seemingly unaware of the effect of his words. 'We're dealing with a man without criminal connections whose motives we don't understand. My most immediate fear is that he may commit a similar crime or crimes unless we apprehend him. I'd feel better in my own mind if I was sure we hadn't neglected any possible line of investigation.'

Bennett was busy drawing a doodle on his notepad. He didn't look up.

It was Sampson who spoke. 'I'm surprised to hear you say that, Angus. Really I am.' His tone had changed to one of puzzlement. 'We all know what happens when you bring outsiders into these cases. Before you know it, every half-baked soothsayer and trick cyclist will be telling us how to solve it.'

'I think you're exaggerating, sir.'

'Am I?' The chief superintendent reached into his top pocket and pulled out a newspaper clipping. 'From this morning's *Express*. I happen to have it with me.' With his other hand he fished out a pair of spectacles and placed them on the end of his nose. 'A lady by the name of Princess Wahletka, a well-known psychic, has offered her services to the police to assist them in solving "the frightful crime of Melling Lodge" – I'm quoting, of course. "They have only to ask, and I am ready to put all my powers at their disposal."' He grinned. 'If you want to take her up, she's appearing nightly at the Empire Theatre in Leeds.'

Two red spots had appeared on the chief inspector's cheeks. 'Excuse me, sir, but you're trying to equate a medical practitioner with a quack.'

'I'm not trying to equate anything, Angus.' The chief superintendent was genial. 'I'm just giving you a friendly warning. So far the press hasn't known how to handle this case — they're as baffled as you are, if you like. Start calling in *psychologists* and you'll hand them an open invitation. Do you know what this is?' He shook the clipping under Sinclair's nose. 'This is the tip of your bloody iceberg, is what it is.'

'Chief Superintendent!' Bennett spoke sharply.

'I'm sorry, sir.' Sampson sat back. The smile remained on his lips.

The deputy drummed his fingertips on the table. He avoided Sinclair's glance.

'Thank you, Chief Inspector,' he said. 'I'll consider your suggestion. Gentlemen, this meeting is concluded.'

He rose from the table.

*

'That was highly educational. I trust you were taking notes.' Sinclair's file landed with a thud on his desktop. 'I thought the clipping was a nice touch. He just happened to have it with him. And did you notice

Bennett back-pedalling for all he was worth? All in all you won't see a finer example of the Ripper complex in action.'

'The *Ripper*, sir?'

'Jack of the same name. By the time he was done there wasn't a smart alec between here and Temple Bar who didn't have a theory as to who he was and how to nab him, and the only point on which they agreed was that the police were a bunch of lame-brained incompetents who couldn't catch cold in an igloo.'

Madden was grinning.

'You may laugh, but there are people in this building who still wake up in a cold sweat thinking about it. They're terrified of opening the door, even a crack.' The chief inspector sat down at his desk. 'Don't blame Bennett,' he said. 'He understands what we're up against. But if we call in an outsider and the newspapers get hold of it – and the chief super will see to it they do – all hell will break loose. Careers are made and lost over cases like this one, and I don't mean yours or mine. Bennett's own future is at stake.'

*

Late that afternoon the telephone rang on the chief inspector's desk. 'Hullo ... yes, he's here. One moment, please.'

He signalled to Madden. Then he got up and left the office. Madden picked up the phone.

'John, is that you?' Helen Blackwell's voice came to him from a long way off. 'Lord Stratton rang Father this morning. He told us what happened to you and Will . . . Are you all right?' Her voice swelled and faded on the trunk line.

'Yes, I'm fine . . .' Surprise robbed him of words. He didn't know what to say to her. 'I'll see you in a fortnight?' he asked anxiously.

Her reply was lost in the crackle of the faulty line.

'What?' he called out. 'I can't hear . . .'

'. . . less than that now . . .' he heard her say. Her soft laugh reached his ears, then the line went dead.

A few minutes later Sinclair returned. With a glance at Madden he seated himself at his desk. 'Och, aye!' he remarked.

3

BILLY STYLES was at Waterloo station a good ten minutes before the time he had been ordered to report; it was only a short ride in the bus from Stockwell, where he lived with his mother. Mrs Styles had been widowed young – Billy's father had died of tuberculosis when he was only four – and she had had to support them both, by working first as a waitress in a tearoom in the high street, then later as a factory hand in a wartime munitions plant. Billy himself had tried to enlist in the last year of the war, when he was eighteen, but had been turned down by the doctor who examined him on the ground that he had weak lungs; a shock to the young man, who had never suspected he had any such flaw in his physical constitution. His suspicion that the doctor was conducting some form of private vendetta against the conscription policy was strengthened when some time later he passed a medical examination to gain entry into the Metropolitan Police without incident. The memory rankled with Billy, who felt cheated of his due.

He had spent the past fortnight working with Sergeant Hollingsworth. Assigned space in a small office beside the chief inspector's, they had toiled over the list of discharged mental patients, dividing it up into regions and dispatching individual rosters to the various police authorities around the country. A number of ex-patients had already been interviewed and the results collated and assessed.

The work was grinding and repetitive, but after experiencing initial boredom with it, Billy had found increasing satisfaction in the process of gradual elimination which he and the sergeant, under Madden's supervision, were engaged in. He had been allowed to study the cumulative file: a history of the case, which Chief Inspector Sinclair kept up to date.

When he read the details of the attack on Madden and Stackpole in the woods above Highfield he felt fresh pangs of jealousy and envy. He felt it was he who should have been with the inspector, rather than the village bobby. Sometimes, in his imagination, he saw himself in the trenches under Madden's command.

The inspector appeared with three minutes to spare and they walked on to the platform together.

'Do you know what this is about, Constable?'

'No, sir.' Billy had to add a skip to his step to keep up with Madden's long stride.

'Let's find a compartment first.'

The telephone call had come the previous evening. Sinclair had looked across at Madden and raised a thumb.

'That was Tom Derry,' he said as he hung up. 'He's a chief inspector now – head of the Maidstone CID. We worked on that Ashford murder together. He thinks he may have something for us.'

Derry had read the item about the Melling Lodge

murders in the *Police Gazette* two days previously, but had not made the connection in his mind right away.

'He didn't handle the case himself,' Madden explained to Billy as the train drew out of the station. 'But then he recalled one or two details from the file. We'll find out more when we talk to him.'

Billy listened in silence. Pride stirred in him. For the first time he felt Madden was treating him as a colleague. He was tempted to join in, to offer some observation of his own, but decided, on balance, it would be better not to speak. If the inspector wanted his opinion he would ask for it.

'Where do you live, Constable?'

They had the compartment to themselves. The train moved at a steady clip through the green fields and hedgerows of Kent, a countryside still unmarred by the spreading stain of pink and white suburban villas.

'Stockwell, sir.'

'With your family?'

'Just my mother, sir. My father's dead.'

'Was he killed in the war?'

'No, sir. He died before.' For some reason he couldn't rationalize, Billy felt ashamed. It was as though he wished his father had perished in the conflict, rather than from a common disease. He wished, too, that he himself had worn a soldier's uniform, if only for a day. 'My uncle Jack now – Mum's brother – he was killed on the Somme.'

Billy hesitated. He could read nothing from the inspector's expression. Yet he knew he had been in the same battle. It was common knowledge at the Yard.

One of the sergeants had told him Madden's battalion had been in action on the first day. Out of seven hundred men, the sergeant said, fewer than eighty had survived to answer their names at the evening roll-call. Billy couldn't conceive of such an event, of so many men being cut down in such a short space of time, and he wanted to ask the inspector about it. But when he looked at Madden's face as he stared out of the window he decided it might be better not to.

*

Derry's office at Maidstone Central Police Station overlooked a corner of the market square. A profusion of pink geraniums overflowed two terracotta pots on the ledge outside his window and the chief inspector was busy watering them when Madden and Styles were shown in. He parked the can on the ledge outside and came over to shake their hands.

'How's Mr Sinclair? Bearing up? Be sure to give him my regards when you see him.' He had a bony, intelligent face and a swift glance, which showed mild surprise at the youthful appearance of Styles.

'Mr Sinclair wanted to come himself, sir. But the assistant commissioner called a meeting this morning.'

'Here's the file,' Derry said. He handed Madden a buff folder. 'But let me give you the gist of it so you'll know why I rang the Yard.'

He directed his visitors to a pair of chairs and then seated himself behind his desk.

'It happened in the first week of April when I chanced to be on leave. I was only away for a fortnight, but by the time I got back it was all over. The detectives handling it felt they had a cast-iron case. They were even more sure when the fellow topped himself.'

'He was in custody, was he?' Madden inquired.

'They were holding him in the cells downstairs. He tore his shirt into strips and managed to hang himself from the bars.' Derry shook his head regretfully. 'I looked over the file, of course, but I have to say I didn't feel any doubts at the time. It seemed solid. Based on what I read, I reckon he would have swung.'

Madden balanced the folder on his knee. 'But you changed your mind when you saw our item in the *Gazette*?'

'I wouldn't go that far. Let's say I'm in *two* minds right now. I just have a nasty feeling we might have picked up the wrong man.'

'Even though he hanged himself?' Madden was surprised.

Derry shrugged. 'Caddo — that was his name — always admitted stealing the goods he was caught with. Perhaps he thought he couldn't escape conviction on the murder charge either, though he did maintain the woman was dead when he entered the house, and he never changed his story. Still, whatever happened he was going to spend a spell in prison.'

'I see he was a gypsy.' Madden had opened the file.

'A full-blooded Romany. They do say you can't lock them up for any length of time. They won't abide it.' Derry reached behind him and brought in the watering-can from the ledge outside. 'Caddo lost his wife a couple of years back. He was alone. A man can come to the end of himself, don't you think?'

Madden didn't look up from the file.

'He owned a horse and caravan.' Derry brushed off his hands. 'He used to visit the district regularly – it's near a village called Bentham, about ten miles east of here. He had an arrangement with a local farmer, a tenant of the Bentham Court estate, and used to camp on his land for a few weeks in return for mending his pots and pans and doing other odd jobs.'

'Any past history with the police?' Madden was paging through the folder.

'Nothing serious. There was an allegation of sheep-stealing a few years ago, but nothing came of it. A case of grab the nearest gypsy, if you ask me. The trouble started when the man he dealt with left the region and a new tenant took over the farm. Chap called Reynolds. He didn't care for gypsies, it seems, and he told Caddo when he turned up at the end of March that he'd give him a week to find a new site and then he wanted him off his land. They had a blazing row in front of witnesses. Caddo was heard to make threats. Next thing, Reynolds went to the bobby at Bentham and accused Caddo of having poisoned his dogs.'

Madden looked up sharply.

'What?' Derry raised a ginger eyebrow.

'That was something we left out of the *Gazette* item, sir. The dog at Melling Lodge was poisoned a few weeks earlier. Do you remember what was used on Reynolds's animals?'

Derry nodded. 'Strychnine,' he said. 'How about the other?'

'The same.' Madden weighed the file in his hand. The two men looked at each other. Derry clicked his tongue in chagrin.

'Damn it!' he said. He looked away.

'Did they search his caravan?' Madden wondered.

'The bobby did. Nothing turned up. Of course, he could have got rid of the stuff. Anyway, the constable spoke to him sharpish. Told him Reynolds wanted him off his land within twenty-four hours. It was a Saturday. The murder happened the same evening.'

'Caddo admitted going over there, to Reynolds's farm.' Madden was back in the file. 'He said he didn't have anything special in mind.'

'That was his first statement.' Derry pointed at the folder. 'He made another later and he was more forthcoming. Admitted he meant to do Reynolds harm. Said he thought of setting fire to his barn.'

'That would have been what time?'

'After six, Caddo said. It was starting to get dark. His story – his second version – was that he approached the house and saw lights on and the back door standing open. He waited a few minutes and then went closer. He didn't see anyone about. He'd lost his nerve about firing the barn – so he said – but he thought he might slip inside and help himself to whatever he could find. When he got to the door he noticed the lock had been smashed, but he couldn't hear anything so he went inside. He took a bag from the kitchen and started putting things in it – a clock from the mantelpiece, some knives and forks from a canteen of cutlery. He found his way to Reynolds's study, opened his desk and pocketed twenty quid and a gold watch.'

'Where was Reynolds all this time?'

'Less than a mile away, looking for some sheep. With his dogs dead he was having a hell of a time running his flock and a number of them had strayed. He had a neighbour with him, fellow called Tompkins, who'd come over to lend a hand. Tompkins saw Mrs Reynolds before they went off, so that put the husband in the clear. Both men were out of sight of the house for an hour – that could well have been a factor.'

'Might have saved their lives,' Madden remarked.

Derry cocked his head. 'You think it was your man?'

'It could be, sir.' Madden scowled in frustration. 'So what did Caddo do then?'

'He went upstairs, just to take a look, he said, to see if there was anything worth lifting. His story is he found Mrs Reynolds's body in the bedroom and got out of the house as fast as he could and ran all the way back to his camp-site. They picked him up in his caravan on the Ashford road next morning.'

Madden was wondering. 'Since you didn't know about the poisoned dog, what made you think there might be a connection with Melling Lodge?'

'The murder itself,' Derry replied. 'The woman having her throat cut that way and her body thrown across the bed. And . . . well, this is a strange thing to say, you'll think . . . but the fact that she *wasn't* raped. Just like your Mrs Fletcher.'

'That struck you as strange?'

Derry nodded. 'He dragged her out of her bath and threw her on the bed. *Why?* She was naked, a good-looking woman, too. I mean, why *didn't* he rape her?' He looked uncomfortable. 'Hell of a thing to find yourself wondering,' he muttered.

'If it's any consolation, sir, Mr Sinclair had the same reaction.' Madden returned to the file. 'What about the murder weapon?' he asked.

'According to our pathologist, probably a cut-throat razor. Caddo had one. It was tested, but nothing came up.'

'Prints?'

'None.' Derry got to his feet. 'I dare say you'd like to have a look at the place, Inspector.'

'I would, sir.' Madden ordered the papers in the file. 'What would be the best way of getting there?'

'I'll take you myself,' Derry said. 'This business is like a bone in my throat. I have to know one way or the other.'

*

It turned out Derry had his own motor-car – one of the new 20 h.p. Ford five-seaters. The cars were being offered on the market at only £205 and Billy had a secret yearning to possess one, though he hadn't learned to drive yet.

They left Maidstone by the Sheerness road, but soon

turned off it and drove through the rolling chalk uplands of the North Downs. The August sun was hot on their faces and the breeze in the open car was welcome. At Bentham, a village nestling in the fold of a green valley, Derry stopped outside a set of wrought-iron gates. He pointed up a long, straight drive, treeless but flanked at its furthest point by a pair of ornamental ponds. In the background, a handsome Palladian façade was visible.

'Bentham Court,' he said. 'The guidebooks call it an architectural gem. A family named Garfield own it now. Reynolds is one of their tenants.'

They drove on for another mile, then branched off the road on to a narrow rutted track that ended at a patch of bare earth beside a chalky stream.

'This was Caddo's camp-site. Reynolds's farm is a mile or two away.' Although he hadn't handled the case, the chief inspector seemed to have taken the trouble to familiarize himself with the details. 'There's a path that runs along the stream.'

They returned to the road and continued on the winding paved surface until they came to another dirt track, which Derry took, steering the car down a gentle gradient to the stream bed, which he crossed slowly, the water creaming about the wheels, and then ascending the grassy slope on the other side. A slate-roofed farmhouse with a whitewashed barn behind it came into view. Sheep dotted the green contoured landscape on either side of the roadway. As Derry pulled up near the house, a man in rough clothes came out of the barn. He stopped some distance from the car and stared at them. There was no hint of greeting in his manner.

'Mr Reynolds?' Derry got out of the car. 'We haven't met. I'm Chief Inspector Derry, from Maidstone. This is Inspector Madden, and Detective Constable Styles. They're from London.' When the man didn't respond, he asked, 'Would you like to see our warrant cards?'

Reynolds shook his head. 'I thought I'd done with you lot.' He came closer, but didn't offer to shake hands.

'Inspector Madden has some questions to ask you. And we'd like to have a look around, if that's all right?'

'I don't understand.' He was about forty, Billy judged, but somehow older. Unshaven and wearing a dirty, collarless shirt, he looked like a man who had lost interest in how he appeared to others. His eyes were dull and uncaring. 'I thought the bastard hanged himself.'

'Can we go inside for a moment? We won't bother you for long.'

'No,' Reynolds said flatly. He glared at them.

Madden spoke: 'I understand how you feel, Mr Reynolds, but please oblige me.' Billy was struck by the gentle tone of his voice. 'I'm working on another case and I believe there may be a connection. You'd be doing me a great service if you'd help us.'

The man didn't reply at once. He stared into Madden's deep-set eyes, until Billy began to think that some silent communication was passing between them. Abruptly he turned away. 'Go in, if you want to,' he said, over his shoulder. He walked off.

Madden led the way through the front door, which opened into a small brick-paved entrance hall where they had to pick their way through a litter of muddy boots. Beyond was a sitting-room smelling of stale cigarette smoke. Sunlight streaming through smeared window-panes fell on a heap of dirty laundry lying on the floor in the middle of the room. An overturned ashtray spread its contents over the surface of a low wooden table where a pile of dirty plates and cutlery was stacked.

The house was like the man, Billy thought. Something had gone. Snapped. He followed Madden and Derry to the kitchen at the rear of the house, where the inspector examined the back door: a fresh section of wood in the jamb, still unpainted, showed where the lock had had to be repaired.

They returned to the hallway and went upstairs. The low-ceilinged bedroom displayed the same signs of neglect as the rooms below. The double bed was unmade, the bedclothes pushed aside, and the glassed top of the dressing-table was dulled by a thin coating of dust. Two framed photographs stood on the mantel-piece above the fireplace. One showed a smiling young woman with a wreath of flowers in her fair hair. The other was a picture of Reynolds in a private's uniform. Billy saw the dark buttons on the tunic and knew what they meant. Reynolds had served in the Rifle Brigade. *Black-buttoned bastards.*

The bathroom was across a narrow passage and Madden walked from one room to the other. Billy saw that he was pacing out the distance between the big ball-and-claw-footed bath and the bed. It looked to be about twelve feet, the young constable reckoned. He saw what Derry had meant. Why drag the woman all the way to the bed and *not* rape her? If he'd wanted to kill her, why not do it in the bathroom? He realized that the same questions could indeed be asked about Mrs Fletcher's murder.

Before they left the bedroom his eye was caught by a leather-bound volume on the bedside table. He glanced at the title. It was a collection of poems by a writer Billy had never heard of. Opening the book, he found an inscription in the flyleaf: *To my dearest darling girl, with all my love, Fred.*

Outside, Madden stood in front of the house and let his gaze wander over the gently sloping hillside. The chalk downland was bare of cover.

'Shall we talk to him now?' Derry asked. He had just seen Reynolds appear from a fold of land below them. He had a young dog at his side. When it trotted away, he summoned it back, slapping his thigh, making the animal come to heel.

'In a moment,' Madden replied.

He walked round to the side of the house. Derry and Billy followed. They found him gazing up the hillside behind the farmhouse at the crest of the ridge, about half a mile away, where a small coppice of beeches stood.

'There!' The inspector pointed. 'I want to have a look at that first.'

As they walked up the cropped grass of the shallow incline Madden told the chief inspector about the dugout in the woods on Upton Hanger. 'We haven't made that public – we're being careful about what we put out. He used a rifle and bayonet for four of the five killings. And we think he was wearing a gas mask when he broke in.'

Derry grunted. 'Sounds to me like you've got a weird one,' he commented.

Billy, walking a respectful two paces behind them, thought that was putting it mildly.

The coppice covered only an acre or two. The leaf-carpeted ground beneath the trees showed no sign of having been disturbed. Madden stood in the shade at the edge of the treeline and looked down at the farmhouse. The barn behind it was set a little to one side, and from where he stood he had a clear view of the kitchen door and the backyard. Watching him, Derry saw the crease of frustration notched in his forehead.

'This is the spot . . .' Madden glanced left and right along the bare crest of the ridge. 'We know he likes to watch them first.'

He took off his hat and mopped his brow with a handkerchief. Derry noticed the ragged scar running along his hairline. The sense of familiarity he usually felt when he met another policeman was missing with Madden. He recognized that this grim-faced inspector was different.

'Sir?' Styles's voice reached them from inside the wood. 'There's something here, sir. A cigarette tin, I think . . .'

Madden spun on his heel and strode over to where the constable was standing behind a low bank. As he approached Billy went down on his haunches.

'Don't touch it!'

The two older men joined him. He pointed, and they saw the glint of metal in the deep shade beneath the bank. Madden crouched down.

'You're right, Constable.'

Taking a pencil from his jacket pocket he lifted the cylindrical cigarette tin off the ground and held it up.

'No label,' Billy said regretfully. He felt he'd earned the right to make a comment.

'The man we're after smokes Three Castles,' Madden explained.

'If it's his it's been here since early April. You won't get a print off it now,' Derry remarked.

'True. But we'll take it with us, anyway. Constable – handkerchief!'

Billy reached into his pocket, recalling, as he did so, the shame he had felt the last time he'd been required to produce one. As Madden was passing the tin over to him, he paused and looked at it more closely, holding it up to the light. 'Do you see that burn mark?' he asked Derry, and the chief inspector nodded. The inside of the tin was blackened. 'I want to search this patch of ground. We're looking for a piece of cloth, probably burned or charred. Anything that would serve as wadding. This tin's been used as a Tommy cooker. You can brew a cup of tea on it if you haven't got a stove handy. The troops used to put wadding at the bottom and soak it in methylated spirits.'

Billy, with the tin safely stowed in his pocket, was already examining the ground around him. Madden and Derry joined in the search. To Billy's chagrin, it was the chief inspector who found what they were looking for.

'Isn't this what they call two-by-four?' Derry was down on his heels brushing away the dead leaves.

Madden picked up the ball of charred cloth. A small square of flannel, unconsumed by the flames, was still visible. He took out his own handkerchief and wrapped it around the burned fragment. Then he returned to the spot where Billy had found the tin and got down on his knees. The other two watched as Madden laid his long body against the low bank in front of him and peered over the rim. They were a dozen yards from the edge of the coppice. Nevertheless, the inspector had a clear line of sight through the trees to the Reynolds's farmhouse below.

'There . . . that's it!' Madden growled his satisfaction.

When they went back down the hill Reynolds was nowhere to be seen. As before, his figure emerged suddenly from a hidden hollow in the slope. The dog was trotting at his heels. It stopped and pricked up its ears as they approached. Reynolds waited, hands in pockets, his face expressionless.

Madden wasted no words. 'Can you remember what

time it was, Mr Reynolds, when you left the house and when you returned? It matters to me how long you were absent.'

Reynolds blinked. He swallowed. 'We left the house, Ben Tompkins and I, just after half past five and came down here looking for strays. We were back soon after half past six. Say twenty to seven at the latest.'

'It was dark by then?'

He nodded.

'You were out of sight of the house all the time?'

'Pretty well. We were further down.' Reynolds turned and pointed away. 'There's a dip in the land, it's not obvious from here.'

'I know you didn't see anything,' Madden said. Billy was surprised again by his tone. His manner with Reynolds now was businesslike, impersonal. Yet Reynolds was responding readily to his questions. 'But did you hear anything? It's important.'

'No, I already told the police.' For the first time he seemed eager to help.

'Nothing at all? Think hard.'

Reynolds frowned. 'What *sort* of thing?'

Madden shook his head. 'I'm not going to say. I don't want to put it in your mind.'

Reynolds stared at him. 'I know I didn't hear anything,' he said. 'But I remember Ben saying something . . .'

'What was that?' The inspector leaned closer.

'We'd found a ewe caught by her leg in a cleft down by the stream. We were just easing her out when Ben looked up. I remember now . . .' He kept staring at Madden. 'He said, "Did you hear that? It sounded like a whistle."'

*

It was after seven when Madden got back to the Yard. Sinclair was waiting in his office.

'We're lucky Tom Derry's in charge at Maidstone. There aren't many who would have smelled a rat.' They stood together at the open window and watched as a pleasure-steamer, strung with coloured lights, moved slowly downriver. 'But is it our rat?'

'I think it is, sir. The razor, the dogs, the whistle.'

'And the fact she wasn't raped?'

'Especially that.'

The sounds of a jazz band drifted up to them through the gathering dusk.

'No evidence of a bayonet this time,' the chief inspector remarked.

'That doesn't mean he wasn't carrying one. You can't see the front door of the house from the coppice. He couldn't have known whether Reynolds was at home or not.'

'So, assuming it was our man, he must have been ready to kill him, too, and he'd have wanted better than a razor for that. The razor's for the woman.'

'It looks that way,' Madden agreed heavily.

Sinclair turned from the window with a sigh and went to his desk. 'I must get home. Mrs Sinclair is threatening divorce on the grounds of desertion.' He eyed his colleague. 'And so should you, John. Get some rest.' The chief inspector viewed Madden's pale face and sunken eyes with concern. Did the man never sleep?

'There were differences, though.' Madden sat down at his desk and lit a cigarette. 'He was in more of a hurry than he was at Melling Lodge. He was in and out of that house in a matter of minutes. There was no sign of him when the gypsy arrived just after six. And there was none of the preparation. He must have poisoned the dogs on Friday night – Reynolds found them on Saturday morning. He killed Mrs Reynolds the same evening.'

'He took his time at Highfield,' Sinclair agreed. 'Perhaps he's getting a taste for it.' He shuddered at the thought.

'But it wasn't done on the spur of the moment,' Madden insisted. 'He knew the lie of the land. He lay up in the wood waiting for sunset. He must have picked out the coppice on an earlier visit.'

'An earlier visit . . .' Sinclair echoed the words. 'But why did he go there in the first place? Or Highfield, come to that. And what was it that caught his eye? What brought him back?'

He slid a pile of papers into an open drawer.

'I keep telling myself it's the women. It *must* be the women. But he never touches them. So could it be something else?' He looked at Madden questioningly.

The inspector shook his head. 'I don't know,' he said. 'I just don't know.'

4

MADDEN LEFT Scotland Yard in the early evening
and walked along the Embankment to Westminster.
With summer drawing to an end the city was filling
again. Sitting on the upper deck of an omnibus bound
for Bloomsbury he looked down on pavements
crowded with young women, typists from government
offices hurrying home at the close of the working day.
He could remember a time before the war when the
same sidewalks would have held only clerks in bowler
hats and high stiff collars. He liked the change that
had come about.

Late that morning a telegram had been delivered to
his desk by one of the commissionaires. It was from
Helen Blackwell. CAN YOU MEET ME IN LONDON
THIS EVENING QUERY. She gave an address in
Bloomsbury Square and a time: six o'clock.

The two weeks were only just up and Madden
hadn't dared to hope that he would hear from her so
soon.

Earlier, at the regular Monday conference in Bennett's office, he had given an account of his trip to
Maidstone and the conclusions he and Sinclair had
drawn from it.

'We think it's the same man.'

Chief Superintendent Sampson had responded with incredulity. 'Now look here, Madden, you've got a gypsy who hanged himself in police custody. That sounds like a pretty fair admission of guilt to me. And where's the connection with the Highfield murders? Granted a woman had her throat cut in each case. But the man who killed those people at Melling Lodge also robbed the house. We *know* that. The stuff taken from the farmhouse was lifted by the gypsy. You can't have it both ways.'

'The Bentham case was reported in the newspapers,' Sinclair interjected. 'I believe our man might have read about the robbery and decided to do the same at Melling Lodge. I still think he was trying to mislead us.'

'You *think*. You *believe*.' Sampson scratched his head. 'The trouble with this inquiry is it's all guesswork.'

'Nevertheless, we have to consider the possibility that these two cases are linked.' The chief inspector was insistent. 'And, if they prove to be, the implication is serious. Even chilling. It means we have a man committing murders, seemingly at random, for motives which are a mystery to us. I repeat, it may be necessary to look at fresh ways of approaching this investigation.'

Watching Bennett's face, Madden couldn't gauge his reaction. The deputy assistant commissioner listened without comment.

*

The address Madden had been given was that of a handsome Victorian house in Bloomsbury Square with a brass plate beside the door on which the words 'British Psycho-Analytical Society' were engraved. A receptionist was seated at a desk in the otherwise bare entrance hall.

'I'm afraid you're a little late for Dr Weiss's address,' she told Madden. 'It must be almost over by now.'

He explained his presence.

'Dr Blackwell? Isn't she the fair-haired lady? You can wait for her down here if you like, or you could go up.' She pointed to the stairway behind her. 'Just slip in quietly, no one will mind.'

Madden went up a flight of carpeted stairs lined with portraits of solemn-looking men in formal attire. When he reached the first floor he heard a voice coming from behind a closed door. He opened it quietly and found himself looking into a large room where perhaps forty people were seated in rows of chairs. Facing them was a short, dark-haired man who stood behind a table carpeted in green felt on which a jug of water and a glass rested beside a pile of notes. He was addressing the gathering.

'. . . but since the issue of abnormality has been raised, may I say that I believe – and here I am quoting Professor Freud again – that the impulses of sexual life are among those which, even normally, are the least controlled by the higher functions of the mind. Generally speaking, we know that anyone who is abnormal mentally is abnormal in his sexual life. What is perhaps more interesting is that people whose behaviour in other respects corresponds to the norm can, under the tyranny of the sexual instinct, lose the capacity to direct or control their lives.'

Madden saw Helen's fair head in the second row of chairs. There were some empty seats at the back of the room and he took one.

'. . . something you said earlier. Does that mean you would sanction perversions?' A middle-aged man in the front row had risen to ask a question. Madden had missed the first part of it. 'More generally, it does seem to me and to others outside the profession that everything in the world of psychiatry revolves around sex. Or perhaps I've misunderstood you, Dr Weiss?'

'It is more likely that I have misled you.' The speaker was smiling. 'My English is not as fluent as I would wish.' To Madden it seemed that he was fully at home in the language, although he spoke with a strong accent. 'But let me say first that, speaking as a psychiatrist, I would not normally use the word "perversion" as a term of reproach in the sexual sphere. To put it bluntly, most of us enjoy some degree of "perversion" from the norm.'

An embarrassed ripple of laughter came from the audience. At that moment Helen Blackwell looked over her shoulder and her eyes met Madden's. His heartbeat quickened. For a moment her face seemed to register surprise. Then she smiled.

'However' – Dr Weiss leaned forward, resting his hands on the table – 'on the more general question, while I would not agree that "everything" in our work has to do with sex, I cannot deny the central position occupied by this most imperious of instincts. Let me be plain. I regard human sexuality as the single most important force in our lives, both as individuals and as members of society. Consider only how it lies at the very root of our capacity to love human beings other than ourselves. Truly, the seed of our happiness.

'But the tale does not end there, sad to say, and this is evident from much of the work being done in my profession. The sexual instinct flows like a river through our lives, and if, for many, it is a broad sunlit stream, for others it can be a source of pain and anguish. A river of darkness. Aphrodite appears to us in many aspects, some of them strange and terrible. We should regard her with awe.

'In this connection, and to answer more fully your earlier question, I cannot do better than draw your attention once more to the writings of Professor Freud, whose work has figured so largely in our discussion this evening. As my old teacher has observed, even the most repulsive sexual acts can be transformed by the human mind into idealized creations. I will close with a quotation from *Three Essays on the Theory of Sexuality*, freely translated: "The omnipotence of love is never more strongly proved than in aberrations such as these. The highest and lowest are always closest to each other in the realm of sexuality."'

The speaker smiled at his audience and bowed. A polite round of applause broke out as he began to collect his notes from the table in front of him. There was a shuffling of feet and chairs. Madden made his way to the front. Helen awaited him, her eyes meeting his when he was still some way off and then holding them in her steady glance as he approached.

'John, dear . . .' She shook his hand. 'I was so afraid you wouldn't be able to come at such short notice.' As people milled about them she moved closer to him. 'I got back yesterday evening and found an invitation to this lecture waiting at the house, so I decided to take a chance and come up.'

She was wearing a dark high-waisted dress with a matching velvet toque. A fringed shawl of red silk was draped loosely about her shoulders. Her glance shifted and he became aware of a figure standing beside them.

'Franz, how lovely to see you again.'

'Helen, my dear . . .' Dr Weiss took her hands in his and kissed them, first one then the other. He was perhaps half a head shorter than she was and she smiled down at him.

'This is my friend John Madden.'

'Mr Madden.' Dr Weiss brought his heels together and executed a brief bow. His dark wavy hair was flecked with grey at the temples. His liquid brown eyes, crinkled at the corners by a smile, held a look of rueful intelligence.

'*Inspector* Madden. John works at Scotland Yard. You must have read about those terrible murders in Highfield . . .'

'Indeed. Our papers carried several reports.' He looked at Madden curiously.

'I stayed with Franz and his family in Vienna before

the war,' Helen told Madden. 'He and Father are old friends and I went there to study German.'

'We still miss you.' Dr Weiss regarded her fondly. 'Mina was devoured by envy at the thought that I might see you on this trip. Mina is my wife,' he explained to Madden. 'She was not alone. Jakob insists that he remembers you well and wants to know when you will return.'

Helen laughed. 'Since Jakob was only three at the time, I find that hard to believe.'

'Some memories we carry in our hearts.' Dr Weiss touched his chest.

'Dear Franz . . . please give them both my love, and tell them I *will* come back and see you all again.'

'But not yet, please!' Dr Weiss held up his hand. 'Vienna is not a place one should choose to visit at present.'

'Are things still so bad?'

'Bad enough. Expressed in our currency, the modest fees I am receiving for these lectures will seem like a fortune.' The doctor smiled wryly. 'An illusory one. They say soon it will take a suitcase of banknotes to buy a loaf of bread.'

'Oh, Franz!'

'Still, we learn through suffering – isn't that what the Greeks have taught us?' He became animated. 'Last winter we had to burn some of our furniture to keep warm. When patients came to the house I would wrap them in blankets and lay them out on the couch. Professor Freud, as you may know, has developed a technique of free association in analysis,' he bent towards Madden again, 'but it's hard for a patient to concentrate on retrieving some memory from the past when all he is wondering is whether he can reach the end of the session without turning into an icicle!'

Helen Blackwell's laughter brought Madden the memory of a grassy bank and the sound of a blackbird's call.

'So here I am, earning a crust as they say.' He glanced about him. 'The Society feels it would be of benefit to introduce psychoanalysis to a wider public in Britain. Well and good, I say. Unfortunately, to most outsiders psychiatry equals Freud equals sex.' He looked droll. 'One has only to mention his name in front of a roomful of Englishmen and half a dozen of them turn red with embarrassment.'

A figure was hovering behind him. Dr Weiss looked round. 'Yes, of course – forgive me. I shall only be a moment longer.' He addressed Helen. 'I leave for Manchester tomorrow. Then Edinburgh. But I shall return to London in a week and I will get in touch with you. Perhaps we could have lunch together? Yes?'

'Of course, Franz. But you must come down to Highfield and see Father again.'

He took her hands and kissed them as before. He bowed to Madden – 'Inspector.' With a smile at them both, he turned and joined a group of men waiting behind him.

Helen took Madden's arm and they moved off down the aisle between the chairs.

'Are you one of those half-dozen, John Madden?'

'Certainly not.'

'Yes, I believe you're blushing.'

They went down the stairs and out into the soft evening light. The plane trees in the square were bowed under the weight of summer foliage. The air was warm and heavy with the dust of the city.

'Would you like to hear about Sophy? She started talking again a week ago. I spoke to Dr Mackay in Edinburgh. So far she hasn't mentioned that night, and when Dr Mackay asked her about it she went silent for another two days. It was a warning – "Keep off!" But she hasn't asked for her mother, and Dr Mackay thinks she knows and accepts that she won't see her again.'

He told her about the drawings. 'We believe the man who broke in was wearing a gas mask. I don't know if you've ever seen one. They're quite hideous. A child would have been terrified.'

They continued slowly around the square. She kept hold of his arm, walking close beside him, her body brushing against his.

'Would you like to have dinner?' he asked, unsure how to proceed. He didn't want her to think he was taking anything for granted.

'Yes, please. I haven't eaten all day.' She looked directly at him. 'Then could we go back to your place? I'm staying with a girlfriend in Kensington. I'd like to take you there, but she's terribly strait-laced and I simply haven't the courage.'

She smiled into his eyes and he smiled back, his

heart lifting. He found it hard to believe there was anything in the world for which she did not have the courage.

*

They sat across from each other in the restaurant. Candlelight brought out the glint of gold in her hair. She told him about her marriage.

'I met Guy when we were students, but he gave up medicine and decided to read law instead. He was still doing that when the war began. Each time he came home on leave it was harder. I had to try to remember why I'd married him, why I'd loved him. When he was killed, all I could think was that I'd failed him and now I'd never have a chance to make it right.'

Madden's wife had been a schoolteacher. They had been shy with each other, still strangers after two years of marriage. He had difficulty now recalling her features, or those of their baby daughter who had died at the age of six months, within days of her mother. During the war he had come almost to forget them, as though their deaths had ceased to matter in the great slaughter going on around him. Later he had tried to recover his feelings, to mourn afresh, but they remained dim in his memory and he never spoke of them now.

Instead, he talked to her about the case. He told her about the murder of the farmer's wife at Bentham.

'We haven't put it out, but we think it was done by the same man. We don't understand his reasons for killing. We can't find a motive that makes sense.'

She wanted to know what had happened to him and Will Stackpole in the woods at Highfield. Lord Stratton had told them little about the ambush and she was shocked when she heard the details. 'You could have been killed, both of you. Was it terrifying, being trapped like that? Were you very afraid?'

'Not really. Not enough—' He stopped, conscious of what he had said. When he didn't go on, she asked, 'Was that how you felt in the war?'

He nodded. He found it hard to speak. 'Towards the end, yes. There seemed no point in being afraid any more. Either you survived or you didn't. But when I felt the same thing up in the woods, it was as though I'd never escaped from it – that feeling that nothing mattered any longer.'

She took his hand in hers.

The past two weeks had not been easy ones for Helen Blackwell. The problem of fitting an affair into her busy, tightly structured life had occupied her mind at length. But she had also found herself wondering whether she was wise, after all, to involve herself with a man so clearly suffering from inner torments.

Her wartime work had taught her much about the effects of prolonged exposure to trench warfare. Everywhere in the land there were men who woke each morning unable to control their trembling limbs and eyelids, who started at the sound of a door being slammed and dived for cover when a car backfired. She knew what mental efforts were required by those who remained active and in command of their lives.

Returning to London, she had not been surprised to

feel a renewal of physical desire when they met. The mysterious bonds of sexual attraction drew her to this silent man. There was no wishing them away. What she was unprepared for was the sudden rush of tenderness that had filled her when she glanced over her shoulder and found his anxious, troubled eyes searching for hers.

*

Later, he took her to his rooms off the Bayswater Road. To the shame of peeling paint and stained wallpaper and the sour smell of rented furniture. Here was a truth he could not hide from her: that he had ceased to care how he lived. A photograph of his dead wife and child, standing on a side table, was all he had salvaged from his past. She asked him their names and he told her. Alice and Margaret. Margaret after his mother, who had died when he was a boy.

When he began to speak, to make some apology for the place he had brought her to, she stopped his lips with hers. 'Come.' She took his hand and led him into the bedroom.

At the sight of her naked body, white and gold and rose-tipped, he started to tremble, and when they lay down together he continued to shake helplessly. She held him in her strong arms, saying nothing, pressing his body to hers, her cheek to his. After a while she began to kiss him, first on his face and throat, then on his chest, her breath warm on his skin. His body was marked by wounds: one shaped like a star under his breastbone, the legacy of a bullet that had passed clean through him, somehow missing his heart, the other a jagged ridge of tissue on his hip from the same shrapnel blast that had torn his arm. Her lips moved freely over his scarred body, until he could bear it no longer. When he reached for her she was ready.

'I've thought about this every day.'

He was inside her in a moment, but this time she checked him. Slowed him. 'It's so lovely . . . let's make it last.'

Even so, for him it was over too soon. Too soon. But she kissed him and held him to her and he heard her soft laugh again.

'What was it Franz was saying?' Breathless beneath him.

He fell asleep and dreamed of a youth named Jamie Wallace who had once been a student at the Guildhall in London. One of the young men with whom Madden had enlisted and trained, he'd been the possessor of a sweet tenor voice and had often entertained the other men with ballads of the day. On the first morning of the Somme he and Madden had found themselves side by side in the forward trench. All night the artillery bombardment had sounded. At sunrise it ceased and a small miracle had occurred. Larks arose from the blasted fields and canals all around and the sky had been full of the sound of them. 'Do you hear that?' Jamie Wallace had asked, his face lighting up. In Madden's dream his lips framed the same silent question. *Do you hear that?* A moment later the whistle had sounded for the start of the attack and the men had gone up the ladders into the lark-filled morning.

Madden awoke in tears to find her asleep beside him, her hair spread out over the pillow. Before undressing she had draped her red silk shawl over the bedside lamp and at the sight of her body, naked and glowing in the rosy light, his grief dissolved. As he drew up the sheet to cover them she reached out in her sleep and he moved quickly, easing himself into the circle of her arms, careful not to wake her.

5

HEFTING HIS LEATHER HOLDALL, Amos Pike climbed over the stile, glancing back as he did so to make sure he wasn't being followed. As always, he was taking a roundabout route to his destination. He had grown up on the edge of a wood where wild things lived – foxes and badgers and a range of smaller predators – and had learned early from his father how skilled most were at disguising their tracks.

When he came to a ditch separating two fields he stepped into it and continued on his way, unseen, walking with long springy strides in the shadow of a hawthorn hedge. Today was Tuesday, not a day he normally had off, but Mrs Aylward had gone to visit her sister in Stevenage for the week, taking the train, and apart from chores in the garden his time was his own until Friday evening. Usually he could count on being free one weekend out of two, though Mrs Aylward would occasionally change her plans at the last minute and when she did so he was expected to conform, cancelling his own arrangements. He did so without complaint. His job had advantages of a rare kind. Unlooked-for opportunities had come his way.

He was approaching a small hamlet, a group of cottages at a crossroads surrounded by fields and orchards, and he paused in the shade of the hedge for several minutes while he scanned the scene. It was nearly one o'clock. Those of the inhabitants who were home would most likely be eating lunch. He didn't wish to be seen by anyone. Satisfied, he walked on and came to a narrow dirt track that led to a gate in the back fence of a small thatched cottage, separated from the rest of the village by an apple orchard and unploughed fields.

He unlatched the gate and went into the garden. Pausing to run his eye over the small patch of lawn and the bed of hollyhocks and sweet peas growing against the cottage wall, he decided to spend an hour later trimming the grass and weeding the bed. He made a practice of keeping the place tidy, reasoning that if he did so it would discourage others from offering the same service to the occupant of the cottage. Pike had no interest in the garden, or its owner. It was the long wooden shed at the side of the lawn that was of concern to him and he aimed by indirect means to keep others away from it.

Depositing the holdall on the ground beside the door of the shed, he unstrapped it and took out a brown-paper parcel, which he carried across the lawn to the kitchen door. He entered the house without knocking.

'Who's there?' The husky quaver came from a room inside.

Pike didn't reply, but he walked from the kitchen through a hallway into a small parlour at the front of the cottage where an old woman sat by the lace-netted window nursing a fat tabby.

'Is that you, Mr Grail?' The eyes she turned towards him were covered with a greyish film. In spite of the heat she wore a woollen shawl tucked over the shoulders of her faded quilted gown. 'I was expecting you last week.'

'I couldn't come, Mrs Troy,' Pike said, in his cold voice. 'I had to work.'

'I ran out of tea.' The timid voice held a note of apology. 'I had to borrow some from Mrs Church.'

Pike frowned. 'You should have said you were short.' He saw her flinch at his words and tried to check the natural harshness of his tone. 'I brought you a packet. Plus some shortbread. You asked for that.'

'Did you bring me any fish?' She spoke in a near-whisper, turning her face away, as though afraid of his response.

'No.' He was losing patience. Her existence meant nothing to him, beyond the fact that it should continue. 'They don't sell fish where I am,' he lied brutally. 'I brought you eggs and bacon and ham. And bread and rice. I'll put it away in the larder.'

A minute later he was outside again, crossing the lawn to the shed. Had Winifred Troy still possessed her sight she would hardly have recognized the structure. Pike had replaced the former roof with sheets of corrugated iron, boarded over the single window and fitted a new door equipped with a heavy padlock opened by a key, which he kept about his person at all times.

The shed dated from a time, some years before, when Mrs Troy and her husband, who had since died, had let the cottage to an artist from the city. With their agreement he had built a studio in the small garden and had used the cottage as a weekend retreat and holiday home. By far the most radical alteration Pike had made was to knock down the end wall and install a pair of stable doors in its place. These opened on to the dirt track which ran through the fields and orchards for half a mile before joining a paved road.

Wrinkling his nose at the musty, airless smell, Pike latched the door shut behind him. It was dark in the shed and he lit a paraffin lamp at once. In the artist's day there had been ample illumination from a pair of skylights in the roof, but these had gone. Amos Pike disliked the idea of being overlooked.

The space inside the shed was mainly given over to a large object, covered with a dust cloth, which stood in the middle of the cement floor. Pike removed the cloth with a flick of his wrist: a motorcycle and sidecar were revealed beneath.

The shed quickly grew hot, the radiation of the lamp combining with the hot sun on the corrugated-iron roof to turn the room into an oven. Pike took off his shirt. His heavily muscled body bore a number of scars, large and small. He put his holdall on a table and took from it a half-gallon tin of red paint and a pair of brushes. He had bought the paint in a hardware store that morning after having been assured by the salesman that it would adhere to metal. He prised off the lid of the tin with a chisel, spread a sheet of newspaper on the floor and sat down cross-legged. He began to paint over the black bodywork.

His movements were precise and, like all his physical actions, governed by a sense of economy and order. This pattern of behaviour had been acquired at an early age and was the result of an event in his life so catastrophic he had only been able to continue his existence by recourse to a system of interlocking disciplines that guaranteed him control over his every waking moment.

Tormented for years by the terror and anguish of his dreams, he had lately found them diminished both in power and frequency. While he could not have framed such a thought himself, it was as though his subconscious had finally worn itself out and ceded the battlefield to his iron will.

Having lived with his grandparents for some years, he had gone for a soldier at the age of sixteen and found a way of life ideally suited to his needs, the strict demands of military practice fitting easily into his own more rigorous code. He had prospered to the extent of his capacities and by the time war broke out had already attained the rank of sergeant. For a while he had been employed as an instructor at a training depot, but when his battalion was posted to the front he had assumed his former position as a company sergeant.

Wounded on several occasions, he nevertheless managed to survive in the lottery of trench warfare, and the summer of 1917 had found him, now a company sergeant major, engaged with his battalion in the

British offensive south of Ypres at the start of the months-long agony that would later be called Passchendaele.

During the bitter struggle for control of the Menin Road, Pike's company had come under heavy fire from the German artillery. Crouched behind a tree stump he saw a man's head blown off as neatly as if it had been hewn with an axe, the trunk stumbling on for several paces before collapsing. Next moment he was flung high into the air by an exploding shell that buried itself in the ground a few yards away.

He awoke to find himself lying in a crater with the battle still raging around him. Concussed and barely conscious, he listened to the fluttering sound of shells as they streamed through the upper air overhead. A great cloud of smoke and dust hung over the battle-field. He saw men running past him on their way back to the lines, but when he opened his mouth to call to them no sound issued from his lips.

He slept for a few hours, but woke towards evening and realized for the first time that he had received a slight wound to his wrist. Although his limbs were undamaged he found he had no desire to move from where he was, lying on the slope of the crater, staring up at the violet sky. From habit he removed the field dressing sewn into the flap of his tunic and poured iodine into the cut on his wrist. He discovered he still had his water-bottle with him and he drank from it.

At that moment he became aware that he was not alone in the crater. A man from his own company named Hallett lay on the opposite slope, curled up on his side, hugging his blood-soaked tunic. He was calling out faintly, begging for water. Pity had never stirred in the icy heart of Amos Pike, and he watched in silence as the man died.

During the night it began to rain, a hard, driving, relentless downpour, which turned the dry, powdery dust of the battlefield into a quagmire. The battle resumed before dawn. German mortar shells whistled overhead. Smoking clods of earth were flung into the crater. By the blanching flare of a rocket Pike saw troops moving forward weighed down with rolls of wire and pigeon baskets, picks and shovels, but he made no attempt to attract their attention.

Morning came. The body of Hallett had vanished. He saw nothing but mud all around him. Mud and the stumps of trees, and bodies, or parts of bodies – nearby he spied a hand holding a mug, nothing more. The crater became a lake of liquefied mud and when he dozed off he slid down the slope and had to claw his way back up, covered in clayey ooze. The rain had stopped and presently the sun came out. Pike slept again. When he awoke he discovered that the mud had formed a hard crust about his body. It would have been a simple matter to break it, but he found he was content to lie where he was, immobile, his limbs held fast in the mud's embrace.

He began to review his life, and as he did so a strange image took shape in his mind. He saw himself wrapped in a winding sheet like an Egyptian mummy, unable to move, the prisoner of a rigid and unforgiving regime that was slowly grinding his life to dust.

He felt a fierce urge to break out, to burst his bonds. Yet the winding sheet spoke to him of death and he knew that if he decided to lie there, unmoving, he would presently die. And that that, too, would be a solution.

He endeavoured to fix his mind on the problem, to come to some kind of decision. As the mud continued to harden about him he heard a sucking sound and Hallett's bloated body surfaced in the crater, coming to rest on the slope beneath his feet. One of the eyes had remained open and it settled on Pike with an accusing glare. He felt an urge to turn away, but found he couldn't do so without cracking the shell of mud coating his neck and jaw. Part of him wished to stay as he was, stiff and unmoving; another part longed for release.

Early next morning a pair of stretcher-bearers found him and brought him back to the British lines, still encased in his suit of mud. He was put in the hands of a medical orderly, who freed him by tapping at the shell with a cook's ladle as though he were cracking an egg, peeling off the covering a piece at a time.

'There!' he said. 'Just like a new-hatched chick.'

The words had a powerful effect on Pike. All of a sudden he felt free. Reborn! A dark urge, like a dragon waking, stirred in his entrails.

The battalion medical officer pronounced him concussed and he was dispatched, via a casualty clearing station, to the base hospital at Boulogne where they kept him for a week and then returned him to his company.

Pike's battalion had been withdrawn from the line and was resting in a rear area near a village in the midst of farming country, some of it still being worked by peasant families.

As soon as he got back he began to cast around.

6

AT THE END OF the week, on Bennett's orders, Sinclair and Madden drew up a report on the current state of the investigation.

The lengthy inquiry into the whereabouts of mental patients discharged from Army wards was nearly concluded. No likely suspects had been identified. Recent purchasers of Harley-Davidson motorcycles living in the Home Counties had been interviewed and the investigation was being broadened to other regions. Second-hand dealers were also being questioned. A description of the man sought had been circulated to police authorities, and Sinclair had sent a separate message to stations in the south of England asking them to instruct rural constables to be on the look-out for motorcyclists travelling by back roads over the weekends. Where possible, they were to be stopped and questioned and a note made of their particulars. The constables were urged to exercise caution.

'Another Friday!' Sinclair stood at the window of his office and stared down at the sluggish tidal flow of the Thames. 'And to think I used to look forward to the weekends! Now I sit waiting for the telephone to ring. I wonder what he's up to, our friend with the size eleven boots.'

Madden had arrived at the office that morning to find the chief inspector glowering over a copy of the *Daily Express*, whose front page was covered with photographs and a story about the R38 airship, which had crashed into the Humber a few days before with the loss of more than forty lives.

'Thank God for all disasters great and small. Any other day it would have been *us* smeared all over the front page.'

He opened the paper and handed it to Madden who saw the headline: *'Melling Lodge Mystery – Murders Still Unsolved – Disquiet At The Yard.'*

'Sampson's been talking to that stoat Ferris.'

The article began by summarizing the information already published about the case and noting that the police remained 'baffled' by the mysterious killings. 'In the opinion of some observers they are no closer now to solving the crime than they were at the start of the investigation.'

It went on:

> A measure of their desperation may be seen in the spreading rumours that certain officers are in favour of seeking help from outside sources.
>
> While such a course has seldom brought benefits in the past – and is strongly opposed by experienced detectives – nevertheless voices are being raised in support of it by some of those most closely connected to the inquiry, which is being conducted by Chief Inspector Angus Sinclair.

'Sampson's chosen his moment,' Sinclair conceded. 'Bennett's seeing the assistant commissioner this afternoon. Parkhurst will want to know what's being done to advance the investigation. You can see the chief super's game. He thinks he's got us stymied. He's waiting for the cry to go up: "Send for Sampson of the Yard!"'

'He's not afraid of it any more?' Madden was surprised. 'He thinks he can crack it?'

'Why not?' Sinclair shrugged. 'Even with the rough description we have – that plus the motorcycle – we've got enough to identify him. Given a little luck.'

'And time,' Madden pointed out.

'Aye . . . time.' The chief inspector looked sombre. 'But what if Sampson's right? What if this man's no more than a thief who lost his head? We could be on the wrong track. We're still guessing. We don't *know* anything.'

'How would you explain Bentham, then?'

'We don't *know* that was him. We can only be sure about Highfield, and perhaps it's as Sampson says. He tossed everything into the dugout in a panic after the killings and only thought later about coming back to collect it.'

It was the first time Madden had seen his superior look discouraged. I don't agree,' he said. 'It's something else. We both felt it at Melling Lodge. He didn't go there to rob and steal, any more than he did at the Reynolds's farm. I still think it's the women.'

'But *why*? What does he want with them?'

Madden had no answer. But he did have an idea in mind.

*

Later, that same day, the inspector took a rare, extended lunch-hour. Helen Blackwell had come up to London.

'I'm supposed to be shopping. We need new curtains for the drawing-room, but somehow I don't think I'll find the right material today.' She laughed and kissed him on the cheek. They had met at a restaurant off Piccadilly. There wasn't a table free immediately and they were sitting on a banquette in the crowded waiting area. On either side of them young women with bobbed hair and brightly painted faces chattered in high-pitched voices. Blood-red nails tipped ash from the ends of cigarettes mounted in long holders. Somewhere out of sight a pianist was playing ragtime. It was a new world to Madden.

'Don't scowl. It makes you look like a policeman.'

He laughed, and she slipped her arm through his.

'I have to be back in Guildford by four. They're short-staffed at the hospital and I'm helping out. I wish we weren't both so busy.'

She was wearing a dress of pleated cotton and a straw hat trimmed with cherries. Madden leaned closer to drink in the scent of jasmine. She examined his face with her clear gaze. 'You're not getting enough sleep. I'll write you a prescription before I go.'

'There's something I want to talk to you about,' he said. 'I've got a favour to ask.'

'What is it?'

'Later.' He didn't want to spoil the moment. He was happy just to be with her, to sit beside her and feel the pressure of her arm linked with his. Without meaning to, he spoke: 'Christ, I miss you.'

She continued looking at him, holding his eyes in her steady glance. Then, not caring that they were in a public place, she leaned over and kissed him on the lips.

Madden felt his face grow warm. 'Let's forget this,' he urged. 'Come back to my place.'

She stood up at once, drawing him with her. 'I was hoping you'd say that.' She was laughing. 'I was going to suggest it myself, but I'm afraid you already think I'm too bold.'

He took her back to his rooms and they made love in the hot afternoon with the curtains drawn across the open window and the sounds of children at play drifting in from the street outside. Afterwards, she lay in his arms, her body warm and damp. She kissed him with open lips, tasting his salty skin.

'Don't let me fall asleep,' she begged. He held her close and felt her heart beating against his.

The seed of our happiness.

The words came into his mind and he recalled where he had heard them. He was reminded, too, that he had a favour to ask of her.

*

When Madden returned to the Yard he found Sinclair sitting behind his desk, puffing at his pipe in a thoughtful manner.

'Sorry I'm late, sir.'

'That's all right, John. There's damn-all happening anyway.' The chief inspector watched a wreath of blue smoke curling upwards from the bowl of his briar. 'I've just been in to see Bennett. He's had his meeting with Parkhurst. The word from on high is "steady as she goes".'

'What does that mean?'

'It means this inquiry stays within the Yard. Parkhurst made that plain. He doesn't want a carnival — his word. No outside experts to be called in. Sampson's got them running scared. We'll have to think of something else.'

7

THE HOTEL WAS IN a side street off Russell Square. Dr Weiss was waiting at a corner table in the almost deserted lounge. The dusty leaves of a rubber plant brushed his shoulders as he rose to greet Madden. 'Inspector, this is a pleasure.'

'It's good of you to see me, Dr Weiss.'

'I am happy to meet any friend of Helen's.'

A gold watch-chain gleamed against the sober black of the doctor's waistcoat. Behind a welcoming smile he cast a curious glance at his visitor. At their last meeting he had noted Madden's dark, shadowed eyes and air of deep-rooted fatigue. He thought that any man who captured Helen Blackwell's interest was fortunate indeed, and he wondered about their relationship.

They sat down at the table. The doctor waited while Madden signalled to a waiter and ordered drinks for them.

'All the same, I was surprised by her call. You wish to discuss the Melling Lodge murders with me? Inspector, I am not a criminologist.'

'I realize that. But this is not an official visit. In fact, I'd be grateful if you wouldn't mention our meeting to anyone.'

'So!' Dr Weiss's brown eyes sparkled. 'But I still don't see how I can be of help.'

Madden hesitated. He was treading on unfamiliar ground. 'There was something you said in your lecture the other night. It's been on my mind ever since. You were speaking of sexual perversions and you said even the most terrible actions could be idealized by the human mind.'

'That is so.' Weiss frowned. 'But I am still at a loss. From what I have read of the murders at Highfield, no sexual motive was involved.'

'No evident sexual motive.'

'I see . . . but you think otherwise?' His curiosity had sharpened.

'The truth is, we don't know what to think. We know the murders were committed by one man. We have a rough physical description of him and we know the make of his motorcycle. But beyond that we're in the dark. We have no idea *who* we're looking for.'

The doctor's greying eyebrows had already lifted in astonishment. 'And you think *I* can tell you that?'

'You could give us an indication.'

'Based on the evidence?'

'It would be a guide, surely.'

'A guide, yes. But to what destination?' Weiss shook his head ruefully. 'Inspector, you don't know what you're asking. The margin for error in such a procedure would be huge. Psychology is not an exact science.'

'I understand that.'

'I could very well point you in the wrong direction.'

'That's a risk I'll have to take,' Madden persisted.

The older man regarded him in silence for several seconds. A faint smile played about his lips. Finally he shrugged. 'Very well then, if you insist.' He resettled himself in his chair. 'Tell me about this man. As much detail as possible, please. The key lies in the details.'

Madden spoke for the next twenty minutes. He related the entire course of the investigation, omitting nothing. He described the ambush that he and Stackpole had survived in the woods above Highfield and the subsequent discovery of the dugout.

'At that point we believed we were dealing with an isolated incident. Recently, however, we have learned that he made a similar attack on a house some months ago. The only person home was a woman and he killed her in much the same way as he killed Mrs Fletcher.'

'In *much* the same way?'

'In virtually the identical manner. He cut her throat and left her body sprawled across the bed. She was in her bath and he dragged her from there to put her on the bed, just as he carried Mrs Fletcher from the stairs. I was reminded of something someone said to me earlier, referring to Lucy Fletcher. That she had been laid out like a sacrifice.'

'You saw an element of ritual in both killings?' Dr Weiss leaned forward. His face was a study in concentration.

Madden nodded. 'That was how they appeared to me.'

'And neither woman was sexually abused in any way?'

'Correct.'

'You tested for seminal fluid?'

'Everywhere. At least in the case of Mrs Fletcher.'

'*On* her body, as well as in the orifices?'

'Yes, why?'

'On the bedclothes?'

Madden frowned. 'I don't know. Is it important?'

'It might be.' Dr Weiss seemed to notice the glass of whisky in front of him for the first time. He took a sip of the drink. 'So! These are the facts.' He looked Madden in the eye. 'Let us deal with your first question – are these murders sexually motivated? To which I would answer yes. Beyond any doubt.'

'Why?' Madden was struck by the certainty of his tone.

'Partly through reductive reasoning. Once you exclude other motives such as revenge or, indeed, robbery, it's difficult to imagine what else could lie behind them. But mainly because of the close similarities in the killing of Mrs Fletcher and Mrs Reynolds. The element of repetition – of ritual, as you rightly surmise – is one of the classic signs of the sexual murder. As I'm sure you're aware, Inspector.'

'Yes, but we're puzzled by the lack of direct evidence. To put it bluntly, why *doesn't* he rape them? Or abuse them in some other way?'

Dr Weiss cocked his head on one side. 'You've considered the possibility that the man is impotent? That these killings are an expression of rage?'

Madden nodded. 'But in that case I would expect him to demonstrate it more clearly, on the bodies of his victims. Merely cutting their throats seems insufficient.'

'I agree.' Weiss nodded crisply. 'But there could be another explanation. He may feel he can't satisfy himself directly. I mean by normal, or even abnormal, penetration.'

'Why would that be?'

'Because he thinks it's forbidden. Taboo. That doesn't mean he's incapable of ejaculation. Only that he can't bring himself to conclude the act in an orthodox manner. Then again, that may be what he is aiming at. To achieve coitus somehow.' Dr Weiss's fingertips played a scale on the glassed table. As though in response the sawing notes of a cello came from the next room where an orchestra had struck up. They were playing an old tune: 'Just A Song At Twilight'.

'But can we be certain?' Madden felt impelled to play the devil's advocate. 'What about the wartime connection? The bayonet, the dugout, the gas mask? Isn't it possible he's simply deranged? That he's react-ing to something he experienced in the trenches?'

Weiss shook his head. 'We must take that into account, certainly. But the seed of these crimes was planted much earlier in life. In childhood. In infancy, perhaps.'

'Can you be sure of that?' Madden was sceptical.

'Sure?' The doctor lifted his shoulders in an elo-quent gesture. 'In my profession one can seldom be *sure* of anything. There's a saying Freud is fond of quoting: "The soul of man is a far country, impossible to explore." But with regard to human sexuality, certain facts are now, *surely*, beyond dispute. For one, it is established very early in childhood. For another, any damage done then is carried into adult life and magnified. About this there can be no doubt.'

Madden was paying close attention. 'But if he was damaged in childhood, as you suggest, wouldn't he have shown signs of it before now? If we accept he went through the war, he must be in his late twenties, at the very least.'

'This is something that is bothering me,' Dr Weiss admitted wryly. 'Have you checked police records before the war as well as since?'

'Yes, there's nothing of this kind on file.'

'Then we must go deeper into speculation.' The doctor shifted in his chair. He slipped a gold watch out of his fob pocket and began to swing it to and fro like a pendulum in front of him. His brow was knitted in a frown. 'Let us suppose this man conforms to a type familiar to psychiatry. Early in his life he would have shown symptoms of sexual disorientation – the infliction of pain on animals, dogs and cats, is one of the most common. With such children the first full sexual experience, I mean orgasm, is often associated with a blood ritual already developed and establishes a pattern difficult to break. We may imagine he underwent some such experience at the start of adolescence. But since he left no trace of himself as a young man, either his sexual desires were very small or he possessed an exceptional degree of willpower and was able to suppress them. Given the ferocity of his present actions, I would tend to discount the first.

'So what are we faced with?' Dr Weiss pondered his own question. 'A man of unusual self-control who has suddenly cast off his shackles and revealed his true sexual identity. For this to have occurred he is most likely to have undergone an experience – what we in our profession term a trauma – of a quite shattering kind. And now we see a very definite connection to his time in uniform. When it comes to injuries wrought to the human psyche, there is no need to look further than the experience of the common soldier in the trenches.'

Weiss paused. His sympathetic glance rested on the inspector. 'I speak only as an analyst,' he said gently. 'My knowledge of this is second-hand – it comes from the many patients I treat in Vienna. Yours, I suspect, is more immediate and more personal.'

Madden made no reply at first. Then he responded with a brief nod.

'So! Having established that, we can at least form a theory as to why the man you seek has begun – begun *now* – to commit these crimes. A theory, mind you!' Dr Weiss raised a warning finger. 'But if we accept it, we can see a possible line of inquiry emerging. What you have told me about his behaviour suggests that the link with his wartime service is more than merely causal.'

'I'm sorry, I don't . . .'

'The killing of these two women derives from some

experience in childhood – or so I believe.' The doctor's features were screwed into a deep frown. 'But the details overlying it – the dugout, the gas mask, the furious attack and bayoneting of the others – these seem like a refinement of the original action. An addition to it even.'

'An *addition*?' Madden was alert at the word. 'You're saying he might have committed a murder of this kind *during* the war?'

'And is now seeking to perfect the act. Yes, that is a possibility.' Dr Weiss nodded vigorously.

'While he was in the trenches?'

'Oh, no!' Weiss shook his head with equal urgency. 'The killing, if it took place, would have been quite separate from the general carnage. The woman is crucial to the act.'

'But while he was a soldier? Behind the lines, perhaps?' Madden felt a spark of excitement. 'We could ask the War Office. It would be in the provost marshal's records.'

'Only if the military authorities investigated it,' Dr Weiss cautioned. 'And only if it actually occurred. Remember, Inspector, this is all supposition.'

Madden smiled grimly. 'To a policeman it sounds more like a lead.'

Weiss acknowledged the remark with a lift of his head. He swallowed what remained of his drink. When his eyes met Madden's again his mood had darkened. 'I find myself in an unusual position, Inspector.'

'Why is that?'

'I have to hope that everything I have said to you is wrong. That this man is not as I imagine him to be.'

'But if he is?'

'Then you should be prepared for the worst. I judge him to be a psychopath, an extreme case. One who has lost touch with reality. He does not see his victims as human beings, but as objects of gratification. Be sure, however, he is not killing at random. Those women meant something to him. Those *particular* women. Otherwise he would not have taken such pains to prepare himself, particularly in the case of Melling Lodge. One must assume he saw them earlier, either in their homes or in the neighbourhood, and was struck by some aspect of their appearance. Whatever it was, it brought him back.'

Dr Weiss paused. He seemed to be collecting his thoughts.

'I can offer you only general pointers,' he went on. 'By all means consider them, but don't confuse what I say with established fact. It is likely he lives in a fantasy, and this will make it difficult to predict his actions. Take his return to Highfield, for example. A foolish decision, on the face of it. But in his own world the reasons would have seemed compelling. Perhaps he wanted a memento of Mrs Fletcher – a piece of her jewellery. A trophy, if you will. It's not unknown in this sort of case.' He looked hard at the inspector. 'I don't say that *was* the reason, mind you. I seek only to indicate the problem you face in trying to understand his behaviour.'

Madden was struck by the doctor's sombre expression.

'Perhaps you recall my remarks the other evening regarding the sexual instinct. Here is a man in whom it has been crushed, almost extinguished, for years. This is the river of darkness I spoke of. Now that it has broken free, nothing will check it. Shame, disgust, morality – these are the normal barriers to perversions and acts of sexual desperation. But against the kind of force I see acting through this man they are helpless. He is driven by compulsion.'

'You're saying he won't stop killing?' Madden nodded. 'We've been afraid of that.'

'No, I'm saying something different.' Weiss shook his head sadly. 'I'm saying he *can't* stop.'

8

'How could you do it, John? Have you taken leave of your senses? Do you know what will happen if this gets out?' The chief inspector's tone was anguished. He paced up and down in front of Madden's desk. The door to the adjoining office was firmly shut. 'If Sampson gets even a sniff of this he'll go straight to the newspapers. My God – I can see the headline now! "Yard Calls In Hun!"'

'Dr Weiss is an Austrian, sir.'

'I doubt the chief superintendent will appreciate the distinction. I can assure you the newspapers won't.' Sinclair paused in his pacing. He stared down at the inspector. 'Have I said something to amuse you?'

'I'm sorry, sir.' Madden sought to compose his features. 'It's just that we never used to think of them that way.'

'What way?'

'You had to come home on leave to hear people talking about Huns and wanting to hang the Kaiser. We used to call them Fritz or Jerry. And we didn't want to hang the Kaiser. We wanted to hang the General Staff. First the Staff, then the Commissariat.'

'Never mind who you wanted to hang.' The chief inspector kept a firm grip on his outrage. It didn't escape him that he had never heard Madden talk this way before. 'You had no right to do what you did. For pity's sake! Why didn't you ask my permission first?'

'Because you wouldn't have given it,' Madden said frankly.

'At least you had that right.'

'You would have had to say no.'

'Ah! Light begins to dawn!' Sinclair's face cleared. 'You didn't *need* to ask. You already *knew* what I was thinking.'

'Well, yes, sir.' Madden was finally embarrassed. 'I thought so.'

'Amazing! I never guessed I was so transparent. Where did you meet this Fritz?'

'At a lecture on psychiatry.'

'Where you just happened to drop in? No, please don't tell me.' The chief inspector's face showed pain. 'I'd rather not know.'

He went to the window and stood with his hands on his hips staring down at the river. After a time he looked over his shoulder. 'Well . . .?'

*

'Excuse me, sir, is this a new development?'

Sampson, late and out of breath, slid into his seat beside the deputy assistant commissioner.

'No, Chief Superintendent. But Mr Sinclair has a fresh line of inquiry he wants to follow up.'

'It's just an idea,' Sinclair explained. He and Madden sat across the table. 'But since it involves going back to the War Office I felt I ought to consult Mr Bennett.'

'The chief inspector thinks it's possible this man might have committed offences, even similar crimes, while he was still in uniform.'

'It's the element of repetition that bothers me.' Sinclair's grey eyes bore a look of blameless innocence. 'Given that he also carried out the assault at Bentham – and I believe he did – then he seems set in a pattern. But when did it start? There's no peacetime record of crimes like these, but we haven't looked at the war years in detail. And the fact that he arms and equips himself like a soldier makes me wonder if he didn't start then. Abroad, perhaps. In France or Belgium. We need to ask the military to check their records.'

There was silence in the room. Finally Sampson spoke: 'Who've you been talking to?' he asked.

'Sir?'

'Have you been discussing this case with anyone?'

'No one outside this building.'

Madden was aware that Bennett's eyes were fixed on him. He stared straight ahead over the deputy's shoulder.

'And you thought all this up yourself?'

'It's no more than a long shot, sir. I don't mind admitting we're clutching at straws.'

Bennett cleared his throat. 'So we'd like them to check the provost marshal's files. I see no harm in that. I'll get in touch with the War Office again. Gentlemen . . .' He rose from the table.

'Well, that was close,' Sinclair remarked, when they

were back in his office. He thumbed tobacco into his pipe. 'For a moment there I thought he had the scent.'

'Sorry to put you in that position, sir.' Madden was feeling remorse. 'He was only guessing.'

'I'm happy to hear it.' The chief inspector struck a match. 'I wouldn't like to think I'd had to do with *two* mind-readers in one day.'

9

HAVING FIRST EXTINGUISHED the paraffin lamp, Amos Pike opened the double doors at the end of the garden shed and stepped out into the cool night air. He wore a belted leather jacket over a khaki shirt, grey flannel trousers and boots. A flat woollen cap fitted snugly on his close-cropped head.

He looked about him. He could see no lights burning in any of the cottages. It was after midnight.

He went back into the shed, released the brake on his motorcycle and pushed the machine to the doorway. There was a slight ramp running down from the floor to the dirt road outside and Pike mounted side-saddle and freewheeled for a few yards until the vehicle came to rest. He set the brake and returned to the shed to close and padlock the doors.

A long canvas bag filled with a variety of objects was wedged in the sidecar. It had once belonged to an angler who had used it for transporting his tackle. Pike had bought it at a street market in Brighton, the same day he had stolen the motorcycle from an alley-way behind a pub. One end of the bag was pushed into the front of the sidecar, the other protruded above the rim of the compartment. He checked now to see that it was secure, then lit the carbide lamp which served as a headlight, fiddling with the gas jet until he was satisfied with the size of the flame. Then he climbed into the saddle and kicked the engine into life, cutting the throttle quickly as the loud *pop-pop-pop* noise shattered the silence of the night. Settling himself on the broad leather seat, he released the brake and set the machine in motion.

He travelled at a steady pace, never exceeding thirty miles an hour. Given the route he had chosen, a snaking tangle of back roads and country lanes, he had the better part of eighty miles to cover in order to reach his destination. Once there, he planned to spend the first part of the day sleeping – it would be Saturday – and then rise and attend to his business. On Sunday he would follow the same routine: first sleep, then work. In the evening he would ready himself for the long ride back. Mondays were his most difficult time. Although short of sleep he would have to carry out his normal duties without giving in to fatigue. Fortunately it was something he was accustomed to doing. He had passed many sleepless nights during the war, lying for hours under artillery bombardments, leading patrols and raiding parties into no man's land. Yet he had never failed to present himself, rifle in hand, ready on the firestep to repel an enemy attack, at the ritual stand-to just before dawn.

A little after four o'clock he entered the outskirts of Ashdown Forest and turned off the paved road on to a rough track. The ancient woodland was scored with forgotten tracks and footpaths, some of them old before the first Roman had set foot in the land, and the way Pike took followed a winding course through forest and field, sometimes almost petering out, but then reappearing in the bobbing beam of his head-light. He rode slowly. He had been this route only once before.

Dawn found him deep in the forest. He drew up beside a great red oak, which spread an umbrella of thickly leaved branches over a clearing fringed with bush and fern. Turning off the track, he steered the motorcycle into a thicket, forcing the branches aside, and stopped in a small dell overhung with holly. He switched off the engine and climbed stiffly from the saddle. From the seat beneath the canvas bag he retrieved a groundsheet, and having spread it on the grass he lay down and fell asleep almost at once.

*

By five o'clock on Sunday afternoon he had completed the first stage of his self-appointed task. Using an entrenching tool – a short-handled pick with a broad-bladed head opposite – he had constructed a dugout similar to the one he had built in the woods above Highfield. There were some differences. He had no sheet of corrugated iron – that had been a chance find – but he planned to fashion a roof of plaited willow and osier on his next visit. Branches cut to measure would serve as rough corduroying to protect the floor from damp.

The dugout was situated in an area of dense brush a mile from where he had parked his motorcycle. He had scouted the area some months before and marked the spot where he meant to dig. After that he had left it untouched while other matters occupied his attention. The task he was engaged on took considerable time, but rather than becoming impatient he found his satisfaction – or, rather, his sense of imminent satisfaction – growing almost daily. He felt like a vessel waiting to be filled. Soon he would overflow . . .

He had discovered this deliberate approach after his attack on the farmhouse at Bentham, which had proved to be a disappointment. He had observed the house and the woman for only a few hours before racing down the slope in a frenzy of excitement. His relief then had been fleeting.

At Highfield he had spent five weekends spread over three months preparing himself. He had observed his prey for many hours. The long period of waiting had given him pleasure of a kind he had never known before. A sense of expectation, slowly ripening, yet indefinitely postponed. Up till the very last moment he had been undecided, and although his physical relief and satisfaction at the climax had been intense, he still felt a sweet regret when he thought of those days.

*

Having made a complete circuit of the bushes surrounding the dugout to ensure it was not visible from any quarter, he struck out in a north-westerly direction, walking for more than two miles through a mixture of woodland and open pasture. His goal was a low hill planted with oak and beech, which he climbed on reaching it.

Searching for a vantage-point, he spent some time moving from one spot to another before settling on a leaf-strewn bank hard by the exposed roots of a giant beech. Beneath him, at the foot of the hill, a water-meadow stretched for a hundred yards to a moss-covered wall. On the other side of the wall lay a handsome stone-built manor house and garden.

From where he sat Pike could trace the outline of a path that crossed the water-meadow, bending in a semi-circle to accommodate the margins of a pond, and then straightening until it reached the house where it met another path running along the outside of the wall. This second footway led to a wrought-iron gate, which opened on to the garden.

Pike's cold eye picked out a route from the gate through a shrubbery to an alleyway that ran between high yew hedges and ended at a lawn in front of the house. A pair of tall glassed doors, similar to the ones at Melling Lodge, gave access to the house. Pike saw himself running up the yew alley at dusk. As he played and replayed the scene in his mind he began to get an erection.

On his only previous visit he had watched the family who lived in the house eating Sunday lunch at a table, shaded by a trellised vine, that stood on a stone-paved patio at the side of the lawn. The leisurely meal had taken nearly two hours to complete, and Pike had sat motionless throughout, tantalized by the flickering cinematographic quality of the scene as sunlight and shadow played on the figures seated beneath the vine. The children had been allowed down from the table before the end of the meal and run shrieking into the yew alley, one chasing the other. Pike had ignored them. He had eyes only for the woman.

He sat for an hour, smoking four cigarettes, without seeing any sign of life. Then one of the glassed doors opened and a maid appeared carrying a heavily laden tray. She began to lay the table. Pike glanced at the sky. Sunset wasn't far off. He wondered how the woman's hair would look by candlelight.

His attention was momentarily distracted by two boys wearing shorts who appeared below him walking barefoot along the path through the water-meadow. They carried rods and lines and they paused for several minutes beside the pond as though debating the merits of fishing it. Eventually they continued on their way and vanished from sight around the corner of the garden wall. Pike knew there was a village less than a mile away. He had driven through it once.

When he looked at the house again he became aware of fresh activity. The door opened and a grey-haired woman in a long skirt stood on the threshold looking out into the garden. A spaniel put its head out of the door beside her knee. Pike frowned. Dogs were troublesome, an unwanted distraction. The woman remained in the doorway for only a few moments, then went back inside the house. The sound of a motor-car engine reached him faintly. The garage and main gate lay on the other side of the house, out of sight.

Pike extinguished his cigarette. Reaching into the deep pocket of his leather jacket he took out a pair of binoculars.

The door opened for a third time. A younger woman wearing a light cotton dress trimmed with red braid stepped out on to the lawn. Pike caught his breath. She was carrying a broad-brimmed straw hat with a trail of red ribbons. He put the field-glasses to his eyes and watched as she shook her head, freeing the hair that clung to her neck.

His mouth had gone dry.

The woman looked up at the sky. Then she glanced over her shoulder and spoke to someone inside the house. Her skin was very fair and Pike imagined it might carry a light dusting of freckles.

A man came out of the house on to the lawn. He said something to the woman and she smiled and moved closer to him. He put his arm around her waist.

The sight brought a low growl from Pike's lips. She belonged to him now.

*

Several hours later he retraced his steps to the hole he had dug and collected his canvas bag. He had already removed some of its contents, including tinned food and a Primus stove. On his next visit he planned to complete the dugout and make it habitable. Then it would be a matter of waiting until the moment was ripe.

It was unlikely he would ever be asked to explain why he had built the dugouts, and in any case would have found it impossible to give a coherent reply. Originally, in the woods above Highfield, he had set out simply to construct some kind of shelter for himself. The dugout had taken shape almost without conscious intention on his part. Once it was completed, however, he saw that it was right. Sitting in the womb-like darkness he had experienced moments of peace and contentment so foreign to his nature he had wondered at first if they were signs of illness.

Thereafter, he had allowed instinct to guide his actions, and it was just such an unconsidered impulse that had taken him back to Highfield only a fortnight after he had broken into Melling Lodge. He had felt a strong need to return and had hesitated only to the extent of remaining close to his motorcycle throughout the night, waiting until dawn came to assure himself that the police were no longer searching the woods.

His subsequent discovery that two men were tracking him – one he had recognized as the village constable – had caused him to react in momentary panic. Up till then he had felt himself to be invulnerable, almost invisible as he went about his business unseen and unsuspected. Now he knew better.

Even so, it never occurred to him to stop. It was beyond his power to do so. The need released in him had come to govern his life, filling his thoughts and forming the sole purpose of his existence. It would die when he did, not before.

But his experience in the woods had induced him

to be more cautious. He had altered his appearance by shaving off his moustache and repainted the bodywork of the sidecar. The changes made him feel more secure. He also believed that his decision to travel late at night, and by little-used roads, was a wise one, and was not unduly alarmed when, sometime after midnight, having crossed the main road to Hastings, he was waved down by a helmeted policeman on a narrow country lane bordered by hedgerows.

The constable was carrying a lamp, which he swung from side to side as he stood planted in the middle of the road. Pike, who was travelling at less than twenty miles an hour, pulled up on the verge. The policeman ordered him to switch off his engine. Pike obeyed. The lamp's beam was bright in his eyes.

'Where might you be heading, sir?' The voice was a young man's. Pike couldn't see his face against the light.

'Folkestone,' he replied.

'Would you give me your name, please?'

'Carver,' Pike said. 'George Carver.'

'Occupation?'

'Gardener.'

'And what would a gardener be doing riding around this time of night?'

'I was spending the weekend with my sister in Tunbridge Wells. My bike broke down and I couldn't get it fixed till late. I've got to get back before tomorrow morning.' The man was beginning to irritate Pike with his questions.

'This isn't the road to Folkestone.'

The fact was incontrovertible. Pike said nothing.

The constable moved the light off his face and shone it on the sidecar. 'What's in the bag?' he asked.

'Tools.'

'Open it, please.'

Pike climbed off the saddle. He took the canvas bag out of the sidecar and laid it on the ground. It was held shut by two leather straps. He began to undo them. As he was working on the second one the light shifted off his hands. He looked up to see the policeman directing his lamp at the sidecar. Pike's eyes followed the beam. He saw the new red paintwork had been scratched, probably when he rode into the thicket. In one spot a broad flake of paint had been removed, revealing the original black surface beneath. Pike went on undoing the strap. The light was back in his face.

'I'd like to see some identification.' The constable's voice had hardened. 'Also proof of ownership of this vehicle.'

'I've got it here,' Pike said, reaching into the bag. He stood up, turning towards the constable, and drove his clenched hand into the pit of the man's stomach. The policeman dropped the lamp. He arched his body. A retching sound came from his lips. Pike withdrew the bayonet and the man clutched at his stomach, lips working. He stepped back and stabbed him a second time, in the chest. The constable fell to the ground. He groaned once and lay still.

Pike picked up the lamp and shone it on the side of the road. A few feet away he saw a gap in the hedgerow. Placing the lamp on the sidecar, he gathered the constable's body in his arms and carried it to the spot. With some difficulty he thrust it through the gap in the hedge into a ditch on the other side.

He returned to the sidecar for the lamp and spent some minutes examining the ground nearby. He found two small pools of blood which he covered with handfuls of dirt taken from the side of the road. Satisfied, he switched off the lamp, wiped it down with a handkerchief and then threw it as far as he could over the hedge into the field beyond.

10

SINCLAIR RETURNED FROM lunch to find Madden
bent over a map spread out on the top of his desk.
Hollingsworth stood beside him.

'I've got the Ordnance Survey map here, sir.' The
sergeant was speaking. 'It's marked. Elmhurst.'

Madden looked up and saw Sinclair. 'We've a
constable down in Sussex, sir. Murdered. He was killed
on a back road on Sunday night.'

'*Sunday?*' The chief inspector joined them, shedding
his jacket. 'Why didn't we hear before?' It was Thursday.

'They only found his body yesterday. I've been
talking to the CID in Tunbridge Wells. The body
was taken there. They could see he'd been stabbed,
but it was only when their pathologist examined the
corpse that he discovered they were bayonet wounds.'

'He's sure about that? The pathologist?'

'Seems to be. He was an Army doctor at Étaples for
two years.'

Sinclair stood at Madden's shoulder. 'Show me.'

Madden checked the Ordnance chart Hollingsworth
had brought against his own smaller-scale map. He
pointed. 'About there. Say twenty miles south of Tunbridge Wells. Very near the main road to Hastings.

The constable – his name was Harris – was stationed at a village called Hythe. There it is, it's marked.'

Sinclair squinted at the Ordnance map. 'Bit off his beat, wasn't he?'

'That's why it took a while to find the body. Elmhurst's four miles away. Apparently there've been reports of organized cockfighting in the district. The detective I spoke to said they think Harris went over there on Sunday night to see if he could catch them at it. He must have been on his way back to Hythe when he ran into trouble.'

'Where was his body?'

'In a ditch by the road. They found traces of blood someone had tried to cover up. Nothing else, I'm afraid.'

The chief inspector bent over the map. 'What do you think? Did he try to stop him? Damn it, I told them to exercise caution.'

'We don't know that it was him.' Madden scowled.

'Yes, but let's suppose it was.' Sinclair drummed his fingertips on the desktop. 'It was late on a Sunday night. He was heading home, back to his job or whatever it is he does. But where did he spend the weekend?' He pored over the map.

'You'd have to know which way he was going.' Hollingsworth offered his opinion. 'Which direction.'

'He was near the Hastings road,' Madden said. 'But he doesn't travel on main roads. So either he'd just crossed it, or was about to. He was going east or west.'

They studied the map in silence.

'Nothing much to the east.' Hollingsworth spoke again. 'Not till you get to Romney Marsh.'

The chief inspector's forefinger came to rest. Madden grunted an acknowledgement. 'Ashdown Forest.'

'How far is it?' Sinclair checked the scale. 'Less than twenty miles. If he was coming from there . . .' He clicked his tongue in frustration. 'Damn and blast! There's ten thousand acres of that. More. We couldn't begin to search it.'

Hollingsworth cleared his throat.

'What is it, Sergeant?'

'A lot of people use those woods, sir. Ramblers, botanists, Scout troops. They could be a help.'

'What we would do well to avoid at this juncture,' the chief inspector enunciated clearly, 'is a massacre of Boy Scouts.'

'Yes, sir, but we could ask them to keep an eye open. Through local police stations. Any sign of fresh digging. All they need do is report it.'

Sinclair looked at Madden, who nodded.

'Good idea, Sergeant. We'll get word out.'

Sinclair waited until Hollingsworth had left the office. Then he spoke: 'I had lunch with Bennett. Nothing from the War Office as yet. He's tried to give them a nudge, but they move at their own speed over there.'

Madden remained bent over the map. Sinclair studied him benignly. 'Take this Sunday off, John. I'll be at home.'

'Are you sure, sir?' Madden looked up. They had agreed that one or other should be within reach of a telephone during the weekends.

'I am. Consult Mrs Sinclair, if you have any doubts. She will assure you that the garden requires my urgent attention.'

The chief inspector had noted an alteration in his colleague's appearance of late, a lightening of the shadows. There seemed to him at least one possible explanation for it. 'If I were you I'd get out of London,' he suggested, with guileless innocence. 'Treat yourself to some country air.'

11

SHE WAS WAITING for him at the station. The red Wolseley two-seater was parked where he remembered it, in the shade under the plane tree. Her tanned forearms resting on the steering-wheel reminded him of the moment beside the stream when they had kissed.

'Father's off shooting pheasants.' She took his hand and pressed it to her cheek. 'We've got the whole day to ourselves.'

The tables outside the Rose and Crown were crowded with lunch-time customers. Heads turned as they drove by.

Helen laughed. 'That'll set tongues wagging.'

But her smile faded as they passed the locked gates of Melling Lodge. 'I get so angry whenever I think about it. There was no *reason* why it should have happened. The vicar saw fit to preach to us last Sunday on the mysterious workings of Divine Providence. I asked him afterwards if he thought the murders were an Act of God. He hasn't spoken to me since.'

Madden put his hand on hers. 'No reason, perhaps. But there might be an explanation. Have you seen Dr Weiss again?' It felt strange to play the role of comforter.

'Franz came down for lunch the day before he went home. He said you'd met, but he didn't say what you'd talked about.'

'I asked him to be discreet. I was breaking the rules by going to him as it was.'

Later, when they reached the house, he gave her an account of his conversation with the psychiatrist, speaking freely, as he always did when they discussed his work, shedding the reserve he would normally have shown with an outsider. He had never felt the need to keep any knowledge from her; he could think of no fact from which she might shrink.

'It's not what I imagined,' she admitted. 'I thought it was blind chance that brought him to that house. If Franz is right, he must have seen Lucy earlier. Does that mean he was in Highfield?'

'Most probably. But we don't know when. Or why he came here.'

*

They ate lunch in the arbour on the terrace, looking out over the sun-bruised lawn. The green leaves of the weeping beech were changing to russet, and beyond the orchard the rising wave of Upton Hanger showed tints of red and gold.

Later, she suggested going for a walk. 'I want to see the place where you and Will were shot at. I asked him to show me, but he refused. He didn't dare say it was no business of a woman's, but I could see he was longing to.'

She waited until the maid had finished clearing the

table and taken the tray inside. 'I've given Mary the afternoon off. We'll have the house to ourselves when we get back.'

Her eyes bore an unmistakable invitation and Madden felt the blood stir within him. He had never known a woman like her. One so open in her desire, so free of shame or pretence. When they set off down the lawn, she called to the dog. 'It's all right, Molly. You can come this time.' Laughing when she caught his eye.

They went through the orchard to the gate at the bottom of the garden. He paused, crossing the stream, to sniff the air. 'We'll have rain later.'

'Why, John Madden! I didn't know you were a country man.' She grasped his hand and let him draw her up on to the bank.

'I grew up on a farm. I didn't move to London until after my father died.' He realized how little he had told her of himself. How much she had taken on trust. 'After Alice and the baby died I left the force. I couldn't continue with the same life. I had an idea of going back to the land.'

'Why didn't you?'

'The war came instead.'

'And afterwards . . .?'

'It didn't seem to matter any more.'

Nothing had, he might truthfully have said, until he had met her.

When they reached the circle of beeches with its bowl of dead leaves – deeper now with the fresh falls of autumn – he recalled the image that had come to him before, of treading on a mattress of dead bodies. At their last meeting she had urged him not to block out his memories of the war. 'That's why your dreams are so intense. You must try to bring all that back into your conscious mind.'

He thought she hadn't understood and had tried to explain. All he wanted to do was put the past behind him.

'I know how you feel. It's like Sophy not speaking about that night. She wants to pretend it never happened. But our minds won't let us do that. We have to remember before we can forget.'

He owed her so much already. The anguish of the past was receding, the abyss no longer yawned at his feet. He didn't know how the miracle had occurred, only that he had found it lying in her arms, and in the assurance of her measured glance. He wanted to tell her these things, but could find no words that would not make some fresh claim on her, a claim to which he felt he had no right. He still thought of himself as damaged. Not a whole man.

He showed her the spot on the path where he and Stackpole had been standing when the first shots were fired and pointed out the thicket on the slope above. 'I think he recognized Will and knew he was a policeman. I was just bending down to look at the footprint when I heard him draw back the bolt of his rifle.'

'What was he doing up there?' She shaded her eyes, scanning the dark line of ilexes.

'We're not sure. He might have returned to collect

what he stole from the house. He'd already started digging.'

'He was mad to come back. He could so easily have been caught.'

'According to Dr Weiss, that wouldn't have stopped him. He says he acts from compulsion.'

She looked at the beech tree where Madden had taken cover, sliding her fingers into the jagged hole gouged in the side of the trunk. When he asked if she wanted to climb up to where the dugout was, she shook her head quickly. 'No, let's get away from here.'

The rain he'd predicted arrived in a blustery squall and they turned for home. By the time they reached the bottom of the ridge and crossed the stream it had become a downpour. The orchard offered no cover and they ran hand in hand to the shelter of the weeping beech. Madden saw that the lights were switched on in the house. Helen had seen them, too.

'Oh, no! Father's back already!'

Laughing, she clung to him under the drooping branches. They were both wet through. When he began to kiss her she responded at once, wrapping her arms about his neck, drawing him deeper into the semi-darkness. 'Can you manage? Tell me what to do . . .'

The sound of their breathing was lost in the drumming of the rain on the leaves.

She was happy afterwards, laughing still, when they stood out of sight of the house and tried to bring some order to their clothing. The rain had stopped.

'I don't know what Father will think.'

He made her stand still while he picked the leaves and twigs from her hair. She stood in front of him with her head bowed.

'Do you remember doing this for Sophy?' she asked. 'I was watching you from the terrace. You looked so solemn, so purposeful. I think I knew then we'd be lovers.'

He smiled in reply, but her words pierced his heart. The tie that bound them seemed fragile to him. Lovers they might be now; they could not be for ever. Only chance had brought them together, and he feared a time would come when he would lose her.

During the war Madden had come to think of his existence as something that would not continue. He had learned to live a day, sometimes even an hour, at a time.

Now, once more, he feared to look ahead.

He could not imagine a future without her.

Part Three

O Love, be fed with apples while you may,
And feel the sun and go in royal array,
A smiling innocent on the heavenly causeway,

Though in what listening horror for the cry
That soars in outer blackness dismally,
The dumb blind beast, the paranoiac fury . . .

Robert Graves, 'Sick Love'

1

WHITE-HAIRED AND FRAIL, but with a curiosity undimmed by age and failing health, Harriet Merrick paused by the pond to count the puffballs of yellow feathers paddling behind their broad-beamed mother. Six. Only the other day there had been eight. Either a fox had been busy, or one of the village cats was finding the water-meadow a happy hunting ground. The afternoon darkened as a cloud moved across the sun. Thunder rumbled close by.

Mrs Merrick glanced at the sky. She debated whether to return to the house. The thought of the scolding awaiting her there brought a smile to her lips. Her habit of taking solitary walks was a matter of concern to her son and daughter-in-law. It had reached the point where she was obliged to slip out when they weren't looking. Mrs Merrick maintained her independence serenely.

She decided to walk on. She was wearing a cardigan over her dress and a sensible straw hat. When she felt the first drops of rain she quickened her pace, then checked and deliberately slowed. Dr Fellows had advised her to take exercise in moderation. 'Don't overdo it,' had been his considered judgement, delivered after a lengthy study of her chart. He told her her heart was 'good for years', though he did not say how many. Harriet Merrick, who had little faith in doctors, thought she was in reasonably good health and might expect to live for a while yet. Unless Providence decreed otherwise.

She was planning to walk around Shooter's Hill – the path she was following circled the wooded knob, a pleasant ramble taking no more than half an hour – but the sudden brisk downpour prompted her to seek shelter beneath the trees bordering the footway. The weather had changed in the last few days. The first showers after the long summer drought had dampened the dust and leaf-mould of the forest floor. Standing under the wide branches of a purple beech she breathed in the soft autumnal scents.

On an impulse she decided to climb the hill, taking the most indirect route she could find, walking back and forth across the slope, following a line of easy contours to the summit. It was something she had not done for two years – Dr Fellows frowned on gradients – and she was pleased when she reached the top without either breathing hard or feeling the familiar warning flutter in her chest. Although it was still raining steadily, the dense canopy of leaves kept her dry. Near the summit she found a place to sit down on a leaf-covered bank beside the exposed roots of a giant beech.

There was a good view of Croft Manor from up here. The house had been in the Merrick family for nearly three hundred years. Her two sons had been born there: William, who had just passed his thirty-sixth birthday; whose withered arm had seemed like a curse, but had proved a blessing. And her darling Tom. On his last leave they had taken a walk in the woods together, the three of them. (Her husband, Richard Merrick, had died when the boys were barely grown.) Tom had made them laugh with his tales of a winter spent in the trenches before Arras. How the hot tea froze in minutes and the bully beef turned into chunks of red ice. When he described a night raid into no man's land he made it sound like an adventure from *Boy's Own*. Volunteers and blackened faces, knives and coshes.

A month later she had awoken in the middle of the night consumed by grief. The emotion was so profound – so far in excess of any nightmare's backwash – that she had roused her elder son and he had tried to comfort her. She lived through the next two days in a state of shock and confusion, unable to equate the psychological disturbance she had suffered with any known reality. Fearful of contemplating what the unknown might hold. On the evening of the second day the telegram had arrived from the War Office. Her darling Tom.

She sat quietly, remembering. Grieving still. The patter of rain on the leaves overhead ceased, and presently the sun came out. Almost at once the glassed doors opened and the children slipped out and went hurrying down the yew alley towards the croquet lawn at the bottom of the garden. They had invented a game of their own, Mrs Merrick had observed, a complicated affair in which the mallets had been discarded and the hoops set up in a seemingly random pattern that only its devisers understood. Before they had reached the end of the alley the figure of Enid Bradshaw, their nanny, appeared in the doorway. She called out to them, or so Mrs Merrick judged, watching the dumb show from afar. The children paused and looked back. Words were exchanged, no doubt on the subject of wet feet, and then Miss Bradshaw retired into the house and the children continued on their way.

Alison, the elder, had Charlotte's fair hair and already, at seven, her graceful gestures. She had never known her father, who had been killed in the first months of the war. William had married the young widow and together they had produced Robert, aged five. Harriet Merrick had watched her diffident son, always conscious of his handicap, grow into full manhood as he took on the responsibility of a dead man's wife and made her his own.

She smiled suddenly. Another person had made her appearance on the lawn. She was dressed in a long skirt that might have seemed old-fashioned even before the war, and her thick grey hair was tied behind her head in a severe-looking bun. Her name was Annie McConnell and she had once been Mrs Merrick's maid when they were both young girls growing up in County Tyrone. Annie had accompanied her mistress to England when she got married and had remained with her ever since. For a while she had been Tom and William's nanny, and after that had filled the post of housekeeper. Now she was simply Annie, part family retainer, part friend. Harriet Merrick loved her dearly.

She watched as Annie strode forthrightly down the yew alley towards the croquet lawn. From a distance her stiff black-skirted figure looked forbidding; to the children it seemed to have the opposite effect. They rushed across the lawn to greet her – Annie had been away for four days visiting her sister in Wellfleet – and threw themselves into her outstretched arms. Mrs Merrick had once spent a whole day weeping in those arms.

She thought now with pleasure of the days they would soon be spending together. William and Charlotte were taking the children to Cornwall to stay with friends. The maids would be sent off. She and Annie would have the house to themselves. They would gossip and reminisce.

Meanwhile, Robert's small hands had been busy in the deep pocket of Annie's skirt. Whatever it was he found there seemed to give him pleasure, and Alison followed his example. Annie shot a guilty glance back in the direction of the house. Apparently contraband was being passed. Not wishing to spy further, Mrs Merrick rose to her feet and dusted off her dress. A slight movement on the slope below caught her eye and she stood still and watched as a pair of red squirrels worked busily, gathering nuts from beneath a walnut tree.

She noticed something else as she started back down the hill: half a dozen cigarette stubs lying in a neat line on the ground near to where she had been sitting. It seemed someone else had found the bank a pleasant place to sit and meditate.

2

FIVE MINUTES AFTER he arrived at his desk on Monday morning Sinclair received an urgent summons from Deputy Assistant Commissioner Bennett. He was gone half an hour and returned with a thick manila envelope on which the heavy red wax seals had been broken. 'From the War Office,' he told Madden, as he tossed him the packet. He stuck his head into the adjoining office. 'Sergeant, in here! You, too, Constable.'

Hollingsworth and Styles came in from their cubbyhole. Sinclair perched on the edge of his desk. There was a light in the chief inspector's eye.

'A criminal attack very similar to the ones we're investigating took place in Belgium in September 1917. A farmer and his wife and family were murdered in their home. The assault bears a remarkable resemblance to the Melling Lodge killings. The husband and his two sons were bayoneted. The wife had her throat cut.'

Billy's whistle brought a glower of disapproval from Hollingsworth.

'An inquiry into the murders was conducted by the investigation branch of the Royal Military Police. From the file, it appears there was little doubt in anyone's mind that the killer or killers were serving British soldiers. What the War Office has sent us is a record of the inquiry. It includes a detailed crime-scene report, a pathologist's findings and a verbatim record of all interrogations.'

Madden frowned at the file cover he was holding. 'The case is marked closed.'

'So it is.' Sinclair slid off his desk and began to pace up and down. 'The chief investigating officer was a Captain Miller. In deciding to terminate the inquiry he wrote a memorandum to accompany the case files in which he explained his decision. It's logged in the file index, but unfortunately it's missing. Nothing sinister there, I'm told – the ministry's snowed under with wartime records. They have a warehouse some-where in London stacked to the ceiling. We're lucky they were able to dig out what they did.'

'Is Captain Miller available?' Hollingsworth asked.

'No, he's dead,' Sinclair answered bluntly. 'His staff car was hit by a stray shell behind the lines. It happened a few weeks afterwards, but by then the case was wrapped up. Let me go on.'

He seated himself behind his desk.

'For whatever reason – we can't be sure from this distance in time – suspicion fell on a battalion of the South Nottinghamshire Regiment. On a company, rather, B Company, and just a small part of that – fifteen men, to be precise. They were all questioned.'

'Were they together?' Madden asked.

'Apparently they all went to the farmhouse for a meal. The battalion was being rested. They'd been in action and taken a mauling and were waiting for replacements. The point, as far as we're concerned, is that these were the only men questioned in connection with the crime. Captain Miller must have had strong reasons for thinking the killer was one of them.'

'Then why was the case closed?' Billy Styles spoke before he could stop himself.

The chief inspector's smile was deceptively inviting. 'Why don't you tell us that, Constable?'

Billy blushed bright red. Hollingsworth, beside him, was grinning.

'Sergeant?'

'Because he must have reckoned whoever did it was dead, sir.'

'Just so.' Sinclair nodded his approval. 'The battalion was back in action a week later. It was that Passchendaele business. Of the fifteen men, only seven came out alive. Colonel Jenkins did some checking. Miller closed the case right about the time the battalion was withdrawn a second time. Which suggests he believed the murderer was one of the eight men who were killed.'

In the silence that followed, the sound of a tugboat's whistle floated in through the open window. Hollingsworth cocked his head. 'Could he have had the wrong man in mind, sir?'

'I wonder, Sergeant.' Sinclair sat forward in his chair. His eye met Madden's. 'Of the seven who came out, only four were alive at the end of the war. Their names and service records are in the file, and Colonel

Jenkins was good enough to check with the Army to find out where they were paid their twenty pounds.'

'Twenty pounds?' Billy didn't understand the allusion.

'That's what the government gave every private soldier who came through the war. A gratuity. Two of them were paid in Nottingham, one in Brighton and the other in Folkestone.'

Madden extracted a sheet of paper from the file and handed it to the chief inspector. 'Here's a list of the names, Sergeant.' Sinclair passed it on to Hollingsworth. 'You and Styles find yourselves a couple of telephones and see if you can come up with four current addresses by lunch-time. But go carefully.' He raised a warning finger. 'Just say we want a word with these people. Don't start any alarm bells ringing.'

The chief inspector waited until they had the office to themselves again. He took out his pipe and tobacco pouch and laid them on the blotter in front of him. His fingers beat a rapid tattoo on the desktop. 'Well, John?'

'Was she raped?'

'She was not.'

Madden grunted. He was studying a fan of documents spread out before him. 'These verbatim interviews – they don't tell us much.'

'"Yes, sir, no, sir, it wasn't me, sir." We'll have to go through 'em, just the same.' Sinclair began filling his pipe. 'Damn it, John, we might have struck lucky. We could come up with a name and a face.'

Madden said nothing. But he was smiling as he went on with his reading.

Sinclair struck a match. 'I've just had a large pat on the back from Bennett.'

'Have you, sir?'

'In front of the chief super, too. He came expecting our usual Monday morning get-together. Instead he had Bennett telling him what my "leap of imagination" had uncovered. I thought Sampson was going to be sick on the carpet.'

Madden was grinning now. 'A leap of imagination, sir?'

'Those were his words. I was overcome. Speechless, you might say.' The chief inspector blew out a cloud of mellow tobacco smoke. 'By the way, how is Dr Weiss? Safely back in Vienna, I trust.'

*

Lunch-time came and went, and it was not until four o'clock that Hollingsworth was able to report success in tracking down three of the four survivors.

'The other bloke, Samuel Patterson, seems to have vanished. He left Nottingham two years ago to take a job as a labourer on a farm near Norwich, but he quit after only a few months and nobody's heard of him since. The Norwich police are trying to trace him.'

The second man paid his gratuity in Nottingham, Arthur Marlow, was a patient in an Army hospital. 'He's got a leg wound that won't heal. He's been bedridden for a year.'

The Brighton police had provided an address for

Donald Hardy, who worked as a solicitor's clerk in Hove. The fourth man, Alfred Dawkins, had had various addresses in Folkestone over the past eighteen months.

'The police don't know where he's living at present, but they know where to find him – that's how they put it.' Hollingsworth scratched his head. 'I let it go at that, sir. Didn't want to stir them up.'

After reflection, Sinclair issued his orders: 'John, you go to Folkestone tomorrow morning. Take Styles with you. Hollingsworth and I will deal with Mr Hardy in Hove. Let's both be clear on one point. If there's any suspicion that either of these two is the man we're seeking, the help of armed officers must be sought before he's approached. I want no more casualties.'

3

BEFORE THEY HAD even left the platform at Folkestone station next morning Madden and Styles learned that Alfred Dawkins was not the man they were seeking. 'That's right, sir, only one leg. Didn't they say?' Detective Sergeant Booth of the Folkestone CID had come to the station to meet them. He was a thick-set man with dark brown eyes and a watchful air. 'Lost it in the very last month of the war, or so I've been told.'

Studying the sergeant, Billy noticed the yellowed fingers of a heavy smoker. His trousers were a little loose at the waist, possibly the result of a diet, Billy surmised. He had resolved to become more observant. To take *note* of things. He knew he was burdened with a wide-eyed quality: a sort of innocence that led him to make daft remarks and ask stupid questions, like the one that had caused him such embarrassment in the chief inspector's office the day before. It was *obvious* why Captain Miller had closed the case, once you thought about it. His trouble was, he didn't think about things enough. Or, rather, he opened his mouth first.

This line of reasoning had been reinforced by a conversation he had had with Madden on the train coming down from London. The inspector had seemed in better spirits. The haunted look Billy had grown accustomed to was less marked. He had gone to the trouble of explaining to the young constable why the case they were on was proving so hard to crack.

'Nearly all murders take place between people who know each other, so there's an obvious connection from the start. But this man kills people he's never met. At least, that's what we think, though we can't be sure. How does he pick them? What took him to Highfield and Bentham in the first instance? Is he a travelling salesman? Does he drive a van, or some other vehicle? Whatever job he has seems to take him around the country. Without a real lead, we have to accumulate all the information we can, all the details, no matter how trivial, because the answer may lie in one of them.'

That chimed with what Billy had been telling himself. *Pay attention.*

They rode through golden cornfields and orchards heavy with fruit. Then the hedgerowed fields stopped abruptly and Billy saw the silver glint of the sea below. Madden pointed to a collection of low buildings on the outskirts of the town.

'That's Shorncliffe Camp. It used to be five, no, ten times the size. The tents stretched for miles. Nearly every British soldier who went to France passed through here. Did you know that, Styles?'

Billy nodded. It was the first time he had heard the inspector speak about the war.

'Towards the end they got up to nine thousand a

day. They marched them down to the town and straight on to the Channel steamers and across to France. At night there were illuminated fishing boats strung out in lines all the way to the French coast.'

On the platform at Folkestone Detective Sergeant Booth explained about Dawkins. (To Billy's satisfaction, he had lit up almost at once.) 'We haven't got his current address, sir. He moves a lot – trouble with landladies. But he's generally down in the port this time of day. I've no doubt we'll find him there.'

'He's not the man I hoped he might be,' Madden admitted. 'But I'd like a word with him just the same.'

Booth had a taxi waiting outside the station. It took them on a winding downhill route through the town. When they reached the port he told the driver to stop. Ahead of them Billy could see the harbour situated in a natural bay carved out of the chalky cliffs. In the foreground a small steamer was tied up at the wharf. A crowd of people, mostly women, were gathered in front of the gangplank. Smoke was issuing from the steamer's red and white funnel. Sergeant Booth pointed. 'There he is, sir, at the foot of the gangplank.'

Through the press of bodies Billy caught a glimpse of a figure on crutches.

'All those women – they're war widows going on a tour of cemeteries in France and Belgium. It's something they started last year. Perhaps you read about it?'

Madden shook his head.

'Alf Dawkins gets himself down here whenever there's a sailing, which is most days in the summer. Stands there on his crutches with his medals pinned on. You'd be surprised how many ladies put half a crown in his hand. Probably worth a couple of quid to him. Afterwards he goes over to the pub' – Booth pointed to a line of buildings a little way down the jetty – 'buys himself a drink. Two or three more likely. That's how we know him. He's been up before the bench. Drunk and disorderly.'

'I don't want to talk to him here. We'll wait in the pub.' Madden's voice was terse.

Twenty minutes later, sitting in a taproom smelling of fish and stale tobacco smoke, they heard the toot of the steamer's whistle. At that moment the pub doors opened and Dawkins swung in on his crutches. Short and stocky, his pale face was disfigured by red blotches. Billy noticed that one of his eyelids blinked with a nervous tic.

Madden rose. 'I'll talk to him alone, if you don't mind.'

Booth raised an eyebrow at his departing figure. 'Doesn't say much, does he?'

Billy wanted to defend the inspector, but he couldn't think of a suitable response.

'Mind you, I wouldn't have his job.'

'What do you mean?'

'This Melling Lodge business?' Booth shook his head. 'Worst kind of case a copper can find himself landed with.'

'Why's that?'

'Because you're dealing with something you don't understand.' The sergeant dipped into his beer. 'Most people do things for reasons and criminals are no different. But this bloke!' He shook his head again. 'With a case like that, it's hard to know where to start.'

Billy watched Madden lead Dawkins away from the bar to a table in the corner. The inspector carried their glasses. He pulled out a chair for the other man and saw that he was comfortably settled.

'I remember a case I was on once.' Booth was speaking again. 'A young woman was murdered, strangled. Her body was found in a field just outside of town. We got the bloke that did it. He kept a diary. It was produced in evidence.'

'Did he mention the murder?' Billy was fascinated.

Booth nodded. 'But it's *what* he wrote – I've never forgotten it. "Warm weather. Rain in the afternoon. I killed a girl today."'

'That was *all*?' Billy was incredulous.

The sergeant shrugged. 'She was his first, thank God. But I remember thinking then, there must be people around us living another life from the one we live. It's as though they're from a different world. To understand them you'd have to get inside their heads, and what chance is there of that?'

Madden took Dawkins's glass to the bar and returned to their table with a fresh drink. He was smiling and nodding at the other man. Dawkins spoke, gesturing with his hands. He patted his trousered stump. He was grinning across the table at the inspector.

'How did you catch him?' Billy wanted to know.

'Through a little thing.' Booth drained his glass. 'He'd taken something from the girl he killed, a brooch shaped like a buckle with a piece of amber mounted in the middle. It was nothing special, but we gave out a description of it. A couple of weeks later a beat constable noticed a girl in the street wearing something similar. He asked her where she'd got it and she told him a young man had given it to her. Turned out he was the bloke.'

'That was lucky.'

The inspector rose and took his leave of Dawkins. Billy saw a banknote change hands.

'Lucky for her,' Booth countered. 'I reckon she would have been his next. But that's how it is with a case like that – or this Melling Lodge business. You won't crack it the usual way. You have to hope something will turn up. Some little thing,' he added, unconsciously echoing the inspector's words earlier. 'You have to keep your eyes open.'

Little was said on the journey back to London. Madden sat gazing out of the window, seemingly wrapped in thought. Billy, aware that another possible lead had turned cold, supposed that was what was on the inspector's mind.

Or was he thinking about all those men who had marched down through the town to the harbour and on to the Channel steamers? the young constable wondered. The route had been renamed after the war, Sergeant Booth had told them in the taxi. Now it was known as the Road of Remembrance. To Billy, recalling Alf Dawkins with his crutches and his nervous tic, begging for half-crowns, it seemed more a case of how quickly people forgot.

*

'Mr Hardy has three children and sings in the church choir. He's short and fat and gets breathless climbing a flight of stairs. I hope you had better luck with Dawkins, John.'

Madden's response caused Sinclair's eyebrows to shoot skywards. 'One leg! Poor devil – but couldn't someone have told us that?'

The chief inspector had returned from Hove an hour earlier. He was seated at his desk, smoking his pipe. Behind him the late-afternoon sun lay like molten fire on the river.

'He remembers the incident well enough. They were all lined up by the sergeant major and marched in one at a time to be questioned. It put a scare into them, Dawkins said, but he swears none of them was guilty. They returned from the farm in a group that night.'

Madden settled behind his desk. He lit a cigarette.

'He said Miller was rough on them. He behaved as though he believed they were hiding something. But after they came out of the line a few days later they never heard another word about the case.'

'I got the same from Hardy.' Sinclair puffed at his pipe. 'What did you make of it?'

The inspector shrugged. 'I wondered why Miller didn't talk to them again. Even if he believed the guilty man had been killed in action he'd still have wanted to question the others to get the full story from them.'

'I had the same reaction.' Sinclair nodded agreement. 'It's obvious Miller no longer regarded them as suspects. He must have had someone else in mind. We've been chasing the wrong fox, damn it!'

'But still someone he thought was dead,' Madden pointed out quickly. 'He closed the case, remember.'

The chief inspector grunted. He shook his head pessimistically. 'I've been wondering what to do next. It occurred to me the Belgian police might be able to help us, so I sent a telegram to the Brussels Sûreté half an hour ago asking them to check their records. After all, those were Belgian citizens who were murdered.' He sighed heavily. 'The trouble is, Brussels was under German occupation at the time and I'm not sure the civilian police were ever involved in the investigation. I've a nasty feeling they'll simply refer us to the British military authorities and we'll be back where we started. With Miller's missing memorandum.'

4

HAROLD BIGGS had been looking forward to spending that Saturday afternoon at the races. He and his pal, Jimmy Pullman, had planned to drive to Dover in Jimmy's second-hand Morris, lose a few shillings on the nags and then look in later at the Seaview Hotel where there was a regular Saturday tea dance. They might, if they were lucky, pick up a couple of girls. But a summons from Mr Henry Wolverton, senior partner in the firm of Dabney, Dabney and Wolverton, on Friday morning put a stopper on that.

'There's something I want you to do tomorrow, Biggs. Old client of the firm. Widow of client actually. Got herself into a state about something. Written me a letter.' Wolverton, a stout middle-aged man with an unhealthily red face, spoke habitually in short sentences as though he couldn't summon up the breath for longer utterances. 'Wants someone to go and see her tomorrow afternoon. Has to be then.' He peered up at Harold over the top of his half-spectacles. 'Out of normal working hours, I know. You don't mind, do you?'

'No, sir,' said Biggs, minding strongly.

'He's got his nerve,' Jimmy Pullman remarked when they met later in the Bunch of Grapes for a lunch-time drink. Jimmy worked in a gents clothing store. 'Catch Mr Henry Bloody Wolverton spending *his* Saturday afternoon traipsing around the country-side. You should have told him where to get off, Biggsy.'

Harold shrugged, pretending unconcern. He accepted a Scotch egg from the plate Jimmy pushed along the pub counter towards him. His job as a solicitor's clerk was the same one he'd held before the war and he'd been happy when early demobilization enabled him to reclaim it. Other men returning later to civilian life had not been so fortunate.

'What do you have to do, anyway?' Jimmy demanded. 'And why tomorrow afternoon?'

Biggs took out the letter Mr Wolverton had given him and squinted through his horn-rimmed spectacles at the nearly illegible handwriting, which meandered drunkenly across the page. 'All she says is she needs someone to do something for her and it has to be tomorrow afternoon. She's underlined "afternoon" sev-eral times. She says it's important. She's underlined that, too.' Biggs sipped his beer.

'And she lives at bloody Knowlton?' Jimmy scowled. 'What's her name?'

Biggs glanced at the letter again. 'Troy,' he said. 'Winifred Troy.'

*

The early-afternoon bus left for Knowlton at a quarter to two, and Biggs reached the bus station with five minutes to spare, having spent the morning working at the office. He just had time to dash back to his lodgings and exchange his dark suit and black bowler for plus-fours and a checked cap. A pair of two-tone shoes, which he'd recently bought at a reduced price through the good offices of Jimmy Pullman, completed his ensemble. He was ready for a trip to the country.

The journey to Knowlton took forty minutes. The bus service, linking Folkestone and Dover via a string of inland villages, was a post-war innovation, and it looked like the business was flourishing. Every seat in the green-painted vehicle was taken and Harold was obliged to share his own with a dough-faced woman in the late stages of pregnancy.

To pass the time – and to take his mind off the disagreeable thought that the short, panting breaths he heard coming from beside him might herald an impromptu birth – he began to conduct a mental exercise. He had recently completed a correspondence course in Pelmanism, a method of memory training designed to eliminate mind-wandering and increase concentration. The course, a popular one in Biggs's set, had been heavily promoted. 'How to Eliminate Brain Fag!' the advertisements trumpeted. Harold was convinced that his memory was sharper as a result and he set out now to recall as much as he could of what he had read in the previous day's newspaper.

The main story on the front page had dealt with the Irish peace talks, which had dragged on in London all summer. A formal conference of the parties was due to open shortly, but diehard elements in Sinn Fein were opposed to any agreement that excluded the province of Ulster from a United Ireland. The report recalled that a shipment of 500 sub-machine-guns destined for Sinn Fein had been seized recently in New York.

There had been further debate in the House of Commons on the government's decision to admit women to the civil service in three years' time. Despite recent rains most of southern England was still in the grip of drought and rigid economies would be necessary for the remainder of the year. The price of whisky had been increased again. A bottle now cost 12/6d.

Most of these stories he had only glanced at (though he seemed to have retained the salient facts!). But there was one item he had read with close attention, a lengthy article dealing with the police investigation into the murders at Melling Lodge in Surrey two months earlier.

Biggs had followed the case with interest from the start. It was a talking point in his office and in the Bunch of Grapes where he usually spent his lunch-hour. The apparently reasonless crime had caught people's imaginations. Some thought it the work of a maniac – Jimmy Pullman held to this view – but Harold felt there was more behind the murders than met the eye. 'It'll turn out to be the person you least expect,' he had predicted. 'Someone like the postman.'

He'd been disappointed initially when the opening words of the article – *Important developments are expected soon in the continuing investigation into the horrific murders at Melling Lodge*' – were not borne out in succeeding paragraphs. Instead, the report detailed the progress of the inquiry to date. Or lack of progress, since it was plain the police had made little headway. The writer questioned whether the investigation was on the right track. If, indeed, it ever had been.

The shock felt at the killings seemed to have induced a sense of 'panic', he asserted. 'Wild theories' had abounded at the outset and even now, when it was increasingly clear that what they were dealing with was 'an isolated incident of senseless violence', there seemed to be an unwillingness, even among experienced officers, to approach the matter in 'a straightforward way'.

Harold was gratified to discover that he was able to retrieve key words and phrases from the text.

A move to seek the help of 'outside experts' had been checked, thanks to prompt action at the 'highest levels' in the Yard. But the investigation had continued to flounder in the eyes of many, who questioned whether proper attention had been given to 'the most basic areas of crime detection'.

A description of the man sought had been available to the police for some time, but there was doubt whether this area of the inquiry had been pursued with 'sufficient thoroughness'. Another 'solid lead' was the motorcycle and sidecar that the murderer was known to have used. It was rare in police work for a physical clue of this nature to yield no results, the reporter declared, leaving unspoken the implication that the detectives in charge of the case had somehow failed to make the most of it.

> Somewhere in England is a man answering to the
> description who owns a motorcycle. Surely it only
> requires a methodical approach by the police of
> this land acting in concert to uncover his identity.

This somewhat dramatic assertion had lodged intact
in Harold's newly improved memory. But he was
puzzled by the article as a whole. He couldn't determine whether the reporter was giving his own opin-
ions or those of the 'informed circles at Scotland Yard'
to whom he referred from time to time. And it was
only right at the very end of the report that the
'important developments' heralded in the opening
paragraph were finally revealed:

> The lack of progress has pointed to the need for a
> fresh approach. It is understood that the officer at
> present heading the inquiry, Chief Inspector Sin-
> clair, will shortly be replaced by the man thought
> best qualified to bring matters to a successful
> conclusion, Britain's most famous detective, Chief
> Superintendent Albert Sampson, better known to
> the public as 'Sampson of the Yard'.

*

Knowlton was not Biggs's final destination. Mrs Troy
lived at a place called Rudd's Cross, which he had
been told was in the vicinity. Inquiring at the village
pub, where the bus deposited him, he learned that in
fact it was more than two miles away and could only
be reached by a footpath that ran through the fields.

As he left the outskirts of Knowlton a distant

rumble came to his ears. Away to the west the thunderheads of a storm were massing. The air was warm and muggy. Harold took off his glasses and mopped his face with a handkerchief. He'd brought no umbrella with him.

He hurried on through the stubbled fields, keeping an anxious eye on the heavens. Pausing at a stile, he removed his cap and patted dry the two bays of bare scalp on either side of his widow's peak. Thunder boomed again, louder this time. His new shoes were starting to pinch.

The bubble of resentment which had been swelling inside him all morning burst into angry recognition that he had let himself be used. Exploited! He might have minded less if there'd been any mention of compensation when Mr Wolverton gave him his assignment.

His bitterness grew as it fastened on this grievance. Only last month his request for an increase in salary had been turned down. He'd felt hard done by then. After years of wartime privation the shops were at last full of goods worth buying. Harold himself had been saving for months to purchase a wireless set – public transmissions by the new British Broadcasting Company were due to start the following year. Further off in his future the mirage of a motor-car shimmered.

Jimmy was right, he thought angrily, as he set off again. It was time he asserted himself.

*

Biggs was at his wits' end. He could make no sense of the old woman's ramblings. She would start on one thing, skip to another, and then lose the thread of both.

'Edna Babb? She's the girl who "does" for you? Have I got that right, Mrs Troy?'

Finding his way to the cottage had proved no problem. It was just as Mr Wolverton had described it, standing on its own, separated by an apple orchard and unploughed fields from the rest of the houses grouped around the crossroads that gave the hamlet its name. But it had taken repeated hammerings on the door with the brass knocker before he heard the shuffle of slow footsteps inside and saw the door handle turn.

'Mr Wolverton?'

The figure peering up at him from the shadowy hallway was old and bent. Her thinning white hair was drawn back in an untidy bun. She wore a thick, knitted shawl wrapped about her shoulders over a long, stained skirt of dark bombazine. Wondering how she could possibly mistake him for his employer, he had given her his name. It was only when he went inside – when she led him into the small parlour and seated herself in a high-backed chair beside the window where a bar of sunlight entering through lace-net curtains illuminated her face – that he noticed the milky, cataract-clouded eyes.

He had pulled up a chair beside hers, and now he sat and listened while she talked of people he had never heard of – of 'Edna' and 'Tom Donkin' and 'Mr Grail' – as though they were old acquaintances of his. While she spoke her hands moved ceaselessly, fondling a cat that had jumped into her lap as soon as she sat down, a large tortoiseshell beast which regarded Biggs steadily through narrow slitted eyelids. Its rasping purr filled the gaps of silence left by the quavering, breathless voice. Listening with half an ear, Harold thought sourly of the likely drenching he was in for later as the thunder rumbled ever closer. The shaft of light filtering through the lace-net curtains had dulled to a leaden beam.

'Tom Donkin took care of the garden?'

The picture was becoming clearer. Donkin was a local man, someone the Babb woman had found to work as a gardener and handyman. It seemed there was something between them, a relationship, but they had fallen out – had a fight in Mrs Troy's words – and Donkin had gone away. He was no longer living in the district and Edna Babb had been trying to discover his whereabouts.

'Looking all over,' Mrs Troy explained. She turned her face towards Harold, milky blue eyes blinking like some blind underground animal's. 'Poor girl. I think she's expecting.'

This had happened some months ago and since then Edna Babb had ceased to be someone Winifred Troy could count on. She still came in to clean, but only intermittently. Once a week, instead of the three times agreed on. Sometimes not at all.

'Why didn't you find someone else?' Biggs asked, increasingly impatient.

It seemed there was no one else, not in Rudd's Cross. Edna 'did' for two other families and they, too, complained of being let down. Sometimes she disappeared for days.

Unmoved by the old woman's predicament, Biggs was just telling himself he could see no way of dealing with the matter – not if the wretched Babb was the only cleaner available – when he discovered to his amazement that this, after all, wasn't the problem. It was merely the background to it. Mrs Troy had learned to cope with Edna's absences. If the house wasn't properly cleaned – and there was plenty of evidence of this in the layer of dust he could see coating the mantelpiece in front of him and dulling the glass front of the silver cabinet across the room – it didn't seem to bother the old woman. The crisis lay in another quarter. To be precise, in the shape of Mr Grail.

Mr Grail?

Harold had forgotten about him. Now he had to sit and listen again as Mrs Troy explained in her halting, back-and-forth way that he was the man who had looked after the garden since Tom Donkin's departure.

But there was more to it than that.

One of Edna Babb's duties had been to shop for her employer in Knowlton, but since she could no longer be relied on Mrs Troy had been forced to seek an alternative source of supplies.

'I told Mr Grail he could use the garden shed – that's what he wanted – but he had to bring me food when he came.'

Why? Biggs wondered. Why on earth not ask one of the village women to shop for her? What was she clinging to so desperately? Was it her independence? She shouldn't be living here on her own, he thought irritably. Didn't she have someone to care for her?

'What can I do for you, Mrs Troy?'

'I want you to tell him to go.' She spoke for the first time with certainty. 'I don't want him coming back.'

Biggs blinked. 'You've spoken to him, have you? Is he giving trouble?'

She shook her head. 'I can't talk to him,' she said. 'I want *you* to tell him.'

Now that he understood at last, Harold didn't trust himself to speak. He'd been dragged all the way out here on his afternoon off just to give some fellow his marching orders! As though to underline his sense of outrage, a loud crack of thunder sounded overhead. It was followed by a patter of raindrops on the roof that swiftly became a downpour. My God, he *was* going to get drenched!

He sought to keep a grip on his temper. 'Where can I find him?' he asked abruptly.

'He usually comes on a Saturday.' She turned her near-sightless eyes on him again. 'Saturday afternoons. That's why I wanted someone here *today*.'

Without a word Biggs stood up and went out into the narrow hallway. He found what he was looking for

– an umbrella, it was standing in a flowered china vase
– and went from there directly through the house to
the kitchen at the back. The smell of stale food assailed
his nostrils. A pile of unwashed plates and dishes lay
on the draining-board of the sink. Through the window he could see the shed, at the bottom, and to one
side, of a small square of lawn bordered by flower-
beds.

He flung open the kitchen door. The rain fell like a
curtain before his eyes. Fuming, he stepped outside,
opening the umbrella as he did so, and splashed across
the already sodden patch of grass to the shed. The
door was barred by a heavy padlock. He hammered on
it.

'Grail!' he called out. 'Grail! Are you there?'

There was no response. He laid his ear to the
wooden door, but he could hear nothing above the
noise of the rain beating on the corrugated iron above
his head and pouring in a stream from the edge of the
roof on to his spread umbrella.

He knocked once more, again without result, and
then plodded back to the house. As he stepped into
the kitchen he saw that the white leather of his new
white-and-tan shoes had turned a muddy brown. Furious, he dried them with a kitchen towel. He returned
to the front room.

'Grail's not in the shed, Mrs Troy. I doubt he'll
come in this storm. Where does he live, anyway?'

She didn't know. Grail had never said. In short
order Harold discovered there was almost nothing she
did know about the man. He'd appeared mysteriously,

several months back, in early spring. He came often on a Saturday but not every week. He usually brought food for her, groceries of some kind, though not always what she asked for.

'Just any stuff,' the old woman said, with sudden, fierce resentment.

So that was it! Grail hadn't lived up to his end of their bargain. Calmer in his mind now, Biggs reflected coolly. As far as he could see, the garden appeared to have been cared for. If it was just a question of the food Grail was bringing, then a word in his ear might do the trick.

Seating himself beside her again he began to put it to her, suggesting that if someone took Grail aside and—

'No! No! No! That's not what I want.' Twin pink roses like fever spots blossomed in the pallor of her cheeks. The hysteria in her voice shook him. 'I don't want to have to deal with that man. *Please! Listen to me!*'

Flushing, Biggs sat back. There was no reasoning with her, he told himself bitterly. She was old and stubborn, and probably feeble-minded. She ought to be in a home. He couldn't see what this fellow Grail had done that was so terribly wrong. Anyone would think he was Satan incarnate! For a moment he wondered if there was something here he hadn't understood. Something she'd left unsaid. But he pushed the thought from his mind. All he wanted was to get the damned business settled and be on his way.

'Well, I can't tell him anything if he's not here,' he said sharply. 'And I can't wait for ever.'

She sat still in her chair, her face turned away from his. The cat's purring had ceased. 'I want Mr Wolverton to come,' she said in a low voice. 'I'll speak to *him*.'

The implied threat in her words brought the blood rushing to his cheeks again. 'There is *something* I can do,' he said quickly. 'I could write him a letter. Mr Grail. I'll leave it in the shed, so if he comes tomorrow he'll find it. I'll tell him he has to go, to quit the premises. There – will that help?'

She said nothing. But her shoulders under the knitted shawl made a faint shrugging gesture.

He stood up, temples throbbing. Old and helpless as she was she'd managed to humiliate him. He felt as though she had slipped a chain around his neck and given it a sharp jerk. He moved away to a small writing desk that stood against the wall behind her chair and sat down. His hand shook as he unscrewed his fountain pen and took a sheet of paper from one of the pigeon-holes.

Dear Mr Grail

Mrs Troy informs me that for some time now she has allowed you the use of her garden shed in return for certain services . . .

The room grew suddenly brighter as he wrote. Glancing up he saw that a beam of sunlight had broken through the lace-net curtains. He was aware that the rain had stopped a few minutes before. The sunshine brought a flash of silver from the glass-fronted cabinet, and Harold's eye was drawn that way. He noticed a pair of tankards standing on a silver salver that occupied the top shelf of the cabinet. The sight of them awoke a recent memory in him. He had gone to an auction in Folkestone with Mr Wolverton to oversee the sale of a deceased client's effects. He recalled the auctioneer holding up a brace of silver mugs, very like the ones in the cabinet.

'Georgian,' the auctioneer had said. They had fetched £120, the pair of them.

> She now finds it necessary to put an end to this arrangement and I am writing to inform you of this. Since no contract exists between you and Mrs Troy I assume that a period of notice of one week from today will be sufficient . . .

A hundred and twenty pounds the pair of them. He could buy a wireless set for £120. For a lot less, as a matter of fact, but the balance could go towards a motor-car.

Harold Biggs sat like a statue, his pen poised above the paper, while the thought of larceny slithered into his mind like an adder and lay there, quietly coiled.

He glanced at the figure in the chair. The old woman seemed to be dozing.

He got up quietly and went out of the room and into the kitchen. His heart was leaping in his chest. He needed time to think. He drew a glass of water from the sink tap and stood at the window staring out. Scattered raindrops fell through sunshine. Blue skies showed on the heels of the clouds, which were moving eastwards. He wouldn't get wet after all.

Dry-lipped he told himself he was entitled to claim payment, to be compensated for his trouble. But it wasn't that. He knew. It was the excitement he felt racing through his veins. The realization that he might be about to do something he had never dreamed of doing. Had never dared to dream of doing. It was like stepping into a new skin. A new person.

He went back to the front room. Mrs Troy hadn't stirred. Her chin lay on her breast. Her eyes were shut.

Biggs held his breath. The cat watched from her lap as he crossed the room silently to the cabinet.

Could he do it? Yes? No?

He opened the glass doors and took out the tankards, one in each hand, hefting them, testing their weight. His eyes, behind his glasses, began to water.

'Mr Biggs? Are you there?'

Harold froze. His back was to her.

Are you there?

He turned his head slowly – and then relaxed with a slow expulsion of breath. Her face was pointing towards the door. She couldn't see across the room. He had banked all on that.

'Mr Biggs . . .?'

Taking care not to make any sound, he replaced the mugs in the cabinet and shut the glass doors. Black spots danced before his eyes.

'Here I am, Mrs Troy.' He crossed the room unhurriedly to the desk. 'I'll just finish this letter now.'

Kindly remove all your belongings and leave the door unlocked . . .

Biggs's pen squeaked faintly on the paper.

I shall return next Saturday, a week from today, to ensure that the shed has been vacated as Mrs Troy requests.

    Yours faithfully,
      Harold Biggs
      (Solicitor's Clerk)

'I've been thinking this over, Mrs Troy.' He spoke to her from the desk as he addressed an envelope in clear capitals: MR GRAIL, BY HAND. 'A letter's not enough, I feel. I ought to handle this in person. I'll be coming back next Saturday to make sure this fellow has got the message. Don't worry, I'll have him out of here, bag and baggage, I promise you.'

Because he didn't want to take the tankards *now*. Not today. He had thought it all out in the kitchen. First, Grail had to be sent packing. Then, anything found missing from the cottage could be laid at his door. He'd be the obvious culprit, a man with a grievance. It was an added bonus, as far as Harold was concerned, that he did not need to trouble his conscience, either. Even if the police got around to questioning Grail they would find no evidence of the theft, no stolen goods, and the matter would be dropped.

Always supposing it came to that. Always supposing Winifred Troy even noticed the mugs had gone missing.

He sealed the envelope, got up and went over to where she was sitting.

'Do you understand, Mrs Troy?' He sat down beside her again. 'This letter's his notice to quit. I'll be back in a week to make sure he's gone. You don't have to deal with him. If he makes any objection refer him to us, to the firm. Tell him we're handling the matter.'

He didn't like it when she turned her face to him. An exchange of glances was part of any conversation. You looked into the other person's eyes and tried to judge their reactions. Mrs Troy's clouded gaze gave no hint of her feelings. Then he felt her fingers close on his.

'Thank you, Mr Biggs.' It was no more than a murmur. 'I'm sorry to have put you to all this trouble.'

Too late, he thought angrily, pulling his hand from hers. He didn't want to think about her, or her life. Or how little of it was left.

'I'll be going now,' he said, getting up. 'I'll see you a week from today.'

He went out of the room without waiting for her response and left the house by the kitchen door, crossing the lawn and pausing at the shed to slip the letter under the door. The puddles in the dirt track outside the wicket gate reflected the washed blue sky.

He stopped for a moment to savour the extraordinary events of the past half-hour. He had walked across the room to the cabinet in her presence and taken out the tankards! He had done what he meant to do. Assert himself! He only wished he could bring it to Mr Wolverton's attention. Somehow ram it down his throat!

As it was, he couldn't even tell Jimmy Pullman what he'd done, or what he planned to do. It would have to remain his secret.

Always in the past he had lacked courage, he thought, needing an explanation for the mediocrity of his life. But he felt if he could do this one thing – return next week and take the tankards – the whole of his future might change. In spite of everything he had a deep-rooted belief in his own good fortune.

'You're a lucky devil.'

Harold grinned at the remembered words. They had been spoken to him by a woman he had picked up one evening in the high street in Folkestone. It was in the second year of the war. He'd forgotten her name now.

They had walked arm in arm from the upper town to one of the pubs in the harbour, down the same winding road that, day by day, echoed to the marching feet of thousands of men on their way to the moored Channel steamers, and to France. (Harold heard them still in his dreams, those marching feet.) She told him her fiancé had been killed at Loos and he had wondered whether this bright-eyed girl with the brassy manner might not feel contempt for a man who, with the help of weak eyesight and a cough he had learned to exaggerate, had worked himself a soft posting in the quartermaster's stores at Shorncliffe Camp. She soon put him right.

'I'll take a live man over a dead hero any day,' she

declared, and proved it to him a few hours later, up against the wall in a dark alleyway behind the pub.

'*You're a lucky devil.*'

He never saw her again, but her words stayed with him. As the war continued, and the casualty lists lengthened, and weak eyes and doubtful lungs were no longer enough to keep a man out of the trenches, Harold had waited for the day when *his* name would be added to the columns marching down daily to the water's edge. It never arrived. He had remained at his post in the quartermaster's stores. And with the passing of time he came to see that what the girl had told him was true, though in a way she could not have imagined. He was specially blessed. Anointed. One of those, who, by fate or accident, was destined to escape the slaughter.

He still had the shiny new shilling he had been given when he enlisted and he had drilled a hole in it and threaded it on to his key ring. Even now, in moments of doubt or indecision, he would find himself slipping his hand into his pocket and running his thumb over the milled edge.

5

AMOS PIKE slipped into the kitchen and deposited the parcel of food he had brought in the pantry. He waited, expecting to hear the old woman's voice from the front room asking who was there. When she didn't speak he went through and found her sitting in her usual place by the window. In the fading light of early evening she seemed unusually pale and shrunken and he looked at her with cold-eyed concern.

'I brought you some things,' he said, in his dead voice.

'Thank you, Mr Grail.'

She sounded breathless, uneasy.

'I got some fish, like you asked.' He studied her face, observing the faint tremor that tugged at the corners of her mouth.

'Thank you,' she whispered again.

Pike's brow creased. He seldom conversed with anyone, but his instincts, like an animal's, were strongly developed.

'Is something wrong?' he asked.

She shook her head at once. 'No, nothing. Thank you for bringing the food.' She kept repeating herself.

He knew she found his presence unsettling, but now there was something else in her manner: a kind of tension, which she was trying to hide. He moved a little closer. He wanted to get to the bottom of this. Distrust and suspicion were the dominant strains of his character, together with his need, and it was this last – the constant thrust of his longing – which caused him to turn away suddenly and leave her sitting where she was.

He would find out later what had upset her.

A last-minute change in Mrs Aylward's itinerary had meant a delay of several hours in his departure for Rudd's Cross. Normally he accepted these occasional disruptions in his plans without emotion. He could afford to take the long view.

But this afternoon for the first time he had felt impatience. The everyday world with its routine of chores and duties was becoming a burden to him. Though he wasn't aware of it, the frail moorings that bound him to common reality were starting to fray.

Twilight was falling when he opened the shed door, and he failed to see the letter lying on the floor at his feet. When he lit the paraffin lamp a minute later he had already stripped the dust cloth off his motorcycle and thrown it aside. It fell on the floor, covering the white envelope.

*

He reached the forest before midnight and slept, wrapped in his groundsheet, beside his motorcycle until dawn. At first light he was on the move, hoisting his heavily laden bag on to his shoulder and striding, silent and ghostlike, through the thick ground mist that swirled about the tree trunks.

He found the dugout as he had left it, apart from a layer of mud that had accumulated at the bottom with the recent rains. He used his entrenching tool to scrape it out, stamping the remaining wet soil into a hard surface, and then went in search of one of the many stands of saplings with which the forest was seeded, returning an hour later with two armfuls of poles, which he trimmed and laid side by side on the packed mud floor, damp-proofing the pit.

At noon he broke off to open a tin of bully beef. All morning he had kept his mind fixed on the minutiae of the jobs he was engaged in: on the branch he was trimming to size, on the neatness of the levelled floor. But he had been conscious all the time of the forces gathering within him: a tidal bore of emotion that throbbed at his nerve ends, making his skin prickle and burn as though lava flowed in his veins.

The sensation was thrilling. But it also made him uneasy. Self-control was the anchor of his life. It had steadied him through years of near-unbearable anguish and aching need, and the fear of losing it now was enough to calm him and keep his mind fixed on the tasks ahead.

When he had finished eating he left the area again, this time heading for a nearby pond, and returned with a sheaf of willow branches. Earlier he had nailed together a rough frame from the remaining saplings and now he began to plait the willow into a lattice to be fixed to the frame. It was painstaking work, and twice he had to return to the waterside for more willow laths, but by five o'clock he had constructed a roof for the dugout and laid it in place.

Collecting his bag and tools he retired into the refuge he had built. Now that his preparations were complete he was able to relax, lighting a cigarette and brewing a mess tin of tea on the Primus stove he had brought on his last visit. While it was still light he went through the contents of his bag, picking out those items he meant to leave behind. The stove he wrapped in oilcloth and stowed in a corner with the tinned supplies, following the pattern he had established, preparing himself for several visits and a long period of anticipation.

But even as he did these things he felt a seed of doubt. He wasn't sure he could wait. His experience at Highfield had been unique, a period when time had seemed suspended, a moment of sweet indecision prolonged to the point where he had temporarily lost the power to act. In retrospect he seemed to have sat for countless evenings in the woods above the village while the excitement mounted in him bit by bit like the slow accretion of coral.

He felt different now. The pressure inside his chest was like a clenched fist. His desire was growing by the day.

The last thing he did before leaving the dugout was to cut fresh brush, which he used to camouflage the site, threading the branches into the surrounding undergrowth, creating the illusion of a dense thicket.

Having made a final inspection of the area to satisfy himself that all was as it should be, he returned to where he had left the motorcycle, taking his bag with him.

Before wedging it into place in the sidecar he unbuckled the straps and took out a piece of meat wrapped in striped butcher's paper, which he slipped into the pocket of his leather jacket, wrinkling his nose at the gamy smell. He had bought it the day before and it was starting to go off.

*

The doors to the drawing-room stood open and the curtains on the windows had been pulled back so that light from inside poured out on to the grass. Two maids were busy with trays, moving back and forth between the house and the table under the trellised vine. Beyond the stretch of lawn illuminated by the lights the garden lay in silvered shadow under the bright moonlight.

Pike sat with his binoculars nailed to his eyes.

He had been watching for more than two hours, propped against the trunk of the beech tree, motionless in a well of darkness untouched by the moon's rays.

The adult members of the family were eating dinner. There were three of them, but two he barely noticed. His attention was fixed on the fair-haired woman facing him, whose bare arms and shoulders glowed like ivory in the flickering candlelight.

Some kind of celebration was in progress. All three

were in evening dress. Champagne had been poured at the start of the meal and glasses raised to the older of the two women. Even from a distance Pike could see the wine froth and sparkle.

He had done this at Highfield. He had sat in the shadows and watched. But try as he might now he couldn't recapture the feeling he had had then: the sense of a pleasure postponed, but within his grasp. A fruit he could pluck whenever he chose.

The beast stirring within him now cared nothing for patience and detachment. Its demands were insistent. He shifted, easing the pressure in his groin.

He turned his attention away from the table to the edge of the lawn, where the yew alley began, and then traced the course of the path that ran the length of the garden to the croquet lawn. Three-quarters of the way along the yew alley a subsidiary path branched out and led to the gate in the mossed wall. Pike's eye came to rest there.

But not for long. Slowly, with all the deliberation he could muster, he made the return journey with his glasses, following the pathway back to the yew alley and then up to the lawn and the house.

He pictured it all in his mind's eye.

The charge, with the rifle and bayonet thrusting ahead!

The glass doors shattering!

He heard the screams. He'd heard them before. They only increased his excitement.

Heart pumping in his chest, he brought the binoculars back to bear on the distant figure of the woman.

His mouth turned dry at the sight of her bare arms. The thought of her body beneath his brought a low growl from his throat.

'*Call me Sadie . . . I want you to call me Sadie.*'

He whispered the words.

At Melling Lodge he had been unable to contain himself. His climax had come too soon, soiling his trousers, while he struggled with the woman on the bed, the shame and the blood and the pleasure all mixed together.

Recalling those moments now, he made a silent vow.

This time it would be different. This time he would call on his iron control.

But the last two hours had shown him he couldn't wait. His need demanded urgent satisfaction. Even tonight would not have been too soon.

He put down his glasses and lit a cigarette, deliberately allowing his body to cool.

The following weekend Mrs Aylward would take the train to London on Saturday morning. He had already been informed of her plans. She would go from there to visit friends in Gloucestershire, returning only the following Tuesday. He would have the whole weekend free, and Monday, too, if he chose.

Pike drew deeply on his cigarette. In a moment his mind was made up.

He had one more thing to do.

Extinguishing his cigarette, he rose and started down the hill, slipping between the trees, catlike in the sureness of his footing, a shadow among the shadows. At the bottom he left the treeline and joined the path that led through the water-meadow, walking silently between the ponds where the moon hung motionless on the dark surface of the water.

When he reached the garden gate he stopped and went down on his haunches. He could hear their voices. The silvery notes of a woman's laugh came to him on the still night air. He thought of her white throat.

He began to whistle. Softly, almost inaudibly at first. Then a little louder. He went on that way, the grating tuneless air growing in volume all the time.

He was rewarded after a minute by the sound of a yelp coming from the direction of the lawn. Then almost at once he heard another noise in which whining, panting and scurrying movement were all mingled, and the dog burst into view on the pathway ahead of him, skidding around the corner from the yew alley, heavy ears flapping.

Growling a challenge, it ran towards the figure crouched behind the barred gate.

*

It was after midnight when he returned to Rudd's Cross, switching off the stuttering engine of his motorcycle when he was still some distance from the cottage. It had given trouble on the ride back, the carburettor needed cleaning. He pushed the machine for the last hundred yards along the puddle-strewn dirt track up to the shed.

Once inside, he wasted no time, not bothering to

light the paraffin lamp, locating the dust cloth by feel in the pitch darkness and flinging it over the motorcycle. He was anxious to get home as soon as possible. A long drive lay ahead of him the following day – Mrs Aylward had a client in Lewes.

Before leaving he cast a glance at the darkened windows of the cottage. He hadn't forgotten the old woman's strange behaviour. Something was troubling her. He must find out what it was.

He would come early next Saturday. There was much to do.

6

Grim-faced, Sinclair strode along the carpeted corridor with Madden at his elbow. 'So Ferris thinks my days are numbered – did you see that piece in Friday's *Express*? "Is it time for a change?" I wonder, does he know something we don't?'

A breakdown in the Underground had delayed the chief inspector's arrival at the Yard by half an hour. He had paused in his office only long enough to empty the contents of his briefcase on to his desk, secure the cumulative file from the drawer where it resided and signal Madden to accompany him.

'Let's leave that till later, John,' he said, when the inspector began to tell him about an idea he had. 'Let's get this over with first.'

Glancing at his colleague's face, Sinclair was pleased to see him looking rested and alert. He allowed himself to wonder whether a visit to Highfield had figured among Madden's weekend activities.

'"Informed circles at the Yard,"' he quoted, as he led the way into the anteroom to Bennett's office. 'That's what Ferris calls his source. Do you think the chief super will have the grace to blush this morning?'

In the event, they had no opportunity to find out.

Bennett was alone in his office. The deputy, dressed in funereal black, stood by the window, hands on hips, gazing out at the morning traffic on the river. He turned when they entered.

'Good morning, gentlemen.' He ushered them to their usual chairs at the polished oak table. Their way led past his desk where a copy of Friday's *Daily Express* was ostentatiously displayed. 'We're on our own this morning.' Bennett sat down facing them. His brown eyes were expressionless. 'Mr Sampson has another appointment.'

Sinclair opened his file. Without haste he began to leaf through the typewritten pages. His neat, contained figure showed no sign of strain or anxiety.

'As you know, sir, we were hoping these wartime killings in Belgium would provide us with information that would assist us in our current inquiries.' The chief inspector raised flint-coloured eyes from the file and looked squarely at Bennett. 'I'm afraid thus far they've proved a blind alley.'

'I'm sorry to hear that.' Bennett shifted slightly in his chair. 'None of these men fits the bill, then?'

'Mr Madden and I have interviewed two of the four survivors of B Company. Neither was our man. The third, Marlow, is in hospital and the fourth, Samuel Patterson, has been traced by the Norwich police. He's working on a farm near Aylsham. His movements are accounted for.'

'Yet these men – and their comrades who were killed – were the only ones Captain Miller questioned?'

'According to the records, yes.'

'And we know he closed the case.' Bennett frowned. 'Then logic suggests he believed one of those killed in battle was the guilty man. That's been your assumption – am I right, Chief Inspector?'

'Yes, sir.'

'But you thought he could have been mistaken? That it might have been one of these four?'

'That possibility was in my mind.' Sinclair nodded. 'But now I've had second thoughts.'

'Oh?' The deputy sat forward.

'I've been struck by the fact that none of these men – none of those who survived – was questioned again after they came out of the line. That doesn't make sense. I've looked at the verbal records of the interrogations carefully. Miller bore down hard on them. It's plain he thought they were hiding something. Even if he believed the guilty man among them was dead he would have had the others in again. He wouldn't have let it go at that.'

Bennett's brow knotted. 'Then the murderer wasn't from B Company after all. Miller must have decided it was someone else.'

'So it would seem,' Sinclair agreed.

'But without that memorandum, we're not likely to discover who.'

'Correct.'

Bennett sighed. He looked away. 'Is there anything else, Chief Inspector?'

'Only this, sir.' Sinclair dipped into the file. Selecting a paper, he pulled it out and held it up before him. 'I sent a telegram to the Brussels Sûreté last week asking them to check their records for us. I was hoping they might have a copy of Miller's report. They don't.' His eye met Bennett's over the top of the sheet of paper. 'In fact, according to their records the case is still open.'

'*What?*' The deputy sat up straight in astonishment. 'I don't understand. What does that mean?'

'Well, for one thing, the British military authorities never informed the Belgian civilian police that the case was closed.'

The two men looked at each other. Perhaps five seconds elapsed. Then Bennett's eyes narrowed. Sinclair, who had a high opinion of the deputy's quickness of mind, saw the realization dawn.

'That damned memorandum! It's not lost, is it? They just won't give it to us!'

Sinclair made a slight gesture of dissent. 'Not necessarily, sir. It may well be lost. *Now.*'

'You mean someone deliberately got rid of it. But we don't know who, or when?'

'That seems likely.'

'The killer himself?'

Sinclair shook his head. 'I doubt that. Unless he was an MP, and even then . . .' He slipped the paper back into the file. 'I spoke to Colonel Jenkins on Friday and asked him to put us in touch with Miller's commanding officer during the war. It's possible he may remember something of the case. Incidentally, Jenkins said they're still hunting for the memorandum at the War Office depot. I've no reason to disbelieve him. There could be a variety of reasons why someone in September 1917 decided it would be better to destroy that piece of paper, particularly if they thought the guilty party was dead. It was a brutal crime and the victims were civilians. No need to point a finger at the armed forces, they might have thought. Let the dead bury the dead.'

Bennett was studying his fingernails. After a few moments he rose and went to the window. He stood with his arms folded looking out. Sinclair glanced at Madden with raised eyebrows. The deputy returned to the table and sat down.

'Let me sum up, if I may.' He cleared his throat. 'There's no point in my tackling the War Office on this, no way of prising that memorandum out of them?'

'I believe not, sir. If it still exists, if they're withholding it deliberately, they'll continue to do so. If not, we'll only antagonize them.'

Bennett nodded, understanding. His frown returned. 'If you only had a name, something to go on . . .' He dropped his eyes. He seemed reluctant to continue. 'Then again, it's quite possible the cases are unconnected. The murders in Belgium, the killings here . . . We can't be *sure*.'

'Indeed we can't, sir.' Sinclair carefully aligned the papers in front of him and slid them back into the folder.

The deputy lifted his gaze. 'Perhaps, after all, it's time to look . . . in a different direction.' His glance conveyed sympathy.

The chief inspector acknowledged the words with a slight nod.

Bennett rose. He turned to Madden. 'Would you leave us, Inspector? I want a word in private with Mr Sinclair.'

*

Twenty minutes later the chief inspector walked briskly into his office. The bulky cumulative file flew from his hands and landed with a resounding thud on his desktop. As though in response, the nervous chatter of a typewriter in the adjoining room fell silent. Sinclair stood before his desk.

'I rather hoped the chief super's non-appearance this morning might signal his dispatch to the Tower for immediate execution. But it seems Ferris was right — we're the ones scheduled for the block.'

'I'm sorry, sir.' Madden scowled from behind his desk. 'I think they're making a mistake.'

'Perhaps. What's certain is Sampson has the assistant commissioner's ear. That's where he was this morning, by the way, doing some last-minute spadework with Sir George, making sure he doesn't change his mind.'

'Is that it, then? Are we out?'

'Not quite yet, though I dare say we would be if Parkhurst wasn't due in Newcastle this afternoon for a regional conference. He won't be back till Thursday. That's the appointed day. He's called a meeting in his office. Bennett and I are invited to attend. You're excused, John.'

The chief inspector took his pipe from his pocket. He perched on the edge of his desk. 'Poor Bennett. He's in the worst position of all, trying to straddle a barbed-wire fence. He knows we're on the right track, even though it keeps going cold. But if he continues backing us he'll find himself exposed. I think he half suspects Sampson's after *his* job.'

'Surely not!' Madden was incredulous.

'Oh, he won't get it.' Sinclair chuckled. 'But our chief super's fantasies know no bounds. Never mind that. You were saying earlier you had an idea. Now would be a good time to hear it.'

The inspector took a moment to collect his thoughts. 'It all depends on how Miller went about his business,' he began.

'I don't follow you.'

'He wouldn't have worked *alone*. He would have had a redcap NCO along with him to take notes and type up his reports. But what we don't know is whether he simply drew a clerk at random from whatever pool was available, in which case it wouldn't be much help to us, or whether he worked with the same man regularly.'

'You mean if they were a team?' Sinclair frowned.

Madden nodded. 'If he used the *same* clerk, then that would be the man who took down the inter-rogations of B Company and typed up the records. He'd be familiar with the case. They might even have discussed it.'

'You're suggesting this mythical clerk might have known what was in Miller's mind. Who he thought the guilty man was.' The chief inspector looked sceptical.

'More than that. He'd most likely have typed up that memorandum. And it wouldn't have been a routine job for him. He'd remember what was in it.'

Sinclair examined the bowl of his pipe. 'So what is it we need to know? The name of Miller's special clerk, if he had one. I'm not sure there's time. Thursday's our deadline.'

'I know, but I've thought of a short cut,' Madden said. 'Miller was travelling in a staff car when he was killed. It's likely he was on an investigation, which means he had a clerk with him, probably the driver. He could be our man.'

'Now you're telling me he's dead!'

'He might be.' Madden was unfazed. 'But we don't *know* that.'

'Nor do we,' Sinclair agreed after a moment. He gave an approving nod. 'You're right, John, it's worth a try. I'll pester the War Office again. I'm in the mood to twist someone's tail.'

7

WHEN SHE CAME to a convenient tree stump, Harriet Merrick paused and sat down, fanning her face with the wide straw hat she had put on to please Annie McConnell. (Mrs Merrick had pleaded in vain that the mild October sunshine was hardly likely to cause her sunstroke!) She was finding the gentle slope to the top of Shooter's Hill heavy going today. A slight pain in her chest, like a bolt tightening, had persuaded her to stop and rest for a while. She waited now for the sensation to pass.

She was reluctant to admit it, but she'd not been feeling herself these past few days. A nagging headache that had started on the night of her sixty-first birthday had continued to plague her since. At her son's suggestion they had taken advantage of the unusually warm autumn weather to dine outside that night, and Mrs Merrick thought at first she might have caught a chill. But the cold she feared did not develop. Instead, her head had continued to ache, keeping her awake at night and allowing her thoughts to wander restlessly in a state of increasing anxiety.

The trouble had started with Tigger's death. Poisoned, Hopley reckoned. He blamed the farmers hereabouts who, he said, were laying down strychnine and other poisons against the foxes, which took a heavy toll of their hen coops. The gardener had come across the poor animal dragging itself on its stomach through the shrubbery in the early morning. Tigger had been missing all night, though Annie had called to him repeatedly before she went to bed.

The children's attention had been distracted while the dog was carried to the potting shed where presently he died. After lunch their father had told them what had happened. They had wept, but then, as children did, dried their tears and taken a lively interest in the funeral arrangements, which Hopley was charged with. That evening they had stood hand in hand with their parents and with Annie while prayers were said and the remains of the spaniel laid to rest in a grave dug behind the croquet lawn.

Their father had assured them he wouldn't let the matter rest there and had already informed the village bobby, Constable Proudfoot, who intended to look into it. The next day Harriet Merrick took her grandchildren aside and promised to buy them a new puppy on their return from holiday in Cornwall.

But, like spreading ripples in a pond, the brutal disturbance to domestic life at Croft Manor continued to claim its victims. On Tuesday night little Robert had become tearful again, and it was discovered he was running a temperature. He had been packed off to bed immediately by his mother while the unspoken thought hung in the air: if it turned out to be anything serious the whole family would have to delay their departure for Penzance at the end of the week.

This in turn seemed to upset Mrs Merrick, as she readily admitted to Annie. 'I don't want them hanging on. I want them to *go*.'

'Will you listen to yourself?' Annie had laughed at her. 'Your own flesh and blood, and you can't wait to see the back of them.'

'I was looking forward to us being here alone. Just you and I, Annie.'

'Now don't you worry, Miss Hattie.' Annie addressed her as Mrs Merrick in front of others, but always as Miss Hattie when they were alone, just as she had for the past forty years and more. 'We'll have plenty of time on our own, you'll see. They'll be off for three weeks.'

'Not if they don't *go*,' Mrs Merrick had pointed out with unanswerable logic, but Annie just shook her head at her.

'What a great silly you are! Always getting yourself worked up for no reason.'

Annie was right – there *was* no reason to be upset. But this, paradoxically, seemed to distress her all the more, and the night before she had hardly closed her eyes for worrying.

'Oh, Annie, I don't know what's the matter with me. Why do I *want* them away from here?' They were walking in the garden together after breakfast. 'I'm starting to feel the way I did when Tom died. Do you remember? I was so afraid then, even before I knew.'

Annie had drawn her into a recess in the yew alley and put her arms around her.

'There, my dear,' she murmured. 'Aren't you

forgetting it's four years since the poor dear boy was killed?'

'How could I *forget*?'

'Almost to the day . . .'

'Oh! Do you think it's *that*?' Mrs Merrick drew back. Tom had been killed in the second week of October. The anniversary was near. 'Oh, I do *hope* so.' She caught her breath at her own words, wondering how she could have said such a thing.

But it was true, none the less, and the thought had comforted her for the rest of the day.

*

She felt better still when she went up to the nursery later with Annie and they found the invalid's temperature had come down. He declared himself fit enough for a game of Happy Families, and although his nanny, Enid Bradshaw, opposed the idea she was overruled by Annie whose writ ran in all departments of the household.

Mrs Merrick smiled as Robert's seven-year-old sister fussed over him, fluffing up his pillows and settling him comfortably in his bed. She giggled with them both when Annie fixed the patient with a glittering eye. 'Now tell me the truth, Master Robert – and may a lie never stain your lips – are you by any chance holding Miss Bun, the Baker's Daughter?'

The game continued until the arrival of Dr Fellows, who pronounced Robert to be on the mend after only the briefest of examinations. 'A case of nerves, I think. Losing the dog must have upset him more than we realized. Poor beast, do you know yet how it happened?'

It was also Mrs Merrick's day for her weekly check-up and Dr Fellows apologized for having come an hour later than usual. 'I was just leaving the surgery when they brought in Emmett Hogg with a broken ankle. It seems he had to hobble and crawl for half a mile before he found help. Fell into a pit in the woods, *he* says.' Dr Fellows lifted an eloquent eyebrow. 'Not many men hereabouts manage to be dead drunk at two o'clock in the afternoon, but Hogg makes quite a habit of it. Now what have *you* been up to, madam?' The doctor lowered his jowly visage over the gauge of his blood pressure apparatus. He pumped air into the cuff around Mrs Merrick's arm. He frowned. 'Been overdoing it again, have we?'

Mrs Merrick, who liked neither being addressed as 'madam', nor being referred to in the first person plural, acknowledged that she had been for a walk earlier that day. She made no mention of Shooter's Hill.

'Take it easy for the next few days,' Dr Fellows advised her. 'We'd better make that a week. No more walks outside the garden until I see you again.'

Mrs Merrick's thoughts were elsewhere. Something he had said had jogged her memory.

'Fell into a pit, you say?'

'That's Hogg's story.' Dr Fellows snapped his bag shut. 'I hae me doots.'

Harriet Merrick winced. 'If it happened in Ashdown Forest he must report it,' she said firmly. 'The police want to know about any fresh digging there. My son was telling me only the other day.'

William was a Justice of the Peace.

'I'm not sure anyone will believe anything Emmett Hogg tells them,' Dr Fellows remarked. He paused at the bedroom door.

'Nevertheless, he must report it. And *you* must make sure he does,' Mrs Merrick added, pleased for once to be in a position to dictate.

8

THE DOOR TO the adjoining office opened and Hollingsworth and Styles entered. Chief Inspector Sinclair, immaculate in grey pinstripe and pearl tie-pin, sat behind his desk. The windows at his back, which so often during the long summer had sparkled diamond-bright in the sunshine, were flecked with rain. Lightning streaked the black sky above Kennington. He motioned the two men to come closer. 'No doubt you've heard the rumours that I'm to be replaced as head of this investigation. I'm sorry to have to tell you they're true. I'm due to see the assistant commissioner in a few minutes. It's my understanding he'll hand the inquiry over to Chief Superintendent Sampson.'

Hollingsworth muttered some words.

'Sergeant?' Sinclair raised an eyebrow.

'Nothing, sir. Sorry, sir.'

'I want to take this opportunity to thank you both for the work you've put in. Long hours, with little to show for it, you may think. But I assure you that's not the case. I've no doubt that the information gathered in this file will eventually lead to the arrest and, I hope, conviction of the man we've been seeking.' He patted the thick buff folder lying on the desk in front of him.

'As to the future, neither Inspector Madden nor myself expects to play any further part in this inquiry. Chief Superintendent Sampson will be putting together his own team and I think it likely he'll want to include you both, given your familiarity with the history and details of the case. I know you'll offer him the same loyalty and devotion to a difficult job you have always given me, and for which I thank you now.'

The chief inspector stood up and held out his hand to Hollingsworth, who shook it. Styles followed suit.

'You'll be informed shortly of any change in your assignments. That will be all.'

The two men returned to the side office, shutting the door behind them. Sinclair resumed his seat and took out his pipe. He glanced at Madden, who had listened in silence at his desk. 'Well, John?'

'I think it's a damned shame.'

'An opinion not shared by Mrs Sinclair, who is pleased at the thought of my spending more time at home. She comforts me with the assurance that I need not fear to find myself less usefully employed in the future. Only the area of my activities will change. Are you familiar with the term "mulching"?'

The grin that came to Madden's face reminded the chief inspector that there was at least one satisfaction he could take from the weeks of labour they had shared. His pleasure at seeing his partner more like his old self had been heightened for a brief time when it seemed likely that Madden's suggestion that they track down Captain Miller's clerk would bear dividends.

Against all odds the War Office had been able to supply them, without delay, with the identity of the driver of Miller's staff car. The names of both men had been on the casualty report.

Corporal Alfred Tozer had survived the blast that killed his superior and in due course had been invalided back to a hospital in Eastbourne where medical records retained since the war gave an address for him in Bethnal Green.

Madden had sped there in a taxi with Hollingsworth only to discover that while it remained Tozer's residence – he lived with his sister and her husband, the three of them running a newsagent's and tobacconist's business together – he was absent from home.

'On a *walking* holiday? In *North Wales*?' The chief inspector had raised his eyes to the ceiling in disbelief.

'He's a rambler, sir. It's how he spends his holiday every year, according to his sister. He visits different parts of the country.'

'How admirable! We must recommend him to the tourist board. So we still don't know whether he was Miller's regular clerk, or even if he has any special knowledge of that case?'

Madden shook his head.

Clutching at straws, Sinclair had telephoned the police in Bangor and asked them to pass the word along to sub-stations in the district to be on the lookout for Tozer. He was to be asked to get in touch with

Scotland Yard at once. The same message had been left with his sister, who was not expecting him back before the weekend.

'I'll put a note in the file, but I don't see the chief superintendent stirring himself to chase up any ideas *we* put forward.'

Their last chance to advance the investigation came that morning with a further message from the War Office regarding Miller's wartime commanding officer in the Military Police. A Colonel Strachan, he was now retired and living in a village in Scotland so remote that even the chief inspector had never heard of it.

The Yard's switchboard had spent most of the morning wrestling with exchanges up and down the country. Sinclair was out of the office when they finally made contact with the colonel, and it was Madden who spoke to him.

'He says he recalls the case and knows it was closed,' he told the chief inspector on his return. 'But he can't remember the name of the man Miller identified as the murderer. He was killed in battle, though. He remembers that much.'

'And how did Miller know it was him?'

'He can't remember that, either.'

'My, my . . .' The chief inspector scratched his head. 'Remind me not to retire too early, John. It seems to have a damaging effect on the brain cells. What did you make of it?'

Madden frowned. 'It's hard to be sure over a long-distance line. His voice was very faint. But I'd say he wasn't bending over backwards to be helpful.'

'Nobbled?' Sinclair inserted a pipe-cleaner into the stem of his briar. He squinted at Madden.

'Possibly. But not by the War Office. He seemed genuinely surprised to get my call. If it was done at all it was done at the time, just as we suspect.'

'But not on *his* initiative?'

'I'm sure not. He was a military policeman. He'd have been breaking the law. No, the order must have come from higher up.'

'From headquarters?'

The inspector shrugged.

'I see a man.' Sinclair extracted his pipe-cleaner and blew through the stem. 'A general, perhaps. Or an overweight colonel with a scarlet hat band and lapel tabs. He's sitting in his office – it's in a *château*, by the way. He's just had a good dinner. The front is a long way off.'

'You're talking about a staff officer.' Madden scowled.

'Am I? Well, this one has a file in front of him.' Sinclair examined the pipe-cleaner. 'A ticklish matter. It's the investigator's memorandum that bothers him. "No," he says, removing it and tossing it aside.' The chief inspector matched words to action, dropping the pipe-cleaner into the wastepaper basket beside him. '"No, I don't think we'll have that."' He looked at his pipe. 'I wonder what the problem was. Perhaps he didn't want the name of the murderer made public. Perhaps it would have been an embarrassment to someone.' He shrugged. 'Anyway, since the man in question was dead it didn't really matter. Justice had been served.' Sinclair put his pipe in his pocket. 'Yes, I'd like to meet that staff officer. I really would.'

He glanced at his watch. 'Time I was on my way.' He rose, collecting the file from his desk. 'They're welcome to this.' He hefted the bulky folder. 'I shan't give Sampson the satisfaction of watching me squirm. The convicted felon made a dignified exit. After all, it's only a job, as the bishop said to the actress . . .'

He started to move around his desk, then halted. With a sudden sharp gesture he slammed the file down. '*No, by God, it's not!*'

Madden started in surprise. The chief inspector stared through the window at the rainswept morning. He spoke in a low, angry tone: 'Somewhere out there is a man bent on murder. It's only a matter of time before he acts. Somewhere there's a woman, a whole family, perhaps, who stand in peril. And now I'm being asked to place this investigation – and the lives of these people, whoever they are – in the hands of a . . . *nincompoop!*'

He snatched up the file, and at the same moment his eye fell on Billy Styles, who was standing in the open doorway to the adjoining office with two cups of tea in his hands. He stared at Sinclair in horror.

'You didn't hear me say that, Constable. Is that clear?'

'Yes, sir.' The young man quailed.

'*Absolutely* clear?'

Billy could only nod.

With a glance at Madden, the chief inspector strode out of the office.

9

AN HOUR LATER Sinclair completed his summing-up of the inquiry to date. He'd been surprised when the assistant commissioner requested it. He had expected the proceedings to be brief, and to be confined to an expression of thanks from Sir George for his weeks of toil, followed by a brisk handover of the file to Chief Superintendent Sampson, who sat beside Parkhurst at the polished oak table with the air of a vulture perched on a branch.

The table was a twin of the one that graced Bennett's office. In other respects the assistant commissioner's rooms were more elaborately furnished. A thick pile carpet covered the floor and the walls were hung with landscapes of the green English countryside. Two windows, overlooking the Embankment, framed a wide mahogany desk behind which hung a large photograph of Sir George with his namesake, King George V. The blurred outlines of a horse walking in the background suggested a racecourse as the likely setting for the picture. Parkhurst, in morning dress, stood with his head slightly bowed and turned attentively towards the monarch, who wore a glazed expression.

The chief inspector sat on his own. Parkhurst faced

him across the table, with Sampson on one side of him and Bennett on the other. The assistant commissioner was in his late fifties. His fleshy cheeks were marked by a network of livid veins. While Sinclair was speaking his glance had wandered about the room, as though unable to settle on anything, in contrast to Sampson, beside him, whose small dark eyes never left the chief inspector's face. Bennett sat apart from both of them, his chair drawn away as though deliberately distancing himself. The deputy's face showed no emotion.

'Allow me to underline the importance I attribute to this recent aspect of the investigation, sir.'

Given the opportunity to explain himself, the chief inspector had abandoned his original intention of washing his hands of the whole business as quickly as possible. He was now enjoying the process of drawing it out, watching Sampson twitch with impatience, observing Sir George trying to screw up his resolve to put an end to the meeting. He would say what he had to say, and be damned!

'It's my belief – and Inspector Madden's – that the man who killed those people in Belgium in 1917 is the same man we're looking for now. The devil of it is we haven't been able to pin down his identity. But we will . . . or, rather, we would have, I'm sure.' Sinclair paused briefly. 'Sir, I cannot urge strongly enough that this line of inquiry should not be abandoned and that we should keep pressing the War Office to provide a name.'

Parkhurst stirred restlessly in his chair. 'All the

same, Chief Inspector, you will admit there's no *necessary* connection between those killings and the ones at Melling Lodge. When all is said and done, you're well in the realm of speculation.'

'Indeed, I am, sir.' Sinclair nodded vigorously. 'But speculation is what this case has forced on us. And speaking of necessary connections, this has been our main problem. I firmly believe there was no personal connection *whatsoever* between the murderer and the people at Melling Lodge, other than the one that existed in his mind, and which we've been trying to unravel.'

Sampson clicked his tongue with irritation. 'Now come on, Angus, we've heard all this before. You've had your run. Right from the start you've insisted this man was no ordinary criminal. There was plenty of evidence to suggest he broke into that house with the intention of robbing it. What happened next was tragic. Terrible. But trying to turn a violent and possibly deranged man into some kind of . . .' He made a gesture of distaste. '. . . some kind of *twisted* force of evil isn't going to help us *catch* him.

'You say he killed that woman in Kent, Mrs Reynolds. But you don't *know* that. Granted, there are some superficial similarities between the two crimes. But what you've done is make an *assumption* because it fits your theory. The same applies to this business in Belgium four years ago. Now you've got him committing a whole string of murders and you've been warning us for weeks he's going to strike again. *When*, may I ask?'

The chief superintendent ran his hand lightly over his brilliantined hair. He leaned forward. 'What's needed here – what's been needed from the start – is the application of normal police procedures. Nothing glamorous and new-fangled. No trying to see into the mind of the criminal, thinking somehow you can read his thoughts. Just good old-fashioned police work. Plenty of sweat, plenty of shoe leather. That's the way to proceed.'

Sinclair had listened to him with an expression of rapt attention. Now he spoke. 'What did you have in mind, sir?'

Sampson sat back. 'I should have thought that was obvious,' he said. 'What do we know about this man? Not a lot, I grant you. But we do know *one* thing. He owns a motorbike. And he uses it. Now, I realize you've gone through that list of recent purchasers provided by Harley-Davidson. But for heaven's sake, man! What about registrations?'

'Motorcycle registrations?' The chief inspector seemed taken aback by the notion. 'Yes, I saw a piece about that in the *Express* the other day. Ferris, was it? He seemed to have the same idea. I wonder where he got it?'

Sampson turned brick red.

'As a matter of fact, sir, it's something I've considered and discarded.' Sinclair turned his attention back to the assistant commissioner. 'Do you know how many motorcycles are registered in the south of England? Close to a hundred and fifty thousand. Even setting aside the enormous burden a procedure like the one Mr Sampson is suggesting would place on the various authorities, I had to wonder what it would achieve. Armed with only the rough physical details we possess – a large man with dark brown hair and a moustache he may or may not have shaved off by now – police officials would presumably have to interview each and every one of these licence holders to see if they approximate the description. And then the thought occurred to me – what guarantee do we have that his vehicle is legally registered? Or that he doesn't keep it hidden somewhere, only using it when he needs to? It's true, this man in many ways is an enigma to us. But whatever else, we know he's not a complete blockhead.' Unlike some others the chief inspector could mention.

Sampson stared at him angrily. His face showed open dislike. 'All right, Sinclair. I think we've heard enough.'

Parkhurst cleared his throat. 'Yes, I believe it's time to—' He broke off at the sound of a loud knock and turned his head towards the door, which had opened. Madden stood framed in the doorway. He held a piece of paper in his hand. A secretary hovered behind his tall figure, making nervous gestures.

'Sorry to interrupt you, sir. It's something urgent.'

'Madden, is it?' Irritation sharpened the assistant commissioner's peremptory tone. 'Can't it wait, man?'

'No, sir. I'm afraid it can't.'

Madden's long legs propelled him across the carpet in a few strides. He went to Sinclair's side and handed him the piece of paper he was carrying. He bent and whispered in the chief inspector's ear. Sinclair gave a slight start. His face lit up. 'Sir, I must ask for this meeting to be suspended.' He rose abruptly.

'What?' Parkhurst gaped at him.

'Now, just a minute—!' Sampson began.

'We're on to him!' Sinclair held up the piece of paper. 'This is our man.'

'You've *found* him?' Parkhurst demanded.

'Not yet, sir. But we have his name.' The chief inspector's eye was bright. 'What's more we'll have a photograph of him before the day's out.'

'A *photograph*?'

'Courtesy of the War Office. He was in the Army, just as we thought. Sir, I must urge you to let me get moving on this. Any delay could be dangerous.' Sinclair gathered his file. He stood poised to go.

'Well, I don't know . . .' The assistant commissioner's watery gaze circled the room. Sampson tried to catch his eye.

'May *I* say something, sir?' Bennett spoke for the first time. 'Chief Inspector Sinclair has handled this inquiry from the outset. He's familiar with every aspect of it. If there's any possibility of a quick arrest, I think we should let him proceed. As he said, delay's the last thing we want to risk at this moment.'

'Sir . . . sir . . .?' Sampson plucked at Sir George's arm. 'We shouldn't be rushed into this.'

'Not now, Chief Superintendent!' Parkhurst snapped with impatience. His glance came to rest on Sinclair. 'Very well, Chief Inspector. Get on with it. But this matter is not concluded – do I make myself clear?'

'Quite clear, sir.'

'And you *will* keep me informed.'

Sinclair was already moving towards the door, with Madden at his heels. As he reached it, Bennett called out, 'By the way, what *is* his name?'

The chief inspector checked. He glanced at the piece of paper in his hand and looked up. 'Pike,' he said crisply. 'Sergeant Major Amos Pike.'

10

'ARE WE SURE about the photograph, John? You're certain the War Office have one?'

'They must have, sir. Colonel Jenkins is chasing it up now. Tozer will explain.'

The two men hastened up the stairs from the first floor and along the uncarpeted corridor to Sinclair's office.

'My God, we'd better be right about this,' the chief inspector muttered. 'Otherwise you and I may be forced to seek refuge in distant parts. In my case, Timbuktu may not be far enough!'

He threw open the door of his office and they went in. Sergeant Hollingsworth sat behind Madden's desk with an open pad before him. Styles stood at his shoulder, while a third man was seated in a chair opposite. Lean and suntanned, with close-cut fair hair, he wore a well-pressed brown suit and a patterned red tie.

'This is Mr Tozer,' Madden said. 'Mr Tozer – Chief Inspector Sinclair.'

The man rose and offered his hand to Sinclair who shook it. A white ridge of scar tissue showed on his face, running from the corner of one eye to below his cheekbone.

'I'm delighted to meet you, Mr Tozer. I take it our message reached you?'

'Yes, sir. Last night when I got home.' He spoke with a marked Cockney accent.

'Your sister wasn't expecting you till the weekend.'

'I came back early, sir. It's been raining for three days in North Wales. When Milly gave me your message I thought I'd come down here in person. I always wanted to see the inside of Scotland Yard. Fact is, I was hoping to work here one day.' He displayed a crooked grin.

'Were you, now?'

The chief inspector shifted Tozer's chair so that it was facing his own desk. Hollingsworth had risen, but Sinclair waved him down.

'Stay there, Sergeant. We'll need a note of this.' To Styles, he said, 'Bring in a chair for Mr Madden, Constable. And then you might fetch Mr Tozer a cup of tea.'

He waited until Madden was seated in a chair alongside his desk.

'You were saying you'd hoped to be a policeman?'

'That's right, sir. I reckoned I was cut out for police work, especially after the time I spent with Captain Miller. But when I came to after our car was hit by that shell I found I had a flipper missing.' He grinned and held up his left arm, displaying the shirt pinned back under his jacket sleeve, covering the stump of his wrist. 'Well, bang went my hopes of joining the Met!'

The chief inspector inclined his head. 'I'm sorry to

hear that. Now, about this name you've given us. Pike. You're sure that's right?'

'I am,' Tozer replied, without hesitation. 'Like I was saying to the Inspector, I remember the whole business clearly. It's not something you'd be likely to forget.' His eyes narrowed. 'Do you mind my asking, sir – but why do you want to know about it now?'

'I don't mind your asking, Mr Tozer.' A smile touched the chief inspector's lips. 'But I'd be obliged for the moment if you'd answer our questions. We're somewhat pressed for time.'

Madden interrupted, 'I came for you as soon as I got Pike's name, sir, and after I'd rung Colonel Jenkins at the War Office. But I dare say you'd like to hear it from the beginning . . .'

'Would you do that, Mr Tozer?' Sinclair turned to him. 'Start with the crime scene, please. Captain Miller was assigned to the case, I assume. Did you work with him regularly?'

'Yes, I did, sir. The captain always used me as his clerk. We seemed to hit it off.'

'And how long had you worked together?'

'Going on six months. From the beginning of 1917. That's when I got posted to the investigation branch. Happiest day of my life, you might say.' Tozer looked up and saw Styles with a cup of tea standing beside him. 'Just put it down, would you, son?'

He displayed his stump with a grin and the constable reddened. He placed the cup and saucer on the chief inspector's desk.

'Your happiest day, Mr Tozer?'

'Yes, sir. I was sent to France in early 1916, so I was there for the Somme, and afterwards.'

'You took part in the battles?'

'Oh, no, sir.' Tozer dropped his blue eyes. 'No, we were posted down the line. The men would go up to the forward trenches, but we had to wait in case any of them turned back. Sometimes they'd lose their nerve, and it was our job to pick them up. No more than boys many of them were . . . but they called them deserters just the same.' He lifted his gaze. 'They used to look at us, the Tommies, as they went by, up to the front. I'd never seen hate like that in anyone's eyes before . . .'

He fell silent. No one spoke. He shifted his gaze from the chief inspector to Madden. 'I reckon you know what I'm talking about, sir.'

Madden moved his head a fraction. 'It's in the past now, Mr Tozer,' he said gently. 'Best to put it from your mind.'

'Thank you, sir. I try to.'

Sinclair let a few moments pass. Then he spoke again: 'So you joined the Special Investigation Branch?'

'Yes, sir . . .' Tozer gathered himself. 'Well, not *as such* – the branch wasn't formed until after the war – but the Military Police were already detailing squads to do investigative work and I got myself posted to one which was attached to a provost company stationed at Poperinge. That's where I met Captain Miller. We were working on another case – a theft of goods in the railyards – when he got the order to drop everything and go directly to St Martens.'

'That was the village closest to the farm, was it not?' Sinclair shifted in his chair. 'How far away was the military camp?'

'Only a couple of miles. It was an area they used a lot for rest camps. Troops coming out of the line would spend about a week there before going back up. This particular battalion – it was from the South Notts Regiment – had been there four or five days.'

'From the file it seems that the soldiers were regarded as the only suspects. Why was that?'

Tozer tugged his earlobe. 'Well, for one thing, there weren't that many civilians around. The war had pretty well cleaned them out. A few of the farms were still being worked and there were people in the village. But the Belgian police and *gendarmerie* had been at work before we got there, checking on their own citizens. They reckoned they could account for all of them. And then there were the bodies, sir. Well, three of them. The husband and the two sons. They'd been bayoneted, no doubt about that. Expert job, too. One thrust each.'

Sinclair glanced at Madden.

'So Miller took over? It became a British investigation?'

'Not entirely, sir. The victims were civilians. But the Belgians had asked for our assistance and it was understood Captain Miller would handle everything on the military side and keep the Belgian authorities informed.'

'The woman who was killed, the farmer's wife,

where did you find her body? Describe the scene, if you will.'

Tozer reached forward for his cup of tea. He took a sip and then replaced the cup on its saucer. He licked his lips. 'She was in the bedroom upstairs, lying across the bed with her skirt and drawers ripped off. Her throat had been cut.'

'The assumption, Captain Miller's assumption, was that she had been raped?' The chief inspector put it in the form of a question.

'Oh, yes, sir. In fact, when he read the Belgian pathologist's report he asked him to go back and re-examine the body. He thought he must be wrong. But the pathologist confirmed there was no trace of seminal fluid and no sign of forcible entry.'

'So the captain was surprised?'

'He was. And not just by that. One of the things he noted, you may have seen it in the file, was the difference between the upstairs and the down. In the kitchen, where the men's bodies were found, you might have wondered how it could have happened. There wasn't a plate broken, just one chair overturned, as I recall. They must have been killed in a matter of seconds. Upstairs was a different story. She'd put up a fight. The mirror was smashed and the curtains torn off one of the windows.' He shook his head regretfully. 'Strong, fine-looking woman she was. Lovely fair hair. Lollondays, they called her in the district.'

'What was that?' Sinclair prompted him.

Tozer blushed. 'That's as close as I can get to it, sir.

It's a French word, means the Dutchwoman. She came from Holland. Spoke a few words of English, we were told. She was a favourite with the lads when they came out of the line. I don't mean she . . .' He flushed again. 'More like a mother, if you take my meaning. She'd cook for them at the farm, lay on omelettes and fried potatoes and the like. Well, she charged, of course, but the men liked to go there from camp.

'This lot from the battalion – fifteen men from B Company – they'd been there earlier, that same week, and they'd booked again to come back that night. We had no trouble getting their names. They owned up straight away. Said they'd gone there and come back in a group.'

'But Captain Miller didn't believe them?'

Tozer pursed his lips, frowning. 'it wasn't like that exactly. See, those lads were the obvious suspects. Or, anyway, the first ones that came to hand. And the captain knew, any time a Tommy found himself face to face with a redcap he'd play deaf and dumb. Like I said, they hated us. So he went at them hard. He reckoned if they'd done it together, one of them would crack. And if they hadn't, if it was just a few of them who were involved, the others were likely to know about it and he'd get at the truth that way. But after he'd had the last one in I remember him saying he didn't think it was them.'

'He'd dismissed them as suspects?' Sinclair was surprised.

'Oh, no, sir. He meant to question them again. But they were off that night, heading back to the front.'

'He didn't try to hold them?'

'Nothing to hold them *on*. But it didn't matter. They weren't going anywhere. Just back to the salient.'

The chief inspector looked at Madden questioningly.

'Passchendaele, sir. That's where the battle was fought. Near Ypres.'

'It was just a few square miles of mud and craters,' Tozer explained. 'You crossed over the canal and you were there. Death's Land, the Tommies called it. All there was was mud and corpses. They didn't expect to come back.'

Sinclair stared at his blotter. He was silent for several seconds. 'In this case, seven did,' he said finally. 'Of the fifteen. But Captain Miller didn't interview them again, as far as I can gather.'

Tozer's eyes widened. 'Only seven . . . I didn't know . . . I'm sorry . . .' He glanced at Madden again and sighed. 'No, sir, the captain never asked to see them again. By that time he was on a different track.'

'That's what we thought.' Sinclair sat forward. 'That's what I want to know about.'

Tozer took another sip of tea. He had gone a little pale, Billy Styles thought, watching from his place beside Sergeant Hollingsworth. 'The day after the battalion left, Captain Miller got a message from Poperinge. They were holding a deserter there. He was up for court martial. He claimed he had information about the murders at the farmhouse.'

'What was his name?'

Tozer searched his memory. 'Duckman . . .? No,

Duckham. William Duckham. He was from the same battalion as those fifteen lads, but a different company.'

'Did Captain Miller interview him?'

'Yes, he did. At the detention barracks at Poperinge.'

'Were you present?'

'I was.' Tozer touched the scar on his cheek. 'The lad – Duckham – was in a bad way. He hadn't been with the battalion long. Only gone into the line once, but that was enough and when they came out he'd made a run for it. Poor boy. He was shaking all over, couldn't stop himself. Maybe he thought it would help his case if he told us what he knew . . .'

'Which was?'

'Duckham told the captain he'd got as far as the farm and then holed up in the barn, which was a little way from the main house. Found a spot in the loft behind some hay and lay there during the day. At night he'd come down and forage for food. He couldn't get himself to move any further, he said. He just lay there—'

Tozer broke off to reach for his tea-cup. The chief inspector controlled his impatience.

'The night it happened he heard the men from B Company arrive and leave, though he didn't see them. He was lying low. But after they'd gone he crawled out from behind the hay and was about to climb down the ladder when the barn door opened and someone came in. Duckham heard him moving about down below, but it wasn't till the man switched on a torch that he saw who it was.'

'Pike?' Sinclair asked, in a low voice.

Tozer nodded. 'Duckham knew him by sight. He wasn't in his company, but everyone in the battalion knew Pike. There was a joke that went round, or so he told us. No one in B Company gave a damn about Jerry. It was Pike they were scared of.'

'He was sergeant major of B Company?'

'That's right. Quite a hero in his way. I'll tell you about that in a moment.' Tozer emptied his tea-cup. 'Duckham had his head over the edge of the loft, and since he didn't dare stir he saw everything. He said Pike had a rifle and knapsack with him and the first thing he did was fix a bayonet to the rifle. Then he opened the knapsack and took out—' He broke off, shaking his head. 'You won't credit this, sir, I know the captain had a hard time believing it, but according to Duckham what he did next was put on a *gas mask*.'

Sinclair expelled his breath in a soundless sigh. His eyes met Madden's. Tozer looked from one to the other. He seemed to be expecting more of a reaction from them.

'Go on, Mr Tozer.'

'When he'd done that he stood still for a few moments. Sort of *growling*, Duckham said. Making these noises behind the mask. Next thing he was out of the barn door and Duckham heard a whistle. Just one long blast. He said before he'd even had time to crawl back behind the hay he heard the woman screaming. Then nothing more. He lay where he was and about ten minutes later Pike came back into the barn. Or he assumed it was him, because he didn't budge. After a minute he heard the barn door being shut, but he stayed where he was for another half-hour until he was sure there was no one about. Then he climbed down and went over to the house. When he found the bodies downstairs he just grabbed whatever food he could and ran for it. He was picked up two days later outside Poperinge.'

The door behind Tozer opened suddenly and Bennett put his head inside. His quick glance took in the scene.

'I won't bother you now, Chief Inspector. Fill me in as soon as you can, please.'

He shut the door.

'Well!' Sinclair sat back. 'So Miller knew it was Pike he was after. What did he do next?'

Tozer's eyes crinkled. 'He didn't exactly *know*, sir. All this had come from a man who was up for a court martial. He might have had something against the sergeant major. He might have been spinning a yarn, hoping to save his own skin. Word had got around about the killings.'

'Miller said that?'

'Yes, sir, he talked to me about it. He liked to do that. Think aloud. He wanted to question Pike first. So he made inquiries and he found out the battalion had crossed the canal the night before. That meant they'd be in the line for anything up to a week. If it had been a matter of a day or two he might have waited until they came out. But he felt it was too long, the case was too serious. So we went after them.'

'You crossed into the salient?' The chief inspector showed surprise.

'Oh, no, sir! Thank God!' Tozer shut his eyes as if in prayer. 'The battalion command post was this side of the canal, but that was bad enough. No end of shells falling all around. I thought we were going to cop it for sure. But the captain was a real terrier. Once he'd got his teeth into something he wouldn't let go. There was an officer called Crane in command there, a major.' Tozer nodded, as though in recollection. 'Copped it himself a week later, we heard. Anyway, when Captain Miller said he wanted Pike sent back, Crane flat refused. Said the battalion was heavily engaged and the sergeant major was one of his best men. Now he couldn't do that, you know, refuse. Not in *that* situation. Not if he was a *general*. Captain Miller had the authority. But he took the major aside and explained how things stood. He said he didn't want Pike's name associated with the crime if the charge wasn't true. Which it would be if he had to issue an arrest order. He wanted Pike to have a chance to clear himself. Well, after he'd put it like that, Crane had to agree and he sent a runner up the line straight away with orders for Pike to be sent back.'

'I take it he never appeared.' The chief inspector eased some stiffness from his shoulder. His gaze remained fixed on Tozer's face.

'No, he didn't, sir. We waited there in the command post all night. The runner came back next morning. He'd reached B Company and found that all the officers were dead or wounded. Pike was alive, so he passed on the major's order directly to him.'

'Do you know how that was phrased?' Madden broke his long silence. 'Was there any mention of the Military Police wanting to talk to him?'

'No, there wasn't. I know that for a fact. Captain Miller was with the major when he spoke to the runner.'

'But he'd seen you, hadn't he? The runner, I mean. A pair of redcaps.'

'I reckon so. Mr Miller thought the same thing. He said he must have told Pike. It was the only explanation.'

'For what?' This time it was Sinclair who spoke.

'After the runner had delivered his message he left to return. There wasn't any trench line as such. The troops were dug in in craters. Pike was sharing one with two other men — neither was from the lot we'd questioned, by the way. They both said the same thing later. Right after the runner left, Pike vanished.'

'*Vanished?*'

'He crawled out of the crater and they never saw him again.'

'You mean he headed back to his own lines?' Madden asked.

'No, that was it.' Tozer shook his head hard. 'He went *forward*, in the direction of the enemy. They both said the same thing. It was the last anyone ever saw of him. Till they found his body.'

*

'*His body?*' The chief inspector sat bolt upright. Madden was frowning.

Tozer looked from one to the other.

'Didn't you know he was dead? I thought . . .' He broke off and stared at them. 'Cor! You didn't think he was still alive, did you?' And then, as the truth suddenly dawned on him, '*Christ! It's Melling Lodge!*'

In the hush that followed his exclamation the squeak of Sergeant Hollingsworth's pen was clearly audible. The two detectives looked at each other. It was Sinclair who spoke: 'What makes you say that, Mr Tozer?'

'Because . . . because that's what I thought when I read about it first. I mean it reminded me of St Martens. A lot of people murdered in a house. I saw somewhere the lady had her throat cut. But I didn't think . . . I never thought it was *Pike*!'

The chief inspector made a small adjustment in his position. He rested his forearms on the desk.

'You say his body was found. What do you mean, exactly? Did you see it yourself?'

'Oh, no, sir. It didn't happen like that. Did it, sir?' He appealed to Madden.

'Sometimes there was a lull in the fighting,' Madden explained. 'Both sides would hold off firing and allow the wounded to be collected. Bodies would be picked up at the same time. Otherwise they would lie there.'

'Take Passchendaele now,' Tozer amplified. 'More than forty thousand bodies were never found. I read it in a newspaper. *Forty thousand!* That was the mud, you see.'

'But Pike's was, you say,' the chief inspector reminded him. 'Why? What makes you so sure?'

'It was *reported* found. About a week later, when Captain Miller was writing up the case. It was listed among the bodies brought back.'

Madden spoke again: 'If we're right about this, sir, what it means is they found a body with Pike's identity disc tucked into the puttees or fixed to the braces. Also his pay book, I imagine. And, if he wanted to be thorough, his tunic with his rank and his regimental badges on it. That would certainly have been enough to establish his identity. Do you agree, Mr Tozer?'

The other man nodded.

'There's no reason why anyone from his own battalion should have seen it. In any case, they would have been out of the line by the time it was brought back.'

Sinclair chewed his lip. 'Let's be clear in our minds about this. Granted, he could have switched identities with some body he found on the battlefield. But how could he have got back himself?'

'He might have faked a wound,' Madden suggested.

'Not the easiest thing, I imagine.'

Tozer put up his hand. 'I've just remembered, sir. I

saw Pike's service record – the captain had it. Just before all this happened he'd been in hospital at Boulogne. Concussion, it was. Now that could have been useful.'

'Useful?'

'It's not an easy thing for the doctors to be sure about. There were those that tried to fake it. Men who had it were sent back for observation. Pike would have known that.'

'Sent back to Boulogne?'

'Or Eetaps. Once he was there he could have slipped out of the hospital. It was a dodge deserters tried.'

Sinclair directed a questioning glance at Madden. The inspector shrugged.

'It's quite possible, sir. Of course, he would still have had the problem of getting back to England. But it could be done, provided he had the nerve.'

'Oh, he had nerve all right!' Tozer interjected.

'Yes, I want to hear about that.' Sinclair turned back to him. 'Go on with your story.'

Tozer was silent, collecting his thoughts. Then he resumed: 'We waited there at the command post all day and in the evening a report came back that Pike was missing. One of the officers from another company was among the walking wounded and he told the major what the two men had said, that Pike had left the crater without a word and gone forward. Captain Miller put two and two together. He reckoned Pike was his man and that he'd decided to end it on the battlefield rather than face a charge of murder. So we left and went back to Poperinge, and the captain sat down to write his report. While he was doing that we heard about the body being recovered. Captain Miller put it all in his report. He wrote a memorandum to go with the file, saying he believed Pike was the killer and giving his reasons and recommending the case should be marked closed. He was just finishing it when he got a message from the assistant provost marshal – Colonel Strachan – to send the file up to staff headquarters. The brass hats wanted to see it.'

'The General Staff?'

'Someone there had asked for it – we never found out who.' Tozer shrugged. 'Captain Miller sent the file off, and then a week later he was called in by Colonel Strachan. He came back hopping mad. He said they were going to bury the whole thing.'

'His investigation?'

'No, just his findings about Pike. The case was to be closed as far as the Army was concerned and the file sent to the provost marshal. But the captain's memorandum was removed. The Belgian police weren't to be informed of his findings.'

Sinclair sat back in astonishment. 'Could they *do* that?'

'In the *Army*? In *wartime*?' Tozer scoffed. 'You were just told to get on with it.' He touched the scar on his cheek again, running his fingers lightly over the ridged flesh. 'Captain Miller was given the full story later. Someone at headquarters thought he ought to know the truth. I mentioned about Pike being a hero. Fact was, he'd won the Military Medal in 1916 and then he won it again the following year. Destroyed a

German machine-gun post single-handed. So he was due the bar and since Field Marshal Haig was making a tour of the front around that time, handing out medals, they included Pike in one of the ceremonies. That was just before he got concussed, so it would only have been a month or two before the murders. There was a nice snap of the two of them taken by an Army photographer.' Tozer's grin took on a cynical twist. 'It appeared in some of the London papers. "Field Marshal Decorates Hero."'

'And two months later it's "Field Marshal Hobnobs With Mass Murderer."' Sinclair scratched his nose. 'Yes, I can see how that might have concentrated a few minds.'

'There'd already been reports about the killings in the French newspapers. If they got hold of Pike's name from the Belgian police it wouldn't be long before the facts were out. So they made up a story about a gang of deserters being suspected and there being a big hunt under way for them.' Tozer looked scornful. 'Whoever it was talked to the captain said that since Pike was dead justice had been served and the whole business was best forgotten.'

'And how did Miller feel about that?'

'*Hopping mad!*' Tozer's eyes flashed. 'He said it was a disgrace.'

'Was that the end of it?' Sinclair asked.

'Pretty well. The captain swore an affidavit for the court martial at Poperinge saying Duckham had been of great assistance to him, but it didn't do any good. They shot him just the same. He didn't forget about

Pike. It was always on his mind. Almost the last thing I remember him saying before we got hit by that shell was how he wasn't going to let it rest. He was going to take it up with *someone*.'

Tozer fell silent. He stared at the floor.

Sinclair coughed. 'It's my impression you served under a fine officer, Mr Tozer.'

'I did that, sir.' The blue eyes lifted.

'And I deeply regret the injury you suffered. I think the force is the poorer for it.'

Tozer made a quick bobbing motion with his head.

The chief inspector got to his feet and Tozer followed suit. They shook hands.

'We may need to get in touch with you again. But in the meantime I'd be grateful if you'd keep this to yourself. We'll get Pike's photograph into the newspapers, but we need to be careful what appears in print.'

'Don't worry, sir. I won't breathe a word.'

He shook hands with Madden and nodded to the other two men.

'Constable Styles will see you out.' Sinclair sat down. 'And thank you again.'

Tozer had his hand on the doorknob when he checked and turned to face them. 'There's one more thing I'd like to say, sir . . .'

'Go ahead.' The chief inspector looked up.

'When you catch up with him, with Pike, you'll watch yourself, won't you?'

'Indeed we will,' Sinclair replied. 'And thank you for the warning. But why do you say that?'

'I forgot to tell you before, I should have mentioned it. We met him, the captain and me.'

'No, by God, you didn't mention it.' Sinclair was on his feet again.

'Only we didn't know, of course. Not then . . .' Tozer bit his lip. 'It was when the captain was interrogating those men from B Company. Pike was the man who marched them in.'

'The company sergeant major. Of course! What about him, Mr Tozer?'

'Well, the funny thing is we talked about him afterwards, Captain Miller and me.' Tozer frowned. 'The captain was just saying he didn't think it was any of the lads he'd questioned, and then he laughed and said: "But did you get a look at that sergeant major? Now if he'd been in the line-up . . ." And I knew just what he meant, because I'd had the same feeling myself. As soon as Pike walked in, I thought: Now there's a killer! Eyes like stones.'

11

PIKE WAS ABLE to keep to his schedule that Saturday morning. Mrs Aylward had caught the nine-twenty train to Waterloo, as planned, confirming with her last words to the household staff her intention of returning the following Tuesday. He had the weekend free, and although his employer had asked him to attend to some outdoor tasks on Monday he had no intention of obeying her wishes. He knew that neither the maid, Ethel Bridgewater, nor Mrs Rowley, the cook, would report his absence to their mistress. They took care not to cross him.

It was ten minutes past eleven by his hunter – the watch was engraved with his father's initials and had been his parting gift to him – when he opened the wooden gate in the back fence and stepped into Mrs Troy's garden.

Already his excitement was stirring, throbbing in the pit of his stomach like a deep, slow pulse. He was impatient to be on his way. But he'd been troubled by the memory of the old woman's distress on his last visit. He regretted having departed in haste then without first determining its cause. Unease had plagued him all week.

Now he walked past the shed and went directly to

the kitchen door, entering without knocking as he always did. He deposited the parcel of food he had brought on the kitchen table and continued soft-footed through into the narrow hallway. The door to the front parlour was open. He paused on the threshold and looked in.

She was in her customary chair by the window with the tortoiseshell cat on her lap. The knitted shawl she favoured was draped about her shoulders and a plaid blanket covered her knees. The day was cloudy, the air cool and autumnal. Pike shifted on his feet, making a small sound. He didn't want to startle her.

'Mr Biggs . . .?' She turned eagerly.

'No, it's me,' Pike said gruffly. 'Grail.'

His words had an astonishing effect on her. She started in shock and clutched involuntarily at the cat, which she had been stroking. It let out a yowl of surprise and sprang from her lap. Her eyes stared blindly at him.

'What's the matter, Mrs Troy?' He seldom used her name.

Her mouth opened and shut. She seemed unable to speak.

'Are you sick? Can I get you something?' He had never made such an offer before.

'No . . .' At last she managed to produce a word. 'No, thank you . . .'

Pike checked an impulse to approach nearer. He saw that she was terrified, but couldn't think why. He was accustomed to causing fear in others. In the past he had reduced men bigger and stronger than he to white-faced silence with a single look. They had sensed the menace he presented, terrible in its stillness. But he had never by word or action sought to intimidate *her*. The word 'irony' was not in his vocabulary, but he would have appreciated its significance in this instance. She was the one person who had nothing to fear from him. Her physical well-being was almost as precious to him as his own. He lived in perpetual anxiety that she might die suddenly, ending his occupation of the shed, bringing havoc to his enterprises.

The situation was beyond him. In the whole of his bleak existence he had never learned how to coax or comfort. He could no more have led her gently, by degrees, to the point of revelation than he could have soothed a sick child. He saw only that it was his presence that disturbed her and he acted accordingly, turning on his heel and leaving the room.

But his mind was in turmoil as he paused briefly in the kitchen to put away the food he had brought.

Mr Biggs?

Pike had never heard the name before.

He walked quickly across the small patch of lawn to the shed and unsnapped the heavy padlock. Daylight flooded the dark interior as he flung open the door and at once he noticed the white envelope lying on the cement floor at his feet.

*

Harold Biggs paused in the shadow of the hawthorn hedge to dry the sweat on his forehead. He was thankful that the days were growing cooler. If he was perspiring heavily it was only partly due to the two-mile walk from Knowlton to Rudd's Cross. His nervousness had been increasing all morning.

'You're going out there *again*?' Jimmy Pullman had professed disbelief when Biggs announced his plans for that Saturday in the Bunch of Grapes. 'You should tell old Wolverton to go hopping sideways. What's the old girl's problem, anyway? What's it you're supposed to be doing for her?'

Biggs had been vague in his reply. Some minor legal business, he implied. He didn't tell Jimmy either that Mr Wolverton had given him the whole day off in recognition of his spontaneous offer to return once more to Rudd's Cross in order to deal with the Grail situation.

The thought of the tankards in Mrs Troy's silver cabinet had weighed on Harold's mind all week. Even now, as he approached her cottage through the stubbled fields, he didn't know whether, in the end, he would have the nerve to act on his plan.

But he'd come prepared. He had brought his brief-case, a bulky, old-fashioned article with clumsy straps which he wanted to change for the sleeker, more modern versions now on sale. Today, though, he was glad of its size. The mugs would fit inside it comfortably.

He knocked on the front door of the cottage and then waited patiently, remembering how long it had taken her to get to the door on his last visit. After a full minute he knocked again. There was no response from within.

Biggs walked around the cottage to the kitchen door. As he pushed it open he heard a subdued tapping coming from the direction of the garden shed behind him. The green wooden door was shut, but the padlock had been removed. He could hear someone moving about inside.

So Grail had come, and presumably was getting his things together preparatory to moving out.

Harold felt his stomach tighten. It was all going according to plan. Once Grail had departed, no doubt angry and resentful at having been turfed out at such short notice, he could remove the tankards from the cabinet, safe in the knowledge that their disappearance, if it was noted at all, would be laid to the other man's account.

But he still didn't know if he had the courage to do it . . .

Harold took a deep, calming breath. He went into the kitchen, calling out in a low voice as he did so, 'Mrs Troy, are you there? It's Mr Biggs from Folkestone . . .'

Again there was no reply.

Removing his checked cap, he laid it on the kitchen table alongside his briefcase. Then he went through to the hallway and looked into the parlour. The chair by the window was empty. His glance shifted automatically to the glass-fronted cabinet on the opposite side of the room. The tankards were where he had left them.

Biggs was nonplussed. He couldn't conceive of the old woman having left the house for any reason, particularly in view of their appointment. He had formed a picture of her life in which she was confined to the cottage. It was hard to imagine her even stepping into the garden.

A doorway on the opposite side of the hall stood ajar, giving a glimpse of a dining-table and chairs. Just past it a narrow stairway led to the upper floor. Harold paused at the foot of this. He had detected the glow of two eyes in the darkness at the top of the carpeted stairs, and as his own grew accustomed to the gloom he made out the shape of a cat. He remembered the animal from his earlier visit. It sat there with paws folded looking down at him.

'Mrs Troy?' he called up the stairs.

After a moment's hesitation he climbed to the upper landing, stepping over the cat, which made no move to get out of his way. Two doors stood ajar. A third was shut. He knocked on that and heard a voice respond faintly from within. Harold opened the door and saw Mrs Troy's figure stretched out on a bed, half sitting, half lying, propped against a bank of pillows. She wore the same dark bombazine skirt as before and her upper body was wrapped in a plaid blanket. The curtains had been three-quarters drawn on the window overlooking the back garden and the dull light entering the room left the corners in shadow.

'I'm sorry, am I disturbing you?' Harold hesitated on the threshold. He saw her face turning from side to side, like a plant seeking the sunlight. He recalled the clouded milky gaze. 'It's me . . . Mr Biggs, from Folkestone.'

'Oh, Mr *Biggs*!' The words were accompanied by a gasp of relief. 'I wasn't sure you'd come.'

'I said I would.' He spoke resentfully, as though he had been misjudged.

'He's *here* . . .' Her agitated whisper barely reached his ears. 'Mr *Grail* . . .'

'Yes, I know. I heard him in the shed. I'll just slip down now and have a word with him. See that everything's in order.'

'Mr Biggs . . .' Now a note of anxiety had come into her voice. She held out her hand to him from the bed. He pretended not to see it. He had come here on *business*. He didn't want this human contact between them. But her hand remained there between them and in the end he had to come forward and take it in his.

'Be *careful*!'

'Why? What do you mean?' He recoiled from her clutching fingers.

'Just ask him to go nicely . . . Tell him I'm sorry, it can't be helped . . .'

Nicely! Harold stoked his rising temper. The thought of what he planned to do – of the advantage he meant to take of this frail old creature – made him dislike her all the more. He withdrew his hand from hers.

'Don't worry, Mrs Troy,' he said curtly. A fresh idea had just occurred to him and he hastened to put it into words. 'You just lie there. After I've spoken to Grail I'll make you a cup of tea and bring it up. I can see this is upsetting you. You must stay here and rest.'

He'd been nerving himself all morning to remove

the mugs in the cabinet from under her nose, under her near-sightless gaze, but this was an unlooked-for piece of good fortune. (*'You're a lucky devil!'* He grinned, remembering.) Already he was breathing easier. As he turned towards the door he caught sight of his reflection in the dressing-table mirror: his solid figure, on the verge of being overweight, bulged at the waistline. He drew in his stomach.

'Just leave Grail to me,' he said.

He hurried down the stairs, out through the kitchen and into the garden.

He would do it!

The certainty had come to him as he stood beside the bed and looked down at her helpless figure.

He had found the courage after all!

Impatient now to bring matters to a conclusion – Grail must be sent on his way without further delay – he strode across the small square of lawn and rapped sharply on the shed door.

'Mr Grail?'

Without waiting for a response, he pushed open the door and went inside. A wave of heat enveloped him. The dark interior was lit by a paraffin lamp, which burned brightly on an upturned box in one corner of the room. A man, naked to the waist, was bending down, arranging the folds of a dun-coloured dust cloth over some large, irregularly shaped object in the middle of the shed. Biggs had a fleeting impression he'd been taken by surprise. Then all thoughts were driven from his mind by the sight of the half-clad figure as it rose and turned towards him. The muscular torso, scarred in several places, was shiny with sweat. A high, rank odour like the smell from an animal's cage assailed his nostrils.

'Grail?'

Harold waited for some response from the man, who said nothing. He noticed a metallic object lying on a work-table at the end of the shed. It looked like a piece of machinery, or a motor part. Tools lay beside it.

'Now what's all this?' Biggs put his hands on his hips. 'I take it you got my letter. You're supposed to be moving out of here today.'

He found to his consternation that he couldn't look the man in the face. The single glance he had given him had revealed a close-cropped head and lips drawn down in a thin line. But it was the eyes. They were brown and flat and when Biggs had sought to meet them with his own, to impress his irritation and impatience on this half-dressed ruffian, he had had to look away almost at once. There was something inhuman in his gaze, Harold thought with alarm. The image of an animal came into his mind again. A carnivore. He was forced to move, to ease the cramp that all at once invaded his limbs, and without any conscious intention he walked forward, further into the shed towards the menacing figure of Grail who nevertheless, surprisingly, made way for him, moving to one side and then a little around so that Harold now stood beside the covered object and Grail was closer to the door.

'*Well?*'

The word sprang unbidden to Harold's lips. He spoke because he could not remain silent in the midst of the greater silence that radiated like a force from the other man.

'You're meant to be leaving here,' he repeated helplessly. 'Moving out. Don't you understand?'

Grail's only response was to move again. Harold saw with mounting panic that his way out of the shed was now blocked.

'What are you doing here, anyway?'

He didn't want to know, but he couldn't still his tongue. When he moved himself it was with an involuntary lurch, his cramped leg muscles jerking in a sudden spasm. His foot, dragging along the cement floor, caught in a fold of the dust cloth. Distractedly, he tried to work it free, kicking out in desperation, tugging at the cloth, which gradually worked loose from the object it was covering.

When he saw what was revealed beneath it Harold went deathly pale. He stared in horror at the handlebars of the motorcycle – the machine was still half covered by the cloth – and the red pointed nose of the sidecar. At that same instant he recalled, with an emotion akin to grief, the article he had read in the newspaper the previous Friday.

He looked up into the flat brown eyes. He couldn't hide his knowledge from them, he was too afraid. And now he found his own gaze held fast by the lifeless stare. A warm stream of urine ran down his leg inside his plus-fours.

Harold saw the face of his mother – she had died in

the last year of the war. Other images flocked to his mind. He saw the girl he had picked up in the high street, Jimmy Pullman leaning on the bar in the Bunch of Grapes, Mr Wolverton's freckled scalp, the cat's eyes glowing at the top of the stairs . . . His life sped by like the frames of a hand-cranked cinematograph in a penny arcade.

And all the while he stared into Grail's eyes.

At the last, like a drowning man clutching at a spar, he put his hand in his pocket and felt for his key ring and his good-luck shilling.

It brought him no comfort in his agony. Even as he ran his thumb frantically back and forth along the milled edge, Grail moved towards him and he knew then, with the finality of death, that his luck had run out.

12

THE CHIEF INSPECTOR spoke: 'This is a photograph of the man in question. Amos Pike. We hope to have a better impression of him available within the next few days, but for now we'd be grateful if your newspapers would publish this picture in a prominent position. When you do so, please make it clear that he is not to be approached by any member of the public for any reason, but that the police should be informed of his whereabouts without delay.'

Sinclair paused. His gaze swept over the assembled reporters, two dozen of them, who were seated down both sides of a long table in one of the Yard's conference rooms. He was sitting at the head himself, with Madden on one side of him and Bennett on the other. Earlier, Sinclair had wryly suggested to the deputy assistant commissioner that he absent himself from the gathering. 'My head's on the block here, sir. No need for yours to join it.'

'Do you believe this is the man we're seeking?'

'I do.'

'Then in that case I'll take the chance.' Bennett produced a wintry smile.

'I would like to add something to what I've just

said. It's most unlikely Pike is living under his own name.'

'Why would that be?' The lanky figure of Ferris looked up from his notebook at the far end of the table.

Regarding the man with dislike, which he took care to conceal, Sinclair drew what satisfaction he could from the reflection that today was Saturday and Ferris's newspaper, a daily, would have to wait until Monday before coming to grips with the story. The Sundays would have the first bite of it.

'Pike was reported killed in the war. We have reason to believe he survived it.'

'What reason? Can you tell us?'

'No,' the chief inspector said bluntly, aware that he *had* none, that he was acting purely on supposition. An admission he was not about to share with the likes of Reg Ferris.

The delay in summoning the press had been caused by the time it had taken the War Office to lay its hands on a photograph of the sergeant major. Thursday afternoon and Friday morning had passed without word or sign, causing Sinclair to mutter darkly about hidden hands at work within the military.

'By God, if they try to cover this up again I'll take it to the newspapers. See if I don't!'

Finally, midway through Friday afternoon, the photographs arrived. It was not the usual booted and khaki-clad courier who brought them, but Colonel Jenkins himself, full of apologies and explaining that many wartime pictures remained uncatalogued and it had taken until now to unearth Pike's.

'In fact, we have two, but one's not much use.'

He laid them on Sinclair's desk. The chief inspector groaned. 'I might have guessed . . .'

In one of the prints the well-known figure of Field Marshal Haig was receiving the salute of a soldier – presumably Pike – who stood before him. The raised arm with the hand touching the cap covered all but a small portion of the man's face.

In the second picture the field marshal leaned forward to pin a decoration on the tunic of the soldier whose full profile had been caught by the camera. But even this was of limited value. The combination of the cap's peak, pulled down low over the eyes, and an old-fashioned gravy-dipper moustache that hid the mouth, reduced Pike's identifiable features to a short nose and a prominent thrusting chin.

After his momentary disappointment, the chief inspector had swung into action. Styles was dispatched with the second print to the Yard's photographic laboratory, which had been standing by since Thursday, with instructions to reproduce copies of the photograph, shorn of the field marshal's figure, in large numbers.

Meanwhile, Sinclair commandeered a police artist and sent him, together with Hollingsworth, to see Alfred Tozer in Bethnal Green.

'I should have thought of it while he was here,' the chief inspector castigated himself. 'I put too much faith in what the War Office would produce.'

'We've also got those survivors from B Company,' Madden reminded him. 'Dawkins and Hardy. They'll remember Pike all right.'

'I'd rather stick with Tozer for the time being,' Sinclair maintained. 'He was trained as a policeman and he's got the instincts of a copper. "Eyes like stones." Let's get a sketch from him first, then we can test it on those others.'

Colonel Jenkins, listening to them, asked, 'Then Pike's the man Captain Miller believed was the killer? The one he wrote about in that lost memorandum.'

Sinclair regarded the slight, erect figure sitting ramrod-straight on a chair before him. The colonel's manner had altered since their first meeting. Gone was the edge of impatience, verging on rudeness, which he'd displayed then. Now he seemed disposed to be agreeable. It cut no ice with the chief inspector.

'Not lost. Deliberately destroyed by an officer serving on the General Staff,' he said coldly. 'We have all the facts.'

The colonel was at a loss for words.

'Don't be concerned, I'm not instituting an inquiry. For the present,' Sinclair added.

'That should give them a few sleepless nights,' he confided to Madden after Jenkins had departed. 'Do you know? I'm beginning to understand why you felt the way you did about that lot. We might have caught up with Pike by now if we'd had Miller's report from the outset. If he kills again, then whoever destroyed it will bear part of the blame. And may he rot in hell!'

The chief inspector was questioned by the journal-
ists about Pike's background.

'He enlisted in the Army in 1906, giving his age as
eighteen, though he may have been younger. From
that point on he was a professional soldier. In due
course he reached the rank of sergeant major and
distinguished himself during the war. He was decorated twice for gallantry.'

'But before that?' one of the reporters asked. 'What
about his family? His parents?'

'His parents are dead.' The slight hesitation in
Sinclair's reply passed unnoticed. 'The Nottingham
police are making further inquiries on our behalf.'

'He comes from there?'

'From Nottingham? No, from somewhere in the
district, I believe. We're still seeking information in
that regard.'

The chief inspector had advised Bennett and Madden in advance that he planned to be less than frank
on the subject of Pike's past history. 'Let them dig it
up for themselves. The longer we can keep this from
turning into a shocker, the better. I've asked the Notts
police not to be unduly helpful and I only hope they
manage to delay things a little.'

Sinclair's own request for information had brought
a reply the previous day from the Nottinghamshire
force which had shocked him. Pike's father had been
hanged in 1903 for the murder of his wife. 'They're
sending me the file, but it sounds like a clear-cut case.
He confessed to the murder in open court.'

'Did he . . .?' Madden hardly dared to ask.

Sinclair nodded bleakly. 'Yes, he cut her throat.'

Bennett, too, was shaken by the discovery. 'My God! His lawyer will have a field day!'

The chief inspector glanced at Madden beside him. 'Yes, and I dare say your Viennese friend would have had something to say on the subject.'

'What Viennese friend might that be?' Bennett inquired innocently, and had the rare satisfaction of seeing Angus Sinclair turn scarlet with embarrassment. 'Or shouldn't I ask?'

Before the press conference ended Ferris held up his hand once more. 'I'd like to ask Mr Bennett a question. We understood Chief Superintendent Sampson was going to take over direction of this investigation. Has there been any change in plans?'

'*We?*' Bennett appeared baffled. 'I do recall reading something to that effect in your journal, Mr Ferris, but nowhere else.' He waited until the laughter had died down. 'As you see, Chief Inspector Sinclair is still at the helm and likely to remain so. He has the full confidence of both the assistant commissioner and myself.'

'But what about Mr Sampson?' Ferris persisted. 'I don't see him here today. Hasn't he been advising on this inquiry?'

'The chief superintendent is indisposed.' Bennett's tone was bland. 'But we hope to have the benefit of his expert assistance again before long.'

'Severe indigestion,' Sinclair confided to Madden, when they returned to his office. 'His wife rang in this morning. Comes of having your nose out of joint, I'm told.'

He leaned back in his chair, hands laced behind his head. 'All we can do now is wait. His picture will be in the Sundays. Pray God someone recognizes him. And pray God this is the last weekend we have to sit through waiting for the phone to ring.'

His glance moved from Madden, who was at his desk, to Hollingsworth and Styles, who stood facing him, awaiting orders.

'Well? Have we forgotten anything? Is there something more we can do?'

Madden shifted in his chair.

'Yes, John?'

'I was thinking, sir – that batch of photographs we're sending down to Highfield. Why don't I take them? I know most of the villagers and I could help Constable Stackpole to get them spread around.'

Sinclair frowned. It was the only way he could keep a straight face. 'I could send one of the others. I hate to impose this on you, John.'

'I don't mind, sir.'

'Well, if you're sure . . .'

A little while later, after the door had shut behind Madden's departing figure, Hollingsworth and Styles in their cubby-hole were startled to hear the sound of humming coming from the adjoining office. The song was an old one and they were both familiar with the words which presently reached them, carried on the chief inspector's surprisingly tuneful tenor:

'Taking one consideration with another,
A policeman's lot is not a happy one . . .'

Billy Styles nudged the sergeant. 'Hark at the guv'nor. He's gone mad as a maggot.'

'None of that lip, Constable,' Hollingsworth growled, though he was more than half inclined to agree.

13

THE CANVASS OF Highfield residents brought little result. Although they walked the village from end to end knocking on doors, only one household yielded a positive response, and as Stackpole remarked, you had to wonder if May Birney wasn't overstretching her imagination.

'You think she might be trying too hard?' Madden asked. 'Because she was right about the whistle?'

The constable had been at the station to meet him and together they had put up copies of the poster in the ticket hall and waiting-room. Frowning, Stackpole had stared hard at the heavily moustached face. 'I know *I* haven't seen him, sir. At least, not that I recognize.'

As they walked into the village he told the inspector he had a message for him from Dr Blackwell. Madden had rung the house from London but failed to reach her.

'She asked if you could pass by her surgery later. She's had to go to Guildford. They had some typhoid cases brought into the hospital there and they needed help.' Stackpole smiled under his helmet. '*You*'re looking well, if I may say so, sir.'

'Am I, Will? I can't think why. We've been working like the devil.'

The Birney family lived above their store in the main street. Neither parent had recognized the face on the poster, but May, pink-cheeked from having been caught in the middle of washing her bobbed brown hair, looked hard at it for ten seconds and then said, 'I've seen him before.'

'Now, don't be hasty, girl.' Mr Birney rubbed his bald spot anxiously. 'You don't want to mislead the inspector.'

'The moustache was different.'

'He had a moustache?' Madden sat forward in the chintz-covered armchair. 'You're sure of that?'

'Yes, sir. But not as big as this one. But I'm positive it's the same man. I remember the chin.'

'So you saw him from the side, in profile?'

May Birney nodded.

'Try and picture him without the cap,' the inspector suggested, but she shook her head at once.

'No, he was wearing a cap. That's how I remember him.'

'What sort of cap?'

She didn't know. She couldn't recall. 'Just a cap. It was pulled down low over his eyes, like in the picture.'

'It can't be a military cap,' Madden remarked later, when they paused on the village green to confer. The autumn afternoon was drawing in. Lights were starting to come on in the cottages flanking the grass triangle. 'If there's one place we won't find Pike it's in the Army.'

'There's lots of other kinds, sir. Charabanc drivers, chauffeurs, delivery-men. They all wear caps of one sort or another. And what if it was just an ordinary cloth cap? Most of us have got one of those.'

'Whatever he was wearing, I think she saw him. Talk to her again, Will.'

Madden had noticed the red two-seater parked in front of one of the cottages across the green. Stackpole had seen it, too. 'There's Dr Blackwell now. You'll find her in her surgery, sir. She rents rooms from old Granny Palmer. I'll leave some posters in the pub and the church hall as I go by.'

*

The doctor's waiting-room was empty. The inner door stood ajar. He paused on the threshold.

She was sitting behind a desk writing in a note-book, her brow creased in a frown of concentration. Lamplight gave a glow to her fair skin and he could see the fine golden hairs on her forearms where she had rolled back the sleeves of her white blouse.

'Is that you, John?'

When she looked up and saw it was him, she rose and came straight into his arms. He kissed her. She stood back to study his face. He had always felt she had the power to see into him.

'You're sleeping better.' The doctor spoke approvingly. 'Have you had any luck with your poster?'

He took one from the manila envelope he was carrying and showed it to her. She glanced at it for a few seconds and then shook her head.

'May Birney thinks she's seen him, but she can't remember where.'

He put his arms around her again. Her neck smelled faintly of jasmine. He could never find the words he wanted.

'Let me finish what I'm doing. I won't be long.' She returned to her chair. 'How soon must you go back? Can you stay for dinner? Can you spend the night?'

'The night . . .?' He hadn't expected it. 'I've got nothing with me.'

'Never mind that. I'll find whatever you need. But I warn you, the house is full of relations. Father invited a whole shoal of cousins for the weekend. I can only put you in the old nursery.' She paused. Their eyes met. 'We'll have to be quiet,' she said, smiling. 'Aunt Maud's in the room next door and she's got ears like a bat.'

The joy he felt whenever they were together was tempered by the knowledge of what it would mean to lose her. He knew he would never meet anyone like her again.

She picked up her pen. 'I'm filling in my day-book, my record of patients. I didn't have time this morning. The hospital in Guildford rang and asked me to go in.'

'Typhoid, Will said.'

'Food poisoning.' She made a wry face and went back to her notebook.

He looked about him. A glass-fronted cabinet held medical books and bandages, rolls of lint and wool, splints and surgical gauze. Behind her a partition divided the room and on the other side was a dispensary with shelves of glass-stoppered bottles. A faint smell of antiseptic hung in the air. He saw that she was watching him.

'This is my life,' she said softly. She coloured and looked down.

Her life?

She had given his back to him.

When he spoke the words seemed to come of their own accord, as if he were simply breathing. 'I love you,' he said.

She looked up, still flushed. 'So you've got a tongue, John Madden . . .' Her eyes were bright in the lamplight.

It was as though a wave had lifted him and carried him to her side. He was shaking like a leaf.

'My darling, it's all right . . . Didn't you know . . .?'

She held him fast in the circle of her arms. He heard a noise somewhere near, but he clung to her. She was whispering something in his ear.

'What?' He loosened his hold.

'*Sir, are you there?*' Stackpole's voice sounded loud in the outer room.

'What is it, Will?' He tore himself from her arms.

'*Sir, they've found him!*' The constable burst in on them. He was red in the face and panting.

'Who?'

'*Pike!*'

'*Where?*'

'Ashdown Forest. They're watching him now. At least, they think it's him, that's all I know.' He was breathing hard. 'Guildford have been trying to reach me. Sir, the chief inspector wants you back in London right away . . .!'

*

She took him in her car to the station. He wanted time to speak to her. The words that for so long had been dammed up inside him were ready to overflow. But the whistle of the approaching train sounded as she drew up outside the station.

They kissed in the darkness.

'Promise me you'll take care. Come back as soon as you can.'

Holding her for a moment in his arms he realized with a surge of happiness that the burden of anxiety he'd carried since their first time together had slipped from his shoulders unnoticed.

The fear he'd always had that each meeting might be their last.

Part Four

It may be he shall take my hand
And lead me into his dark land
And close my eyes and quench my breath . . .

I have a rendezvous with death . . .

Alan Seeger, 'Rendezvous'

1

Sinclair rose from behind his desk. He surveyed the men assembled before him. Besides Hollingsworth and Styles they included six uniformed officers – two of them sergeants – all selected for their skill in marksmanship.

'To those of you who have been summoned from your homes to the Yard this evening, I apologize,' he began. 'But as you will see in a moment the matter is extremely grave.'

The door opened and Bennett came in. He was dressed in evening clothes, the gold studs gleaming in his shirt front. Hollingsworth, who was seated at Madden's desk, rose and offered his chair to the deputy assistant commissioner. The others stood grouped in a semi-circle.

'Three days ago a woodcutter named Emmett Hogg fell into a pit in Ashdown Forest. Unfortunately he didn't bother to report it until today, even though rural constables throughout southern England have been spreading the word for some time now that they want to be informed about any fresh digging in forest areas. At our request, I might add.

'Hogg made his report to the village bobby at Stonehill – that's in the Crowborough district – and this afternoon the constable went out to inspect the site, taking a friend with him, a local gamekeeper. Luckily, as it turned out, because when they got near the keeper spotted some movement in the bushes. The constable – his name's Proudfoot – decided not to approach immediately, another piece of good judgement, and after a while they spotted a man moving about in the area. They were some distance away and the site was in the middle of thick undergrowth. But at a certain moment they got a clear view of him. He was carrying a rifle.'

A murmur went around the group. Sinclair caught Bennett's eye.

'Not a shotgun,' the chief inspector declared emphatically. 'A Lee-Enfield. They saw him clear the breech and check the firing mechanism. Both men are clear on that point.'

He glanced down at his desk.

'Some of you will have seen the photograph we began circulating today of the man we wish to question in connection with the murders at Melling Lodge. It's possible, even likely, that the individual observed by Proudfoot in Ashdown Forest this afternoon is Amos Pike, the man we're seeking.'

The murmur, this time, was louder.

'In requesting information about any unauthorized excavations we asked the various police authorities to impress on their constables the need to exercise caution. Proudfoot acted with good sense in not approaching this man. What he did was leave his friend watching from cover while he returned himself to

Stonehill and telephoned the central police station at Crowborough. They in turn rang Tunbridge Wells where I'm glad to say the local CID chief thought it worth while to get in touch with me right away.'

Sinclair paused to collect his thoughts.

'The situation now is as follows: Proudfoot has returned to join the keeper and will keep watch on the site for the rest of the night. In the meantime, the Sussex police are putting together a force of uniformed officers, some of whom will be armed. As you will be. We'll rendezvous with them at first light and surround the area.

'To anticipate your questions, I did consider taking action along these lines tonight, but decided against it. The presence of up to two dozen policemen stumbling around in the woods in darkness seemed to me more likely to alert this man and drive him off than achieve any useful end.

'As a precaution, however, in the event that he might be planning to attack some household tonight, a number of constables were dispatched to Stonehill from Crowborough earlier today. The site of the pit is about three miles from the village and the police will patrol houses in the district all night, making no attempt to hide their presence. After considerable thought, I've decided not to alert the villagers. Anything we say to them will only create panic and add to our difficulties.'

One of the sergeants held up his hand. 'What if he slips away in the meantime, sir?'

Sinclair shook his head. 'That's the one thing I'm

not concerned about. Always supposing it *is* Pike, we
believe he's engaged in constructing a military-type
dugout in the forest. It's what he did in the woods
above Melling Lodge before he attacked the house. He
takes his time over building it. Provided he's not
disturbed there's no reason to think he won't be back.
And when he does, we'll be waiting for him.

'But let me say straight away – I don't *expect* him to
leave tonight. Tomorrow is Sunday, a day of rest, and
I've no doubt he'll want to put it to use.'

The sergeant spoke up again: 'Did Hogg get a good
look at the pit, sir? Could he describe it?'

'The answer to both questions is no.' Sinclair's
expression was wry. 'It appears Hogg was dead drunk,
which may explain why he fell into the hole in the
first place. He doesn't seem to have noticed anything,
except that it was a hole that wasn't there before.'

The sergeant grunted. 'What time do we move
tomorrow, sir?'

'I want you all on duty at a quarter to five. Spend
the night here if you wish, or go home. But don't be
late. We'll draw weapons from the armoury and proceed to Stonehill by motor-car. The Yard has put two
vehicles at our disposal.' The slight ironic emphasis
given by the chief inspector to the numeral was
noticed only by Bennett. 'I have something further to
say to you.'

He paused deliberately and let his gaze settle on
each officer in turn. When he spoke again it was in an
altered tone.

'I have every intention of arresting Amos Pike, if it is he, and bringing him before the courts. But be under no illusion. This is likely the most dangerous man you will ever be asked to face. His military record was outstanding, but while that may have been of benefit to his country, it's no comfort to us. He's a hardened killer, with no reason not to kill again. Keep that in mind. He may well choose to resist arrest. If he fires on you with his rifle, or refuses to drop it on command, you are to shoot him. If he threatens you with rifle and bayonet, you are to shoot him. You will shoot to kill. I take full responsibility. Is that clear?'

Silence greeted his pronouncement. Then a low mutter came from the semi-circle.

'Very well. That will be all for now. We'll meet tomorrow morning.'

He watched as the men filed out. Styles, at a signal from Hollingsworth, followed the sergeant into the side office and shut the door behind them. Bennett rose. 'Well, Chief Inspector!'

They regarded each other in silence.

'I must call the Sussex chief constable.' The deputy moved towards the door. 'Where's Madden, by the way?'

'He spent the afternoon in Highfield, sir. He rang me from Waterloo half an hour ago. I told him to go home and get some sleep. He'll be here first thing tomorrow.'

Bennett paused at the door. 'Looking better lately, I thought.'

'Sir?'

'Inspector Madden. Less . . . less *hunted*, if you take my meaning.'

'Yes, I do, sir,' Sinclair agreed. He smiled for the first time that evening.

2

BREAKFAST WAS LATE at Croft Manor that Sunday morning. The silver chafing dishes, which were customarily placed on the sideboard punctually at half past eight, had not yet appeared when the three adult members of the Merrick family gathered in the dining-room. (The children ate upstairs in the nursery.) Annie McConnell, who was in the habit of casting an eye over the breakfast table when she came downstairs to see that all was in order, sped off to the kitchen to investigate. She returned with some startling news.

'Did you know the village was crawling with policemen last night, sir?' she asked William Merrick, who said he most certainly did not.

'Yes, and more arrived today. Two carloads from London, they say, and a van from Tunbridge Wells. More than twenty coppers in all.' Annie's eyes were bright with the news. 'And now they've gone off into the forest, the whole pack of them.'

Word had been brought to the house by Rose Allen, one of the maids, and Mrs Dean, the cook, who both lived in the village, a mile away. The excitement there had been the cause of their late arrival and consequent delay in preparing breakfast.

'They're at it now,' Annie assured the family, with

a special smile for Mrs Merrick. She was concerned about her mistress, who seemed particularly disconcerted by what she had just heard.

Annie had to wait until after breakfast to discover what the trouble was and then chided herself for not having guessed it in the first place.

'William will just use this as another excuse to put off leaving for Cornwall. First they were going on Friday, then it was Saturday. Now who knows when he'll decide to start?'

They were taking their usual post-breakfast turn in the garden. Annie had ceased to wonder at her mistress's increasing anxiety over the delay in her family's departure on holiday. She sought only to comfort her. 'Now don't go putting ideas into Master William's head,' Annie counselled. The boys had always been 'Master William' and 'Master Tom' to her, long after they had grown up. 'Let him slip along to the village and find out what's going on. Chances are, it's all a great fuss about nothing.'

Earlier William had donned his cap, backed the Lagonda out of the garage and driven into Stonehill to discover, as he put it, 'what the devil this is all about'.

He returned an hour later, in no better mood than when he had left. His wife and mother were waiting in the morning room to hear what he had to tell them.

'It's the most extraordinary business.' William seated himself on the settee beside Charlotte. 'Half a dozen police constables were sent here from Crowborough last night, and the others arrived at dawn, and just as Annie says they all marched off into the forest and haven't been seen since.'

William had obtained the information from an elderly police sergeant from Crowborough, who had been left behind at the village hall to receive and act on any messages sent back. He had professed ignorance of the purpose of the operation, but assured William that, 'Everything's in hand, sir, and there's nothing to worry about.'

From other sources William had learned that word had been put about in the strongest terms that no one was to accompany the police, who had been last seen heading off in the direction of Owl's Green, on the other side of the village, nor attempt to follow in their tracks. Explanations would be made in full in due course.

'The one man who might have told me something was nowhere to be seen,' William Merrick complained bitterly. 'I mean Proudfoot. Apparently *he*'s there with them. According to his wife he was out all night.'

Harriet Merrick listened with sympathy to her son. He was a man of consequence in the district, a Justice of the Peace. It was clear he felt he should have been consulted. She saw him instinctively rub his withered arm, and almost in the same instant, as though acting on a signal, his wife turned to him, putting her hand on his.

'Don't worry about it, darling. I bet you it turns out to be nothing.'

'Nothing! With twenty policemen tramping about the countryside!' William made his annoyance plain.

'Nothing that'll come to anything, I mean.'

William rose. 'I'm going to ring Richards,' he declared, referring to a magistrate they knew in Crowborough. 'I want to get to the bottom of this.' He went out.

Charlotte looked at her mother-in-law with raised eyebrows. 'Don't worry, I'll get him moving, I promise.'

Mrs Merrick didn't know whether her daughter-in-law was aware of her irrational wish to see them all depart. She had done her best to disguise it, restricting herself to repeated admonitions to them not to waste the precious days of their holiday and drawing their attention to reports in the newspaper describing the glorious Indian summer that the west of England was still enjoying. But perhaps Charlotte sensed something more. Harriet Merrick had always meant to be a good mother-in-law, but her resolutions had never been tested. From the start she'd been touched by Charlotte's instinctive understanding of the special burden her son bore – his guilt at having survived the war in which his brother had died was but one manifestation of it. They'd been allies from the first day.

Charlotte ran her hands through her hair. She was thinking of having it bobbed in the prevailing fashion, but both William and his mother had begged her not to.

'I'm going to see to the children's packing,' she announced. 'Then I'll have all the cases brought down. In the end we'll simply *have* to leave.'

A few minutes later Annie joined her mistress in

the morning room bearing a silver tray on which a bottle, a spoon and a glass rested.

'Time for your medicine, Miss Hattie.'

Mrs Merrick made her customary fuss. 'I don't think it does me the slightest good. And it tastes quite foul.'

'You'll drink it none the less.'

The teaspoon containing a greyish liquid hung poised in the air before Mrs Merrick's mouth. Since she knew from experience it would remain there till Doomsday she opened her lips. 'Disgusting!'

Smiling, Annie handed her the glass of water. 'So you haven't been imagining things, after all.'

Mrs Merrick swallowed. 'What do you mean?'

'Policemen tramping about in the forest. Quite a to-do.'

'Oh, *that*!' Harriet Merrick dismissed the matter with a wave of her hand. She gazed into Annie's deep green eyes. 'I had such a strange dream last night,' she said softly. 'I was walking in the forest and I saw Tom. He was in the trees ahead of me and when I called out he turned and beckoned, and I was coming closer and closer, but I couldn't quite reach him, and then I woke up . . . It'll be four years on Tuesday.'

'I know, my dear.' Annie took her hands.

'And then I lay awake for the rest of the night and all I could think of was how much I wanted William and Charlotte and the children to go *away*.'

Mrs Merrick removed her glance from her companion's eyes and stared down at their linked hands.

Annie sighed. 'It's a strange one you are. My poor

dead mother always said you had the gift. No more than a child you were then. Little Hattie from the big house.'

Mrs Merrick smiled. 'Never mind the gift . . . What shall we do when they've gone? Let's be wicked. Let's light a fire in the drawing-room and roast potatoes in the ashes, the way we used to.'

'That's wicked, is it?'

'We'll sit in the garden and talk and gossip . . .' Harriet Merrick looked into the face of her old friend. 'Oh, Annie, I'm so glad you'll be here with me.'

The green eyes opened wide. 'And where else would I be?'

*

The morning dragged on. William remained closeted in his study. The household, disrupted by the delay, was at sixes and sevens. Had all gone according to plan, parents and children, with the addition of Miss Bradshaw, the nanny, would have set out at ten o'clock in the Lagonda intending to reach Chichester in time for lunch. (The family's regular attendance at Sunday service had been suspended for once.) There William and Charlotte had arranged to spend the night with a schoolfriend of Charlotte's before leaving early next morning for Penzance. Other arrangements were dependent on these. At Harriet Merrick's insistence the entire household staff had been given the full two weeks off. She and Annie would manage alone, although Mrs Dean would come over from the village now and again to cook a meal for them. The three maids were poised to depart, but until the master had made a final decision everything hung in abeyance.

At a quarter to eleven Charlotte knocked on the study door and went in. Ten minutes later she emerged and hurried straight to the kitchen to deliver instructions before rejoining her mother-in-law in the morning room.

'We're leaving. I've asked Cook to make up a picnic hamper and we'll have lunch on the way to Chichester. William's ringing the Hartstons now to tell them we won't be there till this afternoon.'

'Dearest Charlotte . . . you're a genius. How did you manage it?'

'It wasn't that difficult. William had more or less decided himself. He's had no satisfaction telephoning people. No one seems to know what's going on in Ashdown Forest. He's still quite cross, but his attitude now is, "If they don't want to tell me anything they can jolly well deal with it themselves."'

The two women smiled conspiratorially.

'The children will love the idea of a picnic,' their grandmother predicted.

'That's what I thought. I'm going to call them down now.'

She went out and Harriet Merrick was left rejoicing.

3

EYES NARROWED under the brim of his grey felt hat, Sinclair peered through a screen of leaves at the clump of trees and thick bushes half a mile away. Open pasture lay between the tangle of holly and hawthorn where the chief inspector crouched with Madden on one side of him and Inspector Drummond, a plain-clothes detective from the Tunbridge Wells CID, on the other. The expanse of grassland, thinly sprinkled with young oaks, offered no cover and prevented them from approaching any closer to the site of the pit into which Emmett Hogg had fallen.

'It's pretty well surrounded by open land, sir.' Constable Proudfoot, crouching behind them, answered Sinclair's unspoken question. 'When I came back from Stonehill yesterday evening I made a circuit of the area. Took me a good while – I had to be sure of staying out of sight. That thicket there's like an island. There's no way you can get near it on any side without being seen.'

The village bobby, a stocky young man with cropped fair hair and a peeling nose, had been waiting at Stonehill to guide them through the woods to their present position, a walk of about three miles, he claimed, though to the chief inspector, increasingly anxious as the morning wore on, it seemed longer.

'You've been on your feet a good while, Constable. Twenty-four hours and more. How are you bearing up?'

'Well enough, sir.' Proudfoot grinned and rubbed his bristly chin. 'I could do with a shave, though.'

The group of policemen had been bent behind the bushes, watching, for twenty minutes when they were rewarded by the sight of movement in the thicket.

'There!' Madden and Proudfoot spoke in the same breath.

Sinclair saw clearly the upper half of a man's body take shape amidst the undergrowth. He had his back to them and he bent down almost at once, then straightened, then bent again as though he were dragging something through the brush.

'I believe he's dark-haired.' Madden spoke quietly. His eyes were narrowed to slits.

'Well, that's a relief,' the chief inspector said at last. 'At least we know he's still there. Now, let's get back to the others. We must decide what to do next.'

Two minutes later they had retreated into the shadow of the forest and rejoined the squad of uniformed policemen who were sitting under cover in a shallow depression some way in from the edge of the treeline. They numbered twenty-two in all. In addition to the six armed men Sinclair had brought — nine with Madden, Hollingsworth and himself — there were a further six officers bearing arms among the Tunbridge Wells contingent.

Inspector Drummond, too, was armed. He had been waiting for them with his men outside the village hall in Stonehill, a short, black-haired man with ice-blue eyes. He measured his fellow detectives. 'Chief Inspector Smithers sends his regards, sir. He would have come himself, but he said there was no point in *two* chief inspectors getting in each other's hair. He wishes you the best of luck.'

'My thanks to you both,' Sinclair responded drily.

They had paused in the village only long enough to assemble the men before following Proudfoot into the forest. The handful of villagers who had emerged from their cottages to take in the extraordinary sight of a score of coppers gathering on the green in the dawn light had been told sternly by Proudfoot not to venture on their trail.

Thankful at being able to stretch again after his long spell of crouching, Sinclair asked the constable to draw a rough plan of the thicket and the surrounding terrain. Proudfoot took out his notebook and busied himself for a few minutes. He handed the result to the chief inspector who squinted at it, with Madden and Drummond peering over his shoulder. The rough pencil sketch showed a semi-circle of woods surrounding the thicket and open pastureland. Where the woods ended the constable had marked the terrain down as 'broken country, scattered bushes'. This section included a stretch of water, which he named as Stone Pond.

'That's on the far side of the thicket from where we

stand, sir.' Proudfoot indicated what he meant on the drawing. 'No need to worry about the pond – it's as good as a wall. It's the land on either side of it that's our problem. No trees to provide cover, just a few scattered bushes and flat ground.'

'All the same, we'll have to get men over on that side and then have everyone advance at the same time.' The chief inspector squinted at the sketch. 'Now, this keeper, Hoskins. Where's he, exactly?'

Proudfoot pointed with his pencil.

'This stretch of woods we're in here – it bends around to the left and runs as far as that small hill.' He tapped the pad. 'I told him to get up on top of there and stay put. If our man leaves the area at least Hoskins will know what direction he takes.'

'But he knows not to interfere?'

'He does, sir.'

'Very well.' Sinclair glanced at Madden. 'John, what do you think? You've had experience of this sort of thing.'

Madden trod on his cigarette. 'If you put armed men in a circle and bring them in to a central point they'll end up shooting each other. Better to concentrate them at three points and have the other officers filling in the gaps. Here – let me show you.'

He took the notepad from Sinclair's hands and borrowed the constable's pencil. The others watched as he drew a rough triangle on top of Proudfoot's plan.

'If we place the armed officers at each angle they'll be shooting towards the opposite base of the triangle, not at each other. If shooting starts, the unarmed men must drop to the ground and stay there until ordered to advance.'

Sinclair studied the combined drawing. 'Yes, I understand,' he said. He looked up. 'Would you see to that, John? The positioning of the men?'

'Yes, sir, of course.' The inspector thought for a moment. 'They'll have to start advancing at an agreed time,' he said. 'There'll be no way we can signal them without giving away our presence. I would suggest four o'clock this afternoon.'

'Good Lord!' Sinclair glanced at his watch. 'That's more than five hours off. Can't we be ready before then?'

'Probably.' Madden shrugged. 'But for some reason these things always take longer than one thinks. Also, the light will be better later. There'll be less glare.' His glance went to the line of uniformed officers seated nearby in the shade. 'If that man over there is Pike, he'll shoot at us from cover. But he can only be on one side of the thicket at a time. The men must be told to advance quickly if they're unopposed. Once they're in the brush, he loses the advantage of his rifle. But they must watch for the bayonet then.'

4

CROUCHED ON his haunches in the dugout, Pike began to lay out his things. From the capacious leather bag he drew his uniform – shirt, breeches, tunic – and placed them on the broad step cut into the rear of the excavation. His neatly rolled puttees were added to the pile. Next came the gas mask.

His movements, measured and unhurried, gave no clue to his mental state, which for many hours had been battered by doubt and indecision. His normally stony emotional structure was fractured by extremes of feeling that produced at almost the same instant a hot flush of impulse towards action and an icy realization of the dangers that hung over him.

Travelling on his motorcycle from Rudd's Cross the day before, he had several times been on the point of turning back and returning to the hamlet. To the garden shed and Mrs Troy's cottage where a situation now existed that required his urgent attention.

But his need drew him on, and in the dark recesses of his soul this seemed to have its own logic. He had no other business than the one he was engaged on. It was the sole aim of his wasted life and, seen from that perspective, even the need to protect himself paled into unimportance.

Nevertheless, his agitation had already produced small but significant changes in his behaviour. He had begun his journey from Rudd's Cross in the usual manner, following a complicated route of back roads and country lanes, avoiding major thoroughfares. But after an hour he had lost patience and, with a recklessness foreign to his nature, had joined the main road, taking the coastal highway to Hastings, then swinging north towards Tunbridge Wells. Bent over the handlebars, and with his cap pulled low over his eyes, he had ridden at a steady thirty miles an hour without incident until he reached a turn-off that took him westwards into Ashdown Forest.

It was late afternoon when he arrived – still daylight – but he strode uncaring through the woods to the site of the dugout, his bag hoisted on his shoulder. His thoughts were fixed on the hours that lay ahead. Above all, on the following evening. Everything else was shunted to the back of his mind, to be dealt with later.

On reaching the dense thicket he found the brushwood he had used to camouflage the digging undisturbed except in one corner where some of the branches had fallen into the pit. He examined the spot carefully. Although it seemed likely that wind and rain had shifted them, he spent the next twenty minutes searching the area for any signs of a human intrusion. A footprint. A cigarette stub. He found nothing to arouse his suspicion.

His sleep that night was troubled. For the first time in years an old nightmare returned and he had woken drenched in sweat. The air inside the dugout seemed stifling and he had climbed out and stood motionless in the thick brush listening to the night sounds: the stirring of leaf and branch, the distant cry of an owl. He remembered nights spent in the woods with his father. The waning moon, close to the end of its cycle, hung low in the eastern sky.

At first light he rose, determined to regain his poise, and settled at once into a routine of small tasks on which he could fasten his mind. He had the whole day to fill.

First he cleared all the brushwood, now yellowed and browning, that he had used to camouflage the dugout, gathering it into a large bundle which he later dragged through the thicket until he was some distance from the site of his digging where he began to distribute it – a piece here, a piece there – to make it seem like casual deadwood. Midway through it occurred to him there was no point in what he was doing. He didn't intend filling in the dugout later, or attempting to hide it, as he had on Upton Hanger. The police must have found his earlier excavation. They would know what to look for now. Yet in spite of this he completed the task he had set himself before moving on to another.

Twice during the morning he had paused to scout the surrounding landscape. He had chosen the patch of stunted oaks and dense underbrush because of its featurelessness and lack of any practical use. No one could have any reason for entering it, he reasoned. (None but himself.) Crouched at the fringe of the bushes, he had scanned the woods and stretches of open land encircling the thicket. On the second occasion he had caught a glimpse of a figure moving through the trees. It appeared for only a few seconds and then vanished. He remained with his eyes fixed on the spot for several minutes, but saw nothing more to attract his notice.

At one o'clock he broke off to heat a tin of stew on his spirit stove and brew a mess tin of tea. Then he cleaned and put away his utensils and began to unpack his bag.

Examining the gas mask he frowned at the discovery of a small tear in the canvas hood beside one of the straps. Obsessively tidy, he would have mended it on the spot if he'd had needle and thread with him. The first time he had used a mask, in his attack on the farmhouse in Belgium, he'd worn it simply to hide his identity in case he left survivors. He had blown his whistle to cause confusion. (But it was his own pulses that had been set racing!)

At Bentham, in Kent, he had burst into the house bareheaded. It had been a mistake. In the bedroom upstairs, when he dragged the woman from her bath to the bed, she had looked into his eyes. Screaming, she had begged him to stop and Pike had found he could not endure the sensation of having his face uncovered to her gaze.

The shame of it.

He had killed her quickly. Nothing had gone well at Bentham.

Although he could easily have devised a more convenient cover for his face, he recalled the fierce satisfaction of his first assault, when he had worn full military uniform, and soon afterwards he had broken into an Army surplus warehouse in Dover and stolen what he needed, including a gas mask. At Melling Lodge the woman's screams had left him unmoved. It was only the excitement of having her in his arms, crushed beneath him on the bed – excitement which had boiled up and overflowed too soon – that had prevented him from achieving the goal he hoped to attain that night.

The afternoon wore on. The light in the dugout dimmed as the sun declined. Overhead the bright blue autumn sky of the morning had paled. Fleecy clouds shaped like scallops drifted in from the west.

Pike took up his rifle. He had stolen the weapon from a barracks in Caterham when he was working for a construction crew installing a new plumbing system in the camp. For more than two years after his return from France – he'd smuggled himself aboard an empty supply vessel in Boulogne harbour – he had lived hand to mouth, picking up odd jobs, sometimes breaking into houses to steal food and money. It was only after he had obtained his post with Mrs Aylward that the grim purpose he had found for his existence began to take shape in his mind.

He had already checked the firing mechanism – he did it as a matter of course whenever he unpacked the bag – but from habit he settled down to clean it, drawing pieces of two-by-four through the barrel with a weighted cord, oiling the breech. He checked the magazine to see that it was fully loaded.

When everything else was done he reached into his bag again and brought out a flat leather case, fastened with brass catches, and a whetstone wrapped in shammy. He had saved the honing of his razor until last.

He took it from the padded case. The ivory handle was yellowed with age. The blade glinted blue in the pale sunlight. It had been in his family for three generations. Together with his hunter timepiece it was the only souvenir he had of his father.

5

DETECTIVE CONSTABLE STYLES walked grim-faced
along the woodland path, two paces behind Inspector
Drummond who in turn followed in Madden's tracks.
Billy was sulking. He had felt humiliated all morning,
ever since he had been barred by Chief Inspector
Sinclair from drawing a revolver along with the other
men of the Scotland Yard contingent. Billy had
stepped up to the grilled counter to sign the book,
but at that moment the chief inspector, who was
standing nearby talking to Madden, glanced over his
shoulder and said to the armoury sergeant, 'That won't
be necessary,' giving no further explanation, and leaving Billy little option but to do a smart about-turn
and walk away with his face on fire and thoughts of
homicide not far from *his* mind. He had received
training in the use of firearms as a uniformed constable
and, as far as he knew, had passed the course satisfac-
torily. The chief inspector had no *right*, he reckoned.

It hadn't helped when Hollingsworth, checking his
own weapon, had winked at him. 'Don't take on, lad.
The guv'nor knows what he's doing. It's for your own
protection.' He grinned. 'And ours.'

Billy hadn't said a word to anyone since, but
unfortunately nobody seemed to have noticed. Least of

all Madden, beside whom he had been wedged in one of the two cars that had brought the men down from London. The inspector had sat silent throughout the trip, gazing out of the window, lost in thought.

They were walking now in single file through the woods, a line of uniformed policemen strung out behind the three detectives. Madden had chosen a route well away from the treeline, which bent in a slow curve until it met the wooded knoll where the gamekeeper was said to be posted. No longer, though! Glancing up from the leaf-strewn path Billy spotted a man wearing rough tweeds and carrying a shotgun hurrying towards them. Madden had already seen him and brought the column to a halt.

'Hoskins, sir!' the man called out as he drew near.

'Madden's the name. Is he on the move?'

'No, sir.' The keeper came up beside them. He was in his forties with red, weathered cheeks and a stubbled chin. 'But there's trouble over on the other side, near the pond. You can't see 'em from here but it looks like a troop of Girl Guides. They're settling down by the water.'

'Christ!' The exclamation came from Drummond.

Madden thought. He beckoned to Billy. 'I want you to run back the way we came. Tell the chief inspector what Hoskins has told us and say I've ordered you to work your way round till you get to the pond. Stay out of sight as long as you can, but if you have to show yourself take off your hat and jacket and roll up your sleeves. Try to look like someone out for a Sunday-afternoon stroll. Find out who's in charge of those Guides and get them moved away.' Madden thought some more. 'You'll probably have to show your warrant card, so you can say this is a police operation and we require the area to be cleared. Stay there when they've gone. I'll be round later after I've got the men posted on this side. Understood?'

'Yes, sir.' Billy was already on his way. *Now* he would show them.

Within ten minutes he was back at the shallow bowl where the chief inspector sat in the shade beside Sergeant Hollingsworth smoking his pipe. Half of the uniformed squad remained with him. It was planned that Sinclair would lead one of the armed groups and Drummond and Madden the other two. It was going to take a while to get all the men positioned. Billy explained what the new problem was and how Madden proposed to deal with it.

'I think I know who that lot are.' Constable Proudfoot had stayed behind with the chief inspector. 'I'd better go along and have a word with them.'

'Please, sir.' Billy spoke up. 'Mr Madden doesn't want any uniforms spotted.' He hoped he was right. 'He told me if I had to show myself I should take off my jacket and try to look . . . unofficial.'

'I'm sure you'll manage that all right, Constable.'

The ghost of a smile crossed the chief inspector's lips. Billy was trying to work out exactly what he *meant*.

'Get along with you, then.'

He took to his heels again. He believed he could work his way round to the pond in twenty minutes, no more, but once the trees gave out he was forced into an ever-widening circle, seeking dead ground out of sight of the thicket, and it was fully half an hour before at last he saw ahead of him the flicker of blue-skirted figures and beyond them the glint of sunlight on water.

He was on a well-trodden footpath shielded by a line of laurel bushes, which led directly to the pond. The bushes gave out well short of the water's edge, but Billy felt the time had come to show himself. He took off his hat and jacket – and, as an afterthought, his collar and tie – transferred his wallet to his hip pocket and then made a bundle of his discarded garments and tucked them under a bush. Rolling up his sleeves he walked rapidly along the path until he reached the end of the line of laurels, where he slowed his pace to a stroll. Hands in pockets he approached the group of Guides, who were busy collecting sticks and brushwood from the ground. He counted up to two dozen. Four of the older girls were kneeling beside a tripod with a kettle hanging from it in readiness for the fire that would be lit beneath. As Billy came up one of them rose.

'Yes, young man? What can I do for you?'

Under her blue felt hat she was revealed as a woman in her mid-fifties with a tight-lipped look that suggested a temper barely under control. Hostile brown eyes examined him from behind wire-rimmed spectacles.

'I'm sorry to disturb you, miss . . . madam.' He was flustered by the sight of the belted uniform adorned with badges. 'I'm going to have to ask you to leave this area.'

'*What did you say?*' The woman appeared to levitate before Billy's startled gaze. 'Are you aware this is public land? You have no right whatsoever—'

'No, please—' he interrupted her, 'you don't understand. I'm a policeman.' Over her right shoulder he could see the stunted trees and tangled brush of the thicket. It was no more than two hundred yards away.

'I don't believe you.' The scornful gaze took in his bare forearms and braces. His collarless shirt. 'You look like a scruff to me.'

Billy reached into his hip pocket for his wallet – and then froze. Something had moved in the thicket. He caught a glimpse of a man's figure crouching at the fringe of the brush. Sun glinted on metal. He looked again, but like a mirage the figure had vanished. He moved deliberately, edging around so that his back would be turned to the thicket.

'What are you doing? Why are you moving like that?' The woman's eyes narrowed with suspicion. '*Cynthia! Alison!* Come over here.'

She spoke over her shoulder. Two of the girls kneeling by the tripod rose and joined them, standing behind her like bodyguards. They were in their early teens and plainly nervous and unsure of themselves and the situation.

Billy held out his hand, hoping the gesture would not be seen from the thicket, which was now behind him.

'This is my warrant card. Please look at it carefully.'

The woman peered suspiciously at the square of white cardboard as though it might be a scorpion he was offering her. Finally she took it from his hand.

'In that thicket behind me – please don't stare at it – there's an armed man whom we mean to arrest,' he began.

The woman looked up from the card. Her glance went immediately over his shoulder. The two girls were looking in the same direction.

'There are twenty policemen in the woods beyond—'

'I warn you, young man, if you're making this up . . .!'

Billy was becoming desperate. He wanted to take hold of this old bitch and shake her hard. He wanted to tell her to stop being pig-headed and self-important and *listen to what he was saying*. But he had had the example of Madden before him for the past two months and he recalled the inspector's words to him at Highfield.

'I assure you I'm not making it up,' he said quietly. 'You've seen my card. I work at Scotland Yard. Some of the policemen over there are armed. It's possible that shots will be fired in the next half-hour. I want you to get these children together and take them away from here immediately.' He stared back at her.

'Please, miss . . .' One of the girls at her shoulder shuffled nervously.

'Oh, very well!' She thrust Billy's card back at him. 'But I warn you, young man, you haven't heard the last of this!'

She spun round on her heel and put her hand into the patch pocket sewn on to her uniform. In the nick of time Billy saw what was about to happen.

'No, don't!' He grabbed hold of her wrist as she brought the police whistle up to her lips. 'You mustn't use that whistle!'

'*Take your hand off me!*' Her lips had gone white with rage. 'Did you see that, Cynthia? This officer . . . this *so-called* officer manhandled me. I'm going to report him and you will be my witness. *Manhandled!*' she repeated, seeming to relish the word.

Red-faced with anger himself, Billy said nothing. He watched as she turned away from him and clapped her hands. 'Girls! Get into line! We're leaving! This man has spoiled our afternoon.'

The blue uniforms gathered. Billy felt the weight of their disapproval. When they had lined up in twos the woman cast a final glare at him.

'Mr Styles,' she said. 'Yes, Mr *Styles*. I shan't forget that name.'

The Guides marched away down the footpath. Billy was hardly aware of their departure. All his thoughts were focused on the presence in the thicket behind him. He knew he was being watched. *A hardened killer . . .* The chief inspector's words came back to him. He remembered what had happened to Madden and Stackpole in the woods above Highfield and he felt an overpowering urge to move. *To run!*

Instead, he forced himself to stroll up and down the edge of the pond for a few minutes. When he spotted a flat stone on the ground he picked it up and skimmed it across the water's surface. Then another. His knees were shaking and his mouth had gone dry.

Finally, as though bored with the amusement, he ambled back along the footpath. As he reached the cover of the laurels his knees gave way and he stumbled and fell to the ground. His cigarettes were in his jacket and he wanted one badly. But for a while he simply sat where he was in the shade of the bushes blinking away the sweat that ran down his forehead, waiting for his heartbeat to slow.

He marvelled how the minutes he had just passed had seemed to stretch into years.

6

WILLIAM MERRICK lifted his head from under the silver bonnet of the Lagonda. His brow was disfigured by a smear of oil. He rubbed his withered arm, massaging the hand that would never do quite what he wanted of it. Shutting his eyes for an instant, he shook his head as though to clear it, then dipped back under the bonnet.

His mother watched from the window of her bedroom in despair. The suitcases, which had been strapped to the wings of the long chassis, had been removed and stood on the gravel driveway. The rest of the luggage, a small mountain of it, was still packed in the dicky. But for how long?

Mrs Merrick looked at her watch. It was nearly half past four.

They had been on the point of leaving – the entire household, Hopley included, had gathered on the doorstep to wave goodbye – when the car's motor had simply died. Mrs Merrick had heard it shudder and cough as William reached up to fit his goggles over his eyes, and the next moment it had fallen silent.

After a couple of attempts to crank it back to life – the car was an old model with no self-starter – he had ordered everyone to get out, unbuckled the straps holding the suitcases and lifted up the bonnet.

Charlotte had climbed out of the front seat and the children and their nanny from the back. For a while everyone stood around watching William at work. Then they had drifted away. Only Harriet Merrick had remained on the doorstep, as though transfixed, disbelieving, until Annie came out to rescue her.

'Now take that look off your face, Miss Hattie,' she said severely, as she led her mistress back into the house. 'Give the poor boy a chance. He'll not get it mended if you stand there watching him.'

She settled Mrs Merrick in her room, where she was left to reflect bitterly on the fact that only six months before they had had a chauffeur – one Dawson – and that during his reign the Lagonda had never given a day's trouble. But Dawson had left to return home to Yorkshire and since then William had felt able to handle the car himself, with occasional help from Hobday, the village mechanic. It had been clear to Mrs Merrick for some time that her son overrated his skill and knowledge in the matter of managing an automobile – there had been a number of embarrassing breakdowns – but she had thought it wiser to hold her tongue. Now she wished she had been less reticent.

Rose and the upstairs maid, Elsie, were packed and ready to leave themselves and they had promised to send Hobday back to Croft Manor as soon as they reached the village. But the only emissary who arrived from Stonehill was the mechanic's twelve-year-old son, who reported that his father had gone to Crowborough for the day and wouldn't be home till nightfall.

So William had laboured on, his tools in their oilskin cover laid out on the ground by his feet. Meanwhile, Charlotte busied herself rearranging the day. The children had been placated with a picnic in the garden, which their mother and Annie supervised. Sandwiches were sent out to William. Mrs Merrick remained in her room.

At two o'clock Charlotte rang the Hartstons in Chichester to say they would be arriving later than expected. She added a rider that they might not get there at all that afternoon, in which case they would stop off briefly on their way through the following day.

Mrs Merrick came down at four o'clock to join her daughter-in-law in the drawing-room. Charlotte was still in her travelling clothes, her long fair hair drawn up in a net. Tea was served to them by Agnes, one of the downstairs maids, who had volunteered to stay on an extra day.

Despite her daughter-in-law's sympathetic presence Mrs Merrick found it almost impossible to speak. A feeling of terror had gripped her as she lay on her bed. The dread, to which she could put no name nor ascribe to any cause, reminded her vividly of the agony of mind that had awoken her on the night of her younger son's death in France four years before. She had tried to tell herself it was the anniversary – now so close – that had brought back the memory of the pain she had suffered. But even as her mind accepted the explanation, some other part of her, something deeper and darker, from the very depths of her being, rejected it.

'I'll go and speak to William again.'

As Charlotte prepared to rise they heard footsteps in the hall outside. They went past the door to the cloakroom. After a minute they returned. The door opened and William Merrick put his head in. 'We're getting there,' he said.

He shut the door before either of them could speak. The two women looked at each other, sharing the same thought. Quite soon it would be too late to leave. They would have to spend the night at Croft Manor.

Harriet Merrick could bear it no longer. Excusing herself, she returned to her room upstairs. For a while she stood at the window watching her son at work beneath the bonnet, hoping to see him turn the crank and hear the engine cough into life.

Then that, too, became unendurable and she went quietly downstairs and out into the garden. The sun lay low in the western sky. Soon the wooded slopes of Shooter's Hill would lose shape and definition and appear only as a dark mass against the dying light.

From the bottom of the garden she heard the children's voices. They must be playing on the croquet lawn, she thought. Hopley touched his hat to her from the shrubbery. Why hadn't he gone? she thought distractedly.

Why were they all still there?

She heard a light footstep on the grass behind her and turned to find Annie approaching with a wrap in her hands. 'There's a chill in the air. Just put this round your shoulders now.'

Mrs Merrick accepted the garment, drawing it tightly about her. Already she felt the cold.

'It'll soon be dark,' she said. 'It won't be long now.'

7

PIKE PUT ON his cap, pulling the rim down to within an inch of his eyeline, using his first and second fingers to measure the distance in a gesture made automatic by the years he had spent in uniform.

He did up the top two buttons of his tunic and then ran his hands lightly over his body from head to foot – cap, tunic, trousers, puttees, boots – in a further involuntary action to which he gave no thought. His rifle stood propped against the side of the dugout. His gas mask, rolled into a bundle and tied with a piece of cord, lay on the bunk bench beside him. There was nothing further he had to do. Now he could only wait.

Although it was still light outside, the plaited willow roof and the surrounding screen of brush prevented the late-afternoon sun from entering the dugout, and Pike sat unblinking in the near-darkness. He was waiting for nightfall.

At Melling Lodge he had attacked at sunset. The thick woods of Upton Hanger had covered his approach and he had been able to hide in the bushes by the stream until the moment was ripe. Here in Ashdown Forest more patience was called for. His route to Croft Manor took him through stretches of

open country as well as woods and he was too con-
spicuous a figure in his military dress to risk being
seen.

By day at least the forest seemed well populated.
Throughout the afternoon he had made regular sorties
out of the dugout to scan the surrounding countryside
and he had seen, at different times, ramblers in the
distance, a man with a butterfly net and a troop of
Girl Guides. None of them had lingered in the area
and none, he believed, would still be abroad after dark.

Pike reached down for the stone jar of rum at his
feet and lifted it to his lips. As the syrupy liquid
slipped down his throat, settling in a warm pool in
the pit of his stomach, his thoughts went back to the
war years. To the many times he had sat, as he did
now, in trench or dugout, waiting to accompany
patrols and raids into no man's land, or in the hours
leading up to a general attack.

He had not expected to survive the conflict. After
his first few times in action he had seen that, for him,
death or crippling injury was unlikely to be long
delayed. He had been a soldier of almost suicidal
bravery. The anguish that dogged his days, repressed
and barely acknowledged though it was, had nevertheless driven him to risk his life repeatedly. It would
have taken a more reflective man than Amos Pike to
have recognized in these acts of desperation the grim
aspect of a death wish.

But although struck down several times by bullets
and shell fragments he had returned each time to his
battalion where he was regarded with awe that quickly

shaded into fear among those who came into close contact with him.

His memories flowed back and forth . . . He saw the bodies of the dead lying in their hundreds and smelled the sickly-sweet stench of corruption . . . he saw the dead body and smelled the scent of roses . . . he recalled the warmth of sweet white flesh pressed to his and the pleasure that so soon turned to shame.

And now he could feel the heat stirring in him, the blood flowing in his loins, and without being aware of it he began to move back and forth on his seat, while a sound – half moan, half chant – issued from his lips. His eyes were shut tight. The black wings of the past beat about him and he saw himself, too, like a bird, rising and soaring free, escaping the prison of his days—!

His movement stopped in a heartbeat – his eyes flicked open.

He had heard a noise outside the dugout.

A rustle in the underbrush?

Or had it come from further off?

He rose, his instincts on a knife edge. Taking hold of his rifle he stepped out from under the cover of the plaited willow and stood motionless in the fading light, barely drawing breath.

Listening . . .

8

BILLY STYLES lit another cigarette. He glanced at his watch. Still twenty minutes to go. He looked along the line of laurels to where Madden was sitting with his back to the bushes facing a group of five uniformed officers, all of them armed, who were seated on the opposite side of the footpath. Billy was with a party of four – sergeant and three constables – none of them carrying revolvers. They were closest to the pond and had been ordered by Madden to advance, keeping the water on their flank.

It was not until nearly four o'clock that Billy had caught his first glimpse of the inspector and the squad of policemen he brought with him. They had followed the same route he had taken, making a wide circle to avoid being seen from the thicket, and then joining the footpath that led to Stone Pond.

Billy had hastened to meet them. He gave Madden a brief account of his difficulties with the Guides and reported his sighting of the figure at the fringe of the thicket.

'Did you see his weapon?' Madden's frown seemed permanently etched on his features.

'No, sir. Just something shining, like metal.'

The inspector rubbed the scar on his forehead.

'Remember, if he starts shooting you're to drop to the ground and await orders. That goes for all unarmed men.' He glanced around. 'The rest of you should find what cover you can and return fire. But *listen* for my orders. Stay alert.'

Billy learned from one of the two sergeants accompanying Madden that their advance on the thicket had been postponed by an hour. It was now set for five o'clock. Part of the delay had been caused by the difficulty of getting the men into position between the wooded knoll where Hoskins had kept watch and the far side of the pond, where the ground was flat and bare of cover. Then, just when Madden had returned to where Sinclair was waiting to lead the rest of the men around to *this* side of the thicket – where Billy was – a party of ramblers had stumbled upon them, upwards of two score the sergeant said, and the police had had their work cut out gathering them together and shepherding them away from the area. As a result, the chief inspector had delayed the start of the operation from four o'clock to five. It could be no later because of fading light.

Madden left them briefly to walk to the end of the row of laurels where he crouched and peered through the bushes. When he returned he divided the party into two groups, telling the men that no whistles would be blown to mark the start of the advance.

'Watch for my signal. It'll be at five o'clock exactly. We'd better synchronize our watches.'

Madden was speaking to the sergeant in charge of the unarmed squad, but Billy checked his own wristwatch and set it to the inspector's mark. It came to him that his wish to see action – the feeling of resentment he'd always felt at missing the war – might be about to be satisfied. He was pleased to discover he felt no fear, just a faint suggestion of emptiness in the pit of his stomach.

The two parties separated.

Billy sat on the ground with his group in the shade of the laurels. They were all from Tunbridge Wells. One of the younger constables, a man with something of Billy's own colouring – red hair and freckles – said he couldn't see what all the fuss was about.

'Two dozen coppers to catch one bloke. That's hardly fair odds, if you ask me.'

His sergeant was busy filling his pipe. When he had it lit he responded. 'One bloke and one rifle,' he said. 'That's what all the fuss is about. If he takes it into his head to start shooting, then you and I, Constable Fairweather, will be sitting ducks.'

Billy lit another cigarette. He was annoyed to see his hand was shaking as it held the match.

*

Billy stared at the dial of his wristwatch. The minute hand was only a fraction off the vertical. He watched as the second hand began its final revolution and then lifted his eyes and glanced down the long row of laurels. He saw Madden rise to his feet.

The inspector peered through a gap in the bushes. Then he took off his hat and moved it in a sweeping motion above his head. The line of blue-uniformed officers rose on signal. Billy scrambled to his feet and heard the other men around him do the same.

The two parties of policemen broke through the line of bushes and advanced on the thicket, now a darkening mass of greenery in the early-evening light. Billy saw ahead of him a stretch of empty heath dotted with small bushes and hollows. He heard the sergeant telling the men in an even tone to spread out further to the right, closing the gap between themselves and the edge of the pond.

As they continued to move inwards he glanced to his left and registered, with a slight shock, the sight of the policeman nearest to him among Madden's group walking with his revolver pointed straight ahead. He noted that the inspector, who was advancing a few paces in front of the blue line, was unarmed.

Billy was struck by how clearly he seemed to see everything. It was partly the limpid evening light, which enhanced the outlines of objects, but he felt, too, that his own senses had sharpened to an extraordinary degree. He seemed to see blades of grass, individual and distinct, beneath his feet. When a flock of wood pigeons flew overhead he picked out the white and grey feathers of the swiftly moving bodies and heard the creak of their wings. The sky above had taken on a deep metallic sheen. The air was cool and fresh—

CRACK!

The sound of the shot brought him up short, and at the same instant he saw the sergeant, on his right, throw up his arms with a cry and fall to the ground.

CRACK-CRACK-CRACK!

Billy flung himself face down, dimly aware of another sound his ears had registered. It had come and gone without echo and with the swiftness of thought, ripping the air above him like cloth.

Phew-phew-phew!

Half dazed with shock he heard Madden's voice shouting commands. More gunshots sounded, but of a different calibre, and closer at hand, and he realized the armed men were firing back. He turned his head, keeping his cheek pressed to the ground, and saw the sergeant a dozen paces away lying on his side. His face was a ghastly white, the features contorted with pain. Billy began to crawl towards him. As he got closer he saw that the wounded man was clutching his left leg and tugging at his trousers. His bared shin was bathed in blood.

'Sarge? Are you all right?'

The voice came from beyond the prone figure and Billy caught sight of Fairweather's helmeted head bobbing close to the ground. They reached the sergeant together.

'. . . bastard shot me . . . my leg . . .'

The sergeant's pupils were distended by shock.

The rifle sounded again, but from further away, and this time Billy heard no accompanying whistle in the air above. He rolled over. Madden had risen to one knee. He was scanning the thicket a hundred yards ahead. He signalled to the men to stop shooting. The crackle of revolver fire now came from the far side of the tangled brush. Madden rose suddenly and Billy caught the faint sound of his voice calling to the men around him. 'Come on!'

The inspector began to run towards the thicket, followed by the line of blue-clad officers. Billy glanced at the sergeant. Fairweather was bent over him, loosening his trousers and easing them down over his legs. His eyes met Billy's. 'Go on, if you like. I'll see to him.'

Billy got to his feet and raced after the receding line. The gunfire had ceased, but he heard the piercing note of a police whistle. As he pounded over the bumpy ground, stumbling in the hidden hollows, he saw Madden vanish into the fringe of the thicket. The sound of shouting reached him. Orders were being bellowed.

Billy plunged into the brush on the heels of a heavy-set constable, who had fallen behind the others. The shouting was closer now. Then a single rifle shot sounded, followed by a babble of voices. He heard Madden's roar above the rest.

'*Hold him! Put him on the ground! Handcuffs!*'

Billy ploughed his way through the bushes towards the hubbub and came on a seething wall of blue uniforms. He saw Madden and Inspector Drummond crouched beside the figure of a man lying face down in a clearing in the brush. His wrists were handcuffed behind his back. A rifle lay on the ground beside him.

Madden rose to his feet, and at that moment Sinclair appeared, bareheaded, pushing his way through the bushes. He was breathing heavily. Their eyes met. Madden shook his head. He called across the clearing.

'It's not him, sir. It's not Pike.'

'Over here, sir!'

The shout came from Billy's right. A constable with his helmet skewed burst from the tangled undergrowth. He beckoned urgently to Drummond, who rose and followed him into the brush. A moment later they heard the inspector's stifled exclamation. 'Christ on crutches!'

Madden's long legs took him across the clearing ahead of the chief inspector. Billy hurried along behind them. They came on Drummond, hands on hips, peering down into a deep pit where the constable stood balanced on a stack of wooden boxes with rope handles attached to their ends. He was trying to prise the lid off one of them, but it was nailed shut.

'Those are rifles.' It was Madden who spoke. 'Lee-Enfields. Stolen from a military depot, I should think.'

'Wouldn't you know it!' Drummond shook his head in disgust. He glanced at the chief inspector. 'What do you think, sir? Offhand I'd say we'd caught ourselves a bog-trotter.'

Sinclair said nothing, but his gaze was bleak.

They returned to the clearing. Drummond bent down and rolled the handcuffed man over on his back. Billy saw an unshaven face topped by thick black curls. The man wore workman's boots and trousers and a torn fisherman's sweater. He looked to be in his early twenties. Drummond jabbed him in the ribs with the toe of his shoe.

'What's your name, then, Paddy?'

The young man gave no sign of having heard the question. He kept his gaze fixed on some imaginary point in the distance.

'They must have left him to mind the store.'

Drummond jabbed him again, harder this time. Then he looked up and caught Sinclair's eye on him and flushed guiltily.

'Excuse me, sir. I'll be back in a minute.' Madden was on the move almost before Billy realized it, striding through the brush in the direction from which they had come. He scurried after the inspector. Dusk was falling, but there was still enough light in the sky to see the three uniformed figures toiling across the field towards them, cradling a fourth man in their arms. Billy broke into a trot, trying to keep up with the inspector's long strides.

'You were told to stay down till further orders in the event of shooting, Constable.'

'Yes, sir. I know, sir. I'm sorry, sir.'

The look Madden gave him was unreadable.

As they came up to the others Billy saw that the sergeant's head was lolling on his chest. He was breathing in quick gasps, but he rallied when he saw Madden's face bent over him. 'I'm all right, sir. Took a bullet in the calf. It bled a bit.'

His legs were bare, one of them roughly bandaged with what looked like a pair of bloodstained handkerchiefs tied together. Madden made the men lay him down on the grass. He took the sergeant's trousers and folded them into a rough pillow.

'I want you to stay here, Sergeant. Just lie quietly. I'm going to have a rough stretcher made out of some branches and then I'll be back for you. Try to relax. Breathe easy.'

The expression on Madden's face reminded Billy of the day they had gone to Folkestone and he had watched the inspector talking to the one-legged soldier. *Dawkins.* That was his name.

They rejoined Sinclair in the clearing and Madden put a pair of constables to cutting branches. The chief inspector drew him aside. 'I've decided to leave the rifles where they are. This is Special Branch's business. I'll have the place watched until they can get their own people down here.'

Madden nodded. 'They hadn't started filling in the hole. Whoever left that stuff may be back with more.'

Sinclair's glance shifted to their handcuffed prisoner. He was sitting up now, but his gaze remained a blank.

'I've sent a couple of men back to Stonehill with Proudfoot to fetch torches and flares. Let me know as soon as the stretcher's ready.'

He looked up at the sky. Billy, who was standing nearby, followed his glance and saw that the stars were already appearing in the gathering gloom.

The chief inspector sighed.

Hollingsworth came into the clearing. He had Sinclair's hat in his hands and was brushing it off.

'Here it is, sir. I found it.'

'Thank you, Sergeant.'

Sinclair took the hat, but continued to stand bare-headed staring up into the darkness.

'Only two casualties, sir.'

'*Two?*'

'One of the constables fell and hurt his wrist. Looks like a break. They're seeing to him.'

Sinclair was silent.

'We were lucky, sir.' Hollingsworth tried to console his superior. 'It could have been worse.'

'Could it, Sergeant? Could it?'

To Billy it seemed clear that the chief inspector held a different opinion.

*

The Stonehill village hall echoed to the voices of a score of policemen. Folding chairs had been handed out from a stack at the rear of the building and most of the men had taken the opportunity to rest. They were sitting in groups with cups of tea in their hands and plates of sandwiches balanced on their knees. The food and drink had been provided by the women of the village at the request of Constable Proudfoot, who was now occupied in keeping at bay the crowd that had been gathering all evening on the green outside.

The stocky constable stood on the steps of the hall swaying on his feet. Billy didn't know how he kept going. He was feeling the effects of exhaustion himself and was sitting with Fairweather and another constable from Tunbridge Wells, drinking tea and smoking cigarettes. Billy had taken off his shoes and was massaging his toes. The other two watched enviously. Regulations forbade them to remove any items of uniform without good reason and they doubted that a pair of aching feet would be held to meet the requirement.

The wounded sergeant – Billy had discovered his name was Baines – and the constable with the broken wrist were both on their way to Crowborough in an ambulance, which Proudfoot had summoned when he returned to the village. He had sent the other two men back with flares and torches, which the main party had needed to light their way.

The Stonehill hall, like the church hall at Highfield, boasted a raised dais, and it was there that their prisoner was being held under guard. His wrists were still handcuffed – but in front of him now – and he'd been fed and allowed one of the folding chairs to sit on. He had not yet given up his name, but a letter had been found in his pocket addressed to a Mr Frank O'Leary, care of a hotel in Liverpool.

Both name and address had been passed on to Special Branch by Sinclair, who had settled by the telephone in Proudfoot's cottage as soon as they got back. Three officers from Special Branch were already on their way from Tunbridge Wells, and more would follow from London first thing in the morning. In the meantime, two of the armed contingent from the Sussex police had been left on the wooded knoll overlooking the thicket, keeping watch, while a third officer was standing by to bring back any message from them. Inspector Drummond had volunteered to spend the night at Stonehill until Special Branch arrived to take over.

The chief inspector had rung Bennett at his home and given him a brief report on the unexpected outcome of the operation. The London detachment would be returning home shortly.

All this information had come to Billy courtesy of Sergeant Hollingsworth, who had joined them, pulling up a chair and lighting a cigarette.

'The guv'nor's in a proper bate. There's no use telling him he'll get a pat on the back from Special Branch. He thought he had Pike in his sights. But now?' Hollingsworth shrugged. He glanced at Billy with a grin. 'I heard you were playing ducks and drakes over on the pond this afternoon, young Master Styles.'

'What?' Billy reddened.

'That's what the lads posted up on the hillock told us. That Inspector Drummond said you must be barmy.'

Billy set his jaw. If the sergeant thought he was going to try to *explain*! Then he remembered what the woman had said – that she was going to lay a complaint against him – and he realized he might have to explain, whether he liked it or not.

On the other side of the room Sinclair put down his cup on the table beside the tea urn. He'd been talking to Drummond. Madden sat near them, bowed over his thoughts. The chief inspector walked towards the doorway at the rear of the hall with Drummond at his heels. Hollingsworth rose and went after them, and Billy followed, trying to tie his shoelaces at the same time. As he came through the doorway on to the steps he saw that Sinclair was speaking to Proudfoot.

'I want you to go home now, Constable, and go to bed. Everything's taken care of. There's nothing more for you to do at present.'

Proudfoot, red-eyed and unshaven, seemed disposed to object. He was shaking his head.

'I'd just like to say that in my estimation you've not put a foot wrong.' The chief inspector regarded him steadily. 'And that's from the time you spotted that man in the brush yesterday and decided to ring Crowborough. I shall include all of that in my report, and more. You may be sure a copy of it will be sent to the chief constable.'

'Thank you, sir, but . . .' Proudfoot struggled to find the words he wanted to say.

'Go on now, man.' Drummond clapped him on the shoulder. 'You've done more than your share. I'll be here all night and if any crisis develops, well, I'll know where to find you, won't I?'

Billy looked over their heads and saw that the crowd of villagers on the green was thinning. Across the road and on the far side of the turf lights burned in cottage windows. When he glanced at Proudfoot again he saw that the constable's gaze was turned away and was pointing in the other direction, up the street. Billy looked that way and made out the figure of a man on a bicycle pedalling through the darkness towards them. The light on his bike wobbled as he lifted his hand and waved.

'Who's that?' Sinclair asked, in a tense voice.

'Hobday, sir. He's our local mechanic. Owns a garage.'

The figure was closer now and they heard his voice. He was shouting something. Billy was suddenly aware of Madden standing at his shoulder.

'. . . the manor . . . the manor . . .' it sounded like to Billy.

The man was pedalling as hard as he could, drawing closer.

A frown creased the chief inspector's brow.

'What's he saying?'

'Something about Croft Manor, I think . . .'

Proudfoot stumbled down the steps. The others hurried after him. As the bicycle careered down the road he stepped out into the street and held up his hand like a traffic policeman. The rider braked and slid to a halt with his front wheel protruding between the constable's spread legs. He was gasping for breath, half choking.

'. . . *murdered . . . bodies . . . all dead . . .*'

This time Billy heard every word clear. As he did the chief inspector's response, softly spoken though it was.

'Dear God!' Sinclair murmured, his voice breaking. 'Dear God!'

9

It was not until later that Billy heard a full account of how the village mechanic had come to be at Croft Manor. Hollingsworth had taken his statement while Sinclair was ringing the Yard and he had told Billy about it while they were sitting on the front steps of the house after midnight, taking a quick smoke break, while the blue uniforms milled about in the darkness of the driveway.

Hobday had returned that evening from Crowborough, where he was visiting a sick relative, to be told by his young son that Mr Merrick was having trouble with the Lagonda again. He'd rung the manor but failed to reach anyone. According to Mrs Gladly, who ran the village exchange, the phone was giving out an engaged signal. The receiver was off the hook, she told Hobday, but there was no one on the line.

He'd eaten a bite of supper and then tried ringing the house again, with the same result, and had been inclined to leave it at that, except soon afterwards one of the maids who lived in the village, Rose Allen, had passed by his home and urged him to go out to the manor. She didn't know whether or not the family had got away that afternoon, but if the car was still not working then Mr Merrick would need help with it that night so as to be able to leave first thing in the morning. Rose didn't know about any trouble with the telephone.

Hobday's own car was locked away in his garage. He decided to cycle out to the manor. Lights were burning in the house when he arrived, but he got no response by ringing the doorbell and so had walked around the house to the kitchen door which he knew would be unlocked, and gone inside.

Pausing only to call out, 'Anyone at home? Anyone there?' he had passed through the kitchen to the main passageway that led to the drawing-room.

The door was open. Hobday looked in.

The first thing he saw was the double doors to the garden smashed in with the glass of both panes lying strewn on the carpet.

The second was the body of Agnes Bertram, the upstairs maid, sprawled on the hearth rug. He spied another body on the sofa by the fireplace, that of the elder Mrs Merrick.

At the far end of the drawing-room the door to the hall stood open and somehow Hobday's shaking legs carried him across to it.

He got no further. One glance through the door was enough. One look at the carnage there in the hall and he fled.

*

The mechanic's incoherent words had been cut short by the chief inspector, who ordered Madden to Croft

Manor at once, taking Proudfoot and Styles with him.

While their car was being whistled up from across the green Billy heard Sinclair issue an order to Drummond. The Sussex inspector was to ring his headquarters at Tunbridge Wells with an urgent request on the part of Scotland Yard to have all motorcyclists stopped and questioned throughout the night. The order should cover the entire county of Sussex and once that was done it should be extended, by request to other police authorities, to the adjoining counties.

'You must absolutely stress to them the need to act with caution.' Sinclair's consonants took on an added edge. 'The very greatest degree of caution. This man is extremely dangerous. But he must be stopped.' And then, as though speaking to himself, the chief inspector had added, 'God only knows when it happened. I fear we're already too late.'

To Madden, as the inspector was boarding the car, he said, 'I must get hold of the police surgeon. Then the Yard and the chief constable. I'll be with you as soon as I can.'

Inside the car Proudfoot was muttering about 'the children', mumbling to himself, so tired – and now suffering from shock in addition – that he seemed unable to fix his mind on any one thing.

'Whose children?' Madden was with the constable in the back. Billy sat up front with the driver, but twisted around in his seat so that he could listen.

'Mr and Mrs Merrick's . . . but they're supposed to

be off on holiday . . . meant to leave today . . . Hobday didn't say . . . all dead he said . . . all dead . . .'

'The Merricks are the family who live at Croft Manor?' Madden's voice was patient, coaxing.

'That's right . . . always been Merricks at the manor . . . There's old Mrs Merrick and her son, that's Mr William, and *his* wife and their girl and boy . . . and there's Annie . . . Annie McConnell . . . and the maids and the nanny . . . No, *wait*!' The constable's brow knotted in pain as he strove to concentrate. 'I heard all the staff had been given the time off . . .' He fell silent, nodding. Then he spoke again: 'All dead he said . . . all dead . . .'

They were driving down a dark tunnelled lane beneath over-hanging branches. The driver slowed as a pair of iron gates appeared in his headlights. Proudfoot jerked forward in his seat. 'There it is,' he said. 'That's the manor.'

Billy sprang out of the front. One of the gates was standing half open and he drew them both wide, then followed the car down a short driveway, which ended by turning back on itself around a circular flower-bed. Madden was already at the front door as he joined them.

'Locked.'

Proudfoot led them at a trot around to the side of the house where light fell through an open door on to a bricked yard and on to the wall of a kitchen garden beyond it. Madden halted them at the door. 'Follow me. Don't touch anything. Watch where you step.'

He led them through the lighted kitchen to a door

which gave on to a passageway. Billy tried to stay on his heels, but by the time he had stepped out of the kitchen the inspector was already turning into a doorway several paces down the passage. When Billy got there himself he stopped on the threshold.

Madden was bending over a woman's body in front of a fireplace, and Billy was overwhelmed by his earlier memory of the drawing-room at Melling Lodge.

The body of the maid on the floor — the smashed French windows.

Here it was again, like a scene of horror replayed in all its ghastly details.

'Check the body on the couch. See if she's alive.'

The inspector's peremptory tone jerked Billy back to the present.

A sofa stood with its back to him. It wasn't until he went around it that he saw the grey-haired woman who was stretched out there. He fumbled for her wrist. Blue eyes stared at him unblinking. She wore a silk blouse stained in the centre with a circle of blood the size of a saucer. On the carpet at his feet Billy noticed several potatoes. *Potatoes?* He could find no pulse in her wrist.

Madden was already moving. He had left the body on the hearth rug and was skirting the area of broken glass, heading for a door at the opposite end of the drawing-room. Billy followed him, but the inspector stopped in the doorway, blocking his view of what lay beyond. He stood there for several seconds, then turned around.

'Constable!' He spoke past Billy's shoulder.

'Sir?'

Billy glanced back and saw Proudfoot standing by the body of the grey-haired woman.

'I want you to check all the rooms downstairs.' Madden's voice carried a note of command. 'Never mind what's in the hall. Do you mark me?'

Proudfoot stared at him for a moment. Then he nodded. 'Yes, sir.'

'Come along,' Madden said to Billy. He turned and went through the doorway and Billy saw they were entering a spacious hall with a double staircase to the left coming down from the upper floor. As Madden headed that way Billy glanced to his right and saw a wall splattered with blood. Blood lay in pools on the polished stone floor, too, and the carpet had been dragged aside and swept into an untidy heap. There was a body there.

'Hurry up, Constable!' Madden spoke sharply. He was already half-way up the staircase. Billy ran up the steps behind him. When they reached the upper floor the inspector turned to him. 'Check the servants' rooms upstairs. Meet me down here.'

Billy hastened along the passage to a narrow stairway. He went up to the floor above where he found two maids' rooms and a bathroom, all empty. At the end of the corridor was a nursery decorated with flowered wallpaper containing two beds. A rocking-horse stood by the window. Billy gave the room only a glance and then hurried back downstairs.

'Sir, there's no one up there!' His shout echoed down the empty passageway.

'In here, Constable.'

Madden's voice came from near the end of the corridor. Billy found him in a large room furnished with a double bed. Two paintings hung above the headboard, portraits of young children, a girl and a boy. The inspector stood at the foot of the bed, his gaze fixed on them.

'Sir, they got away!' Billy couldn't hide his elation.

'So they did.' The smile on Madden's lips lingered for only a moment, but the young constable savoured it. 'Come on! We must get back.'

They found Proudfoot in the hall below. He was standing some way from the body, his gaze fastened to it.

'There's no one else down here, sir.' He didn't look up as they hurried down the staircase.

'I take it the lady on the couch is old Mrs Merrick?' Madden's voice was loud in the flagstoned hall.

Proudfoot seemed to start at the sound. He looked up then. 'Yes, sir. It is.'

'And who is that?' The inspector pointed.

The constable moistened his lips. 'That would be Annie McConnell,' he replied. His voice shook. 'She was once Mrs Merrick's maid, I believe, but now . . . I don't know . . . they were more like friends . . .'

Madden regarded him from the bottom of the staircase. 'I have a question for you, Constable. How would you describe young Mrs Merrick?'

'Describe . . .?' Proudfoot tilted on his feet. His glance had begun to glaze over.

'Her appearance?' The inspector walked over to

where he was standing. 'Would you call her good-looking?'

The constable swallowed. 'Yes, sir. I would call her good-looking.'

Madden said no more.

Billy, moving closer, got his first clear sight of the body on the floor and couldn't suppress a gasp of dismay. Although the long black skirt and ripped blouse indicated the remains were those of a woman, there was no way of telling from her face, which had been torn to pieces as though by a wild animal. The flap of one cheek hung loose and red. There was an eyeball lodged in it. Her nose had been smashed almost flat and beneath the bloody mess her teeth showed through shredded lips.

Despite the wave of nausea that gripped his stomach the young man forced himself to absorb every detail. He saw a telephone with the receiver off the hook lying on the floor not far from the body. A table and chair had been upturned.

Madden, meanwhile, stood with head bowed studying the scene. When he turned away finally, Billy expected to see that distanced look in his eyes, that 'other world' gaze by which the inspector appeared to separate himself from all around him. But Madden's glance held only pain and sadness. He put his hand on Billy's shoulder.

'Come away, son,' he said.

10

SHORTLY AFTER one o'clock the following day Bennett arrived by car from London. The deputy assistant commissioner was surprised to find the leafy lane leading to Croft Manor empty of both press and rubberneckers. The constable on duty at the gates informed him that the chief inspector had had it cleared.

'He's told the reporters to wait for news in Stonehill, sir. And the villagers have been asked not to congregate.'

The day had dawned grey and misty, as though signalling the arrival of autumn. Bennett, black-coated and black-hatted, paused before the front steps to look about him. He was surprised again – this time because he saw no sign of police activity. Sinclair explained that the gardens had already been searched.

'Madden has the men out in the woods now. They're looking for the dugout.'

The chief inspector met Bennett at the door and escorted him to the morning room, which he had made his headquarters. The deputy took in the other man's pale, unshaven cheeks. He reflected that it was the first time he had ever seen Angus Sinclair with a hair out of place.

'You look exhausted, Chief Inspector. Have you had any sleep?'

'A couple of hours here on the couch, thank you, sir.'

'How about Madden?'

Sinclair merely shrugged.

Bennett wasted no time. He was already undoing the straps of his briefcase as they entered the morning-room.

'I've something for you. New pictures of Pike.'

Tozer's collaboration with the police artist had resulted in a pair of sketches, which the Yard's photographic department had begun producing in poster form. In one of them, the face was as Tozer remembered it, complete with heavy moustache. In the other, the artist had reproduced the same features stripped of facial hair. Sinclair took copies of each over to the window to examine them in the light.

'He's caught something in the eyes, hasn't he? But I wonder about the mouth – that can only be a guess.'

'We're getting them out to the newspapers today,' Bennett told him. 'They should be in tomorrow's editions.'

He waited until Sinclair came back from the window and then sat down in an armchair, indicating to the chief inspector to do the same. 'You wouldn't mind having the press off your neck, I dare say.'

Sinclair's look was answer enough.

'That's what I thought. I'll speak to them before I go back. What's more, I'll tell them all information from now on will come out of the Yard, in London.'

'Thank you, sir.'

'Now fill me in.' Bennett sat back. 'I want to know everything. And so does the commissioner. I have to report to him when I get back. And you'll have to come up to London on Wednesday, I'm afraid. It's a command performance. You and I and Sir George as well. We're all summoned to appear.'

Sinclair sat silent for a few moments, ordering his thoughts. Bennett was used to seeing him with his file in front of him. Now he watched as the chief inspector drew from his mind a summary of the situation.

'We have teams of detectives from London and Tunbridge Wells in place. Some of them are going through the house now, dusting for fingerprints and collecting other evidence. We'll shortly be starting the same process as we followed at Highfield, questioning the villagers as to who or what they might have seen in the past few days and weeks. We'll be showing them these new pictures of Pike along with the earlier one.

'Important items of physical evidence are already in our possession, notably a gas mask.'

'By God!' Bennett sat up. 'Pike's, do you mean?'

'We believe so.' Sinclair spoke in a monotone. 'It was found in the drawing-room this morning under a cabinet. Flung there, perhaps. I'll show it to you.'

He rose and went to a table on which a cardboard box rested. He brought the box over to Bennett and took off the lid.

'You can pick it up, sir. The eyepieces have been tested for prints.'

Bennett held up the khaki canvas hood studded with round glassed eyeholes and a rubber nozzle for breathing.

'Normally the nozzle would be attached to a box respirator,' Sinclair explained. 'Either it was pulled free, or else he doesn't bother with one. And you'll see it's torn behind.' He showed Bennett the ripped canvas. 'There's no doubt one of the victims struggled with him. Annie McConnell. The pathologist found traces of skin under her fingernails when he examined the body this morning. She must have marked him. I pray it was on his face.'

'It was her body you found in the hall?'

'It was. From some bloodstains detected on the carpet in the drawing-room it looks as though he may have bayoneted her there, as he did the other two, but failed to kill her outright. When he came down from upstairs – I'm speculating now – we think he found her trying to use the telephone in the hall.'

Bennett winced. 'Is that why he mutilated her body in that way?'

'Possibly.' Sinclair shrugged. 'But Madden has a different theory. I'll tell you what he believes in a moment. May I continue, sir?'

'Please do.'

'We can't be sure exactly when the attack occurred, except that it must have been after a quarter past five, which was when Mr William Merrick and his family left by car for Chichester. That time's been fixed by the gardener, who was here. Apparently Merrick had had trouble getting the car started and had all but decided to spend the night here – they were going away on holiday – but old Mrs Merrick wanted them out of the house for some reason. She'd been on about it all day.' Sinclair shook his head wearily. 'I can't make that out, sir. But thank God they left.'

'Amen!' Bennett murmured.

'We returned ourselves to Stonehill with our prisoner shortly before seven o'clock. Hobday, the mechanic, went out to Croft Manor at about eight. I haven't had the pathologist's report yet on time of death so again I can only speculate. We know Pike attacked Melling Lodge and the farm at Bentham around sundown. I'm assuming he broke in here soon after dark and was gone from the house before we got back to the village. In any case, the request I made to various county authorities to stop and question motorcyclists has had no result. I ordered it suspended this morning. I'm afraid he had ample time to get well away before we were alerted.'

Bennett was becoming increasingly concerned. Listening to Sinclair's dead voice he realized that the man was deeply depressed.

'What else . . .?' The chief inspector's gaze wandered about the room. 'Madden's team has found a collection of cigarette stubs – all Three Castles – on a hill close by. It's a good vantage point, apparently. We'll have them tested. And we may have another footprint to compare with the cast taken at Melling Lodge. The technicians of the photographic department have lifted some marks off the stone floor in the hall. They use oblique lighting – it's a new development.' He paused deliberately. 'And then there's the matter of the dog. The family had one. It was poisoned a week ago. I had the remains dug up this morning. Ransom will examine them. The Sussex force offered us their own pathologist, but I wanted Ransom again.'

'Quite right, Chief Inspector.' Bennett was watching him closely.

'I could have asked, you know, sir.' Sinclair's eye met his superior's. 'It slipped my mind, but that's no excuse.'

'Asked what?'

'When I got down here yesterday morning, I could have inquired as to whether any dogs in the district had been poisoned lately. The village bobby knew all about it.' The chief inspector's face showed pain. 'In fact, I wonder now if I haven't been wrong all along in withholding that piece of information from the public.'

'And I tell you you've no cause to blame yourself on either count.' Bennett spoke more harshly than he meant. 'If you broadcast that sort of warning we'll have the police being summoned every time a dog throws up. And as for the other, you came here believing you were about to arrest Pike. To arrest him or see him shot down. *That*'s what was on your mind.'

'True, sir.' Sinclair nodded assent. 'But I should have inquired just the same.'

Bennett looked away. 'Have you spoken to William Merrick?' he asked.

'I have. We managed to get in touch with the people they were staying overnight with in Chichester and he came back at once. He's staying with friends nearby. We had a meeting in the early hours of this morning.'

'What did he have to say?'

'A great deal,' Sinclair replied heavily. 'He's bitterly angry, and I can see why. He wanted to know how it was possible for his mother and two members of his household to be murdered in this fashion when there were upwards of a score of policemen in the vicinity. A question to which even the Delphic oracle might feel pressed to provide an answer,' he added, with a flicker of his old spirit.

Bennett had heard enough. 'Let me say something.' He stood up and began to pace about the room. 'Quite apart from the tragedy, this is an appalling piece of misfortune. Because of the incident of that man falling into the pit, you've been cruelly misled. But had he not done so your position would be no better. Worse, in fact. What happened here would have happened just the same' – he gestured with his hand – 'and you would have learned about it in London and had to start from scratch. Instead, you were here – on the spot. Make the most of that, Chief Inspector.'

Sinclair regarded him in silence for a moment or two. Then he nodded. 'Thank you, sir. I mean to,' he said quietly.

'One further point. I had a brief conversation with the assistant commissioner before coming down this morning. I put it to him that the theory we'd heard advanced that the perpetrator of these crimes was no more than a thief with a bent for violence was pitifully wide of the mark. It's quite clear he's a criminal psychopath, just as you have indicated from the start. Had your views encountered less opposition, I suggested, this investigation might have been concluded by now and at least one tragedy averted. Sir George did not disagree. This is your case, Chief Inspector. Though whether you'll thank me for telling you that . . .'

Bennett raised an eyebrow, and Sinclair shrugged.

'You mentioned earlier that Madden had a theory about why the McConnell woman's body was damaged in that way. I'd like to hear it.' The deputy was standing by the window, looking out. 'But I see he's coming now, so perhaps we should wait.'

Sinclair rose from his chair and joined him. Emerging from the yew alley, dark-jowled and haggard, the tall inspector came striding through the mist like the very spectre of Death.

Bennett spoke. 'I was mistaken about him. You picked the right man for this inquiry.'

A minute later there was a knock on the door and Madden entered. 'Good morning, sir,' he said to Bennett. He turned to Sinclair. 'We've found the dugout. It's about two miles off. There's been no attempt to fill it in. He left a few items behind – a tin of stew, an empty rum jar. I've had them collected for examination.'

'Sit down, John.' The chief inspector pointed to a chair. Madden obeyed.

'It's like the one we found at Highfield,' he went

on. 'Made with care and an eye for detail. Looking at the Ordnance map, I'd say it's no more than a couple of miles from the pit we found yesterday. That was due south of Stonehill. The dugout's more to the west.'

'My God!' Bennett shook his head in disbelief. 'You might almost have stumbled on him.'

Sinclair returned to his chair and sat down.

'I told Mr Bennett you had a theory why Annie McConnell's body was savaged,' he said to Madden. 'He'd like to hear it from you.'

Madden turned to the deputy. 'I believe it resulted from rage, sir. Fury. The woman Pike came for was the younger Mrs Merrick. When he found she wasn't in the house he must have gone berserk. Miss McConnell was probably trying to use the telephone when he came back downstairs. But even if that angered him, killing her would have been a simple matter. What he did to the body suggests to me some much stronger emotion at work.'

Bennett nodded, understanding.

Sinclair spoke. 'I'm forced to agree with the inspector,' he said. 'Though I don't care for the implication it carries.'

'Implication?'

'It seems that Pike takes many weeks to prepare for these attacks. By the time he's ready he must be near boiling point. Only on this occasion he was frustrated. I can't pretend to understand his state of mind. But I tremble at the thought of it.'

'He was primed to attack, you mean, and that won't have changed?' Bennett looked grim.

'He could be ready to strike at any time,' the chief inspector agreed. 'We *must* find him. And soon.'

11

WHEN PIKE CAME INTO the kitchen on Tuesday morning he found Ethel Bridgewater already there. She was sitting with a cup of tea on the table in front of her reading the newspaper, which, in Mrs Aylward's absence, she had not had to take upstairs that day. Ethel's fine head of hair was piled up under her lace cap in a new way, but Pike barely noticed it. His thoughts, agonized and bloody, ranged far beyond the confines of the kitchen.

He was ravenous. He hadn't eaten a proper meal for thirty-six hours. Having poured himself a cup of tea he cut three thick slices of bread from the loaf on the kitchen counter and sat down opposite the maid, who was holding the open newspaper in front of her face.

When Pike lifted his head he received a shock that went through his nervous system like a bolt of electricity.

He saw his own eyes staring at him from the front page of the newspaper.

Stunned witless, it took him several seconds to realize that what he was looking at wasn't a photograph but an artist's impression.

The caption was printed in bold letters: MAN SOUGHT.

Beside it, filling the whole of the next column, was a story headlined: 'KILLER STRIKES AGAIN'. A sub-heading bore the words: '*Police Net Spread In Southern Counties*'.

Pike's jaws moved automatically as he chewed his bread. He couldn't make out the small print of the report. But beneath the picture, in darker lettering, he read his own name: *Amos Pike*.

Another shockwave went juddering through him. He stared at the letters in disbelief. The police knew his name!

But *how*?

He was dead. Army records had him listed among the fallen. He was sure of it.

But they had his name. And they knew what he looked like.

Pike put his cup to his lips while the thoughts flailed about inside his head. It hardly mattered to him that the sketch, now that he looked at it, did not, in fact, portray his features with any degree of accuracy. True, the eyes were those that stared at him every day from his shaving mirror. But his own head was squarer than the one shown in the drawing and his mouth quite different. The artist had failed to catch his thin, tightly drawn lips which, in any case, had been altered by a wound he had suffered during the war. A shell fragment had struck his cheek, severing a nerve and causing one corner of his mouth to droop. The effect was to give his face a skewed look. But none of that mattered . . .

Pike touched the fresh scabs on his neck. He felt

his self-control deserting him. Each day now it was worse, each day harder to maintain his poise. The shell he had built for himself so painfully over the years was starting to crack. What lay beneath he could only sense as yet, but the intimation of it left him fearful.

He who had never known fear the way other men did.

Ethel Bridgewater reached the end of the newspaper. She folded it and turned back to the front page.

Pike dropped his eyes – the eyes she must be looking at now.

How could she not recognize them?

But then he lifted them again, fastening his gaze on the paper masking her face. He waited to see how she would react. Better to know now. A vein throbbed in his temple.

After two minutes, perhaps three, she laid the paper down on the table and gave it a little push, as though offering it to him. She did not meet his eyes. But, then, she never did.

Her hands went to her hair, patting and shaping the coiled tresses. Her glance went to the kitchen clock on the wall. Then she stood up, brushing the crumbs off her white slip, and left the room.

Pike relaxed with a slow exhalation of breath. He had been ready to kill her.

*

After breakfast he returned to his room above the old stable and lay down on the narrow bed. Mrs Aylward was not due back until after lunch and he had the morning free if he chose. His head ached. The dull thudding pain had started on the ride back from Ashdown Forest and seemed linked to the frenzied excitement that had gripped him when he raced down the yew alley, rifle at the ready.

Just as his emotion then had found no release, but continued to throb undiminished at his nerve ends, so he seemed unable now to escape from the scenes that ran through his mind over and over again like images on a flickering screen.

He heard the sound of his whistle – a single piercing blast!

He felt the yew hedge brush by on either side of him as he charged towards the lighted room!

He saw the heel of his boot strike the centre of the latched doors, which burst inwards in a shower of broken glass!

As he broke into the room he saw two figures to his right and wheeled that way. A woman in the black of a maid's uniform was kneeling by the fireplace. She half rose, turning towards him, her mouth forming the O of a scream, but his bayonet was ready, quick and deadly, sliding in and out of her black-clothed breast before she had time to utter a sound.

He turned to the other figure, an older woman who was sitting on the couch, expecting to find her cowering and twisting away. Instead she sat upright, unmoving, as though rooted to the spot. The surprise of it caused him to hesitate for a moment and in that instant he was struck from behind, a vase shattering on his hooded head, and then two hands were scrabbling at his neck, striving to get beneath the canvas and, when that failed, taking hold of the cloth itself and tugging furiously at it. Momentarily dazed, he reacted with a vicious backwards jerk of his elbow and heard the grunt of pain behind him. But the fingers held on to the gas-mask hood, which began to tear at the back so that the mask swivelled around on his head and all at once he was blinded, with the glass eyeholes wrenched to one side and his eyes covered by bare canvas.

Dropping his rifle, he lashed back savagely – first with one elbow, then the other – and broke free of the clutching fingers. He dragged the gas mask off his head and flung it aside. Turning, he found his attacker coming at him again. *It was a woman!* He barely had time to register astonishment – he saw a thin lined face and blazing eyes – before her fingernails raked his neck, stabbing for his eyes.

He struck her with his fist and she gave a cry and dropped to her knees.

Quickly he seized the rifle from the floor and thrust the bayonet into her breast. She toppled over and lay still.

He swung round to the couch – and could hardly credit what he saw before him.

The woman hadn't moved. Her face, ashen with shock, was lifted to his. Wide blue eyes gazed at him unafraid.

He thrust quickly at her, turning his head away as he did so. He couldn't bear to face her without the mask. When he looked again she was lying on her side on the couch, the eyes still staring, but empty now.

He ran from the room.

In the hall outside he found a staircase that took him to the floor above where he raced up and down the passage, flinging open doors. Only empty rooms met his eyes. Furious and disbelieving, he ascended to the floor above that to search the servants' quarters, but with the same result. In the end there was nothing left for him to do but go downstairs again.

From the half-landing of the staircase he saw the woman he thought he'd killed – the one with the blazing eyes – dragging herself across the stone floor in her long black skirt. He reached her just as her hand grasped the telephone on the table and he smashed the rifle butt into her face and ran her through and then hit her in the face again and stamped on her with his heavy boots. His fury could not be contained. Growling and snarling he savaged her lifeless body.

He had never behaved in such a way. Not in any of his previous attacks on civilians. Not even when he had stormed a German machine-gun post single-handed during the war and bayoneted the crew and three other men he found in the dugout.

Never!

He lost control.

Sickened and half dazed by the emotion that continued to swirl in his brain – the pulsing need that had brought him to the house was unassuaged – he had quickly searched the remaining rooms downstairs and then departed, stumbling back down the yew alley and leaving the garden by the gate that led to the water-meadow.

He was in haste to get away, not simply to avoid discovery, but to put as much distance as he could between himself and what he had done. The image of the woman's battered face, the eye dislodged from the socket, pursued him like one of the Furies through the moonless night. He saw, too, the other eyes that had looked on him, wide and blue and unafraid.

Not until he reached the dugout did he remember his gas mask, lying discarded on the floor of the drawing-room, but by then it was too late to return for it.

His bag was already packed, such items as he was not taking with him wiped clean of fingerprints.

Within twenty minutes he was kicking the motorcycle's engine into life and beginning the long ride back. He reached the Hastings road without incident, but had to wait at the intersection while a military convoy rumbled by. As soon as the last tarpaulin-covered lorry had passed, he pulled out and settled down at the rear of the convoy, tucked almost under the tail-light of the bulky vehicle ahead, travelling south at a steady twenty miles an hour.

Short of Hastings he abandoned the cover of the convoy and thereafter travelled by lanes and back roads until he arrived at Rudd's Cross a little before midnight.

Pausing on the outskirts of the hamlet to extinguish the carbide lamp of his headlight, he sat quiet in the saddle for some time watching for any sign of life in the huddled cottages. It was late. He saw none.

Mrs Troy's cottage, too, was in darkness as he approached it, pushing his machine along the dirt track up to the doors of the garden shed. The headache that had started while he was still in Ashdown Forest hammered at his temples. But sleep was a long way off. His night's work was only beginning.

12

AT SEVEN O'CLOCK on Wednesday morning, soon after Sinclair had left for London by car to attend the conference called by the commissioner at Scotland Yard, the telephone rang in the public bar of the Green Man in Stonehill.

The landlord, Henry Glossop, would normally have risen by that hour, but both he and his wife had had difficulty sleeping since the terrible events at Croft Manor and they had both consulted Dr Fellows, who had prescribed sleeping draughts.

Glossop heard the phone but lay in bed for a while, hoping someone else would answer it. The building was full of police. The four rooms at the opposite end of the corridor from where he and his wife slept were all occupied by detectives. Overnight bags packed with clean clothes had been sent from London and Tunbridge Wells the day before and distributed to the various recipients.

The phone continued to ring. With a sigh, Glossop rose, put on his flannel dressing-gown and slippers and shuffled down the linoleum-carpeted stairs to the shuttered, beer-smelling taproom where the bell still pealed monotonously.

The caller, yet another policeman, was ringing

from Folkestone, in Kent. He was polite but insistent, and half a minute later Glossop found himself toiling back up the stairs trying to recall which of the rooms housed the tall detective inspector from London.

*

'I just hope this doesn't turn into a wild-goose chase, sir. That's all I hope.'

Detective Sergeant Booth had put on weight. Billy noticed it right away, as soon as the sergeant stepped out from under the awning at Folkestone station and hastened up the platform to greet them. The trousers that had hung loosely at their last meeting now fitted snugly about his waist. For a thick-set man he was surprisingly light on his feet.

'Don't worry about that,' Madden reassured him.

'And how are *you*, Constable?' Booth gave Billy a wink.

'Fine, thank you, Sergeant.'

In fact, he was still feeling drowsy from having dozed off in the compartment. It had taken them three hours, with changes, to reach Folkestone. Billy was suffering from lack of sleep, and so was the inspector, to judge from his deeply withdrawn gaze and white marble-like features. But Billy, who had worked at Madden's side for the past two days, had yet to see him flag, even for an instant.

Booth led them out of the station to a car parked in the road outside, a Wolseley four-seater painted dark blue.

'Chief Inspector Mulrooney's given us one of the station cars for the day, sir.' The sergeant let Madden into the passenger side. 'Not a luxury we normally enjoy.'

Just like the Yard, Billy thought, as he jumped into the back.

'It's the devil of a place to get to.'

'How long will it take us?' Madden asked.

'With the car, no more than half an hour.'

As they drove away from the station Billy looked back and saw the sea, flat and calm under the low grey sky. He marked where the road wound down the hillside to the harbour below – the Road of Remembrance – and recalled what Madden had told him: how the men had marched down in their thousands from the camp on the bluff to the steamers bound for France.

The inspector was speaking again: 'I need to get in touch with Mr Sinclair. He was on his way up to London earlier. The commissioner's called a meeting. Can I ring him from the cottage?'

'I'm afraid not, sir.' Booth steered the car past a wagon loaded with straw baskets piled high with apples. They were out of the town, driving between hedgerows. 'There's no phone in the house, nor in the village. But Knowlton's nearby. Would you like to stop off there first?'

Madden pondered. Then he shook his head. 'No. Let's go straight to Rudd's Cross.'

*

Billy knew only the bare bones of the story, what Madden had told him on the train. But listening to the inspector's questions now, and Booth's answers — leaning forward from the back seat with his chin almost resting on the sergeant's shoulder-blade — he was able to gain a full picture of the chain of circumstances that had led to their hurried departure from Stonehill earlier that morning.

It had started on Monday with a cleaning woman called Edna Babb, who worked for an old lady named Mrs Troy who lived in Rudd's Cross, which was where they were headed now. When Edna arrived at Mrs Troy's cottage the first thing she noticed was that the doors of the silver cabinet in the parlour were standing open and several items missing from it. When she went upstairs she found her employer lying dead in bed. There was nothing to indicate that Mrs Troy had met a violent end, but Edna had been sufficiently upset to hurry across the fields to Knowlton, two miles away, to report her discovery to the village bobby, Constable Packard.

Packard had returned with her directly to Rudd's Cross, where they were joined by the police surgeon. His brief examination of Mrs Troy's body led him to suspect death by asphyxia, which he estimated to have occurred some forty-eight hours earlier. Packard had sealed the house forthwith and returned to Knowlton where he telephoned a report to the central police station at Folkestone.

'I was assigned to the case and went out later that

day with a detective constable,' Booth said. 'We arranged for the body to be taken to Folkestone for examination by the pathologist, along with the pillows on the bed, and we also took fingerprints off the cabinet. I had a word with Babb, who lives in Rudd's Cross, and she told me about this man Grail who's been using the garden shed. The shed was padlocked shut, but I reckoned the circumstances were suspicious enough to warrant breaking in, so I got hold of a screwdriver and took off the latch. The shed was empty, apart from some garden tools.'

'How did Grail come to be using the shed?' Madden asked. 'Was he renting it from Mrs Troy?'

'Not exactly, according to Babb. They had some arrangement whereby Grail took care of the garden and brought her food from time to time.'

'But she never met him? Edna Babb, I mean.'

'Never set eyes on him, she said. He always came at the weekends. I didn't think anything about it at the time, but I realized later, next day, talking to people around there, that he must have taken damned good *care* not to be seen.'

Booth was getting ahead of his story. He went back to Monday afternoon. At that point the police hadn't been sure what they were dealing with, whether murder, or death by natural causes. It would depend on the pathologist's report, which wouldn't be available until later. As for the items missing from the cabinet, they didn't know yet whether these had been stolen or whether Mrs Troy had removed them herself for some reason. Booth had gone back to Folkestone for the night, intending to return to Rudd's Cross the following day to question the inhabitants.

'I found the station had had a call that afternoon from a firm of solicitors. One of their employees was missing, a man called Biggs. He'd gone out to Rudd's Cross on Saturday to attend to some business for Mrs Troy, who was a client of the firm. For the second Saturday running, apparently. What she wanted was for him to get rid of Grail. After his first visit he reported he'd left a letter giving the fellow his marching orders and he'd volunteered to go back the following week to see him off the property.'

'Kind of him,' Madden observed drily. 'You thought it might have been Biggs who lifted the silver?'

'That was a possible explanation, sir. In a sense it still is. Biggs was supposed to meet a friend in Folkestone on Saturday evening, but never showed up, and no one's seen hide nor hair of him since. Nor any sign of the silver.' Booth blew his horn to warn a couple on a tandem cycle ahead of their approach. The road was narrowing. 'But it strikes me as being far-fetched. If Biggs stole the silver it must mean he smothered Mrs Troy first. But he hardly seems the type. Solicitor's clerk, no record with us. I'm inclined to think he ran foul of Grail.'

Billy, in the back seat, wet his lips. He glanced at Madden, but the inspector's face showed no expression.

Booth continued his story. On arriving at the station the following morning he discovered that the pathologist had confirmed the initial diagnosis. Mrs Troy had died from asphyxiation. Saliva traces on the pillow confirmed his finding. The case was now a murder inquiry and Booth was dispatched to Rudd's Cross with a forensic team. While the others were busy examining the cottage, he had gone from house to house questioning the inhabitants.

'That's when I began to think there was something off about this Grail. No one had seen him close up. A few times he'd been spotted in the fields, coming or going, but apart from the fact that he was reckoned to be a big bloke, no one could say what he really looked like. It made me wonder. I decided to take another look at that shed.'

Booth paused while he turned off the paved surface on to a narrow dirt track that ran between apple orchards where pickers armed with the same type of straw baskets Billy had noticed earlier were busy under the laden trees. A girl with her hair bound up in a red scarf waved to him and Billy tipped his hat and smiled back.

'I'd opened the side door the day before, but there was another door at the front, stable-type, top and bottom, also padlocked. I went to work on that and got it open. I'd only seen the inside in semi-darkness before – the window was boarded over. It wasn't until I had both doors open and light flooding into the place that I saw how clean it was.'

'*Clean?*' Madden glanced at the sergeant. They were travelling slowly now, easing over the ruts in the lane. Billy saw a cottage ahead of them, on the right.

'Spotless, sir.' Booth returned the inspector's look. 'Someone had swept and washed the floor until there wasn't a speck of dirt or dust to be seen. But having the light shining in like that made all the difference.' He grinned. 'I saw *something*. It was right in the middle of the floor.' He nodded as they drew up beside the house. 'This is Mrs Troy's cottage. You'll see what I mean in a moment.'

They climbed from the car. Booth opened a gate in a hedge and led the way into a small garden. It was well-tended, Billy noticed, the flower-beds weeded and the edges of the lawn trimmed. The sound of the gate squeaking on its hinges had brought a uniformed policeman around from the other side of the thatched cottage. He touched his helmet.

'All quiet, Constable?'

'Yes, Sarge.'

'We've finished with the house for the time being,' Booth told Madden. 'But I thought it best to leave a man here. We may need to look at that shed more closely.'

The wooden structure occupied a corner of the garden. The metal latch hung loosely by a single screw.

'Let's look at it now,' the inspector said.

Booth opened the door and they followed him inside. Though the day was cool the air felt warm and smelled musty under the corrugated-iron roof. Billy made out the dim shape of a work-table at the back of the shed. A fork and a spade stood propped against the wall beside it. Then the room brightened as the sergeant pushed open the double doors at the far end, first the top leaf, then the bottom. Billy peered down at the floor. It was made of cement and looked white and clean, just as Booth had said. He didn't see the mark until the sergeant pointed it out to them.

'It's very faint, sir. But you can just see the outline.'

Billy picked it up then. It was like a shadow on the pale surface. Madden got down on his hands and knees. He peered at the floor closely, then put his nose close to the cement and sniffed.

'I tried to pick out some of the stuff with the point of a knife.' Booth bent over him. 'I'm not sure if there was enough to test.' He shrugged. 'Anyway, I sent it off to the government chemist last night. Don't know when we'll hear from *him*.'

Madden rose to his feet. He looked at the open doorway at the end of the shed.

'Too narrow for a car,' he observed.

'That's what I thought.' Booth mopped his face with a handkerchief. The fresh air coming in from outside smelled of apples. 'So if that was a patch of oil before he cleaned it up, seems to me it could only have come from a motorcycle standing there.'

Madden grunted. It was hard to tell what he thought.

'And there's something else, sir.' Booth was grinning now, like a conjuror displaying his best trick. 'It wasn't till the idea of a motorbike came into my mind that I thought to look for it. We'll have to go back up the lane a way.'

He led Madden out of the shed and they walked

past the parked car and along the dirt track. Billy, following a few paces behind, spied something ahead of them at the side of the road. When they got closer he saw that a shallow depression in the surface had been marked off with a triangle of wooden stakes, tied together with string. A piece of cardboard fixed to one of the stakes bore a rough pencilled message: POLICE NOTICE – KEEP OFF. He had missed it when they drove by.

Booth was speaking to the inspector. 'This lane we're on is used by farmworkers to get to the fields and orchards. The only cottage it passes is Mrs Troy's. It doesn't *go* anywhere.'

They were standing by the stakes now. The depression held a filling of crusted mud marked with a criss-cross pattern. Booth crouched down, and Madden and Billy did the same. The sergeant pointed with his finger. 'I took a plaster cast of that yesterday afternoon. When I got back to Folkestone I checked it against our book of tyre patterns. It's a standard Dunlop diamond design supplied to motorcycle manufacturers, Harley and Triumph in particular. Someone's ridden a motorbike down this lane in the last few weeks, since the rains started.'

Still Madden said nothing.

'I didn't get the pattern checked till late.' Booth took out a packet of cigarettes and offered one to the inspector, who declined, with a slight shake of his head. 'Chief Inspector Mulrooney had gone home, but I called round to see him and we had a word. I told him what I thought. We wondered if we shouldn't wait for the chemist's report . . .' Booth pulled a face. 'I didn't like the idea of dragging you down here for nothing, sir. Not with what you've got on your hands. But the chief inspector decided the matter was too serious to let any chance slip. Specially after what happened at Stonehill. He said I should ring you first thing in the morning.'

They stood in silence. Booth drew on his cigarette. He glanced nervously at the inspector.

'What do you think, sir?'

Madden glanced down the lane towards the shed. Then his gaze swept the surrounding fields and orchards. Finally he spoke: 'I want to look for a footprint. He might have left one somewhere on this track. Check the puddles.'

They formed themselves into a line and walked back slowly towards the cottage, eyes cast down. Billy noted several patches of mud on his side of the lane, but none bore any footmarks. He was almost level with the garden gate when he noticed that Madden, who was walking between them, in the middle of the track, had stopped. He was down on his haunches, looking at the ground in front of him. Booth had seen him, too.

'Have you found something, sir?'

The inspector's muttered reply was unintelligible. He was peering closely at the saucer of dried mud before him.

'Fetch me some grass, would you, Sergeant?'

Booth tugged a handful from the verge and brought it over to him. Madden fashioned a makeshift brush from the blades and began to flick surface dust and grit from the mud base. He bent down and blew away the dirt. Billy crouched beside him. Gradually the outline of a footmark appeared. First the sole, only lightly sketched on the crusty soil. Then the full print. Madden blew away more loose grains of earth. The deeper impression of the heel grew clear. Billy saw that the outer rim of the oval shape had a piece missing. He heard the soft sigh that issued from the inspector's lips.

The young man never forgot the scene. He carried with him for the rest of his life the image of Madden as he glanced up and met the sergeant's rapt gaze. And in later years, whenever the scent of harvest apples came to him he would hear the inspector's murmured words: 'It's him. It's Pike.'

13

BOOTH PARKED THE CAR in the forecourt of the village pub beside a sign depicting St George slaying the dragon. The three men walked quickly down the street, Billy and the sergeant having to stretch their legs to keep up with Madden's long strides. Knowlton seemed like a busy centre. Besides the usual butcher, baker and general store the narrow street boasted a dressmaker and an antique dealer, side by side, and further down a shop that sold bric-à-brac. Billy barely had time to glance in the windows as they swept by.

As though in keeping with the ambitions of the place, the village bobby maintained an office in the front room of a cottage at the end of the street. Packard, a man in his late forties with greying hair and worry-lines etched deep into his broad forehead, showed no surprise at seeing Booth. But his eyes widened on learning the inspector's identity, and when Madden told him why they were there the constable paled visibly.

'We think this man Pike may live in the district.'

Packard opened the middle drawer of his desk and took out a copy of the police poster. 'This arrived yesterday, sir. I can't say I know this man.'

'Have a look at these, would you?' Madden passed

him the two artist's sketches he'd brought with him. 'And I need to use your telephone urgently.'

Billy watched Packard's expression as he studied the drawings and saw at once that he didn't recognize the face. The constable had vacated his desk so that Madden could make his call.

'He's not a man who draws attention to himself.' Madden spoke with the telephone held to his ear. He'd placed a call to Stonehill via the Folkestone exchange. 'You won't find him buying a round of drinks in the pub. He probably has no friends.'

Packard shook his head. 'I saw one of these in the newspaper today. I'm sorry, sir . . .' He handed the sketches back. The inspector began speaking into the phone, but the conversation didn't last long, and he hung up.

'Mr Sinclair's not back from London yet. They're expecting him shortly.'

He looked at his wristwatch. Billy instinctively did the same. It was a quarter to one.

'Let's see if we can work out the timing of this.' Madden addressed Booth, who sat in one of two straight-backed chairs placed in front of the desk. Packard had taken the other. Billy stood behind them. 'Pike must have gone to Rudd's Cross on Saturday morning to prepare for his trip to Ashdown Forest. Suppose Biggs came on him in the shed and they got into an argument. Whatever happened, it ended with Pike killing him, and once he'd done that he had to dispose of Mrs Troy as well. He couldn't afford to leave a witness to his presence there.'

The inspector lit a cigarette. Booth was already smoking.

'Now the sensible thing would have been to clear up and move out during the weekend. But we know he went to Ashdown Forest. He's not a sensible man, not rational in the way you or I would understand it. He does what he's driven to do.

'So let's say he returned to Rudd's Cross on Sunday night. He could have been back by midnight and that would have given him several hours of darkness in which to clean the shed and dispose of Biggs's body. What about the silver?' Madden frowned, pursing his lips. 'I think he took that, too. He likes to lay false trails. He's tried it before. His father was a game-keeper, you know.' The inspector's glance was still on Booth. 'My guess is he's buried them somewhere, Biggs and the silver both.'

The sergeant extinguished his cigarette. 'But where could he have gone on his bike from Rudd's Cross?' he asked. 'There was an alarm out all over Kent. Motorcycles were being stopped on the road right through Monday morning. They're still making random checks.'

Madden nodded. 'Not far, is the answer. And he must have travelled by back roads and lanes. He knows the district. I'm convinced he lives close by. Whenever he wanted to use the motorcycle he had to get to Rudd's Cross and if he lived too far away it wouldn't be practical. They don't know him *there*, and if Constable Packard's right he isn't well known in Knowlton either. We think he has a job that involves travelling. Something that takes him around the country, in the Home Counties, at least.'

Listening to them, Billy longed to make a contribution. He was jealous that Madden addressed his remarks to Booth. Of course, the sergeant was an experienced detective, and the way he'd been able to read the signs at Rudd's Cross must have impressed the inspector. But the young constable felt left out, just as he had at Highfield that first day.

Madden glanced at his watch again. 'I don't know about you,' he said, 'but we had no breakfast. Let's get a quick bite in the pub, then I'll come back and ring Stonehill again. I *must* speak to Mr Sinclair.'

He was already on the move, rising and striding from the office. The others followed him out into the street, where the inspector carried on talking over his shoulder to Booth and Packard. Billy hung back.

'What's worrying me is Pike may decide to leave the district, just up stakes and go, and we'll have to start afresh. He may not be rational always, but he's no fool. He must know that once Mrs Troy's body is discovered the police will be looking for Grail . . .'

He walked on, his voice fading.

Billy stood rooted to the spot.

He stared at what was before his eyes.

'Constable!'

Billy started. He looked round. Madden was standing some way up the street looking back.

Billy beckoned to him. His heart was racing.

Madden put his hands on his hips, the gesture

underlining his impatience. But he started back, walking rapidly with the others trailing in his wake.

'*Sir!*' Billy called out, when he was still a few paces off. '*Sir, look!*'

The inspector came to a halt beside him. He followed with his eyes the direction Billy was indicating. Booth arrived panting on his heels.

'What is it?' the sergeant demanded. He peered into the window of the bric-à-brac shop. A bewildering variety of objects met his gaze: a grandfather clock, a tray of glass marbles, cushions of various shapes and sizes, a set of hunting prints . . . 'What are you looking at?' he asked.

'Do you see that painting of a house on the wall over there?'

Madden spoke in a conversational tone, and Booth understood he was meant to look past the window display to the wall at the back of the shop. He nodded.

'It's Melling Lodge.'

Billy's heart turned a somersault. He was afraid he'd been mistaken. 'It was that figure on the fountain . . .' The words poured out as he found his tongue. '. . . the boy drawing his bow, I remember it, and the front of the house with the bench fixed in the wall . . .' He went silent again. He could feel the inspector's eyes on him.

'Well spotted, Constable.'

'Thank you, sir.'

Billy didn't look up. He was afraid Madden would see his tear-filled eyes. (Tears of *relief*, he told himself.)

But he felt Booth's elbow in his ribs. The sergeant was grinning at him.

'What did I say, lad? *Little* things.'

*

'He calls himself Carver, sir. He's a chauffeur. He works for a lady named Mrs Aylward. Hermione Aylward. She's a painter. Her house isn't far from Knowlton. He's our man all right.'

Billy had watched Constable Packard turn bright red earlier when the same fact became clear. The constable had quickly volunteered to go to the pub and fetch some sandwiches for them. Billy reckoned he must have been ashamed at not having recognized Pike's face from the poster or drawings. Sergeant Booth took a more charitable view.

'It's the uniform,' he explained, while Madden was placing his call to Stonehill. 'You look at this Carver and you see a chauffeur. Specially if he's a bloke who never does anything to attract attention, never meets your eye. You've got no reason to look at him close or watch him. *He*'s the one doing the watching.'

Madden was speaking into the phone. Billy pictured the chief inspector listening at the other end of the line, his grey eyes intent.

'The pattern's clear. All the facts fit. Mrs Aylward gets about a good deal. Her speciality is children's portraits. Do you recall that painting above the fireplace in the drawing-room at Melling Lodge? Mrs Fletcher with the two children? She did that. And there were individual portraits of the children in the Merricks' bedroom at Croft Manor. I expect we'll find they're her work as well. She's quite well known, apparently.'

That wasn't how Miss Grainger had put it, Billy reflected. (*Dorothy Grainger, prop.*, the sign above the door of the bric-à-brac shop had stated.) Sporting a monocle, she had met them in breeches and a man's sports jacket, appearing through a curtained doorway to announce that the store was closing for lunch and they would have to return later. Madden had shown her his warrant card.

'Dear me! What *has* Hermione been up to?' Miss Grainger had close-cropped hair and a smoker's cough, and Billy had concluded she must be one of *them* (without knowing quite what that meant). Her heavy-featured face was scored with lines of discontent. He goggled when she lit a cigar.

'A painter of note? Come now, Inspector! Let's not go overboard. Gainsborough won't stir in his grave, I assure you. Turner sleeps untroubled.'

Billy hadn't a clue what she was talking about, except it was plainly intended to be insulting towards Mrs Aylward. Somehow Madden had kept his patience.

'Would you tell us about *this* painting?' he had asked.

Now he spoke to the chief inspector: 'The children's portraits are commissioned, but she does other work as well – houses, landscapes and so on – and holds an exhibition from time to time. She must have done the painting of Melling Lodge on the side, when Mrs Fletcher and the children were sitting for her.'

The inspector had not thought it necessary to make the obvious point. That Pike would have driven Mrs Aylward to Highfield and thus had his first glimpse of Lucy Fletcher.

Miss Grainger had admitted to having a commercial arrangement with Hermione Aylward. The artist's unsold paintings were displayed in the shop at knock-down prices. However, the significance of the Melling Lodge picture had not escaped either of them.

'Directly after the murders she told me to raise the price from the usual twenty-five pounds to two hundred and to make sure people knew what the subject was. She wanted me to put up a sign, but I refused. After all, there's such a thing as good taste. Since then we've hardly been on speaking terms.' Miss Grainger produced a satisfied smile. 'And, as you see, there have been no takers.'

The question of Mrs Aylward's chauffeur had arisen early in the interview. Madden had asked if she travelled by car.

'Indeed she does. In a damned great Bentley! You'd think royalty was approaching.'

'Then I take it she has a chauffeur?' Madden had asked noncommittally.

Miss Grainger had shrugged. 'Of course. Carver — isn't that his name?' This to Constable Packard, who had nodded. And then flushed as the realization came to him.

Billy didn't understand why the inspector hadn't shown her the pictures of Pike. It was another thing Sergeant Booth had had to explain to him.

'And let her know it's Carver we're interested in? The word'll be around Knowlton before the afternoon's out. There's no need to tip our hand. We've not set eyes on him yet.'

But they knew where he was, near enough.

'At this moment, on his way back from Dover, sir. He took Mrs Aylward over there to a luncheon. They're expected back at the house by tea-time. She'll be spending the evening in.'

Madden had rung the house earlier, posing as a client interested in hiring the artist's services. He had found only the maid at home.

'I left a message saying I'd ring again later.'

Madden was silent for a while, listening to the chief inspector. He grunted and nodded, as though they were sitting face to face. Twice he looked at his wristwatch.

'We'll be in Packard's office, sir. We'll wait for you here.' He nodded again. 'I agree. We must act as soon as possible.'

Madden hung up the receiver. He looked at Booth and Billy, who were sitting facing him across the desk.

'The chief inspector's on his way. He'll pass by Folkestone and collect a squad of armed officers. As soon as they arrive, we'll go out to the house. We'll take him there.'

14

PIKE LEFT OFF digging in the compost pit and started back across the lawn towards the house. The road outside was hidden from his gaze by a privet hedge, but he kept his eye on the gate as he walked across the leaf-strewn grass. A short driveway led to the front door and beyond it was another stretch of straggly lawn bordered by a shrubbery and a brick wall. Pike's glance swept the garden.

When he passed the conservatory he saw Mrs Aylward's portly, middle-aged figure bent over a tub of hothouse peonies. The double doors to the adjoining studio were shut behind her, but Pike could see the lights switched on inside the house. The evening was drawing in.

He needed to keep busy, to have his hands occupied and his mind fixed on details, no matter how small or trivial. His head felt raw inside. His thoughts gave him pain.

Several times in the past two days he had felt himself losing touch with his physical surroundings. On one occasion he had had a sudden vision of the ground opening under his feet and himself, his consciousness, tumbling into blackness, spinning away like a dead leaf. He had bitten his lip hard, drawing blood, forcing himself to feel the pain of *here* and *now*.

Hourly he expected the police to arrive at the house. He had given himself things to do in the garden so that he could keep watch on the front gate. But if he strayed too far from the stables he might be cut off from his escape route.

His mind, as though on a pendulum, swung between rage and fear.

If they came for him he would make them pay dearly!

But his anger was as nothing to his dread at the thought of capture. He had always promised himself he wouldn't be taken alive. He could never endure the shame of appearing in court, of hearing the charges against him read out in public. An even greater terror, barely acknowledged, lay beneath the surface of his thoughts.

What did they know of his past? Would he be called to account for it?

His first intimation of the net being spread for him had come the previous day at Folkestone station when he had gone there to collect Mrs Aylward. He saw his own face on a poster affixed to the noticeboard in the ticket hall.

Less than half an hour later, when driving his employer home, they had come on a police roadblock on the outskirts of town. A line of motorcycles was drawn up at the side of the road and the drivers were being questioned.

Pike, at the wheel of Mrs Aylward's Bentley, was

waved through, but already he had felt the iron jaws of the trap closing on him.

He knew he had to leave the district. Once Mrs Troy's body was discovered the police would be going from door to door searching for Grail. Even if they didn't connect him with Pike, the face on the poster and in the artist's sketches published in the newspapers would be fresh in their minds.

But his motorcycle, hidden for the present in a field behind the stables, was useless to him now. Even the bus seemed fraught with peril. How did he know the police weren't stopping public vehicles as well?

He had lain awake most of the night, seeking a solution to his dilemma. It came to him the following morning, but by that time he was half-way to Dover.

The answer lay in the car he was driving! Dressed in his chauffeur's uniform he could go where he chose and not be stopped. They were looking for motor-cyclists.

The idea struck him with such force he almost pulled off the road at once in order to deal with the lesser problem of Mrs Aylward's presence in the back seat. But he checked himself in time. He needed several hours' start before the alarm was raised, and that could only be achieved if he travelled by night. He would leave when the household was asleep and his absence would not be noted until morning. Once he was well away, he could abandon the car, and then . . . and then . . . ?

His mind clawed at the question. But this time he could find no answer.

The future was blank.

Henceforth he must live as an outlaw, his face displayed in police stations and public buildings throughout the land, while the beast within him grew stronger and more demanding.

The future was chaos.

*

Pike went through the stone-pillared gateway into the stableyard. The lights were on in the kitchen, where the maid was preparing Mrs Aylward's dinner. He understood from some remarks he'd overheard that Mrs Rowley, the cook, wouldn't be coming in that evening. She had telephoned to say she was unwell. It made no difference to him. He planned on leaving the house – and Mrs Aylward's employment – within the next few hours.

The Bentley was parked across the cobbled yard in the old stables. Pike shut the doors behind him and switched on the light. His room on the floor above was swept clean. Nearly everything he wanted to take with him was already packed in the car. His clothes and his military uniform, together with his rifle, were stowed in the boot. Earlier that day, while Mrs Aylward was lunching in Dover, he had purchased a five-gallon can and filled it with petrol as a fuel reserve. The can shared the back seat with a tarpaulin-wrapped bundle, which served to wedge it securely in place.

He was almost ready to leave. He needed only to retrieve his canvas bag, which was still in the sidecar of his motorcycle. He had had to make two trips from

Rudd's Cross on Sunday night to clear the shed and remove all traces of his presence from the cottage. He hoped the police were still puzzling over what had occurred there. (How would they interpret the disappearance of Biggs?) His bag contained the silver ornaments he'd taken from Mrs Troy's cabinet. He wanted to get well away from Knowlton before he disposed of them. There was just a chance – the slimmest of possibilities – that Carver the chauffeur would not be linked in the minds of the police to either Pike or Grail. That his absconding with Mrs Aylward's Bentley would be marked down as straightforward theft. He meant to leave as few clues to his identity as possible. The longer he could keep them guessing the better.

Pike unbolted the rear door of the stables and stepped outside. Darkness was falling. A high brick wall only a few paces from where he stood marked the boundary of the property. Beyond it was a field, which also belonged to Mrs Aylward – it had come with the purchase of the house and had been used by the previous owner as a paddock for his horses. Now it served no purpose and was overgrown. Pike had parked his motorcycle at the bottom of it under the cover of overhanging bushes.

There was an iron gate in the wall, giving access to the field, but Pike walked past it to a smaller, wooden gate, which opened on to a path that ran alongside the field in the shadow of an untrimmed hedge. Just as it was natural for him to use the cover of the hedge, so he walked soft-footed, making hardly any sound as he padded through the darkness.

He had gone no more than twenty yards when he heard a cough, and stopped dead in his tracks.

The sound came from his left, where the field stretched. He crouched down at once, reaching for the bayonet that swung from his belt, motionless in the inky shadows. After a minute he heard a man's voice. He was speaking softly and Pike couldn't hear what he was saying. He fixed his gaze on the direction from which the sound had come. Beyond the edge of the field, at the far limit of the horizon, the sky was the colour of pearl, glowing faintly with the last rays of the sun. Against this pale backdrop – and visible only for a second, as the man changed position on the ground – he presently glimpsed a familiar shape: the unmistakable outline of a policeman's helmet.

Pike dropped to his stomach and, without pausing, began to crawl back the way he had come. He was practised in the action – he had done it countless times – but the peril he faced now seemed far greater than the dangers he had risked among the mud-choked shell-holes and barbed wire of no man's land. In little more than a minute he was back at the wooden gate. He slid through it on his belly and only when he had regained the protection of the brick wall did he spring to his feet and run to the stable door.

The situation was clear to him. He had understood all in a flash. These were not officers coming to the house on routine inquiries. The presence of the police in the field meant there were others nearby. In all likelihood the house was already surrounded. They knew who he was and had come to arrest him.

His mind screamed a silent refusal.

They would never take him.

His first impulse was to seize his rifle and bayonet and charge the constables crouched in the grass. Shoot them! Bayonet them! Break through their flimsy cordon and run free into the night.

Madness bloomed like a red flower in his brain. But sanity still had a foothold there, and he paused, panting, beside the Bentley.

Where would they go first? To the house, or the stables?

The answer was obvious. They knew where to find him. Mrs Rowley would have seen to that. The cook who was unwell, who wouldn't be in that evening.

He went quickly to the main doors and opened them a crack. The stableyard was empty. So was the lighted kitchen. Either the maid was upstairs, busy in Mrs Aylward's bedroom, or the police were already inside, clearing the house of its occupants. He switched off the light in the stable and opened the doors wide. He needed to create a diversion. Luckily the means were at hand.

Running back to the car, he took the can of petrol from the back seat and began to spray the liquid about, splashing the walls of the building and the wooden partitions between the old stalls. He emptied half the can in this way and put the remainder back in the car.

Pausing only to check that the yard was still empty, he raced to the far end of the stables, struck a match and set fire to the heap of junk and old furniture stored there. Flames sprang up at once. He seized a burning picture frame from the pile and tossed it into the nearest stall, and then ran back to the car.

It took only seconds to crank the engine into life. Pike settled behind the wheel. He had no plan, only a compelling need to break free of the trap closing about him, a desperate desire that burned as hotly in his brain as the fire that roared the length of the stables now, leaping from stall to stall. He waited until the flames were almost on him before putting the car into gear.

As the heavy vehicle rolled slowly out of the doorway a piece of flaming wood from the rafters fell on the canopy, setting it alight.

Pike swung out of the stableyard through the stone-pillared gateway. The course of the drive wound around the projecting conservatory to the front door, but as he began to turn the corner he saw the headlights of a car at the front gate, and he wrenched at the steering-wheel, dragging the Bentley off the gravelled driveway on to the lawn.

He was intending to make a wide circle on the grass and return to the stableyard from where he could leave by the back gate that gave on to the field. His own headlights had picked out a number of helmeted figures running across the grass towards him. A sudden blast of heat on his neck made him look round and he realized the car was on fire. Flames from the burning canopy licked about his head.

The men ahead of him dropped to one knee, as though on command. Next moment the windscreen shattered, and as he swung hard on the wheel again, pulling the car around, he heard the sound of gunshots and felt a stabbing pain in his upper arm.

Pike drew back his lips in a snarl. Pain meant nothing to him. He accepted it as his due. But he had to duck his head to avoid the heat of the flames overhead, and as the bonnet of the Bentley came round he saw other blue-clad forms issuing from the stable-yard. A bullet sang past his ear and buried itself in the upholstery behind him.

Directly ahead of him was the lighted conservatory where Mrs Aylward stood framed in one of the panes like a giant moth, her white face staring out into the garden. They were firing from both sides now. Bullets rang on the car's chassis. A shard of glass from the broken windscreen struck him on the forehead. Blood trickled down into his eyes.

Pike held the car to its course. Foot clamped to the accelerator pedal, he saw Mrs Aylward step back from the glass and then stumble to one side, ponderous in her movements, struggling to escape the huge mass of metal that thundered towards her.

Roaring his rage, he drove straight at the glass-house.

Come what may, they wouldn't take him alive!

15

'CEASE FIRE!'

The bellowed order was drowned in the crash of breaking glass as the car plunged head-on into the conservatory, bringing down the entire structure in its wake as it ploughed straight on, smashing through the double doors and knocking a hole in the side of the house.

Madden sprang to his feet – he'd lain down flat when the shooting started – and ran through the line of marksmen towards the shattered greenhouse. Billy Styles was at his heels. They arrived at the same moment as a pair of uniformed constables coming from the other direction, from the stableyard. A huddled shape lay in one corner under a mantle of broken glass.

'That's Mrs Aylward – get her out of here,' Madden called to the two policemen. 'Take care, she may be badly cut.'

He ran on over crunching glass to where the car was jammed in the wall. Its momentum had taken it most of the way through into the studio beyond. Only the rear protruded. Black smoke streamed through the broken doors above it. The canopy of the Bentley was still blazing.

'It's no good. We can't get through here.'

Madden caught hold of Billy's arm and pulled him away. He stepped over the broken shards of a window-pane and ran around to the front of the house. The door was open and they went in and found a police sergeant already there with a constable. They were casting about in the hallway, unsure where to go.

The inspector pushed past them and turned to where the studio must be. He opened a door. Smoke poured out of the darkened room into the hall. The flicker of flames was visible inside and Madden caught a glimpse of the black bulk of the Bentley before he was driven back by the pungent fumes.

The two policemen were crowding at his back. Behind them was a staircase. Madden called to Billy, who was waiting in the hallway. 'Go upstairs. See if there's anyone there. Get them down.'

Pulling a handkerchief from his pocket, he turned back to the studio. But as he started towards the door he caught a whiff of petrol borne on the billowing smoke cloud.

'*Look out!*' Madden flung himself to one side.

With a *whoosh* a huge tongue of flame erupted suddenly into the hallway. One of the policemen gave a cry and staggered backwards. A tapestry hanging on the wall beside the stairs caught fire. The lintel above the door was already ablaze.

'*Out!*' Madden shouted. '*Everyone out!*'

He pushed the two officers towards the front door, but turned himself to the staircase where the banisters had now caught fire. As he started up a figure appeared in the smoke above him. It was Billy. He had a body slung over his shoulder in a fireman's lift. He staggered as he sought to keep his footing on the smouldering stair-carpet.

'It's all right, sir,' he called out. 'I can manage.'

Walking backwards, Madden shepherded him down, keeping him close to the wall, away from the blazing banisters. The body was that of a young woman in maid's clothing. Her long hair had come loose and the inspector batted sparks from it as he guided the young constable towards the front door. As Billy stumbled out on to the driveway a cheer went up from the assembled policemen.

Coughing, Madden caught sight of the chief inspector walking fast across the lawn towards them. He had Hollingsworth at his side. Booth stood in the driveway yelling at a group of officers who had just come hurrying around the corner of the house. 'What are you doing here? Go back to the yard. Stay at your posts.'

The men turned tail and disappeared.

'John?' Sinclair was at his elbow.

'He's trapped in the car, I think, sir.' Madden spat a mouthful of smoky saliva on to the gravel. 'I couldn't get into the room. The whole house is going up.'

As he spoke, one of the front windows exploded and flames leaped into the night. The policemen gathered in the drive drew back.

'It'll be hours before we can get in.' Booth had joined them.

Madden's eye picked out the figure of Billy Styles

kneeling on the grass beside the young woman he'd carried from the house. She was also on her knees, bent over, retching. Billy supported her with his arm about her waist.

A uniformed sergeant appeared before them. 'I've sent a man down the road to look for a telephone, sir. He'll call for an ambulance and the fire brigade.'

'Thank you, Sergeant,' Sinclair said. 'What about Mrs Aylward?'

'Her cuts don't look too bad, sir. They're mostly on her back. She must have managed to turn away. But she's in shock. We've got her covered up and lying down over there on the grass.'

The chief inspector looked about him. Light from the blazing house illuminated a broad swathe of lawn. Some of the policemen had sat down. Cigarettes were being lit. He shrugged and took out his own pipe.

'Well, there's nothing we can do now except wait.'

*

By midnight the fire had burned itself out. But it was well after dawn before the commander of the fire engine sent from Folkestone gave permission for them to enter the smoking ruins of the house.

In the meantime, two ambulances had arrived, one for Mrs Aylward and her maid, the other for Billy Styles, who was found to have burned hands as well as blisters on his face and neck.

'I'm fine, sir,' he pleaded with Madden, who nevertheless ordered him into the vehicle and shut the doors on his protests.

Sinclair, watching the scene from a distance, was chuckling when the inspector rejoined him. 'Do you know? I think that young man might make a copper, after all.'

A watch was kept on the house all night. Sinclair had brought a dozen uniformed officers with him from Folkestone and the sergeant in charge had organized them into shifts. Madden and the chief inspector retired to one of the cars and snatched a few hours of fitful sleep.

The first flush of dawn brought a new arrival: Chief Inspector Mulrooney, from Folkestone. A big, florid man with a jovial manner, he greeted his London colleagues warmly. 'A good night's work, I trust.'

The Folkestone chief had arranged for a delivery of tea and sandwiches from Knowlton, and the men gathered about the van in a group, yawning and stretching.

Shortly after eight o'clock, following an inspection of the house, the fire chief came over. There had been little that he and his men could do. The blaze had been well out of control by the time they arrived and, like the police, they had spent the night watching and waiting.

He spoke to Sinclair: 'You can pop in now, sir, but only for a minute. It's still hot as a furnace in there.'

The chief inspector and Madden donned boots, helmets and heavy coats lent by the other firemen. At the last moment, Mulrooney decided to accompany them. 'Why should you fellows have all the fun?'

The fire chief and one of his squad, armed with

axes, led the way in through what was left of the front door. The walls of the house still stood, but the roof had been destroyed and daylight streamed in through blackened beams. All about them the skeleton of the house stood smoking. The heat was intense.

Following Madden's directions they picked their way through the debris-strewn hallway to the studio. The hulk of the Bentley, standing in the middle of the ruined room, was hidden by rafters from the collapsed ceiling and chunks of masonry that gave off heat like live coals. The acrid smell of smoke was mingled with other odours.

The two firemen attacked the heap with their axes, hauling pieces of carbonized wood and stone off the car. First the stove-in bonnet was uncovered, then the iron frame of the windscreen. Working quickly, they cleared the driver's area and stood back.

A dreadful sight was revealed. Sitting at the steering-wheel – seemingly welded to it – was a charred human figure. White bone gleamed through blackened flesh. Empty eye sockets stared. The teeth were bared in a lipless grin.

'My God!' Sinclair murmured. He'd never seen anything like it.

Madden, to whom such apparitions were all too familiar, looked away.

Only Mulrooney seemed undisturbed. He nodded with evident satisfaction.

'Now there's a sight to gladden the eye!'

16

THE ROAD TO MRS AYLWARD'S house ran through orchards and winding hedgerows. Little more than a mile from Knowlton, both house and stables were invisible from the lane, hidden behind a high privet hedge and surrounded by fields and orchards.

'Pike must have liked it here,' Bennett commented, as a policeman waved them through the front gate on Friday morning. 'No prying eyes.' He had come down from London by train. Sinclair had met him at Folkestone station and together they had driven out to Knowlton.

When he saw the blackened ruin the deputy shook his head. As their car drew up in front of the house a booted figure in blue overalls came out on to the front steps carrying a bucket of charred debris.

'We couldn't start searching the place until late yesterday,' Sinclair explained to him. 'So far we've found Pike's rifle and razor. They were both in the boot of the car. The razor was wrapped in some clothing. There's no doubt he was about to skip. My feeling is we got here in the nick of time.'

'A pity about the house.' Bennett gazed about him. They were out of the car, standing in the driveway. A police van was parked nearby.

'Yes, but I don't believe we could have handled it any other way,' the chief inspector declared. Pale and exhausted though he looked, Bennett was pleased to see that his customary poise and confidence had returned. 'Both Madden and I were afraid he might leave, and we were right. He would have got rid of the car once he'd escaped. Then we'd have been back to searching for him. And who knows what he might not have done in the meantime?'

His look challenged the deputy, who conceded with a nod and a smile. 'I'm not criticizing you, Chief Inspector. I'm just thinking of Mrs Aylward. She's lost her home, poor woman.'

'And been frightened out of her wits, into the bargain,' Sinclair agreed grimly. 'But I couldn't telephone her and warn her we were coming. Chances are, she would have panicked, and Pike would have picked *that* up in the blink of an eyelid.'

'Have you spoken to her yet?'

'Only briefly, sir, on doctor's advice. I saw her at the hospital in Folkestone. She's confirmed the visits to Highfield and Stonehill – she did paintings for both families. Bentham was different. She'd had an earlier portrait commission in the district and she'd noticed a house near the village worth painting. Bentham Court – Madden remembers seeing it from the road when he went there. A Palladian gem, to quote the lady. She got permission from the owners to spend the day there. She thinks she remembers Pike going off to look for petrol. He must have seen Mrs Reynolds in the village and followed her home. Got the lie of the land.'

'How long had he worked for her?'

'About a year. He came with no references, but she gave him a month's trial and he proved satisfactory. She was thinking of dismissing him, though. She said she found him "a heavy presence".' The chief inspector raised a droll eyebrow. 'That's a gem in its own right. I'm saving it for my memoirs.'

He led Bennett around the house to the ruins of the conservatory and showed him the hole in the wall where the Bentley had lodged. 'I had it carted away to Folkestone this morning. We removed the body yesterday. That was a nasty business.'

'Where is it now?'

'With the pathologist in Folkestone. I didn't think it worthwhile dragging Ransom down here. There's little enough either of them can do. Not with what's left.'

They walked on through the stone-pillared gateway into the yard. Sinclair pointed across the heap of blackened rubble that marked the place where the stables had stood.

'We found his motorcycle hidden at the bottom of that field. There was a bag in the sidecar with Mrs Troy's silver in it. I can't believe he meant to leave it there. Perhaps he hadn't had time to collect it before we arrived.

'Madden's over at Rudd's Cross today completing inquiries there. We've pieced that part of the story together pretty well. The Folkestone police are searching the area for Biggs's body. It should be close by. Pike had a lot to do that night. He couldn't have gone far with it.'

They walked back to the car.

'The commissioner wants a full report,' Bennett said. 'And we'll have to decide how much to release to the press. They're clamouring for details.'

That morning's papers had carried the news of Pike's death. A bald statement issued by Scotland Yard had said the police were no longer seeking anyone in connection with the murders at Melling Lodge and Croft Manor.

'Will there be many loose ends?'

'Enough.' Sinclair put on a long face. 'How did Pike fake his death? How did he get back from France? How did he live before he found a job with Mrs Aylward? Has he done things we don't know about?' He gave Bennett a dark look. 'As to his background, I'm hoping that file from the Nottingham police will be of help. It's sitting on my desk in London. I haven't had a chance to look at it yet. But there are some things we'll never know. What set him off? Why did he start killing? And why those particular women?' The chief inspector shook his head with a sigh. 'Questions, nothing but questions. And no clear answers. It's the sort of thing Socrates used to enjoy, they tell me. But Socrates wasn't a policeman.'

*

After a brief visit to Folkestone central police station to thank Chief Inspector Mulrooney for his assistance, Bennett caught an early-afternoon train back to London. He had named the following Wednesday as the day on which Sinclair would present his report to the commissioner.

'That should give us enough time to wrap things up, sir. I'll leave tomorrow, but I'm going to Stonehill first. We need an account from the Merricks for the record of Mrs Aylward's visit and whether either of them recalls seeing Pike on that occasion. Chief Inspector Derry, from Maidstone, is doing the same at Bentham for us. I'll speak to him over the weekend.'

'What about Madden?' the deputy asked.

'He'll return to London tomorrow afternoon and go down to Highfield on Sunday.'

'*Sunday!*' Bennett was moved to protest. 'For heaven's sake, the man's been working non-stop. Hasn't he earned at least one day off?'

'He has indeed, sir,' Sinclair replied solemnly. 'And I only wish you could persuade him of it.'

'Ah! I see! It's *his* idea?'

'He insists on going himself. But that's Inspector Madden all over. A slave to his sense of duty.'

Quick-witted though he was, Bennett realized he'd missed something in this last exchange. But he could deduce no more from the chief inspector's pious demeanour as they shook hands than that, in some fashion, his leg had just been well pulled.

*

Sinclair left early the following day for Stonehill. Madden's departure for London was delayed till the afternoon. Sergeant Booth accompanied him to the station. They stopped off at the hospital on the way to inquire after Constable Styles and were directed to one of the wards. Billy was sitting up in bed in hospital pyjamas with his hands bandaged and his face white with cream. He appealed to Madden, 'There's nothing wrong with me, sir. Can't you get me discharged?'

'It's out of my hands, I'm afraid. I've already asked. They're keeping you in till Monday.'

Even Madden's smile, rare thing that it was, couldn't lighten the young man's dejection. Nor was he cheered a few minutes later when a nurse arrived with a glass jar of violets, which she placed on his bedside table.

'From the young lady in Ward B,' she said to Billy, with a simper.

'What's this, then?' Booth's brown eyes twinkled.

'Miss Bridgewater's the young woman the constable saved from the fire,' the nurse explained. 'She's hoping he'll go and visit her in her ward so she can thank him in person.'

'Constable!' Madden's frown was back.

'Do I *have* to, sir?'

'You've just said there's nothing wrong with you.'

Billy looked to Booth for support, but found none.

'Make the most of it, lad,' was the only advice received from that quarter. 'When it comes to the fair sex, you're never a hero for long.'

17

MRS AYLWARD'S Bentley was well remembered in Highfield, the lady less so, though both Alf Birney and his daughter recalled her coming into the shop to make a purchase.

'Late April it was,' Stackpole told Madden. 'May Birney remembers her buying a bunch of daffodils and asking the way to Melling Lodge.'

The car had been parked in the street outside the shop and it was there that Miss Birney had had her glimpse of Pike.

'She saw him standing in the road beside the car, side-on, just like she told us. He was wearing his chauffeur's cap. It's all come back to her now, she says.'

The inspector had arrived to find his work mostly done. Stackpole had taken fresh statements from the Birneys. He had them in his tunic pocket, ready for Madden's perusal.

'Oh, and I have a message for you from Dr Blackwell, sir,' the constable added, with an unusually wooden expression. 'She says she'll be back in her surgery by three.'

'Thank you, Will,' Madden replied, equally stiff-faced.

He had telephoned Helen the night before and discovered she was committed to accompanying her father to a luncheon party in Farnham that Sunday. 'But I'll drop him at the house when we get back and meet you in the village. Keep an eye out for my car. My darling, I long to see you.'

Madden, tongue-tied as always, could only murmur that he loved her, but that seemed enough.

Stackpole had been waiting on the station platform to greet him. The tall constable's smile had warmed the grey autumn day. 'It's good to have you back, sir. The village is a different place since we heard the news. There are some people waiting to shake your hand, I can tell you.'

A good many of them seemed to have gathered at the Rose and Crown, where Stackpole suggested they look in for a bite of lunch. Having wrung at least a dozen palms, Madden sought refuge in the familiar surroundings of the snug bar, which Mr Poole, the landlord, had kept private for them. While the constable ordered beer and sandwiches, he settled down to read the Birneys' statements.

'It shook me when I realized how long ago it was he first came here.' Stackpole had removed his helmet. A pint of amber bitter nestled in his big hand. 'Late April, according to Miss Birney. He must have kept coming back after that.'

Madden grunted. He was still busy reading.

'From May to the end of July – that's three months. What was he doing up there in the woods? Building a dugout, I know, but after that . . .?'

The inspector had gone silent. Stackpole stole a glance at him. 'What is it, sir?'

Madden's forefinger rested on a line in the statement he was reading. 'Dr Blackwell . . .?' A frown creased his forehead.

The constable looked over his shoulder. 'That's May's statement, is it? Yes, she remembers the doctor being in the shop that morning. It was just before Mrs Aylward came in. That was when she noticed Pike outside.'

' "I saw him through the shop window. He was standing looking back up the street, staring hard at something. He just stood there like a statue . . ." '

'Yes, sir?' Stackpole still hadn't grasped the inspector's point.

'Looking at what, Will? Staring at *whom?*'

Understanding dawned slowly in the constable's eyes. 'Christ!' he said. He'd turned pale.

'They resembled each other, didn't they? She told me once people used to take them for sisters.' Madden sat with his head bowed. 'Pike saw her first, Will. Before he ever set eyes on Lucy Fletcher.'

The inspector raised his eyes. 'Was that why he was up in the woods for so long? Couldn't he make up his mind between them? We've always wondered why he came back. He had his bag with him, so we thought he'd come to collect something. But that wasn't it. He was bringing what he needed.'

His companion reached over and pressed his arm. 'Don't, sir,' Stackpole urged him. 'Put it from your mind. It's over now.'

Madden's face was stricken. 'This stays between us,

Will,' he said quietly. He fastened his gaze on the constable. 'Not a word to Dr Blackwell about it. *Never!* Do you hear me?'

*

They found Tom Cooper, the Fletchers' gardener, trimming the hedge in front of his own cottage at the end of a lane off the paved main road. He took off his cracked leather gloves to shake the inspector's hand. 'I was that pleased to hear he was dead, sir, though I wish you'd caught him. I was hoping to see the bastard swing.'

Cooper told them something they hadn't known before. Mrs Aylward had taken two days to complete the painting and had spent the intervening night in a hotel in Guildford.

'I only saw the chauffeur the first day, when they arrived. He took the lady's things from the car into the hall. Mrs Fletcher showed him where to put them. Then he parked the car in the drive. Next time I came by it was empty, and I didn't see him again. I thought he must have gone into the village.'

'*That's* where he went,' Madden said later, as they walked back up the lane. He nodded behind them towards the woods of Upton Hanger, bright with the colours of autumn. The morning mist was gathering again, starting to weave silvery threads among the tips of the Scotch pines lining the crest. 'He knew by then he'd be coming back. He was scouting out a site for his dugout.'

They reached the corner. Looking up the road, the inspector caught sight of the small red two-seater coming towards them. He raised his arm. Stackpole saw the light in his eyes and grinned under his helmet.

She drew up beside them. 'Hullo, you two.' Her deep blue glance rested on Madden. 'I've just bumped into young Jem Roker. He was looking for me. His father's fallen off a haystack and broken his arm. I'll have to go out there.' She smiled into his eyes. 'A doctor's life . . .'

'Will you be long?' he asked anxiously.

'Not more than an hour. But I've got to stop in at the surgery first. Come along there for a moment.'

They followed the car as it turned off the road on to the track that circled the green. The door of the doctor's waiting-room was ajar when they got there. Stackpole hung back.

'I'll wait for you here, sir.' He studied the grey sky as though it held some feature of interest.

Madden went inside and found Helen in her office. She came from behind her desk into his arms. He held her to him, wordless. The thought of the peril that had come so close to her sent a shudder through him he couldn't control.

'John, what is it?'

'No . . . nothing . . . I'm just . . .' He abandoned all hope of words and clung to her.

She kissed him. 'Those poor people at Stonehill . . . I lay awake all night trying to imagine what you must be doing . . . I wanted you with me, I don't want you going away any more . . .'

He tightened his hold on her and they kissed again.

'I've something to show you,' she said. She led him

back to the desk and picked up an envelope that was lying there. 'This is from Dr Mackay in Edinburgh. She says Sophy has started talking about her mother again. Still nothing about that night, but it won't be long, Dr Mackay thinks.' Helen took out a folded sheet of paper from the envelope and handed it to him. 'This is something Sophy did. Dr Mackay thought I'd like to see it.'

Madden smoothed out the paper in his hands. It bore a child's drawing done in crayon of a lake with mountains in the background. Yellow-billed ducks floated on the blue water. Giant birds flapped overhead.

'What are those?' he asked, pointing.

Helen frowned. 'Highland cattle?' she hazarded.

Madden laughed. 'Of course.'

'It's a happy picture, don't you think?'

'Yes, I do.' He took her in his arms again. They stood unmoving for several moments. Then she spoke.

'Let's get married soon,' she whispered. 'Let's not wait. There's so little time.'

'Time . . .?' He didn't understand her, and drew back a little to study her face. 'We've all the time in the world now.'

'No, it's going, it's passing every second, can't you feel it?' Laughing, she challenged him with her eyes. 'Marry me *now*, John Madden.'

He returned her straight gaze, unblinking. 'By God, I will!' he vowed.

*

Stackpole was waiting on the green a little way from where the Wolseley was parked. Madden put the doctor's bag on the passenger seat besides the splints and bandages that Helen had brought out from the surgery. She got into the car.

'When you've finished go straight to the house. Father's spending the afternoon in Farnham, so you won't find anyone there. But Molly will be pleased to see you. Just let yourself in. The front door's not locked.' She held his gaze for a moment. 'I'll be back as soon as I can.'

With a wave to the constable, she drove off.

Their last call of the afternoon was on the Fletchers' cook, Ann Dunn, who lived on the opposite side of the green. She, too, remembered Mrs Aylward's visit to Melling Lodge. 'When lunch was ready in the kitchen, I sent for the chauffeur, but he wasn't in the car. We thought he must have gone to the pub.'

Mrs Dunn brushed a lock of hair from her forehead with a flour-dusted arm. She had found new employment with the village baker. The pleasant smell of newly baked bread filled the small cottage. 'I've just remembered now. It was poor Sally Pepper I sent out to look for him.'

The afternoon light was beginning to fade as they recrossed the green. Glancing at the inspector, Stackpole saw his eyes filmed over with thought and he smiled to himself again. The smoke of autumn fires hung in the still air. When they reached the constable's cottage they found Mrs Stackpole herself, hair bound up in a yellow scarf, busily raking dead leaves into a bonfire.

'Here I am, Will Stackpole, doing your work as usual.' She smiled a greeting to Madden. 'There was a call from Oakley while you were gone. Dick Wright says he's lost another pair of chickens. And they pinched some food from his kitchen, too. He still says it's gypsies.'

'Gypsies!' Stackpole snorted with derision. 'Whenever anything's lifted hereabouts, it's always the gypsies.'

Mention of Oakley jogged the inspector's memory. 'What became of our friend Wellings?' he asked. 'Did you charge him in the end?'

'Never had a chance to, sir.' Stackpole discarded his helmet and began to unbutton his tunic. 'He did a midnight flit. Packed up and slipped away without a word. It hardly seemed worth the trouble to try to get him back. The pub's been shut ever since.'

Madden caught sight of a curly head framed in an upstairs window of the cottage. 'Hullo, Amy,' he said.

Mrs Stackpole spun round. 'What are you doing there, young lady? Get back to bed this instant!'

The child's head vanished.

'Amy's down with the measles,' her mother explained. 'Dr Blackwell said she'd look in later on her way home.'

Stackpole busied himself with the rake. 'Perhaps you'd like to wait here for her, sir,' he said casually.

'No, I don't think so, Will.' The inspector adjusted his hat. 'I'll be on my way.'

'You're leaving *now?*' The constable looked aghast.

'Not this moment.'

'Then we'll be seeing you again?'

'I shouldn't be surprised.'

Turning at the garden gate he was in time to see Mrs Stackpole jab an elbow into her husband's ribs. Grinning, he raised an arm in farewell.

18

THICK GREY CLOUDS hung close to the earth, brushing the tops of the tall beech trees. Away to his left the woods of Upton Hanger were no more than a dark shadow in the deepening dusk. Madden walked down the lane in a cocoon of mist-wrapped silence, buoyant with a happiness that sent his spirits soaring and lightened his step on the damp ground underfoot.

Pausing at the locked gates of Melling Lodge, he looked down the elm-lined drive, but it was already too dark to see the house. He recalled the day he had driven through the gates in Lord Stratton's Rolls-Royce, and all that had happened since.

But as he walked on his mood changed. The euphoria began to drain away and was replaced by a low current of unease, which at first he attributed to the dank air and gathering mist, reminding him, as they did, of freezing nights spent in no man's land, waiting to ambush an enemy patrol.

At the same time he was aware of a nagging voice at the back of his mind. Madden was gifted with unusual powers of retrieval; it was one of his strengths as a detective; there was little he heard that he forgot. But his attention had strayed from his work that afternoon. His thoughts had wandered. He had the uncomfortable feeling of having missed something important. Of having heard, but not listened.

The lane narrowed, the hedgerows drawing in on either side. He came to where the road began a long turn to the right. Ahead of him was the footpath that ran through the spur of woods to the side gate of the garden; the path Will Stackpole had shown him on his first visit.

Hesitating for a second, he decided to stay on the paved road, reasoning that Helen might catch up with him in her car, and after five minutes came to the main gates, which were open. Beyond them, the drive stretched away like a dark tunnel.

He started down the avenue of limes, dead leaves rustling beneath his feet. The trees on either side still bore a heavy burden of autumn foliage and he spied a faint gleam of gold in the blackness overhead. At the end of the tunnel the white shape of the house showed dimly, the outline blurred and softened by the thickening mist.

Madden stopped.

He had heard a noise in the bushes flanking the line of trees. A rustle louder than the whisper of leaves beneath his feet.

'Molly, is that you? Here, girl!' He called to the dog.

The noise ceased at once. The inspector stood unmoving in a darkness dense with silver mist. Utter silence had fallen all around him. Then he felt something brush his cheek and he lifted his hand quickly—

A leaf, spiralling down from the branches above, came to rest on his shoulder.

He heard the rustle again, quick and furtive, and this time recognized the sound as that of a small, scurrying animal. Prey or predator, he could not tell, but it was gone in a moment.

His anxiety had not abated and he began to comb his memory, running through the events of the afternoon, the conversations he had held, trying to track down the errant phrase that lurked like a fugitive at the back of his mind, refusing to show itself.

Was it something Stackpole had said?

He reached the end of the drive and crossed the short expanse of gravel in front of the house. The portico light was out, but the door was unlocked, as promised, and he went inside, switching on the light in the entrance hall. The way to the drawing-room led through the hall and across a passage and he went there without pausing.

The drawing-room was in darkness, but there was enough light coming from the hall to make out the various table lamps. As he began to switch them on, a reflection of the room sprang up in the wide bow window overlooking the terrace where the curtains had not been drawn. He caught sight of his own figure in the gold-framed mirror above the mantelpiece and frowned, remembering.

Not the constable. His wife!

It was something Mrs Stackpole had said.

Madden opened the door to the terrace and stepped outside. The mist was thicker on this side of the house, covering the lawn and cloaking the orchard at the foot of the garden.

He whistled and called out the dog's name twice: 'Molly! Molly!'

No answering yelp came from the silvered blackness. Mist lapped at the flagstoned terrace.

The hairs on the back of Madden's neck rose. Like other long-term survivors of the trenches he had developed an instinct for danger that some had called a sixth sense but was, in fact, a learned reaction to small events and anomalies: a flicker of light in the depths of no man's land; the thrum of a barbed-wire strand in the darkness.

To things that were not as they should be.

He whistled again, and this time he heard a faint whine. The noise came from close at hand – near the foot of the terrace steps, which were hidden in mist – but overlapping it came another sound from behind him: the high-pitched note of the Wolseley's engine approaching down the drive towards the house.

'Dick Wright says he's lost another pair of chickens. And they pinched some food from his kitchen, too.'

Madden whirled and made for the door, slamming and locking it behind him, and then sprinted across the drawing-room, running for the hallway and the front door.

Racing to head her off.

Before he had crossed the room he heard the pounding of footsteps on the terrace and turned to see his own reflection in the bow window shatter as a body came hurtling through it, smashing wood and glass, landing on the floor beyond the window-sill and then driving onwards towards him without a pause. He had time only to register the pale, blood-streaked face and the long pole that Pike held crossways in front of his body like a barrier before the man was on him!

Too late the inspector saw the gleam of the bayonet tipping the pole. He tried to fling himself to one side, but Pike followed the movement, and as Madden staggered backwards he made a darting, snakelike thrust, driving the blade deep into the inspector's body, then wrenching it out with a savage turn of his wrist.

Madden collapsed to his knees with a groan and toppled over. He lay unmoving.

*

Leaving her car's motor running, Helen Blackwell hurried into the house. As she ran through the lighted hallway she called to Madden: 'John, they want you back in London. That man who was burned wasn't Pike. He's not dead—'

She came into the drawing-room and stopped. Her eyes went from the smashed window to Madden's body on the floor, seeing both in the same instant. For the space of a heartbeat she stood rooted. Paralysed by shock. Then, as she opened her mouth to cry out, a hand was clamped across her lips from behind and her arms were pinned to her side. Hot breath blasted in her ear; bristles tore at her neck.

She knew who it was – who it must be. The knowledge came in a flash and, though terror-stricken, she fought back at once, throwing her body from side to side, trying to unbalance her assailant. Strong as he was she sensed weakness in him. His hoarse breathing bore a note of exhaustion. Mingled with the incoherent growling that came from his lips she heard grunts of pain.

Reeling about the room, crashing into furniture, sending stools and side tables spinning, they came before the mirror over the fireplace and Helen caught a glimpse of her attacker behind her. She saw a bloodstained forehead and lips drawn back over snarling teeth. She also saw a dark stain on the upper arm of his khaki shirt. Wrenching a hand free from his clawing grip she punched her knuckles into the mark with all her strength.

Pike let out a roar of pain and released her. But before she could react, a blow from behind sent her stumbling into the fireplace where her forehead struck the projecting ledge of the mantelpiece and she fell back, stunned, on the hearth rug, blood flowing from a deep cut above her eye.

Snarling with pain, Pike seized her under the armpits and dragged her inert form over to the sofa. He was moaning, half crying, muttering the same words over and over: 'Sadie . . . oh, Sadie . . .'

Blood from his forehead dripped on to her blouse. He pulled her hair from under her body, where it was trapped, and spread it about her shoulders.

'Oh, Sadie . . .'

He ripped the buttons of her blouse, then reached down to drag up her skirt. As he pulled it above her knees he was caught from behind by his shirt and lifted and spun around. A tremendous blow to the side of his jaw sent him staggering backwards and he tripped over one of the tumbled stools and fell flat on his back.

'*You murdering swine!*'

Stackpole stood over him in his shirtsleeves. As Pike tried to clamber to his feet, grasping at the back of an armchair, the constable struck him another clubbing blow, knocking him face down on the carpet.

'*Bastard!*'

He grasped the back of Pike's shirt in one hand and his leather belt in the other and hauled him up on to his hands and knees. As the dazed man flailed about, trying to find his bearings, Stackpole ran him across the floor and pitched him head first into a glass-fronted cabinet. Glass and china shattered, spilling on to the carpet. Pike's head emerged from the cabinet dripping with blood. The constable threw his body aside.

Breathing heavily, his face suffused with rage, he looked about him. Dr Blackwell was stirring on the sofa, raising her head, blinking blood from her eye—

'Look out – !'

Her cry made him turn quickly and he saw Pike on the floor behind him gripping a long pole with both hands. His strike was so swift Stackpole had no chance to avoid it. The tip of the bayonet caught the constable in the thigh and he stumbled to one side and fell over a chair, landing heavily on his back.

Dazed, he saw Pike, his bloodied face twisted with

pain, hauling himself to his feet. He was leaning on the pole, pushing himself upright, when all of a sudden the prop was snatched from his hands and he crashed to the floor again. The figure of Madden rose to his knees behind him. He held the pole in his hands. The inspector's front was drenched in blood. His face was ghastly pale.

Pike lay groaning on his back. He seemed to have come to the end of his strength. As Stackpole clambered up he saw that Madden, too, was on his feet. The inspector stood swaying over the man stretched out on the floor. He lifted the bayonet-tipped pole in unsteady hands.

'Do it, sir!' Stackpole urged him hoarsely. 'Kill him! Send the bastard to hell!'

'John – !' Dr Blackwell called to him from the sofa. Her voice was pleading.

Madden held the point of the blade an inch from Pike's chest. The brown eyes met his through a mask of blood. They showed no emotion.

'Amos Pike!' Madden's voice was faint. 'I'm placing you under arrest.'

The eyes flared. The bloody face contorted. Before the inspector could stop him Pike reached up and seized the pole from his failing grip. With a single thrust he drove the point downwards into his own chest, impaling his body to the floor. Blood fountained from his lips. His body gave a last convulsive heave and was still.

Madden sank to his knees and fell sideways to the floor.

'John . . .' Helen Blackwell scrambled across the floor to his side. 'My darling . . .' She knelt beside him, tearing at his blood-soaked shirt.

Stackpole hobbled towards them. A sudden drumming on the floor made him check. Pike's heels beat a spasmodic tattoo on the carpet. The constable plucked the bayonet-tipped pole from his chest. He saw it was a roughly trimmed sapling. The long sword bayonet had been wired to one end. He raised it, prepared to strike again. The drumming ceased.

'Is he dead?' Dr Blackwell didn't look up.

'Dead as he'll ever be.'

'Will, go to the phone. Ring Guildford hospital. They must send an ambulance with a nurse right away. *Immediately*. When you've done that, fetch my bag from the car. *Hurry!*'

The constable was already on the move, half limping, half running. When he returned a few minutes later he found her in the same position, kneeling beside the inspector, flicking blood angrily from her eye, pressing a pad of silk that must have come from her underclothing to Madden's side.

'Open my bag. You'll find a dressing inside.'

Stackpole did as he was bid. She quickly replaced the makeshift pad. Then she took his hand in hers and held it firmly on the surgical dressing.

'Keep it like that. Don't press too hard. I have to fetch a bandage from upstairs. I'll only be a moment.'

Shocked by the sight of Madden's bloody torso and ashen face, Stackpole couldn't check the words that came to his lips: 'Will he . . . is he going to . . .?'

'*No!*' she said fiercely. 'He's not going to die, do you hear me?' She turned her pale, bloodstained face to his. 'We're going to keep him alive. You and I.'

Barely aware of the pain from his injured leg, the constable knelt beside Madden's body, holding his hand steady on the dressing. The patter of running footsteps sounded overhead. He let his gaze wander about the room. Despite the shambles that met his eye – Pike's body lying stark not a foot away, the smashed glass and furniture all around – and notwithstanding the inspector's dreadful pallor, he felt strangely comforted.

He had known her for many years, since childhood indeed, and long since learned to trust her word and judgement.

19

'HE HAD BIGGS'S BODY in the car with him,' the chief inspector explained. 'Somehow he managed to set it behind the steering-wheel, though that can't have been easy. He was hurt himself, and the room was full of smoke. He was on the point of leaving when we arrived, you know, getting ready to make a run for it. Perhaps he thought it a good idea to take the body with him and bury it in some place where it wouldn't be found. That way he'd keep us guessing. Was it Biggs who had stolen the silver? Was Carver really Pike?'

Dr Blackwell's steady glance told Sinclair she was paying close heed to what he was telling her.

'God knows how he slipped away. We had the place surrounded, but the men were running this way and that, and the stables were on fire, too. It was all confusion. My guess is he went out through the kitchen and across the stableyard.

'But how he survived at all is the real mystery. He drove flat out into the side of the house. The pathologist who examined his body found three cracked ribs and injuries to his head. Plus he had a revolver bullet in his arm. The man had incredible strength and endurance.'

'How did he get to Highfield?' Dr Blackwell's gaze shifted to the white-painted bedstead on the other side of the hospital room. Sinclair noted that her eyes seldom left Madden for long. The inspector was deeply asleep.

'A farmer who lived a few miles from Mrs Aylward's house reported his car stolen during the night. It was found abandoned in a wood near Godalming ten days ago. He must have come the rest of the way on foot. Amazing strength. Amazing perseverance.'

'Will Stackpole says he was stealing food over on the Oakley side of the hanger. A farmer there reported some minor thefts.' Dr Blackwell's gaze returned to the chief inspector.

'He went back to his old dugout,' Sinclair affirmed. 'He couldn't reconstruct it, he hadn't the tools. All he had was his bayonet. But he dug a hole in the loose soil. More of an animal's burrow, really. I wonder how human he was at the end.'

He regretted his words at once and looked at her quickly to gauge their effect. He could only imagine how it might feel to have been the object of so twisted and murderous a passion. But if the doctor was disturbed by the thought she gave no sign of it. 'I realized afterwards he must have come back for me. I have the same kind of looks as Lucy Fletcher. He could have watched us both from the ridge. But what about the others? Mrs Reynolds and Mrs Merrick?' She seemed genuinely curious.

'They were fair-haired, like you.' And good-looking, he almost added, but didn't wish to sound over-familiar. Dr Blackwell's manner towards him had been cool. Remembering her smile from their previous encounters at Highfield, he wondered if he would see it today.

'We were his type, then. One look and he was smitten. The fatal glance. Like Tristan and Iseult.' She spoke with bitter irony. Her gaze went again to the still figure in the bed.

'His mother had the same colouring.'

'His *mother*!' Her eye kindled with renewed interest.

'Yes, we know quite a lot about his past now. Let me finish telling you about the body first.'

Sinclair was starting to enjoy their conversation, which hadn't seemed likely at first. During his frequent visits to Guildford and Highfield over the past fortnight he had called in at the hospital several times, only to find Madden asleep or sedated. On his last visit, a few days before, he had seen Dr Blackwell in her clothes and white doctor's jacket lying stretched out on the only other bed the ward contained, and had crept from the room.

That afternoon he had come on her sitting in a chair beside the inspector's bed with his hand resting in hers on the white counterpane. Madden's eyes were shut. The doctor, too, was nodding, but she started awake as he entered and stood up at once, turning to face him. Sinclair was put in mind of a lioness guarding her wounded mate and he approached the bedside cautiously.

'He's asleep. You're not to wake him.'

Her thick fair hair was tied back tightly in a ribbon,

her face pale above the white doctor's coat. The cut over her eye showed an ugly red scab. He saw she had made no attempt to cover it with powder.

Sinclair was shocked by his colleague's appearance. The inspector's sunken cheeks and chalky skin gave his pallid features the aspect of a death's head.

Dr Blackwell noticed his reaction. 'I know he looks terrible,' she said. 'But he's getting better. It was mainly the loss of blood, the shock. I wasn't sure at first . . . I didn't know whether we could save him. But he's very strong . . .' She touched Madden's cheek and then kissed his forehead. It was as though she needed to reassure herself of his physical presence. 'You don't *know* how strong,' she burst out, anger sharpening her tone.

The chief inspector rather thought he did, but wasn't disposed to argue the point.

'We've no idea, you or I, what men like him suffered in the war, what they endured. To see him like this now . . . !' Her voice broke.

He understood then where her anger came from. He saw that she held him and the whole unsuffering world guilty of indifference to the inspector's long Calvary. And he accepted the justice of this injustice humbly and in silence.

On the point of leaving, he had mentioned his disappointment at not finding Madden awake. 'We've got most of the answers now. John would be interested to hear them.'

'Then why not tell me?' she had suggested coolly.

It afforded the chief inspector some amusement on

his train journey back to London later to reflect that it hadn't even *occurred* to him to demur.

They had taken their chairs over to the window, away from the sickbed. A brisk wind was blowing outside. Golden leaves from the chestnuts lining the street batted against the window-panes. The pale autumn sunshine brought out the shadows beneath Helen Blackwell's eyes.

Now it had shifted and lay on the polished linoleum at their feet, slowly lengthening and moving across the floor towards the sleeping figure in the white bed.

'The Folkestone pathologist naturally examined the body we retrieved from the car. It was badly disfigured. There was little he could learn from it. But one thing bothered him. Army records gave Pike's height as a touch over six feet and his physique as muscular. The body seemed about two inches shorter. I say "seemed" because it was so severely burned the flesh had shrivelled, altering its natural size and, besides, it was fixed in a sitting position, making it difficult to measure accurately.'

'And there was no possibility of checking for distinguishing marks.' The doctor's attention was fully engaged.

'None. But in the course of his examination the pathologist had found something interesting. A key ring that must have been in the pocket of the man's clothing and which had adhered to the flesh of his leg. He gave it to the Folkestone police who tested the keys on the padlocks Pike had used to lock the shed where he kept his motorcycle and found they didn't fit. However, it was equally possible they were for locks at Mrs Aylward's house or in the stables, and there was no way of checking those.

'Then one of the detectives had a fresh idea. He took a good look at the key ring itself. It was made with a shilling piece – a hole had been drilled in the coin – and he remembered that was something men returning from the war had done. The shilling was the King's shilling they were given on enlistment and they kept it as a memento.

'Now Pike had certainly served in the war, but he'd enlisted as a professional soldier years before. Even supposing he still had his shilling, it seemed unlikely to the detective that a man like Amos Pike would have done anything so *sentimental* as to turn it into a key ring.' The chief inspector smiled approvingly. 'That's what I call good detective work. Seeing *past* the evidence. He's a man called Booth. Fine copper. He'd already helped us a great deal.'

'The key ring belonged to Biggs?' Dr Blackwell asked.

'It did. Booth learned that from a friend of his, but not until lunch-time on Sunday. By then I was returning myself from Stonehill by train. I got to the Yard in the late afternoon, found Booth's message waiting for me and tried to ring John in Highfield right away.'

'I was at the constable's cottage when you rang,' Dr Blackwell said. Sinclair already knew that – he had read her statement to the Guildford police. But he let her speak. 'We tried to ring John at my house, but there was no reply, so we decided to go over and fetch him. Pike must have been waiting outside in the garden when John switched the lights on. We found the body of our dog near the terrace.'

'Thank God Stackpole was with you,' Sinclair observed. 'But I wondered why he didn't go into the house when you did? Why he stayed outside?'

'He was opening up the dicky,' she explained. 'He was going to have to sit there on the way to the station. Poor Will, it's a terrible squeeze for him.' She looked away. 'We owe him our lives, John and I. You won't forget that, will you?'

The chief inspector assured her that indeed he would not.

'You mentioned Pike's mother . . .' Dr Blackwell resettled herself. 'I read in the paper his father murdered her and was hanged for it.'

'The press have got on to that,' Sinclair acknowledged. He'd been half hoping she'd forgotten his dropped remark. 'They're digging around for the rest. I dare say it'll all come out in the end.'

He paused. His superiors at the Yard had decreed that some of the facts of the case should be kept from the general public. But he didn't believe the prohibition should apply to her.

'Ebenezer Pike confessed to the killing. He said he'd found his wife in bed with another man. He made the admission in open court. The trial didn't last long. All the same, I was surprised when I read the police file to find no mention of the man caught with Mrs Pike. Not even his name. The implication seemed to be that he'd run off and not been found.'

Dr Blackwell nodded, as though comprehending. 'It was their son, wasn't it? That's who he found her with.'

The chief inspector gazed at her in admiration. He'd made the same deduction himself, though not quite so quickly.

'Yes, his father acknowledged it. But only on condition it wasn't included in his confession. He was adamant on that point, and in the end they had to take what he gave them. I spoke to an inspector who'd worked on the case. He said the boy had been found in the bedroom covered with blood, sitting crouched in a corner. He was naked, like his mother. She was stretched over the bed with her hair hanging down and her throat cut. It was one of those cases nobody likes to think about. The boy was packed off to live with his grandparents. A few years later he went for a soldier—'

Sinclair broke off to stare at the floor. When he lifted his eyes he found that the doctor's forehead was creased with a questioning frown. 'That's not the end of the story, is it?'

He wondered how she had guessed. Or was this an example of so-called women's intuition? A revolutionary thought occurred to the chief inspector: he wouldn't half mind having a Helen Blackwell or two working beside him on the force!

'I read through the file several times, but I wasn't satisfied. Don't ask me why.' He was prepared to claim a modicum of intuition on his own account. 'I took a day off and went down to Nottingham and then out to the village where the Pikes had lived. It's called Dorton. Their cottage was a mile or so away on a big estate where Ebenezer Pike was head gamekeeper. I spoke to the local bobby. The murder was before his time, but he put me on to his predecessor who was still living there, retired.'

Sinclair smiled. 'George Hobbs is his name. He's over seventy, full of rheumatism, but bright as a button. He remembered the case only too well. In fact, he's still in a huff about it.'

'A *huff*?'

'He was the first policeman on the scene. He knew all the characters involved. He was the one they ought to have turned to to get it sorted out. That was George Hobbs's opinion then, and nothing has occurred since to alter it!' Sinclair's smile broadened. 'A wonderful institution, the village bobby. I pray we never lose him.'

The quick glance Dr Blackwell directed towards Madden, who was muttering in his sleep, contrived to suggest impatience without expressing it.

'Hobbs was able to flesh out the picture for me. First, about the Pikes as a family. Ebenezer, the father, was a cold, hard man, he said. He married the daughter of a local farmer, Sadie Grail was her name, and that was interesting. Grail was the name Pike used at the village where he kept his motorcycle. Now, according to Hobbs, Miss Grail was by way of being damaged goods. The young lady had already achieved a certain reputation in the countryside and it seems that marriage by no means curtailed her activities.'

The chief inspector caught Helen Blackwell's eye and shrugged. 'Anyway, they had a son together, Amos Pike, but Hobbs said he had no end of trouble from them. Pike gave his wife a beating on several occasions. She ran away twice. Once she assaulted him with a kitchen knife. Meanwhile, young Amos was growing up – and making of it all, who knows what? *He* was becoming a problem, too.'

'A problem?'

'According to Hobbs, strange things had been found in the woods, small animals sliced up, some hanging from branches. Two cats from the village were killed . . . in unpleasant ways. The finger pointed towards Amos Pike, but no one had caught him at it. He was growing up fast, Hobbs said. A big lad, even before he was in his teens. And there was something else, something between him and his mother, that seems to have upset the constable.'

'What was that?' The doctor's eyes had taken on a distanced look.

'The way she treated him, even in public.' Sinclair made a gesture of distaste. 'I can only tell you what Hobbs told me. She'd run her hands over him, he said. "Not in a good way" – that was how he put it. He thought she did it partly to anger her husband. But there was more to it than that, he reckoned. He called her "a dangerous woman". One has to form one's own picture, I think.'

The chief inspector felt momentarily embarrassed until he realized that Dr Blackwell wasn't similarly affected.

'He was trying to say she corrupted the boy, it sounds.'

'I believe so. On the day in question, the first he heard of the murder was when a local woman called Mrs Babcock arrived at his house in a state of hysterics and said she'd found Sadie Pike lying dead in her cottage. Hobbs rushed out there. On the way he encountered Ebenezer Pike with a bloody shirt-front and carrying his razor. He told the constable he'd killed his wife. When Hobbs reached their cottage he found the scene I've described.

'He sent for outside help immediately and a pair of detectives came from Nottingham. They made it clear they didn't require his assistance, but he went about making his own inquiries none the less. He discovered Pike had been with another keeper near the cottage shortly before the murder. This man couldn't say what time that was, but he remembered hearing the church bell ringing while they were talking.'

Sinclair cocked his head. 'Hobbs was intrigued. He'd heard the bell himself and wondered why it was ringing – it was the middle of the afternoon and there seemed no reason for it. So he asked the vicar, who told him he'd had a new clapper installed and was trying it out. Hobbs went in search of Mrs Babcock again. He asked her if *she* remembered hearing the bell. Apparently she did. After finding Mrs Pike's body she'd gone outside into the backyard and thrown up. It was while she was being sick that she heard the bell ringing. She remembered particularly because she thought someone was sounding the alarm.'

The chief inspector was silent, musing.

'Ebenezer couldn't have been in two places at once. His wife was dead before he ever got to the cottage. Hobbs tried to explain this to the two detectives, but they wouldn't listen. They had their murderer – he'd already confessed. They didn't want to hear about bells ringing in the middle of the afternoon and new clappers. Two slick city lads, Hobbs called them. They must have thought him a yokel.'

Dr Blackwell sat with bowed head. 'She took him to bed and he killed her.'

'So it would seem.' The chief inspector sighed.

They sat in silence for a while. Then Sinclair spoke again: 'Madden met someone recently. Perhaps he told you. A Viennese doctor. He talked about blood rituals and early sexual experience. How patterns could be fixed for life. Those animals found in the woods, the cats . . . I've been wondering . . .' He grimaced. '*Interesting* man, that doctor. I wish I'd met him myself. We need to know more about these matters.'

He glanced at Helen Blackwell. She sat unmoving.

'Well, the boy grew up, but you don't leave that sort of thing behind, do you? It must have been in his mind all these years. I don't say *on* his mind. There's no sign his conscience ever troubled Amos Pike.'

She broke her silence, speaking softly: 'Poor child. Poor man. Poor damned creature.'

He looked at her, astonished. 'Aye, there's that, too,' he conceded, after a moment.

Dr Blackwell rose and crossed the room to Madden's side. She bent over him, adjusting the bedclothes, smoothing the hair on his forehead. She kissed him once more. Sinclair again had the sense of her needing to touch him, to feel the assurance of his live presence. He saw it was time to leave.

As they walked down the corridor to the entrance, the linoleum squeaking beneath their shoes, he remembered a commission he'd been charged with. 'There are many people asking after John. But one in particular wants his name mentioned. Detective Constable Styles. The young man is most insistent. Would you pass that on? John will be glad to hear it.'

'I'll tell him,' she promised.

When they reached the entrance lobby he turned to take his leave, but saw she had something more to say. She was looking to one side and frowning, weighing her words it appeared. Finally she faced him. 'I'd better tell you now. You're not likely to get him back.'

The chief inspector found himself temporarily speechless.

'I mean to keep him here with me if I can. Lord Stratton's selling off some of his farms. Most of the big landowners are. They've had to retrench since the war. I've been thinking we might buy one. John always wanted to go back to the land. He'd be happy living in the country.'

It seemed to Sinclair's addled brain that he'd lost a battle before he knew he was fighting one. 'What does *he* say? Have you spoken to him?' He cast around for ground on which to make a stand. 'He's a damn fine copper, I'll have you know.'

'He's more than that,' she said simply.

The chief inspector took a moment to reflect on this. Then he bowed, accepting the truth. 'Aye, I'll not deny it.'

His reward was to see the smile he had waited for in vain all afternoon.

'Are you and he friends?' She looked at him with new eyes.

'I should hope so!' Angus Sinclair was affronted.

'Then I look forward to seeing you again, very often.' She shook his hand in her firm grip. 'Goodbye, Mr Sinclair.'

As he watched her walk away down the long corridor with urgent strides, the scowl faded from the chief inspector's face and a smile came to his lips. He'd just had a thought that made him chuckle.

All evidence to the contrary, and present circumstances notwithstanding, his friend John Madden was a lucky dog!

Epilogue

Have you forgotten yet? . . .
Look up, and swear by the green of the Spring
   that you'll never forget.

Siegfried Sassoon, 'Aftermath'

IN THE SPRING of the following year, John Madden took his wife to France. Landing at Calais, they hired a car and drove southwards to Arras and thence to Albert, skirting the great battlefields where so many young men had lost their lives in the summer of 1916.

Driving through the flat countryside, a watery world threaded by rivers and canals and criss-crossed by dykes overgrown with weeds and willows, he was surprised to find it at once so familiar and so changed. The peasant women in black skirts and red kilted petticoats, their legs encased in thick stockings, were just as he remembered them. But the roofless farmhouses with smashed windows and blackened walls were now repaired or rebuilt and barns lofty as churches stood freshly painted, gleaming in the spring sunshine.

Signs of the recent conflict abounded. Albert, where they paused to eat lunch, was a town still struggling towards rebirth. Ceaselessly bombarded throughout the war, its population of several thousands had been reduced to little more than a hundred by the time the Armistice was declared. At the small restaurant where they ate – in a street still pitted with craters and where heaps of masonry marked the sites of ruined houses – they fell into conversation with a French Engineer officer. He told them he and his men were engaged in clearing the farms roundabout of mines and unexploded shells and grenades. (They had seen ample evidence of this in the small mountains of metal piled up at intervals along the roadside.) He said the work would go on for years, for decades, so great was the mass of iron lying buried beneath the seemingly unscarred earth. 'A century will not be enough to clear them,' he predicted.

A mantle of green covered the fields, which Madden remembered as dry and powdery. Driving through the level landscape, he recalled how different it had once looked to his eyes. Low ridges then appeared as impregnable bastions; a hillock might be reckoned to cost a thousand lives to take and hold.

No longer blinded by deliberate forgetfulness, his memories roamed freely over the hours that led up to that summer dawn when the world had changed for him. He remembered the pale gleam of moonpennies by the roadside and the shuffle of boots on duckboards as the men moved up the trench line. The sound of the Allied bombardment echoed again in his ears, a night-long inferno of noise and uproar when the earth had shaken and the air had quivered with terrible hammer blows. Most of all, he recalled the gladness he had felt to be there with the other men, the sense of comradeship they had shared in the face of death. It was never to come again.

They had paused at the village of Hamel the previous afternoon so that he could look across at the sinister hill of Thiepval where his own battalion had come to grief. Standing arm in arm with Helen he pointed out where the forward trench had been and told her how he and the other members of his platoon had waited in the pale dawn light for the signal to attack.

He spoke the names of some of them: Bob Wilson, Ben Tryon, Charlie Feather, the Crown and Anchor man; the Greig twins, colliers from Kent, their white cheeks seamed with blue coal dust; Billy Baxter and his cousin Fred, both barrow-boys from Whitechapel. Jamie Wallace with his sweet tenor voice.

He never saw them again. They had vanished, all of them, that morning, advancing into a cloud of smoke and dust as though entering the mouth of hell. But he kept the memory of them warmly in his heart, and they came to him no more in dreams.

*

It was Helen Madden, rather than her husband, who had wanted to make the trip, and who had felt that now was the time to do so before domestic priorities rendered any thought of foreign travel out of the question, at least for a while.

The previous year she had visited the graves of her elder brother and her first husband, who were both buried in Belgium. Now she wished to do the same for David, her younger brother, whose body lay near Fricourt in one of the chain of Allied cemeteries that peppered the killing ground of the Somme river basin.

Some six months earlier the War Office had handed

over care of all military graveyards to the Imperial War Graves Commission. Work had begun at once on turning the cemeteries into places of beauty and pilgrimage and the Maddens found a team of gardeners labouring in newly dug flower-beds bordering the wide unfenced field where the neat lines of wooden crosses were half hidden by early-morning mist. The crosses would soon disappear, to be replaced by white headstones.

Leaving her husband seated on a bench by the warden's hut, where a map of the cemetery was available for consultation, Helen went alone to her brother's grave. She had brought a bunch of white roses flecked with blood-red poppies and she knelt down to lay it on the grassed mound.

Try as she might she could only remember David as a schoolboy, pink-cheeked, full of boyish slang, a noisy presence in the house at holiday time. He had gone straight from school to officers' training camp, but even the sight of him in his awkwardly fitting uniform had not persuaded her of his adult status. She mourned now for his lost manhood, all the sweetness of life denied him at its outset.

When plans for maintaining the cemeteries had first been mooted, voices had been raised in favour of reorganizing them by rank, of separating officers from men. They had been silenced by the near-unanimous wish, expressed at every level of society, that the fallen should be left to lie where fate and circumstance had placed them. In death's great democracy Second Lieutenant David Collingwood had for companions a gunner of the Royal Artillery and a lance-corporal of the Middlesex Regiment. His sister laid a flower on each.

Getting carefully to her feet, Helen Madden looked back to where her husband was waiting. The last of the ground mist had dissolved and the bench where he sat was bathed in silvery sunshine. Although his wound had healed completely and his vigour was almost fully restored, she continued to keep a watchful eye on him. She liked to know he was near at hand.

For his part Madden malingered happily. He'd felt well for some time now, but he enjoyed the many attentions his wife showered on him and thought he might let her cosset him for a little while longer.

Returning to France for the first time since the end of the war, he'd expected to be overwhelmed by memories – the memories she had taught him not to turn from. But although all that past was still fresh in his mind, he could feel it receding, ebbing like a wave that might return from time to time to wash on his shores, but would bring no terrors in its wake.

As to the future, he saw it approaching, noting with pleasure the continued alteration in her tall slender figure as it filled out week by week with the child she was carrying. Her eyes captured his while she was still some distance off, and he rose and waited for her, recalling as he did that it was her glance that had first struck him when they met. How it seemed to express the depths of her character.

Blue, unswerving, magnetic. True north.

The sunlight was bright on her hair as she drew near. She was smiling as she reached to take his arm. 'Come, my love' – pausing to straighten the collar of his coat and touch his cheek with her hand – 'it's time we went home.'

Permissions Acknowledgements

Extract from 'To the War-Mongers' © Siegfried Sassoon (from *The War Poems of Siegfried Sassoon*, Faber & Faber) is reproduced by kind permission of George Sassoon.

'Picnic July 1917' by Rose Macaulay is reproduced by kind permission of the Peters Fraser & Dunlop Group Limited.

Extract from 'Sick Love' by Robert Graves (from the *Oxford Anthology of English Poetry*, Volume II, Oxford University Press) is reproduced by kind permission of Carcanet Press Limited.

Extract from 'Aftermath' © Siegfried Sassoon (from *Siegfried Sassoon, Collected Poems, 1908–1956*, Faber & Faber) is reproduced by kind permission of George Sassoon.

extracts reading groups

competitions books new

discounts extracts

extracts

competitions reading groups

books discounts

new events extracts

events reading groups

books extracts books

new titles reading groups

interviews events

discounts extracts interviews

new books events books

events new events extracts

reading groups

discounts extracts discounts

www.panmacmillan.com

extracts events reading groups

competitions books extracts new